Best of Times, Worst of Times

Best of Times, Worst of Times

Contemporary American Short Stories
from the New Gilded Age

Edited by

WENDY MARTIN *and* CECELIA TICHI

New York University Press   *New York & London*

NEW YORK UNIVERSITY PRESS
New York and London
www.nyupress.org

Library of Congress Cataloging-in-Publication Data
Best of times, worst of times : contemporary American short stories from
the new Gilded Age / edited by Wendy Martin and Cecelia Tichi.
p. cm.
ISBN 978–0–8147–9627–6 (cl : alk. paper)
ISBN 978–0–8147–9628–3 (pb : alk. paper)
ISBN 978–0–8147–6147–2 (e-book)
1. Short stories, American—21st century.   2. United States—Social life
and customs—Fiction.   I. Martin, Wendy.   II. Tichi, Cecelia.
PS648.S5B4655   2010
813'.0108054—dc22   2010033746

New York University Press books are printed on acid-free paper,
and their binding materials are chosen for strength and durability.
We strive to use environmentally responsible suppliers and materials
to the greatest extent possible in publishing our books.

Manufactured in the United States of America
C 10 9 8 7 6 5 4 3 2 1
P 10 9 8 7 6 5 4 3 2 1

Contents

Acknowledgements   ix

Introduction   1
WENDY MARTIN AND CECELIA TICHI

All in the Family

1 Your Mother and I   11
DAVE EGGERS

2 The Ballad of Duane Juarez   18
TOM FRANKLIN

3 In the American Society   27
GISH JEN

4 Gogol   41
JHUMPA LAHIRI

5 Refresh, Refresh   68
BENJAMIN PERCY

6 Smorgasbord   81
TOBIAS WOLFF

Shifting Identities

7 How to Date a Brown Girl (black girl, white girl, or halfie)   97
JUNOT DÍAZ

8 In the Cemetery Where Al Jolson Is Buried   102
AMY HEMPEL

9 Metamorphosis   111
JOHN UPDIKE

10 Think   120
DAVID FOSTER WALLACE

Locations and Dislocations

11   Expensive Trips Nowhere   125
      TOM BISSELL

12   Near-Extinct Birds of the Central Cordillera   146
      BEN FOUNTAIN

13   Shiloh   168
      BOBBIE ANN MASON

14   COMMCOMM   182
      GEORGE SAUNDERS

15   Mines   203
      SUSAN STRAIGHT

Across Divides

16   Skinless   217
      AIMEE BENDER

17   View from a Headlock   226
      JONATHAN LETHEM

18   Brownies   248
      ZZ PACKER

19   Pie of the Month   268
      JEAN THOMPSON

Workdays and Nightshifts

20   A Day   287
      CHARLES BUKOWSKI

21   Scales   296
      LOUISE ERDRICH

22   Something That Needs Nothing   309
      MIRANDA JULY

23   Equal Opportunity   327
      WALTER MOSLEY

24   The Passenger   341
      MARISA SILVER

About the Editors   357

Stories Listed Alphabetically by Author's Last Name

Aimee Bender, "Skinless" (1995)

Tom Bissell, "Expensive Trips Nowhere" (2005)

Charles Bukowski, "A Day" (1990)

Junot Díaz, "How to Date a Brown Girl (black girl, white girl, or halfie)" (1995)

Dave Eggers, "Your Mother and I" (2004)

Louise Erdrich, "Scales" (1982)

Ben Fountain, "Near-Extinct Birds of the Central Cordillera" (2005)

Tom Franklin, "The Ballad of Duane Juarez" (1998)

Amy Hempel, "In the Cemetery Where Al Jolson Is Buried" (1983)

Gish Jen, "In the American Society" (1986)

Miranda July, "Something That Needs Nothing" (2006)

Jhumpa Lahiri, "Gogol" (2003)

Jonathan Lethem, "View From a Headlock" (2003)

Bobbie Ann Mason, "Shiloh" (1991)

Walter Mosley, "Equal Opportunity" (1998)

ZZ Packer, "Brownies" (1999)

Benjamin Percy, "Refresh, Refresh" (2005)

George Saunders, "COMMCOMM" (2005)

Marisa Silver, "The Passenger" (2000)

Susan Straight, "Mines" (2002)

Jean Thompson, "Pie of the Month" (2005)

John Updike, "Metamorphosis" (1999)

David Foster Wallace, "Think" (2001)

Tobias Wolff, "Smorgasborg" (1987)

Acknowledgments

We wish to express deep appreciation to Tyler Reeb, who participated in all aspects of this project from the selection and arrangement of these stories to the compilation of the notes on contributors and the oversight of the process of securing permissions. In addition, he contributed ideas for the Introduction and helped to identify thematic clusters that inform our Table of Contents. His commitment to the vision and values that inspired this project has been steadfast throughout. His work on this project augurs well for his academic career.

We would also like to thank the external reviewers who offered valuable advice on story selection, commended the project, and emphasized its usefulness in the literature and composition classroom. We also thank the students in the Claremont Graduate University English Department seminars on "The Contemporary American Short Story" and "Short Story" for their contributions to this project: Jenny Lau, Hyunhwa Lee, Laura Longobardi, Kristina Munz, Katie Nelson, Adam Rose, Katrina Sire, Rachel Tie, Jan Michelle Andres, Jukyung Bae, Ryan Friedman, Grant Horner II, Douglas Ishii, Stefani Stallard, Karen Beth Strovas, Eric Westrope, and Sharone Williams. And special thanks to Lina Geriguis, Kristina Kraus, Christopher Potts, and Philomon Roh, who made many important contributions to the Introduction, and to Karen Beth Strovas for her assistance in copyediting the manuscript.

Much gratitude goes to Mary Ellen Wanderlingh, Administrative Assistant for the Transdisciplinary Studies Program at the Claremont Graduate University, and to Janis May, Administrative Assistant of the Department of English, Vanderbilt University. Their willingness to help with the preparation of the manuscript, as well as the permissions and disbursement process, has been invaluable. We commend their admirable patience, good will, and exactitude. We appreciate, in addition, the subvention funding made available by Vanderbilt University and the support of the New York University Press editors, Eric Zinner and Ciara McLaughlin.

We are grateful to the writers in this collection for their commitment to the vision that has sustained this project.

Introduction

WENDY MARTIN *and* CECELIA TICHI

"It was the best of times, it was the worst of times." This classic opening line from Charles Dickens's *A Tale of Two Cities* (1859) captures the spirit of the American short stories in this volume. Dickens's proclamation rings true for late twentieth- and early twenty-first century America in fiction and in fact; his assertion of polar extremes fits the American temper of these times. At its best, the United States has sponsored and embraced the digital revolution and finds itself poised for striking new directions in green energy resources, medicine, consumer choices, job categories, housing patterns, and in environmental and other changes. Yet "worst of times" also applies: our nation is reeling from a quarter century of manufacturing shutdowns, jobs outsourced and off-shored, wars, corporations' ever expanding power, and growing wealth disparities that find the rich richer, the poor poorer, and the middle class seriously eroded.

The stories in this collection speak urgently to this complex modern moment and chronicle an America of a second Gilded Age. Extending from the late 1800s to the early 1900s, the first Gilded Age was an era of extravagant wealth and of dark socioeconomic conflict. Named after a novel by Mark Twain and Charles Dudley Warner, the first Gilded Age saw the rise of statistics as a way of measuring social conditions, while the fiction of the era dramatized its woes, shenanigans, and triumphs. Viewing our era as a second Gilded Age gives recent decades an historical point of reference and anchors contemporary America in the flow of history.

Authors of the first Gilded Age constitute a Who's Who of American literature, including Mark Twain, Edith Wharton, Stephen Crane, and others. Their novels and short stories, such as "The Man That Corrupted Hadleyburg," *The House of Mirth*, and "Maggie, A Girl of the Streets" endure as sharp-edged depictions of a time resplendent with wealth amassed from rapidly growing heavy industry, manufacturing, and finance—but rife with labor turmoil, greed, racism, misogyny, oppressive working conditions, imperial wars in Cuba and the Philippines, and an ideology of "survival of the fittest."

Today's fiction writers similarly craft stories that confront the hard facts of contemporary life, revealing many of the same concerns as the writers of the first Gilded Age. While policy makers and social critics once again report their findings in statistics, pie charts, think tank white papers, books, and blogs, numerous fiction writers offer stories that are incisive, frank, confrontational, and spirited. Engaging the hard facts of contemporary society and culture, these writers avoid defeatism while examining race relations, immigration, social class, the workplace, gender relations, the pervasive environment of ads and brands, warfare, U.S. imperialism, and other issues. The stories in this volume draw readers into the lives of characters who are tossed about by social, economic, and political currents that they struggle to comprehend. Authors featured here include men and women, straight and gay, ethnically diverse, and representing different regions of the United States and other places in the world where the nation exerts its military, political, economic, and cultural influence.

The litany of crises that marked the first decade of the twenty-first century caused deep social fractures and also prompted innovative ideas and self-reflection. These crises began with the September 11, 2001, attacks on New York's World Trade Center and the Pentagon. These attacks precipitated U.S. invasions of Afghanistan in 2001 and Iraq in 2003, and the wars proved to be unexpectedly difficult and lengthy. In 2005, in the aftermath of the Hurricanes Katrina and Rita, the city of New Orleans and the Mississippi Gulf Coast became a domestic disaster area; TV and computer screens revealed the suffering and death of American citizens, many of them poor and black. Post-hurricane evacuation and governmental relief efforts proved incompetent and left upwards of 1,500 dead and tens of thousands living in camp trailers for years afterward. In 2008, the nation's financial system nearly collapsed. This worldwide banking crisis, centered in the United States, froze credit and forced millions of homeowners into foreclosure, while savings and retirement accounts plummeted and joblessness soared. In spring 2010, catastrophe once again struck the Gulf Coast when the drilling mechanism of the BP (British Petroleum) rig, *Deepwater Horizon*, failed, causing a lethal explosion and an eruption of tens of millions of gallons of crude oil into the Gulf and onto the coastal beaches and wetlands. Evidence indicated that BP's cost-cutting measures and a failure of U.S. government regulatory agencies were responsible for what some believe to be the worst environmental disaster in U.S. history.

The writers represented in *Best of Times, Worst of Times* began to document the social dislocations of this second Gilded Age well before the turn of the millennium. In a long arc from the 1980s, they created a record of social, political, and economic trends and consequences. By presciently capturing the decades-long social changes that only recently have come to widespread public attention, their stories confirm the truth of poet Ezra Pound's statement that "artists are the antennae of the race." This sociopolitical and economic context merits attention because it serves as the bedrock for these texts.

Many commentators have celebrated the rapid growth of globalization in recent decades, especially the booming 1990s. This era of "supercapitalism," as described by former Secretary of Labor Robert Reich, saw megagrowth and mega-deals as well as rapidly falling costs in communication and transportation that integrated the world of trade. Economists and business leaders projected a future in which the United States would relinquish manufacturing and rely on new jobs in the service and knowledge sectors to sustain our culture of consumption. They praised the efficient free market that brought American businesses and consumers a cornucopia of low-priced goods. Big-box discount retailers epitomized these developments; these retailers became the sole shopping destination for millions of American consumers by undercutting the prices of local Main Street businesses nearly everywhere, selling products from microwave ovens to flat screen TVs, and even food, imported from every corner of the world. Meanwhile, much former American farmland where fruits, vegetables, and livestock were once grown for American tables gave way to sprawling suburban subdivisions, as noted in Bobbie Ann Mason's story, "Shiloh." At the same time, vast acreage in the midwestern heartland was turned over to two feedstock crops, soybeans and corn, largely monopolized by patented seeds from agribusiness giants. This trend, too, was praised for progress and efficiency.

The collapse of the Soviet Union in the late 1980s was celebrated as ushering in the "Pax Americana," leaving the United States the one remaining world superpower and apparently vindicating the value of free trade. In the name of peace, and security and freedom, the U.S. military continued to expand its presence worldwide, sometimes by enlarging bases, at other times by direct force. The recent and ongoing wars in Iraq and Afghanistan come to mind (the Iraq war of 1991, Operations Desert Storm and Desert Shield; the Afghanistan campaign, Operation Enduring Freedom; and the second Iraq war in 2003, Operation Iraqi Freedom). But other military operations have punctuated the era covered in Best of Times, Worst of Times. In 1983, President Ronald Reagan ordered Operation Urgent Fury, the invasion of the Caribbean island of Grenada. The Reagan administration charged that the airstrips of the island nation threatened a "Soviet-Cuban militarization" of the Caribbean and Central America. The U.S. public supported this Cold War campaign to rid the Caribbean of communism, but the invasion was condemned as "a flagrant violation of international law" by the United Kingdom, Canada, and the UN General Assembly. In December 1989, military force was exerted once again as President George H. W. Bush ordered 57,684 troops and aircraft into Panama to depose Panamanian president General Manuel Noriega, a former CIA operative. The official justification for the invasion—Operation Just Cause—included safeguarding U.S. citizens in Panama, defending human rights, combating drug trafficking, and protecting the Panama Canal treaty. A report by Physicians for Human Rights calculated that over 4,000 Panamanians may have been killed and 15,000 displaced.

Benjamin Percy's "Refresh, Refresh" and Jean Thompson's "Pie of the Month" dramatize a point made by social critic Gore Vidal, who has exposed the contradiction of a nation waging "perpetual war for perpetual peace." Their stories address an ideology of militarism and recall the prophetic warning of President Dwight D. Eisenhower, whose farewell address in January 1961 cautioned against a growing "military-industrial complex." President Eisenhower, formerly a career army officer who was named General of the Army for his leadership in World War II, was troubled by a "conjunction of an immense military establishment and a large arms industry." His warning was ignored, and costly militarism expanded unceasingly in the decades ahead, as the United States became the world's biggest exporter of weaponry worldwide and established a military presence across the globe. The historian Chalmers Johnson has described the United States as becoming a global "empire of [military] bases" with the goal of "maintaining absolute military preponderance over the rest of the world." Today, the United States has 761 active military bases in 151 countries around the world and spends more on its military than the next eight industrialized nations put together.

Two other stories in this volume, Tom Bissell's "Expensive Trips Nowhere" and Ben Fountain's "Near-Extinct Birds of the Central Cordillera," record less overt evidence of global interventions by the United States. In Bissell's story, two affluent Americans vacation in Central Asia, only to be confronted by the unforeseen consequences of the former Cold War when the United States waged proxy wars against the Soviet Union and its allied bloc. Fountain's fiction, set in Latin America, reveals an alliance of rebel insurgents with Wall Street financiers, illustrating an international commingling of military force, politics, and money.

American workers and households, meanwhile, have felt embattled at home. Since the 1970s, according to the U.S. Census Bureau and the U.S. Bureau of Labor statistics, the least wealthy 40 percent of American households have lost 80 percent of their wealth, while the top one percent have increased their wealth more than the bottom 95 percent. Economists Robert H. Frank and Philip J. Cook have described this as the "winner-take-all society," which mirrors the "survival of the fittest" ethos of the first Gilded Age. This increasing concentration of wealth at the top can largely be attributed to radical changes in the American workplace in recent decades. With the systematic shutdown of American mills and factories, well-paying manufacturing jobs that provided comfortable lives from post–World War II into the late 1970s disappeared. Skilled labor declined and products that were formerly made in America, from automobiles, computers, and furniture to shoes, toys, and clothing, now come largely from East Asia, where nonunion workers are paid a pittance for arduous toil. Manufacturing jobs declined from around 28 percent of the workforce in 1970 to only around 10 percent in 2006. Between 1979 and 1996, the U.S. Department of Labor statistics show that the United States lost 43 million manufacturing jobs, and another 1.2 million vanished in 2008 alone.

These job losses have had widespread consequences. The projected high-paying service sector and knowledge industry positions have failed to materialize in sufficient numbers, and former unionized middle-class U.S. assembly line workers like the character in Charles Bukowski's story, "A Day," now find themselves employed for a fraction of their former wages, often no more than the U.S. hourly minimum wage—even less for some service workers. Economist Jared Bernstein has observed that "while the economy grew by 15 percent between 2000 and 2006, the inflation-adjusted weekly earnings of the typical, or median, worker were flat." Though consumer products from smart phones to shrimp became increasingly affordable, Bernstein points out that "most of the indicators that matter most to us in our everyday lives—jobs, wages, mid-level incomes, prices at the pump and the grocery store, health care, retirement security, college tuition—are coming in at stress-inducing levels." In 2009, although President Barack Obama proclaimed that "the fight for American manufacturing is the fight for America's future," two of the three largest American automobile manufacturers declared bankruptcy. In the same year, the chairman and chief executive officer of General Electric remarked, "We must make a serious commitment to manufacturing and exports. This is a national imperative." The United States, however, has no industrial policy and furthermore devotes less of its economy to manufacturing than any other industrialized nation except France.

From the 1980s to the present, long-term employment with the prospect of steady growth in income, together with benefits and timely promotions, gave way to contingent work such as temping or short-term contract employment, as seen in Miranda July's "Something That Needs Nothing." Corporate America, according to one business and finance reporter, has become a "white-collar sweatshop," a term echoing the labor peonage of the first Gilded Age. Once–valued employees have been redefined as independent contractors, who bear full responsibility for healthcare insurance and pension savings, even as waves of layoffs idle millions. The labor and economics writer Louis Uchitelle has identified a new figure, "the disposable American" emerging from surging layoffs. Individuals and families are balanced precariously in the new labor market, performing what has been called a "highwire act," as described in Louise Erdrich's "Scales" and Marisa Silver's "The Passenger." To stay aloft during periods of sudden job loss or illness, Americans must often deplete savings set aside for their future or their children's educations. When reemployed, they may have to accept lower pay than before, sometimes in repeated cycles that send their incomes on a relentless downward course.

Ironically, the American prison system experienced robust growth throughout this era of declining prosperity. Susan Straight's story, "Mines," provides a window on what one researcher has called a "prison nation." Areas of the country that experienced job loss from shuttered manufacturing plants or closed military bases often welcomed the building of prisons for the jobs they created. According to the Urban Institute, the U.S. prison population increased by more than one million between 1980 and 2000. By 2009, America imprisoned its citizens at a rate nearly five times the world's average. With four percent of the world's population, the United States housed 25 percent of the world's prisoners, many incarcerated for nonviolent drug offenses, and about 16 percent of these mentally ill. Most prisoners come from racial minority groups. Private for-profit prisons such as the Corrections Corporation of America augmented state and federal facilities and are now listed on the New York Stock Exchange, giving investors opportunities to make money in this market in human misery. A regimen of punishment without rehabilitation has been the hallmark of prison life in recent decades, and once released, convicted felons who have paid their debt to society find themselves without job skills and facing an uphill struggle to gain employment. Walter Mosley's story, "Equal Opportunity," captures the determination of an ex-con to battle the odds, put his life on a new footing, and persist until he achieves his goal.

A closely related problem has been the imprisonment of undocumented immigrants in a detention system that reflects the ambivalence of the American public toward immigrants in general. Estimates indicate that upwards of twelve million undocumented immigrants currently live in the United States. The American public believes these people are hard-working and values their labor in low-wage, low-profile jobs—for example, as domestics, restaurant kitchen help, gardeners, and workers in meat processing plants. However, as whites gradually lose their majority in the United States, the nativism that arose in the first Gilded Age once again asserts itself in such groups as the armed vigilante Minutemen who patrol the U.S.–Mexican border, the Federation for American Immigration Reform, and NumbersUSA. Despite presidential support, in 2006, Congress failed to pass a law granting undocumented immigrants a pathway to U.S. citizenship, and controversy continues over whether these immigrants (as some call them, illegal aliens) are entitled to health care or whether their children (especially those from Mexico and Central America) ought to be educated at public expense.

Immigration issues overlap with stereotypes of race, ethnicity, and class, which tend to complicate issues of status and identity in the United States. Young black males, for instance, are often racially profiled in the media as drug dealers or gangsters. Latina/Latinos also are subject to negative images, as shown in Junot Diaz's "How to Date a Brown Girl." According to the National Association of Hispanic Journalists, 66 percent of all Latino/Latina network newscasts focus on crime, terrorism, poverty, and welfare. Exclusionary images of East Asians also persist, along with resentment toward the academic accomplishments of Asian-Americans in what is dubbed the "smart Asian syndrome," especially in math and science. Stereotypes of whites range from the degrading phrase "white trash" to the elitism indicated by "WASP," reflecting the privileged status that white Anglo-Saxon Protestants have long enjoyed in the United States. Tobias Wolff's "Smorgasbord" addresses these issues of class and caste in the contemporary moment.

Though the "worst of times" are vividly present in this volume, these stories cannot be reduced solely to the crises that have shaped our era: the second Gilded Age is also one of adaptation, resistance, resilience, and survival. In an age of fracture, there also can be affirmation of community, family, and friends. The e-mail technology referenced in Percy's "Refresh, Refresh" allows a son to maintain contact with his soldier father who is away in Iraq, while the plot of Silver's "The Passenger" underscores the value of an infant's life, affirming a commitment to the future. Cruel racial stereotyping is confronted and overcome in Jhumpa Lahiri's "Gogol" and in Gish Jen's "In the American Society," strengthening family bonds. Enduring friendship is a hallmark of Amy Hempel's "In the Cemetery Where Al Jolson Is Buried," and the importance of community activism is emphasized in Thompson's "Pie of the Month," when an unassuming middle-aged woman turns her kitchen into an antiwar center. Characters are sustained by humor as in Dave Eggers's "Your Mother and I," which imagines a better world beyond the vexations of this era. Some of these stories are traditional in form, while others like George Saunders's "COMMCOMM" are distinctly postmodern. Whether the narrative is straightforward or has a playful, self-referential, and fragmented structure, the works in *Best of Times, Worst of Times* comprise a vast panorama of contemporary American lives, summoning us once again to the opening of Charles Dickens's *Tale of Two Cities*: "It was the best of times, it was the worst of times, it was the age of wisdom, it was the age of foolishness, it was the epoch of belief, it was the epoch of incredulity, it was the season of Light, it was the season of Darkness, it was the spring of hope, it was the winter of despair, we had everything before us, we had nothing before us, we were all going direct to heaven, we were all going direct the other way." Whoever we are and whatever our circumstances, these American writers insist that directly engaging life in the United States is their mandate—and ours.

All in the Family

1

Your Mother and I

DAVE EGGERS

Dave Eggers, a writer, publisher, and social activist, was born in Boston, Massachusetts, in 1970. After high school, he pursued a journalism degree at the University of Illinois at Urbana-Champaign. But at age 21, within a span of one year, his father died of brain and lung cancer and his mother died of stomach cancer. Those tragedies forced Eggers to interrupt his studies to raise his eight-year-old brother; he would later chronicle those experiences in his widely popular, lightly fictionalized memoir *A Heartbreaking Work of Staggering Genius* (2000). Buoyed by the success of that work, Eggers founded McSweeney's, an independent multimedia publishing company that produces books, a quarterly journal, a monthly magazine, and a quarterly DVD of short films and documentaries. He is the author of six books, including *How We Are Hungry*, a collection of short stories.

I told you about that, didn't I? About when your mother and I moved the world to solar energy and windpower, to hydro, all that? I never told you that? Can you hand me that cheese? No, the other one, the cheddar, right. I really thought I told you about that. What is happening to my head?

Well, we have to take the credit, your mother and I, for reducing our dependence on oil and for beginning the Age of Wind and Sun. That was pretty awesome. That name wasn't ours, though. Your uncle Frank came up with that. He always wanted to be in a band and call it that, the Age of Wind and Sun, but he never learned guitar and couldn't sing. When he sang he *enunciated* too much, you know? He sang like he was trying to teach English to Turkish children. Turkish children with learning disabilities. It was really odd, his singing.

You're already done? Okay, here's the Monterey Jack. Just dump it in the bowl. All of it, right. It was all pretty simple, converting most of the nation's electricity. At a certain point everyone knew that we had to just suck it up and pay the money—because holy crap, it really was expensive at first—to set up the cities to make their own power. All those solar panels and windmills on the city buildings? They weren't always there, you know. No, they weren't. Look at some pictures, honey. They just weren't. The roofs of these millions of buildings weren't being used in any real way, so I said, Hey, let's have the buildings themselves generate some or all of the power they use, and it might look pretty good, to boot—everyone loves windmills, right? Windmills are awesome. So we started in Salt Lake City and went from there.

Oh hey, can you grate that one? Just take half of that block of Muenster. Here's a bowl. Thanks. Then we do the cheddar. Cheddar has to be next. After the cheddar, pecorino. Never the other way around. Stay with me, hon. Jack, Muenster, cheddar, pecorino. It is. The only way.

Right after that was a period of much activity. Your mother and I tended to do a big project like the power conversion, and then follow it with a bunch of smaller, quicker things. So we made all the roads red. You wouldn't remember this—you weren't even born. We were all into roads then, so we had most of them painted red, most of them, especially the highways—a leathery red that looked good with just about everything, with green things and blue skies and woods of cedar and golden swamps and sugar-colored beaches. I think we were right. You like them, right? They used to be grey, the roads. Insane, right? Your mom thinks yellow would have been good, too, an ochre but sweeter. Anyway, in the same week, we got rid of school funding tied to local property taxes—can you believe they used to pull that crap?—banned bicycle shorts for everyone but professionals, and made everyone's hair shinier. That was us. Your mother and I.

That was right after our work with the lobbyists—I never told you that, either? I must be losing my mind. I never mentioned the lobbyists, about when we had them all deported? That part of it, the deportation, was your mother's idea. All I'd said was, Hey, why not ban all lobbying? Or at least ban all donations from lobbyists, and make them wear cowbells so everyone would know they were coming? And then your dear mom, who was, I think, a little tipsy at the time—we were at a bar where they had a Zima special, and you know how your mom loves her Zima—she said, How about, to make sure those bastards don't come back to Washington, have them all sent to Greenland? And wow, the idea just took off. People loved it, and Greenland welcomed them warmly; they'd apparently been looking for ways to boost their tourism. They set up some cages and a viewing area and it was a big hit.

So then we were all pumped up, to be honest. Wow, this kind of thing, the lobbyists thing especially, boy, it really made your mother horny. Matter of fact, I think you were conceived around that time. She was like some kind of tsunam—

Oh don't give me that face. What? Did I cross some line? Don't you want to know when your seed was planted? I would think you'd want to know that kind of thing. Well then. I stand corrected.

Anyway, we were on a roll, so we got rid of genocide. The main idea was to create and maintain a military force of about 20,000 troops, under the auspices of the U.N., which could be deployed quickly to any part of the world within about thirty-six hours. This wouldn't be the usual blue helmets, watching the slaughter. These guys would be badass. We were sick of the civilized world sort of twiddling their thumbs while hundreds of thousands of people killed each other in Rwanda, Bosnia, way back in Armenia, on and on. Then the U.N. would send twelve Belgian soldiers. Nice guys, but really, you have a genocide raging in Rwanda, 800,000 dead in a month and you send *twelve Belgians*?

So we made this proposal, the U.N. went for it, and within a year the force was up and running. And man oh man, your mother was randy again. That's when your fecundation happened, and why we called you Johnna. I remember it now—I was wrong before. Your mother and I were actually caught in the U.N. bathroom, after the vote went our way. The place, all marble and brass, was full of people, and at the worst possible moment, Kofi himself walked in. He sure was surprised to see us in there, on the sink, but I have to say, he was pretty cool about it. He actually seemed to enjoy it, even watched for a minute, because there was no way we were gonna stop in the middle—

Fine. I won't do that again. It's just that it's part of the story, honey. Everything we did started with love, and ended with lust—

But you're right. That was inappropriate.

We went on a tear right after genocide, very busy. I attribute it partly to the vitamins we were on—very intense program of herbs and vitamins and protein shakes. We'd shoot out of bed and bounce around like bunnies. So that's when we covered Cleveland in ivy. You've seen pictures. We did that. Just said, Hey Cleveland, what if you were covered in ivy, all the buildings? Wouldn't that look cool, and be a big tourist attraction? And they said, "Sure." Not right away, though. You know who helped with that? Dennis Kucinich. I used to call him "Sparky," because he was such a feisty fella. Your mom, she called him "The Kooch."

We're gonna need all three kinds of salsa, hon. Yeah, use the small bowls.

Just pour it right up to the edge. Right. Your brother likes to mix it up. Me, I'm a fan of the mild.

Right after Cleveland and the ivy we made all the kids memorize poetry again. We hadn't memorized any growing up—this was the seventies and eighties, and people hadn't taught that for years—and we really found we missed it. The girls were fine with the idea, and the boys caught on when they realized it would help them get older women into bed. Around that time we banned wearing fur outside of arctic regions, flooded the market with diamonds and gold and silver to the point where none had any value, fixed the ozone hole—I could show you that; we've got it on video—and then we did the thing with the llamas. What are you doing? Sour cream in the salsa? No, no. That's just wrong, sweetie. My god.

So yeah, we put llamas everywhere. That was us. We just liked looking at them, so we bred about six million and spread them around. They weren't there before, honey. No, they weren't. Oh man, there's one now, in the backyard. Isn't it a handsome thing? Now they're as common as squirrels or deer, and you have your mom and pop to thank for that.

It's jalapeño time. Use the smaller knife. You're gonna cut the crap out of your hand. You don't want one of these. You see this scar on my thumb? Looks like a scythe, right? I got that when we were negotiating the removal of the nation's billboards. I was climbing one of them, in Kentucky actually, to start a hunger strike kind of thing, sort of silly I guess, and cut the shipdoodle out of that left thumb.

Why the billboards? Have you even see one? In books? Well, I guess I just never really liked the look of them—they just seemed so ugly and such an intrusion on the collective involuntary consciousness, a blight on the land. Vermont had outlawed them and boy, what a difference that made. So your mother and I revived Lady Bird Johnson's campaign against them, and of course 98 percent of the public was with us, so the whole thing happened pretty quickly. We had most of the billboards down within a year. Right after that, your brother Sid was conceived, and it was about time I had my tubes tied.

Give me some of that cobbler, hon. We're gonna have the peach cobbler after the main event. I just wanna get the Cool Whip on it, then stick it in the freezer for a minute. That's Frank's trick. Frank's come up with a lot of good ideas for improving frozen and refrigerated desserts. No, that's not his job, honey. Frank doesn't have a job, per se.

I guess a lot of what we did—what made so much of this possible—was eliminate the bipolar nature of so much of what passed for debate in those days. So often the media would take even the most logical idea, like private funding for all sports stadiums or having all colleges require forty hours of community service to graduate, and make it seem like there were two equally powerful sides to the argument, which was so rarely the case. A logical fallacy, is what that is. So we just got them to keep things in perspective a bit, not make everyone so crazy, polarizing every last debate. I mean, there was a time when you couldn't get a lightbulb replaced because the press would find a way to quote the sole lunatic in the world who didn't want that lightbulb replaced. So we sat them all down, all the members of the media, and we said, "Listen, we all want to have progress, we all want a world for the grandkids and all. We know we're gonna need better gas mileage on the cars, and that all the toddlers are gonna need Head Start, and we're gonna need weekly parades through every town and city to keep morale up, and we'll have to get rid of Three Strikes and mandatory minimums and the execution of retarded prisoners—and that it all has to happen sooner or later, so don't go blowing opposition to any of it out of proportion. Don't go getting everyone *inflamed*." Honestly, when lynchings were originally outlawed, you can bet the newspapers made it seem like there was some real validity to the pro-lynching side of things. You can be sure that the third paragraph of any article would have said "Not *everyone* is happy about the anti-lynching legislation. We spoke to a local resident who is not at all happy about it . . ." Anyway, we sat everyone down, served some carrots and onion dip and in a couple hours your mother and I straightened all that out.

About then we had a real productive period. In about six months, we established a global minimum wage, we made it so smoke detectors could be turned off without having to rip them from the ceiling, and we got Soros to buy the Amazon, to preserve it. That was fun—he took us on his jet, beautiful thing, appointed in the smoothest cherry and teak, and they had the soda where you add the colored syrup yourself. You ever have that kind? So good, but you can't overdo it—too much syrup and you feel bloated for a week. Well, then we came home, rested up for a few days, and then we found a cure for Parkinson's. We did *so*, honey. Yes that was us. Don't you ever look through the nice scrapbook we made? You should. It's in the garage with your Uncle Frank. Are you sure he's asleep? No, don't wake him up. Hell, I guess you have to wake him up anyway, because he won't want to miss the *comida grande*.

After Parkinson's, we fixed AIDS pretty well. We didn't cure it, but we made the inhibiting drugs available worldwide, for free, as a condition of the drug companies being allowed to operate in the U.S. Their profit margins were insane at the time, so they relented, made amends, and it worked out fine. That was about when we made all buildings curvier, and all cars boxier.

After AIDS and the curves, we did some work on elections. First we made them no more than two months long, publicly funded, and forced the networks to give two hours a night to the campaigns. Around when you were born, the candidates were spending about $200 million each on TV ads, because the news wasn't covering the elections for more than 90 seconds a day. It was nuts! So we fixed that, and then we perfected online and phone voting. Man, participation went through the roof. Everyone thought there was just all this apathy, when the main problem was finding your damned polling place! And all the red tape—register now, vote then, come to this elementary school—but skip work to do it—on and on. Voting on a Tuesday? Good lord. But the online voting, the voting over the phone— man that was great, suddenly participation exploded, from about, what, 40 percent, to 88. We did that over Columbus Day weekend, I think. I remember I'd just had my hair cut very short. Yeah, like in the picture in the hallway. We called that style the Timberlake.

And that's about when your mom got all kinky again. She went out, bought this one device, it was kind of like a swing, where there was this harness and—

Fine. You don't need to know that. But the harness figures in, because that's when your mother had the idea—some of her best ideas happened when she was lying down—to make it illegal to have more than one president from the same immediate family. That was just a personal gripe she had. We'd had the Adamses and Bushes and we were about to have the Clintons and your mother just got pissed. What the fuck? she said. Are we gonna have a monarchy here or what? Are we that stupid, that we have to go to the same well every time? This isn't an Aaron Spelling casting call, this is the damned presidency! I said What about the Kennedys? And she said Screw 'em! Or maybe she didn't say that, but that was the spirit of it. She's a fiery one, your mom, a fiery furnace of—

Ahem. So yeah, she pushed that through, a constitutional amendment.

That led to another busy period. One week, we made all the cars electric and put waterslides in every elementary school. We increased average life expectancy to 164, made it illegal to manufacture or wear Cosby sweaters, and made penises better looking—more streamlined, better coloring, less hair. People, you know, were real appreciative about that. And the last thing we did, which I know I've told you about, was the program where everyone can redo one year of their childhood. For $580, you could go back to the year of your choice, and do that one again. You're not allowed to change anything, do anything differently, but you get to be there again, live the whole year, with what you know now. Oh man, that was a good idea. Everyone loved it, and it made up for all the people who were pissed when we painted Kansas purple, every last inch of it. I did the period between ten-and-a-half and eleven-and-a-half. Fifth grade. Wow, that was sweet.

Speaking of ten-year-olds, here comes your brother. And Uncle Frank! We didn't have to wake you up! *Hola hermano, tios! Esta la noche de los nachos! Si, si.* And here's your mother, descending the stairs. With her hair up. This I was particularly proud of, when I convinced your mother to wear her hair up more often. When she first did it, a week before our wedding, I was breathless, I was lifted, I felt as if I'd met her twin, and oh how I was confused. Was I cheating on my beloved with this version of her, with that long neck exposed, the hair falling in helixes, kissing her clavicles? She assured me that I was not, and that's how we got married, with her hair up—that's how we did the walk with the music and the fanfare, everything yellow and white, side by side, long even strides, she and me, your mother and I.

2

The Ballad of Duane Juarez

TOM FRANKLIN

Tom Franklin's fiction is deeply infused with the histories and cultures of the American South. He was born in 1963 and raised in Dickinson, Alabama, until 1981 when he moved with his family to Mobile, Alabama. While studying for his BA in English from the University of South Alabama in Mobile, Franklin supported himself by working nights at a sandblasting grit factory, a chemical plant, and a hospital morgue, as well as at hazardous-waste clean-up sites. After receiving his BA, Franklin earned his MFA in creative writing at the University of Arkansas in 1998. The following year, he was named the Philip Roth Resident in Creative Writing at Bucknell University. A 2001 Guggenheim Fellow, Franklin has since taught at Knox College, Ole Miss, and Sewanee. The title story in his short story collection *Poachers: Stories* (1999) earned Franklin the Edgar Allan Poe Award for Best Short Story. His writings have also been included in anthologies such as *New Stories from the South: The Year's Best, 1999; The Best American Mystery Stories,* 1999 and 2000; and *The Best American Mystery Stories of the Century.* Franklin has also published two novels, *Hell at the Breech* (2003) and *Smonk: A Novel* (2006).

Ned uses dynamite to fish with. They come swirling to the top, stunned and stupid. You lean over the rail of Ned's expensive boat and scoop them. You drink his beer and smoke his grass. Stay out all night and lie to your wife. Sometimes Ned brings girls, and we know from experience that the moon on the water and the icy Corona from Ned's live wells and the right Jimmy Buffett song on the CD make Ned's girls drip like sponges. You can crawl inside these soft wet girls that Ned finds and sleep there all night. They're intelligent, Ned's girls. They read novels. They're real estate brokers or paralegals or college students.

Where does Ned find these girls?

He's rich. They find him.

I've done the boat thing with Ned like four times, but I'm not rich. In fact I'm poor. I don't shave but I do drink too much and sometimes in the evening I throw moldy fruit through the windows of the house Ned lets me rent, one-fifty a month, though I can't remember the last time I paid. Ned understands. He buys *Playboy* magazines and looks through them once, then gives them to me. That's what it's like to be rich.

Here's what it's like to be poor. Your wife leaves you because you can't find a job because there aren't any jobs to find. You empty the jar of pennies on the mantel to buy cigarettes. You hate to answer the phone; it can't possibly be good news. When your friends invite you out, you don't go. After a while, they stop inviting. You owe them money, and sometimes they ask for it. You tell them you'll see what you can scrape up.

Which is this: nothing.

If you're wondering what somebody like Ned's doing with somebody like me, it's because he's my little brother. I married for love, Ned married for money. Now he pays my light bill; it's in his wife Nina's name. Ned'll come by on Thanksgiving or Christmas day with a case of beer, and he leaves what we don't finish, maybe two cans. He rents movies which we watch on a TV/VCR unit from his real estate office.

In the divorce my ex got everything. Even kept her composure—no crying in front of the judge for her. That was somebody else's department. Thank God there weren't any kids: that's what Ned said. I came home from fishing one morning and she was gone, the damn house empty. I called Ned from a gas station because she'd taken our telephones.

"Bitch ripped off everything except the mallards and the deer heads," I said.

"Well," Ned said, "buck up, big bro. Some people don't have that much."

So what Ned does now is find me these jobs. I cut the grass around some of his rental houses, rake the dead leaves, use the Weed Whacker. I wash his Porsche twice a week when the pollen's thick, and this one time he even let me drive it to get it tuned. In the rearview mirror, I looked like Ned. But it was my eyebrow poking up over his sunglasses and it was me smoking his cigars from the dash pocket and shifting without using the clutch. It was me, Duane, cruising past the downtown hookers standing in their heels to see if there was something in my price range.

Another time Ned let me clean out the attic of a foreclosure, he said keep anything I wanted. Here's what I took: three shotguns, two graphite fishing rods, a tent, a rocking horse, a road atlas, an ice chest, a coin collection, a Styrofoam boulder from one of Nina's plays. When Ned asked if I found anything worth keeping I went, "Not really." I used the coin collection to buy TV dinners and pawned the rest, except for one of the shotguns, a nice Ithaca twelve-gauge pump.

It's been a year since Debra left and I'm still in the getting-over-it stage. I'm drunk every day; that helps. With the TV Ned left I discovered *My Three Sons* and soap operas and PBS. At night I sit and watch. There was this show called *Animals Are Beautiful People*. It was funny as hell. This baboon in the middle of a field picks up a rock looking for something to eat and there's a snake coiled there. The baboon screams, then faints dead away. When he wakes a few minutes later, he picks up the same rock, and there's the snake and whammo, the goddamn baboon faints again.

One night Ned calls. "Hey, big bro, Nina wants to sell the house."

He means the one I'm living in. Holding the remote, the TV muted, I look around.

"But hey, don't panic," Ned says. "The price she wants, they'll never move it. You'll just have this for-sale sign in your yard.

"But you might need to cut that grass once in a while," he says. "You can borrow our lawn mower.

"Another thing," he says. "We're going to the Bahamas for a couple weeks. Will you check up on our place while we're gone? Just drive by a few times, make sure it hasn't burned down.

"There's some cats there, too," he says. "All those damn strays Nina feeds? Won't get 'em fixed either. Says, listen to this, that it interrupts the natural goddamn flow of everything.

"Make you a deal," Ned says. "If all those cats are gone when we get back, I'll pay the responsible party two hundred bucks. All on the Q-T, though. Nina would freak."

On the morning they're leaving for the Bahamas, I'm sleeping on the porch: it's too hot inside, and the flies.

Ned kicks a beer can.

"Hey, bro," he says.

I sit up, blink, see dried vomit on my pants. Brush at the ants working in it.

Ned tosses me a small brown paper bag. "This might come in handy," he says, and winks.

The bag's heavy, like a pint.

Ned squats and socks me in the arm. "We'll have to go fishing when I get back, huh?" He stands up, goes past the for-sale sign. Screeches off in the Porsche.

I open the bag to find a small silver pistol and two plastic boxes of twenty-two cartridges.

Ned and Nina have been gone for a week when I decide it's time to head on over there. I sit up in bed at four in the afternoon and blink at the calendar girl. Finish the beer on the nightstand. The pistol will never work on cats—they'll probably zigzag all over the place and my aim's not that good—so I dig in the closet and find the Ithaca and a box of shells—number eights, birdshot—and go outside, load the stuff into the backseat. I get in front with the pistol, not relishing the idea of all that shooting with my hangover.

There's a line of big black ants, some carrying white things over their heads, going across the dash of the car. Not to mention the water standing in the back floorboard, hatching all these mosquitoes. I put the car in gear and drive to Ned and Nina's big spread in the woods. The magnolia trees and the million-year-old oaks and the Spanish moss. All so damn depressing.

Their lawn's high; Ned'll probably ask me to mow it. I get out slapping at mosquitoes, and four or five cats eye me from the lawn furniture. One yawning from the limb of a tree. There's a sprinkler that I turn on: it makes a ticking sound that alarms the cats. The pistol is snug in my pocket and I take it out, load it. Point it at a fat calico.

"Bang," I say.

I have the house key I copied off Ned's key ring the day he let me take the Porsche. Nina, you can bet, won't like me being inside. I go up the steps, winded at the top, and let myself into the den and sit on the sofa and rest. Rustic as hell. I leaf through a magazine. Try to remember the kind of wood they use to make these big ceiling beams. I get up and wander to the kitchen and take a Heineken from the fridge, put the rest of the six-pack under my arm and start rummaging through the pantry. There's several cans of sardines and tuna that I pocket. Then I notice something else: Ned's Porsche keys hanging on a rack over the sink.

Outside, I open the cans and imitate Nina's squeaky, cute voice: "Here, kitty kitty kitty."

Soon the clueless cats are feasting and purring at my feet, rubbing their shoulders against my ankles. They're half starved. With Ned's Porsche's trunk opened I pick up them one by one by the scruffs of their necks and load them in. They're getting wary now, making these low moaning noises.

But five cats and three kittens are locked away before the smarter ones disappear.

I let myself back into Ned's house and climb upstairs to wash my hands. I look like hell in the bathroom mirror. Those eyes, Christ. Opening the medicine cabinet I find some Tylenol and swallow four. There's some Valium, too, and I empty most of them from the bottle into my shirt pocket. Nina's prescription. There's dozens of bottles of pills in here. Reading their names is like reading Mexican or something. I unscrew some of the caps and sniff inside. Stale. When I find a container of Nina's birth control pills it gives me a semi. A little packet of orange sinus pills looks sort of like the birth control, and I switch them.

Sometimes—and I'm not proud of this—I do a strange thing regarding Nina. I know it's embarrassing, but on nights when Ned's out, I call from a pay phone and wait for Nina to answer. When she says hello, I just hold the line, let her hear me breathing.

"I know it's you, you bitch!" she screams. "You whore!"

Then I hang up, excited and guilty.

Finishing my beer, I go past the door-length mirror into Ned and Nina's bedroom. Their water bed isn't made. I crawl in with my boots on and slosh around: Nina's pillow's sweet smell, a blond pubic hair curling on the quilt.

Going through the nightstand I find seventy-five dollars. In Nina's underwear drawer there are frilly pieces of lingerie that are like Kleenexes they're so delicate. I toss one into the air and let it land on my face. Perfume. There are little fragrant soap balls in the drawer. I lift a thin negligee from the pile and hold it in front of the mirror.

The phone rings.

I stuff the nightie in my pocket and close the drawer, hurry down to the living room where the answering machine is. It beeps and Ned's recording plays and some asshole comes on and asks about the house for sale. Call him, he says, as soon as they get in. I study the machine. A digital number changes from 12 to 13. I press the play button and listen for awhile. There are several calls, that I erase, about the house for sale.

My house.

Outside, you can hear the cats meowing and clawing around in the trunk of the Porsche. I get in and rev the engine, spin off and take curves hard and fast to shut them up.

To be honest, I don't think I've ever killed a cat. Deer, sure. Doves, squirrels, coons. Practically any game animal. Three or four dog accidents with my car and a few dozen snakes, possums and armadillos.

But none of that's the worst thing I've ever done. The worse thing I've ever done was when I woke up in my car after drinking all night with Ned—it was a time I don't remember that much, a week or two after Deb left, *blackouts* are what they call them in jail—and my clothes had a lot of blood on them. I couldn't remember where it came from, so I called Ned and he said he didn't have a clue. Said not to call him at work. Hung up on me. It was my first week renting Ned's place. There was so much blood that I burned the clothes in the fireplace, went outside wearing a bedsheet and watched the smoke coming out of the chimney, worried what my new neighbors would think of a man who burns fires in August and stands in his yard in a sheet.

While I'm paying five dollars for gas at the Jiffy Mart, the clerk squints her eyes and says, "What's that commotion coming out your trunk? Sound like you got you a wildcat in there."

I tell her it's my ex-wife and she laughs a toothless, good-natured laugh.

A drink seems in order next, so I drive the Porsche to the Key West and get a corner table. I finger the pistol in my pocket and think about killing things. Stub out my cigarette in an ashtray shaped like an oyster shell. I glance around. This place is designed to look like an island. Tropical shit, I mean. Every once in a while a fairy floats in thinking it's a gay bar because of how Key West is down in Florida. I guess they don't take the hint from the pickups in the parking lot. The gun racks in back windows. But when they see how the regulars glare at them, they get the picture pretty quick and gulp down their peppermint schnapps or whatever they drink and drop a giant tip for Juarez, the bartender. Juarez for the record isn't foreign: his real name's Larry, but Larry says with a foreign name you get more pussy. Over a shot of tequila, I consider changing my name to something better, tougher-sounding.

I roll my mind over this: What if Ned ever hires me for a real job, to knock off a person, say? Or at the least just beat the shit out of some asshole, maybe some yo-yo who cuts Ned off at a red light and Ned gets the guy's license number. Or maybe somebody's fucking Nina. Ned calling me and saying he's got a big score, yeah, the real thing. Meet him at the Key West. *"It's a doctor,"* he'll whisper in my ear, *"a fat plastic surgeon that's fucking her."*

All I'd have to do is call Ned in the middle of the night and hang up a few times. Get him worried.

"Ten grand," I'll say, and Ned'll go, "Too much," and I'm like, "Hey, Ned? Then pay somebody else, okay, Ned? This ain't some piece of real estate you're buying, Ned. Some piece of ass. This is a professional job, little bro, and if you get some clown who don't know what he's doing, he gets excited by the blood and suddenly you got a body on your hands. Now you're dealing with forensics detectives, Ned, guys pulling hairs off the body with fucking tweezers."

I'm enjoying my little plot until Juarez appears and hits me with more Cuervo. Seeing him reminds me that you need an alias for certain kinds of deals. I pronounce my name out loud and decide my last name's the problem. So I take my cue from Juarez and there on the spot become Duane Juarez. *He* sounds like a dangerous guy, somebody you don't fuck with.

I head to the bar to buy the original Juarez his poison of choice. Pouring, he wants to know what the occasion is, and I tell him I've just made an important decision and we clink our glasses.

"To you," he says. "To Duane."

"Juarez," I add.

"What?"

"Nothing."

Then the subject of cat-killing comes up, and Juarez tells me he grew up on a farm where their mousing cats were always giving birth. Juarez says his old man would stuff a whole damn litter of kittens in a croaker sack and beat it against the ground until the bag stopped moving. Which reminds me that I have a job to do, so I pay my tab with one of Ned's twenties and head outside. There's another cat sitting on the Porsche, attracted, I guess, by the noise or the cat piss smell coming from the trunk.

"Scram," I say, but this one's friendly, and as I pass, it strains its head toward me. "Nice pussy cat," I say, scratching it behind the ears. Then I take it in both hands and toss it into the bushes.

I drive to the woods, down dirt roads, leaving a trail of green bottles. Kudzu, wisteria, honeysuckle. Miles since the last house. I cross a little bridge with ivy and pull off the road into a clearing. Get out feeding shells into the belly of the twelve-gauge. The sky is high and the air is clean and clear and you can hear all these crows. I go to the trunk and open it a crack. Paws and whiskers appear and I swat at them with the gun barrel. They meow and hiss, and finally a whole cat wriggles out. It kicks off the bumper and I slam the trunk, shuck the shotgun's action and lead the cat perfectly as it goes around in circles.

I don't feel the gun's kick, but the cat jackknifes and lands and now it's only half a cat. It flops a couple of times. The woods are bone quiet, everything frozen, the leaves not rattling, the acorns perfectly still on their stobs. I go stand near the cat, which is dead now, and watch the black stuff pooling around its belly. It's a dark gray one with white feet, the kind you'd name Mittens. Some of its fur is moist with blood and I shuck the shotgun; the smoking red shell case lands beside my boot. I think this cat ought to have a name, so Mittens it is. Was.

Back at the trunk, I open the last beer and raise it in a toast, then let another cat out. It hauls ass for the trees.

"Nina!" I yell. The first shot whirls her around but doesn't stop her, and even before the gunshot's faded I've jacked in another shell and I'm batting my way through limbs and spiderwebs in the woods, following her bright red trail. I find her scrabbling up a tree with her sides pumping. When she sees me she howls with her ears flat on her head. She tries to climb higher, but with another shot I send her spread-eagled through the air and she hits the leaves like a tiny bearskin rug.

Then I remember something. It was when we were teenagers, after Ned and I had dropped Nina off from a drive-in movie one night. We both liked her and we'd been drinking and smoking grass. As Ned drove home, we saw beside the road this dead poodle that had belonged to Nina's family for like eleven years—it'd been missing for a day or two. The dog was lying on its side, its legs straight, and—Ned's idea of a joke—we took it back to Nina parents' mansion and stood it there dead on the porch, like a statue. In the car, Ned laughed so hard he started gagging. Then he passed out. When I snuck back to get the dog and bury it, Nina's father caught me in the porch light, my hands around the poodle.

I name the next cat Debra, because it's gray like one Deb used to have, but even as I pull the trigger I feel guilty. I find her wallowing in her pool of blood and shit, gnawing at her shoulder. I decide instead to hang a Mexican name on her. "Maria," I say, taking the pistol from my pocket. But just when I'm about to put Maria out of her misery, I'm struck with a memory of Debra, before we got married, when there was a shitload of love. I don't know why I think of it, but there we are, on the sofa, watching *Mad Max*. I'm getting fresh and Debra's saying okay, okay, we can fool around, but we can't *do it* because she's smack in the middle of her period. So we're kissing and groping until it gets real steamy and she's climbing all over me. Finally she rolls off and stands up, kind of swaying, her nipples hard through her shirt, and I follow her into the bedroom. She throws the covers off and gets a towel and spreads it over the bed. There's this loud zip and she steps out of her skirt. *I hope you like it rare,* she says.

Closing one eye, I squeeze the trigger on Maria and that's that.

At the trunk this time two escape and my beer bottle rolls off the car. Juan the Manx heads for the woods, his body opening and closing like a little hand, and I fire and bowl him over, then shucking the pump whip around and wing—I think—the one jumping into the bushes.

Left now are the kittens, two identical blacks and one solid white. I open the trunk wide: they're cowering behind the spare. All this noise has their fur ruffled, their tails puffy, eyes red, ears flat, teeth bared. "Kitty kitty kitty," I say, and get one of the blacks by the scruff and lift it out and hold it up against the sky. Do it with the pistol right there, specks of blood on my hand and arm.

That was Leigh, one of Ned's girls, and this is Cindy, and there she goes, flung, landing in that tree. But here's Duane Juarez, reloading.

The white kitten is moving. It jumps out, disappears under the car, and here's Duane Juarez dropping to his knees, watching the kitten scramble up into the engine. Duane Juarez on his belly, sliding under the car, and trying to nab the bastard getting bit hard on the knuckle.

Duane Juarez by the Dumpster in the alley behind the Key West, kicking a stranger in the chest. Picking the guy up and breaking his nose with a head butt, Ned behind them, rooting in the shadows. Duane Juarez picking a tooth out of his knuckle and tossing it to Ned for a souvenir.

The woods are as quiet as a back alley. There's only one way to deal with this kind of cat situation. You have to get in the Porsche and rev its engine to a scream. You have to leave the shotgun barrel holding down the accelerator. You have to climb onto the car with the pistol. The hood might buckle with your weight, but it's your job to stand there, ready.

This one's Ned.

3

In the American Society

GISH JEN

Gish Jen, the daughter of first-generation Chinese immigrants, was born and raised in 1956 in Scarsdale, New York, a largely Jewish community. She earned her BA in English at Harvard University in 1977. Her graduate education consisted of a year at Stanford University (1979–80), followed by an MFA in creative writing at the University of Iowa (1983). Jen's writing has appeared in *The New Yorker, The Atlantic Monthly,* and *The Best American Short Stories of the Century.* She has published three novels, *Typical American* (1991), *Mona in the Promised Land* (1996), and *The Love Wife* (2004), as well as a collection of short stories, *Who's Irish?: Stories* (1999). Her short stories and novels engage distinct perspectives on American ambition and identity, at turns maddening and comical. Jen is a recipient of many awards and distinctions, including fellowships with the Radcliffe Bunting Institute and James A. Michener Foundation/Copernicus Society, the Massachusetts Artists Foundation, and the National Endowment for the Arts.

HIS OWN SOCIETY

When my father took over the pancake house, it was to send my little sister, Mona, and me to college. We were only in junior high at the time, but my father believed in getting a jump on things. "Those Americans always saying it," he told us. "Smart guys thinking in advance." My mother elaborated, explaining that businesses took bringing up, like children. They could take years to get going, she said, years.

In this case, though, we got rich right away. At two months, we were breaking even, and at four, those same hotcakes that could barely withstand the weight of butter and syrup were supporting our family with ease. My mother bought a station wagon with air conditioning, my father an oversized red vinyl recliner for the back room; and as time went on and the business continued to thrive, my father started to talk about his grandfather, and the village he had reigned over in China—things my father had never talked about when he worked for other people. He told us about the bags of rice his family would give out to the poor at New Year's, and about the people who came to beg, on their hands and knees, for his grandfather to intercede for the more wayward of their relatives. "Like that Godfather in the movie," he would tell us as, feet up, he distributed paychecks. Sometimes an employee would get two green envelopes instead of one, which meant that Jimmy needed a tooth pulled, say, or that Tiffany's husband was in the clinker again. "It's nothing, nothing," he would insist, sinking back into his chair. "Who else is going to taking care of you people?"

My mother would mostly just sigh about it. "Your father thinks this is China," she would say, and then she would go back to her mending. Once in a while, though, when my father had given away a particularly large sum, she would exclaim, outraged, "But this here is the *U—S—of—A!*"—this apparently having been what she used to tell immigrant stock boys when they came in late.

She didn't work at the supermarket anymore; but she had made it to the rank of manager before she left, and this had given her not only new words and phrases but new ideas about herself, and about America, and about what was what in general. She had opinions about how downtown should be zoned; she could pump her own gas and check her own oil; and for all that she used to chide Mona and me for being copycats, she herself was now interested in espadrilles, and wallpaper, and, most recently, the town country club.

"So join already," said Mona, flicking a fly off her knee.

My mother enumerated the problems as she sliced up a quarter round of watermelon. There was the cost. There was the waiting list. There was the fact that no one in our family played either tennis or golf.

"So what?" said Mona.

"It would be waste," said my mother.

"Me and Callie can swim in the pool."

"Anyway, you need that recommendation letter from a member."

"Come *on*," said Mona. "Annie's mom'd write you a letter in a *sec*."

My mother's knife glinted in the early-summer sun. I spread some more newspaper on the picnic table.

"Plus, you have to eat there twice a month. You know what that means." My mother cut another, enormous slice of fruit.

"No, I *don't* know what that means," said Mona.

"It means Dad would have to wear a jacket, dummy," I said.

"Oh! Oh! Oh!" said Mona, clasping her hand to her breast. "Oh! Oh! Oh! Oh! Oh!"

We all laughed: My father had no use for nice clothes, and would wear only ten-year-old shirts, with grease-spotted pants, to show how little he cared what anyone thought.

"Your father doesn't believe in joining the American society," said my mother. "He wants to have his own society."

"So go to dinner without him." Mona shot her seeds out in long arcs over the lawn. "Who cares what he thinks?"

But of course, we all did care, and knew my mother could not simply up and do as she pleased. For to embrace what my father embraced was to love him; and to embrace something else was to betray him.

He demanded a similar sort of loyalty of his workers, whom he treated more like servants than employees. Not in the beginning, of course. In the beginning, all he wanted was for them to keep on doing what they used to do, to which end he concentrated mostly on leaving them alone. As the months passed, though, he expected more and more of them, with the result that, for all his largesse, he began to have trouble keeping help. The cooks and busboys complained that he asked them to fix radiators and trim hedges, not only at the restaurant but at our house; the waitresses, that he sent them on errands, and made them chauffeur him around. Our head-waitress, Gertrude, claimed that he once even asked her to scratch his back.

"It's not just the blacks don't believe in slavery," she said when she quit.

My father never quite registered her complaints, though, nor those of others who left. Even after Eleanor quit, then Tiffany, and Gerald, and Jimmy, and even his best cook, Eureka Andy, for whom he had bought new glasses, he remained mostly convinced that the fault lay with them.

"All they understand is that assemble line," he lamented. "Robots, they are. They want to be robots."

There were occasions when the clear running truth seemed to eddy, when he would pinch the vinyl of his chair up into little peaks and wonder if he was doing thing right. But with time he would always smooth the peaks back down; and when business started to slide in the spring, he kept on like a horse in his ways.

By the summer, our dish boy was overwhelmed with scraping. It was no longer just the hash browns that people were leaving for trash, and the service was as bad as the food. The waitresses served up French pancakes instead of German, apple juice instead of orange. They spilled things on laps, on coats. On the Fourth of July, some greenhorn sent an entire side of fries slaloming down a lady's *Massif Central*. Meanwhile, in the back room, my father labored through articles on the economy.

"What is housing starts?" he puzzled. "What is GNP?"

Mona and I did what we could, filling in as busgirls and dishwashers, and, one afternoon, stuffing the comments box by the cashier's desk. That was Mona's idea. We rustled up a variety of pens and pencils, checked boxes for an hour, smeared the cards with coffee and grease, and waited. It took a few days for my father to notice that the box was full, and he didn't say anything about it for a few days more. Finally, though, he started to complain of fatigue; and then he began to complain that the staff was not what it could be. We encouraged him in this—pointing out, for instance, how many dishes got chipped. But in the end all that happened was that, for the first time since we took over the restaurant, my father got it into his head to fire someone. Skip, a skinny busboy who was saving up for a sports car, said nothing as my father mumbled on about the price of dishes. My father's hands shook as he wrote out the severance check; and once it was over, he spent the rest of the day napping in his chair.

Since it was going on midsummer, Skip wasn't easy to replace. We hung a sign in the window and advertised in the paper, but no one called the first week, and the person who called the second didn't show up for his interview. The third week, my father phoned Skip to see if he would come back, but a friend of his had already sold him a Corvette for cheap.

Finally, a Chinese guy named Booker turned up. He couldn't have been more than thirty, and was wearing a lighthearted seersucker suit, but he looked as though life had him pinned. His eyes were bloodshot and his chest sunken, and the muscles of his neck seemed to strain with the effort of holding his head up. In a single dry breath he told us that he had never bused tables but was willing to learn, and that he was on the lam from the deportation authorities.

"I do not want to lie to you," he kept saying. He had come to the United States on a student visa but had run out of money and was now in a bind. He was loath to go back to Taiwan, as it happened—he looked up at this point, to be sure my father wasn't pro-KMT—but all he had was a phony Social Security card, and a willingness to absorb all blame, should anything untoward come to pass.

"I do not think, anyway, that it is against law to hire me, only to be me," he said, smiling faintly.

Anyone else would have examined him on this, but my father conceived of laws as speed bumps rather than curbs. He wiped the counter with his sleeve, and told Booker to report the next morning.

"I will be good worker," said Booker.

"Good," said my father.

"Anything you want me to do, I will do."

My father nodded.

Booker seemed to sink into himself for a moment. "Thank you," he said finally. "I am appreciate your help. I am very, very appreciate for everything."

My father looked at him. "Did you eat today?" he asked in Mandarin.

Booker pulled at the hem of his jacket.

"Sit down," said my father. "Please, have a seat."

My father didn't tell my mother about Booker, and my mother didn't tell my father about the country club. She would never have applied, except that Mona, while over at Annie's, had let it drop that our mother wanted to join. Mrs. Lardner came by the very next day.

"Why, I'd be honored and delighted to write you people a letter," she said. Her skirt billowed around her.

"Thank you so much," said my mother. "But it's too much trouble for you, and also my husband is . . . "

"Oh, it's no trouble at all, no trouble at all. I tell you." She leaned forward, so that her chest freckles showed. "I know just how it is. It's a secret of course, but, you know, my natural father was Jewish. Can you see it? Just look at my skin."

"My husband," said my mother.

"I'd be honored and delighted," said Mrs. Lardner, with a little wave of her hands. "Just honored and delighted."

Mona was triumphant. "See, Mom," she said, waltzing around the kitchen when Mrs. Lardner left. "What did I tell you? 'I'm honored and delighted, just honored and delighted.'" She waved her hands in the air.

"You know, the Chinese have a saying," said my mother. "To do nothing is better than to overdo. You mean well, but you tell me now what will happen."

"I'll talk Dad into it," said Mona, still waltzing. "Or I bet Callie can. He'll do anything Callie says."

"I can try, anyway," I said.

"Did you hear what I said?" said my mother. Mona bumped into the broom closet door. "You're not going to talk anything. You've already made enough trouble." She started on the dishes with a clatter.

Mona poked diffidently at a mop.

I sponged off the counter. "Anyway," I ventured. "I bet our name'll never even come up."

"That's if we're lucky," said my mother.

"There's all these people waiting," I said.

"Good." She started on a pot.

I looked over at Mona, who was still cowering in the broom closet. "In fact, there's some black family's been waiting so long, they're going to sue," I said.

My mother turned off the water. "Where'd you hear that?"

"Patty told me."

She turned the water back on, started to wash a dish, then put it down and shut the faucet.

"I'm sorry," said Mona.

"Forget it," said my mother. "Just forget it."

Booker turned out to be a model worker, whose boundless gratitude translated into a willingness to do anything. As he also learned quickly, he soon knew not only how to bus but how to cook, and how to wait tables, and how to keep the books. He fixed the walk-in door so that it stayed shut, reupholstered the torn seats in the dining room, and devised a system for tracking inventory. The only stone in the rice was that he tended to be sickly; but, reliable even in illness, he would always send a friend to take his place. In this way, we got to know Ronald, Lynn, Dirk, and Cedric, all of whom, like Booker, had problems with their legal status, and were anxious to please. They weren't all as capable as Booker, though, with the exception of Cedric, whom my father often hired even when Booker was well. A round wag of a man who called Mona and me *shou hou*—skinny monkeys—he was a professed nonsmoker who was nevertheless always begging drags off other people's cigarettes. This last habit drove our head cook, Fernando, crazy, especially since, when refused a hit, Cedric would occasionally snitch one. Winking impishly at Mona and me, he would steal up to an ashtray, take a quick puff, and then break out laughing, so that the smoke came rolling out of his mouth in a great incriminatory cloud. Fernando accused him of stealing fresh cigarettes, too, even whole packs.

"Why else do you think he's weaseling around in the back of the store all the time?" he said. His face was blotchy with anger. "The man is a frigging thief."

Other members of the staff supported him in this contention, and joined in on an "Operation Identification," which involved numbering and initialing their cigarettes—even though what they seemed to fear for wasn't so much their cigarettes as their jobs. Then one of the cooks quit; and, rather than promote someone, my father hired Cedric for the position. Rumor had it that Cedric was taking only half the normal salary; that Alex had been pressured to resign; and that my father was looking for a position with which to placate Booker, who had been bypassed because of his health.

The result was that Fernando categorically refused to work with Cedric.

"The only way I'll cook with that piece of slime," he said, shaking his huge, tattooed fist, "is if it's his ass frying on the grill."

My father cajoled and cajoled, but in the end was simply forced to put them on different schedules.

The next week, Fernando got caught stealing a carton of minute steaks. My father would not tell even Mona and me how he knew to be standing by the back door when Fernando was on his way out, but everyone suspected Booker. Everyone but Fernando, that is, who was sure Cedric had been the tip-off. My father held a staff meeting, in which he tried to reassure everyone that Alex had left on his own, and that he had no intention of firing anyone. But though he was careful not to mention Fernando, everyone was so amazed that he was being allowed to stay that Fernando was incensed nonetheless.

"Don't you all be putting your bug eyes on me," he said. "*He's* the frigging crook." He grabbed Cedric by the collar.

Cedric raised an eyebrow. "Cook, you mean," he said.

At this, Fernando punched Cedric in the mouth; and, the words he had just uttered notwithstanding, my father fired Fernando on the spot.

With everything that was happening, Mona and I were ready to be finishing up at the restaurant. It was almost time: The days were still stuffy with summer, but our window shade had started flapping in the evening as if gearing up to go out. That year, the breezes were full of salt, as they sometimes were when they came in from the east, and they blew anchors and docks through my mind like so many tumbleweeds, filling my dreams with wherries and lobsters and grainy-faced men who squinted, day in and day out, at the sky.

It was time for a change—you could feel it—and yet the pancake house was the same as ever. The day before school started, my father came home with bad news.

"Fernando called police," he said, wiping his hand on his pant leg.

My mother naturally wanted to know what police; and so, with much coughing and hawing, the long story began, the latest installment of which had the police calling Immigration, and Immigration sending an investigator. My mother sat stiff as whalebone as my father described how the man had summarily refused lunch on the house, and how my father had admitted, under pressure, that he knew there were "things" about his workers.

"So now what happens?"

My father didn't know. "Booker and Cedric went with him to the jail," he said. "But me, here I am." He laughed uncomfortably.

The next day, my father posted bail for "his boys," and waited apprehensively for something to happen. The day after that, he waited again, and the day after that, he called our neighbor's law student son, who suggested my father call the Immigration Department under an alias. My father took his advice; and it was thus that he discovered that Booker was right. It was illegal for aliens to work, but it wasn't to hire them.

In the happy interval that ensued, my father apologized to my mother, who in turn confessed about the country club, for which my father had no choice but to forgive her. Then he turned his attention back to "his boys."

My mother didn't see that there was anything to do.

"I like to talking to the judge," said my father.

"This is not China," said my mother.

"I'm only talking to him. I'm not give him money unless he wants it."

"You're going to land up in jail."

"So what else I should do?" My father threw up his hands. "Those are my boys."

"Your boys!" exploded my mother. "What about your family? What about your wife?"

My father took a long sip of tea. "You know," he said finally, "in the war my father sent our cook to the soldiers to use. He always said it—the province comes before the town, the town comes before the family."

"A restaurant is not a town," said my mother.

My father sipped at his tea again. "You know, when I first come to the United States, I also had to hide-and-seek with those deportation guys. If people did not helping me, I am not here today."

My mother scrutinized her hem.

After a minute, I volunteered that before seeing a judge, he might try a lawyer.

He turned. "Since when did you become so afraid like your mother?"

I started to say that it wasn't a matter of fear, but he cut me off.

"What I need today," he said, "is a son."

My father and I spent the better part of the next day standing on lines at the Immigration office. He did not get to speak to a judge, but with much persistence he managed to speak to a special clerk, who tried to persuade him that it was not her place to extend him advice. My father, though, shamelessly plied her with compliments and offers of free pancakes, until she finally conceded that she personally doubted anything would happen to either Cedric or Booker.

"Especially if they're 'needed workers,'" she said, rubbing at the red marks her glasses left on her nose. She yawned. "Have you thought about sponsoring them to become permanent residents?"

Could he do that? My father was overjoyed. And what if he saw to it right away? Would she perhaps put in a good word with the judge?

She yawned again, her nostrils flaring. "Don't worry," she said. "They'll get a fair hearing."

My father returned jubilant. Booker and Cedric hailed him as their savior. He was like a father to them, they said; and, laughing and clapping, they made him tell the story over and over, sorting through the details like jewels. And how old was the assistant judge? And what did she say?

That evening, my father tipped the paperboy a dollar and bought a pot of mums for my mother, who suffered them to be placed on the dining room table. The next night, he took us all out to dinner. Then on Saturday, Mona found a letter and some money in an envelope on my father's chair at the restaurant.

Dear Mr. Chang,
You are the grat boss. But, we do not like to trial, so will runing away now. Plese to excus us. People saying the law in America is fears like dragon. Here is only $140. We hope some day we can pay back the rest bale. You will getting intrest, as you diserving, so grat a boss you are. Thank you for every thing. In next life you will be burn in rich family, with no more pancaks.

> *Yours truley,*
> *Booker + Cedric*

In the weeks that followed, my father went to the pancake house for crises, but otherwise hung around our house, fiddling idly with the sump pump and boiler in an effort, he said, to get ready for winter. It was as though he had gone into retirement, except that instead of moving south, he had moved to the basement. He even took to showering my mother with little attentions, and to calling her "old girl," and when we finally heard that the club had entertained all the applications it could for the year, he was so sympathetic that he seemed more disappointed than my mother.

IN THE AMERICAN SOCIETY

Mrs. Lardner tempered the bad news with an invitation to a bon voyage bash she was throwing for her friend Jeremy Brothers, who was going to Greece for six months.

"Do come," she urged. "You'll meet everyone, and then, you know, if things open up in the spring . . . " She waved her hands.

My mother wondered if it would be appropriate to show up at a party for someone they didn't know, but "the honest truth" was that this was an annual affair. "If it's not Greece, it's Italy," sighed Mrs. Lardner. "We really just do it because his wife left him and his daughter doesn't speak to him, and poor Jeremy just feels so *unloved.*"

She also invited Mona and me to the goings-on, to keep Annie out of the champagne. I wasn't too keen on the idea, but before I could say anything, she had already thanked us for so generously agreeing to honor her with our presence.

"A pair of little princesses, you are!" she told us. "A pair of princesses!"

The party was that Sunday. On Saturday, my mother took my father out shopping for a suit. Since it was the end of September, she insisted that he buy a worsted rather than a seersucker, even though it was only 10, rather than 50, percent off. My father protested that the weather was as hot as ever, which was true—a thick Indian summer had cozied murderously up to us—but to no avail. Summer clothes, said my mother, were not properly worn after Labor Day.

The suit was unfortunately as extravagant in length as it was in price, which posed an additional quandary, since the tailor wouldn't be in until Monday. The salesgirl, though, found a way of tacking it up temporarily.

"Maybe this suit not fit me," fretted my father.

"Just don't take your jacket off," said the salesgirl.

He gave her a tip before they left, but when he got home, he refused to remove the price tag.

"I like to asking the tailor about the size," he insisted.

"You mean you're going to *wear* it and then *return* it?" Mona rolled her eyes.

"I didn't say I'm return it," said my father stiffly. "I like to asking the tailor, that's all."

The party started off swimmingly, except that most people were wearing Bermudas or wrap skirts. Still, my parents carried on, sharing with great feeling the complaints about the heat. Of course, my father tried to eat a cracker full of shallots, and burned himself in an attempt to help Mr. Lardner turn the coals of the barbecue; but on the whole, he seemed to be doing all right. Not nearly so well as my mother, though, who had accepted an entire cupful of Mrs. Lardner's magic punch and indeed seemed to be under some spell. As Mona and Annie skirmished over whether some boy in their class inhaled when he smoked, I watched my mother take off her shoes, laughing and laughing as a man with a beard regaled her with navy stories by the pool. Apparently he had been stationed in the Orient and remembered a few words of Chinese, which made my mother laugh still more. My father excused himself to go to the bathroom, then drifted back and weighed anchor at the hors d'oeuvres table, while my mother sailed on to a group of women, who tinkled at length over the clarity of her complexion. I dug out a book I had brought.

Just when I'd cracked the spine, though, Mrs. Lardner came by to bewail her shortage of servers. Her caterers were criminals, I agreed; and the next thing I knew, I was handing out bits of marine life as amiably as I could.

"Here you go, Dad," I said, when I got to the hors d'oeuvres table.

"Everything is fine," he said.

I hesitated to leave him alone; but then the man with the beard zeroed in on him, and though he talked of nothing but my mother, I thought it would be okay to get back to work. Just at that moment, though, Jeremy Brothers lurched our way, an empty, albeit corked, wine bottle in hand. He was a slim, well-proportioned man, with a Roman nose and small eyes and a nice manly jaw that he allowed to hang agape.

"Hello," he said drunkenly. "Pleased to meet you."

"Pleased to meeting you," said my father.

"Right," said Jeremy. "Right. Listen. I have this bottle here, this most recalcitrant bottle. You see that it refuses to do my bidding. I bid it open sesame, please, and it does nothing." He pulled the cork out with his teeth, then turned the bottle upside down.

My father nodded.

"Would you have a word with it, please?" said Jeremy. The man with the beard excused himself. "Would you please have a god-damned word with it?"

My father laughed uncomfortably.

"Ah!" Jeremy bowed a little. "Excuse me, excuse me, excuse me. You are not my man, not my man at all." He bowed again and started to leave, but then circled back. "Viticulture is not your forte. Yes, I can see that, see that plainly. But may I trouble you on another matter? Forget the damned bottle." He threw it into the pool, winking at the people he splashed. "I have another matter. Do you speak Chinese?"

My father said he did not, but Jeremy pulled out a handkerchief with some characters on it anyway, saying that his daughter had sent it from Hong Kong and that he thought the characters might be some secret message.

"Long life," said my father.

"But you haven't looked at it yet."

"I know what it says without looking." My father winked at me.

"You do?"

"Yes, I do."

"You're making fun of me, aren't you?"

"No, no, no," said my father, winking again.

"Who are you anyway?" said Jeremy.

His smile fading, my father shrugged.

"*Who are you?*"

My father shrugged again.

Jeremy began to roar. "This is my party, *my party,* and I've never seen you before in my life." My father backed up as Jeremy came toward him. "*Who are you? WHO ARE YOU?*"

Just as my father was going to step into the pool, Mrs. Lardner came running up. Jeremy informed her that there was a man crashing his party.

"Nonsense," said Mrs. Lardner. "This is Ralph Chang, whom I invited extra specially so he could meet you." She straightened the collar of Jeremy's peach-colored polo shirt for him.

"Yes, well we've had a chance to chat," said Jeremy.

She whispered in his ear; he mumbled something; she whispered something more.

"I do apologize," he said finally.

My father didn't say anything.

"I do." Jeremy seemed genuinely contrite. "Doubtless you've seen drunks before, haven't you? You must have them in China."

"Okay," said my father.

As Mrs. Lardner glided off, Jeremy clapped his arm over my father's shoulders. "You know, I really am quite sorry, quite sorry."

My father nodded.

"What can I do? How can I make it up to you?"

"No, thank you."

"No, tell me, tell me," wheedled Jeremy. "Tickets to casino night?" My father shook his head. "You don't gamble. Dinner at Bartholomew's?" My father shook his head again. "You don't eat." Jeremy scratched his chin. "You know, my wife was like you. Old Annabelle could never let me make things up—never, never, never, never, never."

My father wriggled out from under his arm.

"How about sport clothes? You are rather overdressed, you know. Excuse me for saying so. But here." He took off his polo shirt and folded it up. "You can have this with my most profound apologies." He ruffled his chest hairs with his free hand.

"No, thank you," said my father.

"No, take it, take it. Accept my apologies." He thrust the shirt into my father's arms. "I'm so very sorry, so very sorry. Please, try it on."

Helplessly holding the shirt, my father searched the crowd for my mother.

"Here, I'll help you with your coat."

My father froze.

Jeremy reached over and took the jacket off. "Milton's, one hundred twenty-five dollars reduced to one hundred twelve-fifty," he read. "What a bargain, what a bargain!"

"Please give it back," pleaded my father. "Please."

"Now for your shirt," ordered Jeremy.

Heads began to turn.

"Take off your shirt."

"I do not taking orders like a servant," announced my father stiffly.

"Take off your shirt, or I'm going to throw this jacket right into the pool, just right into this little pool here." Jeremy held it over the water.

"Go ahead."

"One hundred twelve-fifty," taunted Jeremy. "One hundred twelve . . . "

My father flung the polo shirt into the water with such force that part of it bounced back up into the air like a fluorescent fountain. Then it settled into a soft heap on top of the water. My mother hurried up.

"You're a sport!" said Jeremy, suddenly breaking into a smile, and slapping my father on the back. "You're a sport! I like that. A man with spirit, that's what you are. A man with panache. Allow me to return to you your jacket." He handed it back to my father. "Good value you got on that, good value."

My father hurled the coat into the pool, too. "We're leaving," he said grimly. "Leaving!"

"Now, Ralphie," said Mrs. Lardner, bustling up; but my father was already stomping off.

"Get your sister," he told me. To my mother: "Get your shoes."

"That was *great*, Dad," said Mona as we walked to the car. "You were *stupendous*."

"Way to show 'em," I said.

"What?" said my father offhandedly.

Although it was only just dusk, we were in a gulch, which made it hard to see anything except the gleam of his white shirt moving up the hill ahead of us.

"It was all my fault," began my mother.

"Forget it," said my father grandly. Then he said, "The only trouble is, I left those keys in my jacket pocket."

"Oh *no*," said Mona.

"Oh no is right," said my mother.

"So we'll walk home," I said.

"But how're we going to get into the *house?*" said Mona.

The noise of the party churned through the silence.

"Someone has to going back," said my father.

"Let's go to the pancake house first," suggested my mother. "We can wait there until the party is finished, and then call Mrs. Lardner."

Having all agreed that was a good plan, we started walking again.

"God, just think," said Mona. "We're going to have to *dive* for them."

My father stopped a moment. We waited.

"You girls are good swimmers," he said finally. "Not like me."

Then his shirt started moving again, and we trooped up the hill after it, into the dark.

4

Gogol

JHUMPA LAHIRI

Jhumpa Lahiri, the daughter of Bengali Indian immigrants, was born in London in 1967 and raised in Kingston, Rhode Island. She received her BA in English literature from Barnard College in 1989 and then went on to secure four degrees at Boston University: MA degrees in English, creative writing, and comparative literature as well as a PhD in renaissance studies. Her first short story collection, *Interpreter of Maladies* (1999), earned her the 2000 Pulitzer Prize for Fiction. The short story featured in this collection, "Gogol," first appeared in *The New Yorker* and was later published as part of Lahiri's first novel, *The Namesake* (2003), which was adapted into a major motion picture. She published a second short story collection, *Unaccustomed Earth*, in 2008. Lahiri is also the recipient of a Guggenheim Fellowship.

In a hospital waiting room in Cambridge, Ashoke Ganguli hunches over a Boston *Globe* from a month ago, abandoned on a neighboring chair. He reads about the riots that took place during the Democratic National Convention in Chicago and about Dr. Benjamin Spock, the baby doctor, being sentenced to two years in jail for threatening to counsel draft evaders. The Favre Leuba strapped to his wrist is running six minutes ahead of the large gray-faced clock on the wall. It is four-thirty in the morning.

He desperately needs a cup of tea, not having managed to make one before leaving the house. But the machine in the corridor dispenses only coffee, tepid at best, in paper cups. He takes off his thick-rimmed glasses, fitted by a Calcutta optometrist, and polishes the lenses with the cotton handkerchief he always keeps in his pocket, "A" for Ashoke embroidered by his mother in light-blue thread. His black hair, normally combed back neatly from his forehead, is disheveled, sections of it on end. He stands and begins pacing, as the other expectant fathers do. The men wait with cigars, flowers, address books, bottles of champagne. They smoke cigarettes, ashing onto the floor. Ashoke, a doctoral candidate in electrical engineering at M.I.T., is indifferent to such indulgences. He neither smokes nor drinks alcohol of any kind. Ashima is the one who keeps all their addresses, in a small notebook she carries in her purse. It has never occurred to him to buy his wife flowers.

He returns to the *Globe*, still pacing as he reads. A slight limp causes Ashoke's right foot to drag almost imperceptibly with each step. Since childhood he has had the habit and the ability to read while walking, holding a book in one hand on his way to school, from room to room in his parents' three-story house in Alipore, and up and down the red clay stairs. Nothing roused him. Nothing distracted him. Nothing caused him to stumble. As a teen-ager he had gone through all of Dickens. He read newer authors as well, Graham Greene and Somerset Maugham, all purchased from his favorite stall on College Street with *pujo* money. But most of all he loved the Russians. His paternal grandfather, a former professor of European literature at Calcutta University, had read from them aloud in English translation when Ashoke was a boy. Each day at teatime, as his brothers and sisters played *kabadi* and cricket outside, Ashoke would go to his grandfather's room, and for an hour his grandfather would read supine on the bed, his ankles crossed and the book propped open on his chest, Ashoke curled at his side. For that hour Ashoke was deaf and blind to the world around him. He did not hear his brothers and sisters laughing on the rooftop, or see the tiny, dusty, cluttered room in which his grandfather read. "Read all the Russians, and then reread them," his grandfather had said. "They will never fail you." When Ashoke's English was good enough, he began to read the books himself. It was while walking on some of the world's noisiest, busiest streets, on Chowringhee and Gariahat Road, that he had read pages of "The Brothers Karamazov," and "Anna Karenina," and "Fathers and Sons." Ashoke's mother was always convinced that her eldest son would be hit by a bus or a tram, his nose deep into "War and Peace"—that he would be reading a book the moment he died.

One day, in the earliest hours of October 20, 1961, this nearly happened. Ashoke was twenty-two, a student at Bengal Engineering College. He was travelling on the No. 83 Up Howrah–Ranchi Express to visit his grandparents in Jamshedpur, where they had moved upon his grandfather's retirement from the university. Ashoke had never spent the Durga *pujo* holidays away from his family. But his grandfather had recently gone blind, and he had requested Ashoke's company specifically, to read him *The Statesman* in the morning, Dostoyevsky and Tolstoy in the afternoon. Ashoke accepted the invitation eagerly. He carried two suitcases, the first one containing

clothes and gifts, the second empty. For it would be on this visit, his grandfather had said, that the books in his glass-fronted case, collected over a lifetime and preserved under lock and key, would be given to Ashoke. He had
already received a few in recent years, given to him on birthdays and other
special occasions. But now that the day had come to inherit the rest, the
day his grandfather could no longer read the books himself, Ashoke was
saddened, and as he placed the empty suitcase under his seat he was dis-
concerted by its weightlessness, regretful of the circumstances that would
cause it, upon his return, to be full.

He carried a single volume for the journey, a hardbound collection of
short stories by Nikolai Gogol, which his grandfather had given him when
he'd graduated from class twelve. On the title page, beneath his grandfather's signature, Ashoke had written his own. Because of his passion for this
particular book, the spine had recently split, threatening to divide the pages
into two sections. His favorite story in the book was the last, "The Overcoat," and that was the one Ashoke had begun to reread as the train, late in
the evening, pulled out of Howrah Station with a prolonged and deafening
shriek, away from his parents and his six younger brothers and sisters, all of
whom had come to see him off, and had huddled until the last moment by
the window, waving to him from the long, dusky platform.

Outside the view turned quickly black, the scattered lights of Howrah
giving way to nothing at all. He had a second-class sleeper, in the seventh
bogie behind the air-conditioned coach. Because of the season, the train
was especially crowded, filled with families on holiday. Small children were
wearing their best clothing, the girls with brightly colored ribbons in their
hair. He shared his compartment with three others. There was a middle-
aged Bihari couple who, he gathered from overhearing their conversation, had just married off their eldest daughter, and a friendly, potbellied,
middle-aged Bengali businessman wearing a suit and tie, by the name of
Ghosh. Ghosh told Ashoke that he had recently spent two years in England
on a job voucher, but that he had come back home because his wife was in-
consolably miserable abroad. Ghosh spoke reverently of England. The sparkling, empty streets, the polished black cars, the rows of gleaming white
houses, he said, were like a dream. Trains departed and arrived according to
schedule, Ghosh said. No one spat on the sidewalks. It was in a British hospital that his son had been born.

"Seen much of this world?" Ghosh asked Ashoke, untying his shoes and
settling himself cross-legged on the berth. He pulled a packet of Dunhill
cigarettes from his jacket pocket, offering them around the compartment

before lighting one for himself. "You are still young. Free," he said, spreading his hands apart for emphasis. "Do yourself a favor. Before it's too late, without thinking too much about it first, pack a pillow and a blanket and see as much of the world as you can. You will not regret it. One day it will be too late."

"My grandfather always says that's what books are for," Ashoke said, using the opportunity to open the volume in his hands. "To travel without moving an inch."

"To each his own," Ghosh said. He tipped his head politely to one side, letting the last of the cigarette drop from his fingertips. He reached into a bag by his feet and took out his diary, turning to the twentieth of October. The page was blank, and on it, with a fountain pen whose cap he ceremoniously unscrewed, he wrote his name and address. He ripped out the page and handed it to Ashoke. "If you ever change your mind and need contacts, let me know. I live in Tollygunge, just behind the tram depot."

"Thank you," Ashoke said, folding up the information and putting it at the back of his book.

"How about a game of cards?" Ghosh suggested. He pulled out a well-worn deck from his suit pocket, with an image of Big Ben on the back. But Ashoke politely declined. One by one the passengers brushed their teeth in the vestibule, changed into their pajamas, fastened the curtain around their compartments, and went to sleep. Ghosh offered to take the upper berth, climbing barefoot up the ladder, his suit carefully folded away, so that Ashoke had the window to himself. The Bihari couple shared some sweets from a box and drank water from the same cup without either of them putting their lips to the rim, then settled into their berths as well, switching off the lights and turning their heads to the wall.

Only Ashoke continued to read, still seated, still dressed. A single small bulb glowed dimly over his head. From time to time he looked through the open window at the inky Bengal night, at the vague shapes of palm trees and the simplest of homes. Carefully he turned the soft yellow pages of his book, a few delicately tunneled by worms. The steam engine puffed reassuringly, powerfully. Deep in his chest he felt the rough jostle of the wheels. Sparks from the smokestack passed by his window. A fine layer of sticky soot dotted one side of his face, his eyelid, his arm, his neck; his grandmother would insist that he scrub himself with a cake of Margo soap as soon as he arrived. Immersed in the sartorial plight of Akaky Akakyevich, lost in the wide, snow-white, windy avenues of St. Petersburg, unaware that one day he was to dwell in a snowy place himself, Ashoke was still reading at two-thirty in the morning, one of the few passengers on the train who was awake, when the locomotive engine and seven bogies derailed from the broad-gauge line. The sound was like a bomb exploding. The first four bogies capsized into a depression alongside the track. The fifth and sixth, containing the first-class and air-conditioned passengers, telescoped into each other, killing the passengers in their sleep. The seventh, where Ashoke was sitting, capsized as well, flung by the speed of the crash farther into the field. The accident occurred two hundred and nine kilometers from Calcutta, between the Ghatshila and Dhalbumgarh stations. More than an hour passed before the rescuers arrived, bearing lanterns and shovels and axes to pry bodies from the cars.

Ashoke can still remember their shouts, asking if anyone was alive. He remembers trying to shout back, unsuccessfully, his mouth emitting nothing but the faintest rasp. He remembers the sound of people half-dead around him, moaning and tapping on the walls of the train, whispering hoarsely for help, words that only those who were also trapped and injured could possibly hear. Blood drenched his chest and the left arm of his shirt. He had been thrust partway out the window. He remembers being unable to see anything at all; for the first hours he thought that perhaps, like his grandfather, he'd gone blind. He remembers the acrid odor of flames, the buzzing of flies, children crying, the taste of dust and blood on his tongue. They were nowhere, somewhere in a field. Milling about them were villagers, police inspectors, a few doctors. He remembers believing that he was dying, that perhaps he was already dead. He could not feel the lower half of his body, and so was unaware that the mangled limbs of Ghosh were draped over his legs. Eventually he saw the cold, unfriendly blue of earliest morning, the moon and a few stars still lingering in the sky. The pages of his book, which had been tossed from his hand, fluttered in two sections a few feet away from the train. The glare from a search lantern briefly caught the pages, momentarily distracting one of the rescuers. "Nothing here," Ashoke heard someone say. "Let's keep going."

But the lantern's light lingered, just long enough for Ashoke to raise his hand, a gesture that he believed would consume the small fragment of life left in him. He was still clutching a single page of "The Overcoat," crumpled tightly in his fist, and when he raised his hand the wad of paper dropped from his fingers. "Wait!" he heard a voice cry out. "The fellow by that book. I saw him move."

He was pulled from the wreckage, placed on a stretcher, transported on another train to a hospital in Tatanagar. He had broken his pelvis, his right femur, and three of his ribs on the right side. For the next year of his life he lay flat on his back, ordered to keep as still as possible while the bones of his body healed. There was a risk that his right leg might be permanently paralyzed. He was transferred to Calcutta Medical College, where two screws were put into his hips. By December he had returned to his parents' house in Alipore, carried through the courtyard and up the red clay stairs like a corpse, hoisted on the shoulders of his four brothers. Three times a day he was spoon-fed. He urinated and defecated into a tin pan. Doctors and visitors came and went. Even his blind grandfather from Jamshedpur paid a visit. His family had saved the newspaper accounts. In a photograph, Ashoke observed the train smashed to shards, piled jaggedly against the sky, security guards sitting on the unclaimed belongings. He learned that fishplates and bolts had been found several feet from the main track, giving rise to the suspicion, never subsequently confirmed, of sabotage. "HOLI-DAY-MAKERS' TRYST WITH DEATH," the *Times of India* had written.

During the day he was groggy from painkillers. At night he dreamed either that he was still trapped inside the train or, worse, that the accident had never happened, that he was walking down a street, taking a bath, sitting cross-legged on the floor and eating a plate of food. And then he would wake up, coated in sweat, tears streaming down his face, convinced that he would never live to do such things again. Eventually, in an attempt to avoid his nightmares, he began to read, late at night, which was when his motionless body felt most restless, his mind agile and clear. Yet he refused to read the Russians his grandfather had brought to his bedside, or any novels, for that matter. Those books, set in countries he had never seen, reminded him only of his confinement. Instead he read his engineering books, trying his best to keep up with his courses, solving equations by flashlight. In those silent hours, he thought often of Ghosh. "Pack a pillow and a blanket," he heard Ghosh say. He remembered the address Ghosh had written, somewhere behind the tram depot in Tollygunge. Now it was the home of a widow, a fatherless son. Each day, to bolster his spirits, his family reminded him of the future, the day he would stand unassisted, walk across the room. It was for this, each day, that his father and mother prayed. But, as the months passed, Ashoke began to envision another sort of future. He imagined not only walking, but walking away, as far as he could, from the place where he was born and where he had nearly died. The following year, walking with a cane, he returned to college and graduated, and without telling his parents he applied to continue his engineering studies abroad. Only after he'd been accepted with a full fellowship, a newly issued passport in hand, did he inform them of his plans. "But we already nearly lost you once," his bewildered father had protested. His siblings had pleaded and wept. His mother, speechless, had refused food for three days. In spite of all that, he'd gone.

Seven years later, there are still certain images that wipe him flat. They lurk around a corner as he rushes through the engineering department at M.I.T. They hover by his soulder as he leans over a plate of rice at dinner-time, or nestles against Ashima's limbs at night. At every turning point in his life—at his wedding, in Calcutta, when he stood behind Ashima, encir-cling her waist and peering over her shoulder as they poured puffed rice into a fire, or during his first hours in America, seeing a small gray city caked with snow—he has tried but failed to push these images away: the twisted, battered, capsized bogies of the train, his body twisted below it, the terrible crunching sound he had heard but not comprehended, his bones crushed as fine as flour. It is not the memory of pain that haunts him; he has no memory of that. It is the memory of waiting before he was rescued, and the persistent fear, rising up in his throat, that he might not have been rescued at all. At times he still presses his ribs to make sure they are solid.

He presses them now, in the hospital, shaking his head in relief, disbelief. Although it is Ashima who carries the child, he, too, feels heavy, with the thought of life, of his life and the life about to come from it. He was raised without running water, nearly killed at twenty-two. He was born twice in India, and then a third time, in America. Three lives by thirty. For this he thanks his parents, and their parents, and the parents of their parents. He does not thank God; he openly reveres Marx and quietly refuses religion. Instead of thanking God he thanks Gogol, the Russian writer who had saved his life, when the nurse enters the waiting room.

The baby, a boy, is born at half past five in the morning. He measures twenty inches long, weighs seven pounds nine ounces. When Ashoke arrives, the nurse is taking Ashima's blood pressure, and Ashima is reclining against a pile of pillows, the child wrapped like an oblong white parcel in her arms. Beside the bed is a bassinet, labeled with a card that says "Baby Boy Ganguli."

"He's here," she says quietly, looking up at Ashoke with a weak smile. Her skin is faintly yellow, the color missing from her lips. She has circles beneath her eyes, and her hair, spilling from its braid, looks as though it had not been combed for days. Her voice is hoarse, as if she'd caught a cold. He pulls up a chair by the side of the bed and the nurse helps to transfer the child from mother's to father's arms. In the process, the child pierces the silence in the room with a short-lived cry. His parents react with mutual alarm, but the nurse laughs approvingly. "You see," she says to Ashima, "he's already getting to know you."

At first Ashoke is more perplexed than moved, by the pointiness of the head, the puffiness of the lids, the small white spots on the cheeks, the fleshy upper lip that droops prominently over the lower one. The skin is paler than either Ashima's or his own, translucent enough to show slim green veins at the temples. The scalp is covered by a mass of wispy black hair. He attempts to count the eyelashes. He feels gently through the flannel for the hands and feet.

"It's all there," Ashima says, watching her husband. "I already checked."

"What are the eyes like? Why won't he open them? Has he opened them?"

She nods.

"What can he see? Can he see us?"

"I think so. But not very clearly. And not in full color. Not yet."

They sit in silence, the three of them as still as stones. "How are you feeling? Was it all right?" he asks Ashima after a while.

But there is no answer, and when Ashoke lifts his gaze from his son's face he sees that she, too, is sleeping.

When he looks back to the child, the eyes are open, staring up at him, unblinking, as dark as the hair on its head. The face is transformed; Ashoke has never seen a more perfect thing. He imagines himself as a dark, grainy, blurry presence. As a father to his son. Being rescued from that shattered train had been the first miracle of his life. But here, now, reposing in his arms, weighing next to nothing but changing everything, is the second.

Because neither set of grandparents has a working telephone, the couple's only link to home is by telegram, which Ashoke has sent to both sides in Calcutta: "With your blessings, boy and mother fine." As for a name, they have decided to let Ashima's grandmother, who is past eighty now, who has named each of her six other great-grandchildren in the world, do the honors. Ashima's grandmother has mailed the letter herself, walking with her cane to the post office, her first trip out of the house in a decade. The letter contains one name for a girl, one for a boy. Ashima's grandmother has revealed them to no one.

Though the letter was sent a month ago, in July, it has yet to arrive.

Ashima and Ashoke are not terrible concerned. After all, they both know, an infant doesn't really need a name. He needs to be fed and blessed, to be given some gold and silver, to be patted on the back after feedings and held carefully behind the neck. Names can wait. In India parents take their time. It wasn't unusual for years to pass before the right name, the best possible name, was determined. Ashima and Ashoke can both cite examples of cousins who were not officially named until they were registered, at six or seven, in school. Besides, there are always pet names to tide one over: a practice of Bengali nomenclature grants, to every single person, two names. In Bengali the word for "pet name" is *daknam*, meaning literally the name by which one is called, by friends, family, and other intimates, at home and in other private, unguarded moments. Pet names are a persistent remnant of childhood, a reminder that life is not always so serious, so formal, so complicated. They are a reminder, too, that one is not all things to all people. Every pet name is paired with a "good name," a *bhalonam*, for identification in the outside world. Consequently, good names appear on envelopes, on diplomas, in telephone directories, and in all other public places. Good names tend to represent dignified and enlightened qualities. Ashima means "she who is limitless, without borders." Ashoke, the name of an emperor, means "he who transcends grief." Pet names have no such aspirations. They are never recorded officially, only uttered and remembered.

Three days come and go. Ashima is shown by the nursing staff how to change diapers and how to clean the umbilical stub. She is given hot saltwater baths to soothe her bruises and stitches. She is given a list of pediatricians, and countless brochures on breast-feeding and bonding and immunizing, and samples of baby shampoos and Q-Tips and creams. The fourth day there is good news and bad news. The good news is that Ashima and the baby are to be discharged the following morning. The bad news is that they are told by Mr. Wilcox, compiler of hospital birth certificates, that they must choose a name for their son. For they learn that in America a baby cannot be released from the hospital without a birth certificate. And that a birth certificate needs a name.

"But, sir," Ashima protests, "we can't possibly name him ourselves."

Mr. Wilcox, slight, bald, unamused, glances at the couple, both visibly distressed, then glances at the nameless child. "I see," he says. "The reason being?"

"We are waiting for a letter," Ashoke says, explaining the situation in detail.

"I see," Mr. Wilcox says again. "That is unfortunate. I'm afraid your only alternative is to have the certificate read 'Baby Boy Ganguli.' You will, of course, be required to amend the permanent record when a name is decided upon."

Ashima looks at Ashoke expectantly. "Is that what we should do?"

"I don't recommend it," Mr. Wilcox says. "You will have to appear before a judge, pay a fee. The red tape is endless."

"Oh dear," Ashoke says.

Mr. Wilcox nods, and silence ensues. "Don't you have any backups?" he asks. "Something in reserve, in case you didn't like what your grandmother has chosen."

Ashima and Ashoke shake their heads. It has never occurred to either of them to question Ashima's grandmother's selection, to disregard an elder's wishes in such a way.

"You can always name him after yourself, or one of your ancestors," Mr. Wilcox suggests, admitting that he is actually Howard Wilcox III. "It's a fine tradition. The kings of France and England did it," he adds.

But this isn't possible. This tradition doesn't exist for Bengalis, naming a son after father or grandfather, a daughter after mother or grandmother. This sign of respect in America and Europe, this symbol of heritage and lineage, would be ridiculed in India. Within Bengali families, individual names are sacred, inviolable. They are not meant to be inherited or shared.

"Then what about naming him after another person? Someone you greatly admire?" Mr. Wilcox says, his eyebrows raised hopefully. He sighs. "Think about it. I'll be back in a few hours," he tells them, exiting the room.

The door shuts, which is when, with a slight quiver of recognition, as if he'd known it all along, the perfect pet name for his son occurs to Ashoke.

"Hello, Gogol," he whispers, leaning over his son's haughty face, his tightly bundled body. "Gogol," he repeats, satisfied. The baby turns his head with an expression of extreme consternation and yawns.

Ashima approves, aware that the name stands not only for her son's life but for her husband's. She'd first heard the story of the accident soon after their marriage was arranged, when Ashoke was still a stranger to her. But the thought of it now makes her blood go cold. There are nights when she has been woken by her husband's muffled screams, times they have ridden the subway together and the rhythm of the wheels on the tracks makes him suddenly pensive, aloof. She has never read any Gogol herself, but she is willing to place him on a shelf in her mind, along with Tennyson and Wordsworth. When Mr. Wilcox returns with his typewriter, Ashoke spells out the name. Thus Gogol Ganguli is registered in the hospital's files. A first photograph, somewhat over-exposed, is taken that broiling-hot, late summer's day: Gogol, an indistinct blanketed mass, reposing in his weary mother's arms. She stands on the steps of the hospital, staring at the camera, her eyes squinting into the sun. Her husband looks on from one side, his wife's suitcase in his hand, smiling with his head lowered. "Gogol enters the world," his father will eventually write on the back in Bengali letters.

Letters arrive from Ashima's parents, from Ashoke's parents, from aunts and uncles and cousins and friends, from everyone, it seems, but Ashima's grandmother. The letters are filled with every possible blessing and good wish, composed in an alphabet they have seen all around them for most of their lives, on billboards and newspapers and awnings, but which they see now only in these precious, pale-blue missives.

In November, when Gogol is three months old, he develops a mild ear infection. When Ashima and Ashoke see their son's pet name typed on the label of a prescription for antibiotics, when they see it at the top of his immunization record, it doesn't look right; pet names aren't meant to be made public in this way. But there is still no letter from Ashima's grandmother, and they are forced to conclude that it is lost in the mail. The very next day a letter arrives in Cambridge. The letter is dated three weeks ago, and from it they learn that Ashima's grandmother has had a stroke, that her right side is permanently paralyzed, her mind dim. She can no longer chew, barely swallows, remembers and recognizes little of her eighty-odd years. "She is with us still, but to be honest we have already lost her," Ashima's father has written. "Prepare yourself, Ashima. Perhaps you may not see her again."

It is their first piece of bad news from home. Ashoke barely knows Ashima's grandmother, only vaguely recalls touching her feet at his wedding, but Ashima is inconsolable for days. She sits at home with Gogol as the leaves turn brown and drop from the trees, as the days begin to grow quickly, mercilessly dark. Unlike Ashima's parents, and her other relatives, her grandmother, her dida, had not admonished Ashima not to eat beef or wear skirts or cut off her hair or forget her family the moment she landed in Boston. Her grandmother had not been fearful of such signs of betrayal; she was the only person to predict, rightly, that Ashima would never change. A few days before leaving Calcutta, Ashima had stood, her head lowered, under her late grandfather's portrait, asking him to bless her journey. Then she bent down to touch the dust of her dida's feet to her head.

"Dida, I'm coming," Ashima had said. For this was the phrase Bengalis always used in place of goodbye.

"Enjoy it," her grandmother had bellowed in her thundering voice, helping Ashima to straighten. With trembling hands, her grandmother had pressed her thumbs to the tears streaming down Ashima's face, wiping them away. "Do what I will never do. It will all be for the best. Remember that. Now go."

By 1971, the Gangulis have moved to a university town outside Boston, where Ashoke has been hired as an assistant professor of electrical engineering at the university. In exchange for teaching five classes, he earns sixteen thousand dollars a year. He is given his own office, with his name etched onto a strip of black plastic by the door. The job is everything Ashoke has ever dreamed of. He had always hoped to teach in a university rather than work for a corporation. What a thrill, he thinks, to stand lecturing before a roomful of American students. What a sense of accomplishment it gives him to see his name printed under "Faculty" in the university directory. From his fourth-floor office he has a sweeping view of the quadrangle, surrounded by vine-covered brick buildings. On Fridays, after he has taught his last class, he visits the library, to read international newspapers on long wooden poles. He reads about American planes bombing Vietcong supply routes in Cambodia, Naxalites being murdered on the streets of Calcutta, India and Pakistan going to war. At times he wanders up to the library's sun-filled, unpopulated top floor, where all the literature is shelved. He browses in the aisles, gravitating most often toward his beloved Russians, where he is particularly comforted, each time, by his son's name stamped in golden letters on the spines of a row of red and green and blue hardbound books.

Ashoke and Ashima purchase a shingled two-story colonial in a recently built development, a house previously occupied by no one, erected on a quarter acre of land. This is the small patch of America to which they lay claim. Gogol accompanies his parents to banks, sits waiting as they sign the endless papers. Ashoke and Ashima are amazed, when moving by U-Haul to the new house, to discover how much they possess; each of them had come to America with a single suitcase, a few weeks' worth of clothes. The walls of the new house are painted, the driveway sealed with pitch, the shingles and sundeck weatherproofed and stained. Ashoke takes photographs of every room, Gogol standing somewhere in the frame, to send to relatives in India. He is a sturdily built child, with full cheeks but already pensive features. When he poses for the camera he has to be coaxed into a smile.

In the beginning, in the evenings, his family goes for drives, exploring their new environs bit by bit: the neglected dirt lanes, the shaded back roads. The back seat of the car is sheathed with plastic, the ashtrays on the doors still sealed. Sometimes they drive out of the town altogether, to one of the beaches along the North Shore. Even in summer, they never go to swim or to turn brown beneath the sun. Instead they go dressed in their ordinary clothes. By the time they arrive, the ticket collector's booth is empty, the crowds gone; there are only a handful of cars in the parking lot. Together, as the Gangulis drive, they anticipate the moment the thin blue line of ocean will come into view. On the beach Gogol collects rocks, digs tunnels in the sand. He and his father wander barefoot, their pant legs rolled halfway up their calves. He watches his father raise a kite within minutes into the wind, so high that Gogol must tip his head back in order to see, a rippling speck against the sky.

The August that Gogol turns five, Ashima discovers she is pregnant again. In the mornings she forces herself to eat a slice of toast, only because Ashoke makes it for her and watches her while she chews it in bed. Her head constantly spins. She spends her days lying down, a pink plastic wastepaper basket by her side, the shades drawn, her mouth and teeth coated with the taste of metal. Sometimes Gogol lies beside her in his parents' bedroom, reading a picture book, or coloring with crayons. "You're going to be an older brother," she tells him one day. "There'll be someone to call you Dada. Won't that be exciting?"

In the evenings, Gogol and his father eat together, alone, a week's worth of chicken curry and rice, which his father cooks in two battered Dutch ovens every Sunday. As the food reheats, his father tells Gogol to shut the bedroom door because his mother cannot tolerate the smell. It is odd to see his father presiding in the kitchen, standing in his mother's place at the stove. When they sit down at the table, the sound of his parents' conversation is missing.

Because his mother tends to vomit the moment she finds herself in a moving car, she is unable to accompany Ashoke to take Gogol, in September of 1973, to his first day of kindergarten at the town's public elementary school. By the time Gogol starts, it is already the second week of the school year. For the past week, Gogol has been in bed, just like his mother, listless, without appetite, claiming to have a stomach ache, even vomiting one day into his mother's pink wastepaper basket. He doesn't want to go to kindergarten. He doesn't want to wear the new clothes his mother has bought him from Sears, hanging on a knob of his dresser, or carry his Charlie Brown lunchbox, or board the yellow school bus that stops at the end of Pemberton Road.

There is a reason Gogol doesn't want to go to kindergarten. He parents have told him that at school, instead of being called Gogol, he will be called by a new name, a good name, which his parents have finally decided on, just in time for him to begin his formal education. The name, Nikhil, is artfully connected to the old. Not only is it a perfectly respectable Bengali good name, meaning "he who is entire, encompassing all," but it also bears a satisfying resemblance to Nikolai, the first name of the Russian Gogol's. Ashoke thought of it recently, staring mindlessly at the Gogol spines in the library, and he rushed back to the house to ask Ashima her opinion. He pointed out that it was relatively easy to pronounce, though there was the danger that Americans, obsessed with abbreviation, would truncate it to Nick. She told him she liked it well enough, though later, alone, she'd wept, thinking of her grandmother, who had died earlier in the year, and of the letter, forever hovering somewhere between India and America.

But Gogol can't understand why he has to answer to anything else. "Why do I have to have a new name?" he asks his parents, tears springing to his eyes. It would be one thing if his parents were to call him Nikhil, too. But they tell him that the new name will be used only by the teachers and children at school. He is afraid to be Nikhil, someone he doesn't know. Who doesn't know him. His parents tell him that they each have two names, too, as do all their Bengali friends in America, and all their relatives in Calcutta. It's a part of growing up, they tell him, part of being a Bengali. They write it for him on a sheet of paper, ask him to copy it over ten times. "Don't worry," his father says. "To me and your mother, you will never be anyone but Gogol."

At school, Ashoke and Gogol are greeted by the secretary, who asks Ashoke to fill out a registration form. He provides a copy of Gogol's birth certificate and immunization records, which are put in a folder along with the registration. "This way," the secretary says, leading them to the principal's office. Candace Lapidus, the name on the door says. Mrs. Lapidus assures Ashoke that missing the first week of kindergarten is not a problem, that things have yet to settle down. Mrs. Lapidus is a tall, slender woman with short white-blond hair. She wears frosted blue eye shadow and a lemon-yellow suit. She shakes Ashoke's hand and tells him that there are two other Indian children at the school, Jayadev Modi, in the third grade, and Rekha Saxena, in fifth. Perhaps the Gangulis know them? Ashoke tells Mrs. Lapidus that they do not. She looks at the registration form and smiles kindly at the boy, who is clutching his father's hand. Gogol is dressed in powder-blue pants, red-and-white canvas sneakers, a striped turtleneck top.

"Welcome to elementary school, Nikhil. I am your principal, Mrs.Lapidus."

Gogol looks down at his sneakers. The way the principal pronounces his new name is different from the way his parents say it, the second part of it longer, sounding like "heel."

She bends down so that her face is level with his, and extends a hand to his shoulder. "Can you tell me how old you are, Nikhil?"

When the question is repeated and there is still no response, Mrs. Lapidus asks, "Mr. Ganguli, does Nikhil follow English?"

"Of course he follows," Ashoke says. "My son is perfectly bilingual."

In order to prove that Gogol knows English, Ashoke does something he has never done before, and addresses his son in careful, accented English. "Go on, Gogol," he says, patting him on the head. "Tell Mrs. Lapidus how old you are."

"What was that?" Mrs. Lapidus says.

"I beg your pardon, Madam?"

"That name you called him. Something with a 'G.'"

"Oh that, that is what we call him at home only. But his good name should be—is"—he nods his head firmly—"Nikhil."

Mrs. Lapidus frowns. "I'm afraid I don't understand. 'Good name'?"

"Yes."

Mrs. Lapidus studies the registration form. She has not had to go through this confusion with the two other Indian children.

"I'm not sure I follow you, Mr. Ganguli. Do you mean that Nikhil is a middle name? Or a nickname? Many of the children go by nicknames here. On this form there is a space—"

"No, no, it's not a middle name," Ashoke says. He is beginning to lose patience. "He has no middle name. No nickname. The boy's good name, his school name, is Nikhil."

Mrs. Lapidus presses her lips together and smiles, "But clearly he doesn't respond."

"Please, Mrs. Lapidus," Ashoke says. "It is very common for a child to be confused at first. Please give it some time. I assure you he will grow accustomed."

He bends down, and this time in Bengali, calmly and quietly, asks Gogol to please answer when Mrs.Lapidus asks a question. "Don't be scared, Gogol," he says, raising his son's chin with his finger. "You're a big boy now. No tears."

Though Mrs. Lapidus does not understand a word, she listens carefully, hears that name again. Gogol. Lightly, in pencil, she writes it down on the registration form.

Ashoke hands over the lunchbox, a windbreaker in case it gets cold. He thanks Mrs. Lapidus. "Be good, Nikhil," he says in English. And then, after a moment's hesitation, Gogol's father is gone.

At the end of his first day he is sent home with a letter to his parents from Mrs.Lapidus, folded and stapled to a string around his neck, explaining that owing to their son's preference he will be known as Gogol at school. What about the parents' preference? Ashima and Ashoke wonder, shaking their heads.

And so Gogol's formal education begins. At the top of sheets of scratchy pale-yellow paper he writes out his pet name again and again, and the alphabet in capital and lowercase. He learns to add and subtract, and to spell his first words. In the front covers of the textbooks from which he is taught to read he leaves his legacy, writing his name in No. 2 pencil below a series of others. In art class, his favorite hour of the week, he carves his name with paper clips into the bottoms of clay cups and bowls. He pastes uncooked pasta to cardboard, and leaves his signature in fat brushstrokes below paintings. Day after day he brings his creations home to Ashima, who hangs them proudly on the refrigerator door. "Gogol G." he signs his work in the lower right-hand corner, as if there were a need to distinguish him from any other Gogol in the school.

In May his sister is born. This time, Ashoke and Ashima are ready. The have the names lined up, for a boy or a girl. The only way to avoid confusion, they have concluded, is to do away with the pet name altogether, as many of their Bengali friends have already done. For their daughter, good name and pet name are one and the same: Sonali, meaning "she who is golden." Though Sonali is the name of her birth certificate, the name she will carry officially through life, at home they begin to call her Sonu, then Sona, and, finally, Sonia. Sonia makes her a citizen of the world. It's a Russian link to her brother, it's European, South American. Eventually it will be the name of the Indian Prime Minister's Italian wife.

As a young boy Gogol doesn't mind his name. He recognizes pieces of himself in road signs: "Go Left," "Go Right," "Go Slow." For birthdays his mother orders a cake on which his name is piped across the white frosted surface in a bright-blue sugary script. It all seems perfectly normal. It doesn't bother him that his name is never an option on key chains or refrigerator magnets. He has been told that he was named after a famous Russian author, born in a previous century. That the author's name, and therefore his, is known throughout the world and will live on forever. One day his father takes him to the university library, and shows him, on a shelf well beyond his reach, a row of Gogol spines. When his father opens up one of the books to a random page, the print is far smaller than in the Hardy Boys series Gogol has begun recently to enjoy. "In a few years," his father tells him, "you'll be ready to read them." Though substitute teachers at school always pause, looking apologetically when they arrive at his name on the roster, forcing Gogol to call out, before even being summoned, "That's me," his regular teachers know not to give it a second thought. After a year or two, the students no longer tease and say "Giggle" or "Gargle." In the programs of the school Christmas plays, the parents are accustomed to seeing his name among the cast. "Gogol is an outstanding student, curious and coöperative," his teachers write year after year on report cards. "Go, Gogol!" his classmates shout on golden autumn days as he runs the bases or sprints in a dash.

As for his last name, Ganguli, by the time he is ten he has been to Calcutta three times, twice in summer and once during Durga *pujo*, and from the most recent trip he still remembers the sight of the name etched respectably into the pink stone façade of his paternal grandparents' house. He remembers the astonishment of seeing six pages full of Gangulis, three columns to a page, in the Calcutta telephone directory. He'd wanted to rip out the page as a souvenir, but, when he'd told this to one of his cousins, the cousin had laughed. On taxi rides through the city, going to visit the various homes of his relatives, his father had pointed out the name elsewhere, on the awnings of confectioners, and stationers, and opticians. He had told Gogol that Ganguli was a legacy of the British, an anglicized way of pronouncing his real surname, Gangopadhyay.

Back home on Pemberton Road, he helps his father paste individual golden letters bought from a rack in the hardware store, spelling out Ganguli on one side of their mailbox. One morning, the day after Halloween, Gogol discovers, on his way to the bus stop, that it has been shortened to "Gang," with the word "green" scrawled in pencil following it. He runs back into the house, sickened, certain of the insult his father will feel. Though it is his last name, too, something tells Gogol that the desecration is intended for his parents more than for Sonia and him. For by now he is aware, in stores, of cashiers smirking at his parents' accents, and of salesmen who prefer to direct their conversation to Gogol, as though his parents were either incompetent or deaf. But his father is unaffected at such moments, just as he is unaffected by the mailbox. "It's only boys having fun," he tells Gogol, flicking the matter away with the back of a hand, and that evening they drive to the hardware store, to buy the missing letters again.

Gogol's fourteenth birthday. Like most events in his life, it is another excuse for his parents to throw a party for their Bengali friends. His own friends from school were invited the previous day, for pizzas that his father picked up on his way home from work, a basketball game watched together on television, some Ping-Pong in the den. His mother cooks for days beforehand, cramming the refrigerator with stacks of foil-covered trays. She makes sure to prepare his favorite things: lamb curry with lots of potatoes, luchis, thick *channa* dal with swollen brown raisins, pineapple chutney, sandeshes molded out of saffron-tinted ricotta cheese. All this is less stressful to her than the task of feeding a handful of American children, half of whom always claim they are allergic to milk, all of whom refuse to eat the crusts of their bread.

Close to forty guests come, from three different states. Women are dressed in saris far more dazzling than the pants and polo shirts their husbands wear. A group of men sit in a circle on the floor and immediately start a game of poker. These are all his *mashis* and *meshos*, his honorary aunts and uncles. Presents are opened when the guests are gone. Gogol receives several dictionaries, several calculators, several Cross pen-and-pencil sets, several ugly sweaters. His parents give him an Instamatic camera, a new sketchbook, colored pencils and the mechanical pen he'd asked for, and twenty dollars to spend as he wishes. Sonia has made him a card with Magic Markers, on paper she's ripped out of one of his own sketchbooks, which says "Happy Birthday Goggles," the name she insists on calling him instead of Dada. His mother sets aside the things he doesn't like, which is almost everything, to give to his cousins the next time they go to India. Later that night he is alone is his room, listening to side three of the White Album on his parents' cast-off RCA turntable. The album is a present from his American birthday party. Born when the band was near death, Gogol is a passionate devotee of John, Paul, George, and Ringo. He sits cross-legged on the bed, hunched over the lyrics, when he hears a knock on the door.

"Come in!" he hollers, expecting it to be Sonia in her pajamas, asking if she can borrow his Rubik's Cube. He is surprised to see his father, standing there in stocking feet, a small potbelly visible beneath his oat-colored sweater vest, his mustache turning gray. Gogol is especially surprised to see a gift in his father's hands. His father has never given him birthday presents apart from whatever his mother buys, but this year, his father says, walking across the room to where Gogol is sitting, he has something special. The gift is covered in red-and-green-and-gold-striped paper left over from Christmas the year before, taped awkwardly at the seams. It is obviously a book, thick, hardcover, wrapped by his father's own hands. Gogol lifts the paper slowly, but in spite of this the tape leaves a scab. "The Short Stories of Nikolai Gogol," the jacket says. Inside, the price has been snipped away on the diagonal.

"I ordered it from the bookstore, just for you," his father says, his voice raised in order to be heard over the music. "It's difficult to find in hardcover these days. It's a British publication, a very small press. It took four months to arrive. I hope you like it."

Gogol leans over toward the stereo to turn the volume down a bit. He would have preferred "The Hitchhiker's Guide to the Galaxy," or even another copy of "The Hobbit" to replace the one he lost last summer in Calcutta, left on the rooftop of his father's house in Alipore and snatched away by crows. In spite of his father's occasional suggestions, he has never been inspired to read a word of Gogol, or of any Russian writer, for that matter. He has never been told why he was really named Gogol. He thinks his father's limp is the consequence of an injury playing soccer in his teens.

"Thanks, Baba," Gogol says, eager to return to his lyrics. Lately he's been lazy, addressing his parents in English, though they continue to speak to him in Bengali. Occasionally he wanders through the house with his running sneakers on. At dinner he sometimes uses a fork.

His father is still standing there in his room, watching expectantly, his hands clasped together behind his back, so Gogol flips through the book. A single picture at the front, on smoother paper than the rest of the pages, shows a pencil drawing of the author, sporting a velvet jacket, a billowy white shirt, and a cravat. The face is foxlike, with small, dark eyes, a thin, neat mustache, an extremely large pointy nose. Dark hair slants steeply across his forehead and is plastered to either side of his head, and there is a disturbing, vaguely supercilious smile set into long, narrow lips. Gogol Ganguli is relieved to see no resemblance.

For by now he's come to hate questions pertaining to his name, hates having constantly to explain. He hates having to tell people that it doesn't mean anything "in Indian." He hates having to wear a nametag on his sweater at Model United Nations Day at school. He hates that his name is both absurd and obscure, that it has nothing to do with who he is, that it is neither Indian nor American but, of all things, Russian. He hates having to live with it, with a pet name turned good name, day after day, second after second. He hates seeing it on the brown-paper sleeve of the *National Geographic* subscription his parents got him for his birthday the year before, and seeing it perpetually listed in the high honor roll printed in the towns' newspaper. At times his name, an entity shapeless and weightless, manages nevertheless to distress him physically, like the scratchy tag of a shirt he has been forced permanently to wear. At times he wishes he could disguise it, shorten it somehow, the way the other Indian boy in his school, Jayadev, had got people to call him Jay. But Gogol, already short and catchy, resists mutation. Other boys his age have begun to court girls already, asking them to go to the movies or the pizza parlor, but he cannot imagine saying, "Hi, it's Gogol" under potentially romantic circumstances. He cannot imagine this at all.

From the little he knows about Russian writers, it dismays him that his parents chose the weirdest namesake. Leo or Anton, he could have lived with. Alexander, shortened to Alex, he would have greatly preferred. But Gogol sounds ludicrous to his ears, lacking dignity or gravity. What dismays him most is the irrelevance of it all. Gogol, he's been tempted to tell his father on more than one occasion, was his father's favorite author, not his. Then again, it's his own fault. He could have been known, at school at least, as Nikhil. That one day, his first day of kindergarten, which he no longer remembers, could have changed everything.

"Thanks again," Gogol tells his father now. He shuts the cover and swings his legs over the edge of the bed, to put the book away on his shelves. But his father takes the opportunity to sit beside him on the bed. For a moment he rests a hand on Gogol's shoulder. The boy's body, in recent months, has grown tall, nearly as tall as Ashoke's. The childhood pudginess has vanished from his face. The voice has begun to deepen, is slightly husky now. It occurs to Ashoke that he and his son probably wear the same size shoe. In the glow of the bedside lamp, Ashoke notices a scattered down emerging on his son's upper lip. An Adams apple is prominent on his neck. The pale hands, like Ashima's, are long and thin. He wonders how closely Gogol resembles him at this age. But there are no photographs to document Ashoke's childhood; not until his passport, not until his life in America, does visual documentation exist. On the night table Ashoke sees a can of deodorant, a tube of Clearasil. He lifts the book from where it lies on the bed between them, running a hand protectively over the cover. "I took the liberty of reading it first. It has been many years since I have read these stories. I hope you don't mind."

"No problem," Gogol says.

"I feel a special kinship with Gogol," Ashoke says, "more than with any other writer. Do you know why?"

"You like his stories."

"Apart from that. He spent most of his adult life outside his homeland. Like me."

Gogol nods. "Right."

"And there is another reason." The music ends and there is silence. But then Gogol flips the record, turning the volume up on "Revolution 1."

"What's that?" Gogol says, a bit impatiently.

Ashoke looks around the room. He notices the Lennon obituary pinned to the bulletin board, and then a cassette of classical Indian music he'd bought for Gogol months ago, after a concert at Kresge, still sealed in its wrapper. He sees the pile of birthday cards scattered on the carpet, and remembers a hot August day fourteen years ago in Cambridge when he held his son for the first time. Ever since that day, the day he became a father, the memory of his accident has receded, diminishing over the years. Though he will never forget that night, it no longer lurks persistently in his mind, stalking him in the same way. Instead, it is affixed firmly to a distant time, to a place far from Pemberton Road. Today, his son's birthday, is a day to honor life, not brushes with death. And so, for now, Ashoke decides to keep the explanation of his son's name to himself.

"No other reason. Good night," he says to Gogol, getting up from the bed. At the door he pauses, turns around. "Do you know what Dostoyevsky once said?"

Gogol shakes his head.

"'We all came out of Gogol's overcoat.'"

"What's that supposed to mean?"

"It will make sense to you one day. Many happy returns of the day."

Gogol gets up and shuts the door behind his father, who has the annoying habit of always leaving it partly open. He turns the lock on the knob for good measure, then wedges the book on a high shelf between two volumes of the Hardy Boys. He settles down again with his lyrics on the bed when something occurs to him. This writer he is named after—Gogol isn't his first name. His first name is Nikolai. Not only does Gogol Ganguli have a pet name turned good name but a last name turned first name. And so it occurs to him that no one he knows in the world, in Russia or India or America or anywhere, shares his name. Not even the source of his namesake.

Plenty of people changed their names: actors, writers, revolutionaries, transvestites. In history class, Gogol has learned that European immigrants had their names changed at Ellis Island, that slaves renamed themselves once they were emancipated. Though Gogol doesn't know it, even Nikolai Gogol renamed himself, simplifying his surname at the age of twenty-two, from Gogol-Yanovsky to Gogol, upon publishing in the *Literary Gazette*.

One day in the summer of 1986, in the frantic weeks before moving away from his family, before his freshman year at Yale is about to begin, Gogol Ganguli does the same. He rides the commuter rail into Boston, switching to the Green Line at North Station, getting out at Lechmere, the closest stop to the Middlesex Probate and Family Court. He wears a blue oxford shirt, khakis, a camel-colored corduroy blazer bought for his college interviews that is too warm for the sultry day. Knotted around his neck is his only tie, maroon with yellow stripes on the diagonal. By now Gogol is just shy of six feet tall, his body slender, his thick brown-black hair slightly in need of a cut. His face is lean, intelligent, suddenly handsome, the bones more prominent, the pale-gold skin clean-shaven and clear. He has inherited Ashima's eyes—large, penetrating, with bold, elegant brows—and shares with Ashoke the slight bump at the very top of his nose.

The courthouse is an imposing, pillared brick building occupying a full city block, but the entrance is off to the side, down a set of steps. Inside, Gogol empties his pockets and steps through a metal detector, as if he were at an airport, about to embark on a journey. He is soothed by the chill of the air conditioning, by the beautifully carved plaster ceiling, by the voices that echo pleasantly in the marbled interior. A man at the information booth tells him to wait upstairs, in an area filled with round tables, where people sit eating their lunch. Gogol sits impatiently, one long leg jiggling up and down.

The idea to change his name had first occurred to him a few months ago. He was sitting in the waiting room of his dentist, flipping through an issue of *Reader's Digest*. He'd been turning the pages at random until he came to an article that caused him to stop. The article was called "Second Baptisms." "Can you identify the following famous people?" was written beneath the headline. The only one he guessed correctly was Robert Zimmerman, Bob Dylan's real name. He had no idea that Leon Trotsky was born Lev Davidovich Bronstein. That Gerald Ford's name was Leslie Lynch King, Jr., and that Engelbert Humperdinck's was Arnold George Dorsey. They had all renamed themselves, the article said, adding that it was a right belonging to every American citizen. He read that tens of thousands of Americans, on average, had their names changed each year. All it took was a legal petition.

That night at the dinner table, he brought it up with his parents. It was one thing for Gogol to be the name penned in calligraphy on his high-school diploma, and printed below his picture in the yearbook, he'd begun. But engraved, four years from now, on a bachelor-of-arts degree? Written at the top of a résumé? Centered on a business card? It would be the name his parents picked out for him, he assured them, the good name they'd chosen for him when he was five.

"What's done is done," his father had said. "It will be a hassle. Gogol has, in effect, become your good name."

"It's too complicated now," his mother said, agreeing. "You're too old."

"I'm not," he persisted. "I don't get it. Why did you have to give me a pet name in the first place? What's the point?"

"It's our way, Gogol," his mother maintained. "It's what Bengalis do."

"But it's not even a Bengali name. How could you guys name me after someone so strange? No one takes me seriously."

"Who? Who does not take you seriously?" his father wanted to know, lifting his fingers from his plate, looking up at him. "People," he said, lying to his parents. For his father had a point; the only person who didn't take Gogol seriously, the only person who tormented him, the only person chronically aware of and afflicted by the embarrassment of his name, the only person who constantly questioned it and wished it were otherwise, was Gogol.

"I don't know, Gogol," his mother had said, shaking her head. "I really don't know." She got up to clear the dishes. Sonia slinked away, up to her room. Gogol remained at the table with his father. They sat there together, listening to his mother scraping the plates, the water running in the sink.

"Then change it," his father said simply, quietly, after a while.

"Really?"

"In America anything is possible. Do as you wish."

With relief, he types his name at the top of his freshman papers. He reads the telephone messages his roommates leave for Nikhil on assorted scraps of paper. He opens up a checking account, writes his new name into his course books. "*Me llamo* Nikhil," he says in his Spanish class. It is as Nikhil, that first semester, that he grows a goatee, starts smoking Camel Lights at parties and, while writing papers and before exams, discovers Brian Eno and Elvis Costello and Charlie Parker. It is as Nikhil that he takes Metro-North into Manhattan one weekend and gets himself a fake I.D. that allows him to be served liquor in New Haven bars. It is as Nikhil that he loses his virginity at a party at Ezra Stiles, with a girl wearing a plaid woolen skirt and combat boots and mustard tights. By the time he wakes up, hung over, at three in the morning, she has vanished from the room, and he us unable to recall her name.

There is only one complication: he doesn't feel like Nikhil. Not yet. Part of the problem is that the people who now know him as Nikhil have no idea that he used to be Gogol. They know him only in the present, not at all in the past. But, after eighteen years of Gogol, two months of Nikhil feel scant, inconsequential. At times he feels as if he'd cast himself in a play, acting the part of twins, indistinguishable to the naked eye yet fundamentally different. At times he still feels his old name, painfully and without warning, the way his front tooth had unbearably throbbed in recent weeks after a filling, threatening for an instant to sever from his gums when he drank coffee, or ice water.

Even more startling is when those who normally call him Gogol refer to him as Nikhil. Though he has asked his parents to do precisely this, the fact of it troubles him, making him feel in that instant that he is not related to them, not their child. "Please come visit us with Nikhil one weekend," Ashima says to his roommates when she and Ashoke visit campus during parents' weekend in October, the suite hastily cleared of liquor bottles and ashtrays for the occasion. The substitution sounds wrong to Gogol, correct but off key, the way it sounds when his parents speak English to him instead of Bengali.

At Thanksgiving, he takes the train up to Boston. He feels distracted for some reason, impatient to be off the train; he does not bother to remove his coat, does not bother to go to the café car for something to drink even though he is thirsty. His mother and Sonia have gone to India for three weeks, to attend a cousin's wedding, and this year Gogol and his father will spend Thanksgiving at the home of friends.

He angles his head against the window and watches the autumnal landscape pass: the spewing pink and purple waters of a dye mill, electrical power stations, a big ball-shaped water tank covered with rust. Abandoned factories, with rows of small square windows partly bashed in, ravaged as if by moths. On the trees the topmost branches are bare, the remaining leaves yellow, paper-thin. The train moves more slowly than usual, and when he looks at his watch he sees that they are running well behind schedule. And then, somewhere outside Providence, in an abandoned field, the train stops moving. For more than an hour they stand there while a solid, scarlet disk of sun sinks into the tree-lined horizon. The lights turn off, and the air inside the train turns uncomfortably warm. The conductors rush anxiously through the compartments. "Probably a broken wire," the gentleman sitting beside Gogol remarks. Across the aisle a gray-haired woman reads, a coat clutched like a blanket to her chest. Without the sound of the engine Gogol can hear an opera playing faintly on someone's Walkman. Through the window he admires the darkening sapphire sky. He sees spare lengths of rusted rails heaped in piles. It isn't until they start moving again that an announcement is made on the loudspeaker about a medical emergency. But the truth, overheard by one of the passengers from a conductor, quickly circulates: a suicide has been committed, a person has jumped in front of the train.

He is shocked and discomforted by the news, feeling bad about his irritation and impatience, wondering if the victim had been a man or a woman, young or old. He imagines the person consulting the same schedule that's in his backpack, determining exactly when the train would be passing through. As a result of the delay he misses his commuter-rail connection in Boston, waits another forty minutes for the next one. He puts a call through to his parents' house, but no one answers. He tries his father's department at the university, but there, too, the phone rings and rings. At the station he sees his father waiting on the darkened platform, wearing sneakers and corduroys, anxiousness in his face. A trenchcoat is belted around his waist, a scarf knitted by Ashima wrapped at his throat, a tweed cap on his head.

"Sorry I'm late," Gogol says. "How long have you been waiting?"

"Since quarter to six," his father says. Gogol looks at his watch. It is nearly eight.

"There was an accident."

"I know. I called. What happened? Were you hurt?"

Gogol shakes his head. "Someone jumped onto the tracks. Somewhere in Rhode Island. I tried to call you. They had to wait for the police, I think."

"I was worried."

"I hope you haven't been standing out in the cold all this time," Gogol says, and from his father's lack of response he knows that this is exactly what he has done.

The night is windy, so much so that the car jostles slightly from time to time. Normally on these rides back from the station his father asks questions, about his classes, about his finances, about his plans for the future. But tonight they are silent, Ashoke concentrating on driving. Gogol fidgets with the radio.

"I want to tell you something," his father says, once they have already turned onto their road.

"What?" Gogol asks.

"It's about your name."

Gogol looks at his father, puzzled. "My name?"

His father shuts off the radio. "Gogol. There is a reason for it, you know."

"Right, Baba. Gogol's your favorite author. I know."

"No," his father says. He pulls in to the driveway and switches off the engine, then the headlights. He undoes his seat belt, guiding it with his hand as it retracts, back behind his left shoulder. "Another reason."

And, as they sit together in the car, his father revisits a field two hundred and nine kilometers from Howrah. With his fingers lightly grasping the bottom of the steering wheel, his gaze directed through the windshield at the garage door, he tells Gogol the story of the train he'd ridden twenty-five years ago, in October, 1961. He tells him about the night that had nearly taken his life, and the book that had saved him, and about the year afterward, when he'd been unable to move.

Gogol listens, stunned, his eyes fixed on his father's profile. Though there are only inches between them, for an instant his father is a stranger, a man who has kept a secret, has survived a tragedy, a man whose past he does not fully know. A man who is vulnerable, who has suffered in an inconceivable way. He imagines his father, a college student as Gogol is now, sitting on the train as Gogol had just been, reading a story, and then suddenly nearly killed. He struggles to picture the West Bengal countryside he has seen on only a few occasions, his father's mangled body, among hundreds of dead ones, being carried on a stretcher, past a twisted length of maroon compartments. Against instinct he tries to imagine life without his father, a world in which his father does not exist.

"Why don't I know this about you?" Gogol says. His voice sounds harsh, accusing, but his eyes well with tears. "Why haven't you told me this until now?"

"It never felt like the right time," his father says.

"But it's like you've lied to me all these years." When his father doesn't respond, he adds, "That's why you have that limp, isn't it?"

"It happened so long ago. I didn't want to upset you."

"It doesn't matter. You should have told me."

"Perhaps," his father concedes, glancing briefly in Gogol's direction. He removes the keys from the ignition. "Come, you must be hungry. The car is getting cold."

But Gogol doesn't move. He sits there, still struggling to absorb the information, feeling awkward, oddly ashamed, at fault. "I'm sorry, Baba."

His father laughs softly. "You had nothing to do with it, Gogol."

And suddenly the sound of his pet name, uttered by his father as he has been accustomed to hearing it all his life, means something completely new, bound up with a catastrophe he has unwittingly embodied for years. "Is that what you think of when you think of me?" Gogol asks him. "Do I remind you of that night?"

"Not at all," his father says eventually, one hand going to his ribs, a habitual gesture that has baffled Gogol until now. "You remind me of everything that followed."

5

Refresh, Refresh

BENJAMIN PERCY

Benjamin Percy features Central Oregon's high desert region prominently in his fiction. He was born in Eugene, Oregon, in 1979 and raised in Tumalo, in Central Oregon. Percy began his undergraduate studies at Brown University with an initial major in archeology, but he later shifted his focus to writing. After receiving his BA from Brown University, Percy went on to earn an MFA in creative writing at Southern Illinois University. He is the author of two books of short stories, *Refresh, Refresh*, and *The Language of Elk*. His fiction and literary essays have appeared in *Esquire, Men's Journal, The Paris Review, Chicago Tribune, Glimmer Train*, and *Poets & Writers*, among others. A recipient of the Plimpton Prize and the Pushcart Prize, Percy teaches in the MFA program at Iowa State. Graywolf Press published his novel, *The Wilding*, in 2010.

When school let out the two of us went to my backyard to fight. We were trying to make each other tougher. So in the grass, in the shade of the pines and junipers, Gordon and I slung off our backpacks and laid down a pale green garden hose, tip to tip, making a ring. Then we stripped off our shirts and put on our gold-colored boxing gloves and fought.

Every round went two minutes. If you stepped out of the ring, you lost. If you cried, you lost. If you got knocked out or if you yelled stop, you lost. Afterward we drank Coca-Colas and smoked Marlboros, our chests heaving, our faces all different shades of blacks and reds and yellows.

We began fighting after Seth Johnson—a no-neck linebacker with teeth like corn kernels and hands like T-bone steaks—beat Gordon until his face swelled and split open and purpled around the edges. Eventually he healed, the rough husks of scabs peeling away to reveal a different face from the one I remembered—older, squarer, fiercer, his left eyebrow separated by a gummy white scar. It was his idea that we should fight each other. He wanted to be ready. He wanted to hurt those who hurt him. And if he went down, he would go down swinging as he was sure his father would. This is what we all wanted: to please our fathers, to make them proud, even though they had left us.

This was in Crow, Oregon, a high desert town in the foothills of the Cascade Moutains. In Crow we have fifteen hundred people, a Dairy Queen, a BP gas station, a Food4Less, a meatpacking plant, a bright green football field irrigated by canal water, and your standard assortment of taverns and churches. Nothing distinguishes us from Bend or Redmond or La Pine or any of the other nowhere towns off Route 97, except for this: we are home to the Second Battalion, Thirty-fourth Marines.

The marines live on a fifty-acre base in the hills just outside of town, a collection of one-story cinder-block buildings interrupted by cheatgrass and sagebrush. Throughout my childhood I could hear, if I cupped a hand to my ear, the lowing of bulls, the bleating of sheep, and the report of assault rifles shouting from the hilltops. It's said that conditions here in Oregon's ranch country closely match the mountainous terrain of Afghanistan and northern Iraq.

Our fathers—Gordon's and mine—were like the other fathers in Crow. All of them, just about, had enlisted as part-time soldiers, as reservists, for drill pay: several thousand a year for a private and several thousand more for a sergeant. Beer pay, they called it, and for two weeks every year plus one weekend a month, they trained. They threw on their cammies and filled their rucksacks and kissed us good-bye, and the gates of the Second Battalion drew closed behind them.

Our fathers would vanish into the pine-studded hills, returning to us Sunday night with their faces reddened from weather, their biceps trembling from fatigue, and their hands smelling of rifle grease. They would talk about ECPs and PRPs and MEUs and WMDs and they would do pushups in the middle of the living room and they would call six o'clock "eighteen hundred hours" and they would high-five and yell, "Semper fi." Then a few days would pass, and they would go back to the way they were, to the men we knew: Coors-drinking, baseball-throwing, crotch-scratching, Aqua Velva-smelling fathers.

No longer. In January the battalion was activated, and in March they shipped off for Iraq. Our fathers—our coaches, our teachers, our barbers, our cooks, our gas station attendants and UPS deliverymen and deputies and firemen and mechanics—our fathers, so many of them, climbed onto the olive green school buses and pressed their palms to the windows and gave us the bravest, most hopeful smiles you can imagine and vanished. Just like that.

Nights, I sometimes got on my Honda dirt bike and rode through the hills and canyons of Deschutes County. Beneath me the engine growled and shuddered, while all around me the wind, like something alive, bullied me, tried to drag me from my bike. A dark world slipped past as I downshifted, leaning into a turn, and accelerated on a straightaway—my speed seventy, then eighty—concentrating only on the twenty yards of road glowing ahead of me.

On this bike I could ride and ride and ride, away from here, up and over the Cascades, through the Willamette Valley, until I reached the ocean, where the broad black backs of whales regularly broke the surface of the water, and even farther—farther still—until I caught up with the horizon, where my father would be waiting. Inevitably, I ended up at Hole in the Ground.

A long time ago a meteor came screeching down from space and left behind a crater five thousand feet wide and three hundred feet deep. Hole in the Ground is frequented during the winter by the daredevil sledders among us and during the summer by bearded geologists interested in the metal fragments strewn across its bottom. I dangled my feet over the edge of the crater and leaned back on my elbows and took in the black sky—no moon, only stars—just a little lighter than a raven. Every few minutes a star seemed to come unstuck, streaking through the night in a bright flash that burned into nothingness.

In the near distance Crow glowed grayish green against the darkness—a reminder of how close to oblivion we lived. A chunk of space ice or a solar wind could have jogged the meteor sideways and rather than landing here it could have landed there at the intersection of Main and Farwell. No Dairy Queen, no Crow High, no Second Battalion. It didn't take much imagination to realize how something can drop out of the sky and change everything.

This was in October, when Gordon and I circled each other in the backyard after school. We wore our golden boxing gloves, cracked with age and flaking when we pounded them together. Browned grass crunched beneath our sneakers, and dust rose in little puffs like distress signals.

Gordon was thin to the point of being scrawny. His collarbone poked against his skin like a swallowed coat hanger. His head was too big for his body, and his eyes were too big for his head, and football players—Seth

Johnson among them—regularly tossed him into garbage cans and called him E.T.

He had had a bad day. And I could tell from the look on his face—the watery eyes, the trembling lips that revealed in quick flashes his buck-teeth—that he wanted, he *needed*, to hit me. So I let him. I raised my gloves to my face and pulled my elbows against my ribs and Gordon lunged forward, his arms snapping like rubber bands. I stood still, allowing his fists to work up and down my body, allowing him to throw the weight of his anger on me, until eventually he grew too tired to hit anymore and I opened up my stance and floored him with a right cross to the temple. He lay there, sprawled out in the grass with a small smile on his E.T. face. "Damn," he said in a dreamy voice. A drop of blood gathered along the corner of his eye and streaked down his temple into his hair.

My father wore steel-toed boots, Carhartt jeans, and a T-shirt advertising some place he had traveled to, maybe Yellowstone or Seattle. He looked like someone you might see shopping for motor oil at Bi-Mart. To hide his receding hairline he wore a John Deere cap that laid a shadow across his face. His brown eyes blinked above a considerable nose underlined by a gray mustache. Like me, my father was short and squat, a bulldog. His belly was a swollen bag, and his shoulders were broad, good for carrying me during parades and at fairs when I was younger. He laughed a lot. He liked game shows. He drank too much beer and smoked too many cigarettes and spent too much time with his buddies, fishing, hunting, bullshitting, which probably had something to do with why my mother divorced him and moved to Boise with a hairdresser and triathlete named Chuck.

At first, after my father left, like all of the other fathers, he would e-mail whenever he could. He would tell me about the heat, the gallons of water he drank every day, the sand that got into everything, the baths he took with baby wipes. He would tell me how safe he was, how very safe. This was when he was stationed in Turkey. Then the reservists shipped for Kirkuk, where insurgents and sandstorms attacked almost daily. The e-mails came less frequently. Weeks of silence passed between them.

Sometimes, on the computer, I would hit refresh, refresh, *refresh*, hoping. In October I received an e-mail that read: "Hi, Josh. I'm O.K. Don't worry. Do your homework. Love, Dad." I printed it and hung it on my door with a piece of Scotch tape.

For twenty years my father worked at Nosier, Inc.—the bullet manufacturer based out of Bend—and the Marines trained him as an ammunition technician. Gordon liked to say his father was a gunnery sergeant, and he was, but we all knew he was also the battalion mess manager, a cook, which was how he made his living in Crow, tending the grill at Hamburger Patty's. We knew their titles, but we didn't know, not really, what their titles meant, what our fathers *did* over there. We imagined them doing heroic things: rescuing Iraqi babies from burning huts, sniping suicide bombers before they could detonate on a crowded city street. We drew on Hollywood and TV news to develop elaborate scenarios where maybe, at twilight, during a trek through the mountains of northern Iraq, bearded insurgents ambushed our fathers with rocket launchers. We imagined them silhouetted by a fiery explosion. We imagined them burrowing into the sand like lizards and firing their M-16s, their bullets streaking through the darkness like the meteorites I observed on sleepless nights.

When Gordon and I fought we painted our faces—black and green and brown—with the camo grease our fathers left behind. It made our eyes and teeth appear startlingly white. And it smeared away against our gloves just as the grass smeared away beneath our sneakers—and the ring became a circle of dirt, the dirt a reddish color that looked a lot like scabbed flesh. One time Gordon hammered my shoulder so hard I couldn't lift my arm for a week. Another time I elbowed one of his kidneys, and he peed blood. We struck each other with such force and frequency that the golden gloves crumbled and our knuckles showed through the sweat-soaked, blood-soaked foam like teeth through a busted lip. So we bought another set of gloves, and as the air grew steadily colder we fought with steam blasting from our mouths.

Our fathers had left us, but men remained in Crow. There were old men, like my grandfather, whom I lived with—men who had paid their dues, who had worked their jobs and fought their wars and now spent their days at the gas station, drinking bad coffee from Styrofoam cups, complaining about the weather, arguing about the best months to reap alfalfa. And there were incapable men. Men who rarely shaved and watched daytime television in their once white underpants. Men who lived in trailers and filled their shopping carts with Busch Light, summer sausage, Oreo cookies.

And then there were vulturous men like Dave Lightener—men who scavenged whatever our fathers had left behind. Dave Lightener worked as a recruitment officer. I'm guessing he was the only recruitment officer in world history who drove a Vespa scooter with a Support Our Troops ribbon magnet on its rear. We sometimes saw it parked outside the homes of young women whose husbands had gone to war. Dave had big ears and small eyes and wore his hair in your standard-issue high-and-tight buzz. He often spoke in a too loud voice about all the insurgents he gunned down when working a Fallujah patrol unit. He lived with his mother in Crow, but spent his days in Bend and Redmond trolling the parking lots of Best Buy, ShopKo, Kmart, Wal-Mart, Mountain View Mall. He was looking for people like us, people who were angry and dissatisfied and poor.

But Dave Lightener knew better than to bother us. On duty he stayed away from Crow entirely. Recruiting there would be too much like poaching the burned section of forest where deer, rib-slatted and wobbly legged, nosed through the ash, seeking something green.

We didn't really understand the reason our fathers were fighting. We understood only that they *had* to fight. The necessity of it made the reason irrelevant. "It's all part of the game," my grandfather said. "It's just the way it is." We would only cross our fingers and wish on stars and hit refresh, *refresh*, hoping that they would return to us, praying that we would never find Dave Lightener on our porch uttering the words *I regret to inform you . . .*

One time, my grandfather dropped Gordon and me off at Mountain View Mall, and there, near the glass-doored entrance, stood Dave Lightener. He wore his creased khaki uniform and spoke with a group of Mexican teenagers. They were laughing, shaking their heads and walking away from him as we approached. We had our hats pulled low, and he didn't recognize us.

"Question for you, gentlemen," he said in the voice of telemarketers and door-to-door Jehovah's Witnesses. "What do you plan on doing with your lives?"

Gordon pulled off his hat with a flourish, as if he were part of some *ta-da!* magic act and his face was the trick. "I plan on killing some crazy-ass Muslims," he said and forced a smile. "How about you, Josh?"

"Yeah," I said. "Kill some people, then get myself killed." I grimaced even as I played along. "That sounds like a good plan."

Dave Lightener's lips tightened into a thin line, his posture straightened, and he asked us what we thought our fathers would think, hearing us right now. "They're out there risking their lives, defending our freedom, and you're cracking sick jokes," he said. "I think that's sick."

We hated him for his soft hands and clean uniform. We hated him because he sent people like us off to die. Because at twenty-three he had attained a higher rank than our fathers. Because he slept with the lonely wives of soldiers. And now we hated him even more for making us feel ashamed. I wanted to say something sarcastic, but Gordon was quicker. His hand was out before him, his fingers gripping an imaginary bottle. "Here's your maple syrup," he said.

Dave said, "And what is that for?"

"To eat my ass with," Gordon said.

Right then a skateboarder type with green hair and a nose ring walked from the mall, a bagful of DVDs swinging from his fist, and Dave Lightener forgot us. "Hey, friend," he was saying. "Let me ask you something. Do you like war movies?"

In November we drove our dirt bikes deep into the woods to hunt. Sunlight fell through tall pines and birch clusters and lay in puddles along the logging roads that wound past the hillsides packed with huckleberries and on the moraines where coyotes scurried, trying to flee from us and slipping, causing tiny avalanches of loose rock. It hadn't rained in nearly a month, so the crabgrass and the cheatgrass and the pine needles had lost their color, as dry and blond as cornhusks, crackling beneath my boots when the road we followed petered out into nothing and I stepped off my bike. In this waterless stillness, it seemed you could hear every chipmunk within a square acre rustling for pine nuts, and when the breeze rose into a cold wind the forest became a giant whisper.

We dumped our tent and our sleeping bags near a basalt grotto with a spring bubbling from it, and Gordon said, "Let's go, troops," holding his rifle before his chest diagonally, as a soldier would. He dressed as a soldier would too, wearing his father's overlarge cammies rather than the mandatory blaze-orange gear. Fifty feet apart, we worked our way downhill through the forest, through a huckleberry thicket, through a clear-cut crowded with stumps, taking care not to make much noise or slip on the pine needles carpeting the ground. A chipmunk worrying at a pinecone screeched its astonishment when a peregrine falcon swooped down and seized it, carrying it off between the trees to some secret place. Its wings made no sound, and neither did the blaze-orange-clad hunter when he appeared in a clearing several hundred yards below us.

Gordon made some sort of SWAT-team gesture—meant, I think, to say, stay low—and I made my way carefully toward him. From behind a boulder we peered through our scopes, tracking the hunter, who looked, in his vest and earflapped hat, like a monstrous pumpkin. "That cocksucker," Gordon said in a harsh whisper. The hunter was Seth Johnson. His rifle was strapped to his back and his mouth was moving—he was talking to someone. At the corner of the meadow he joined four members of the varsity football squad, who sat on logs around a smoldering campfire, their arms bobbing like oil pump jacks as they brought their beers to their mouths.

I took my eye from my scope and noticed Gordon fingering the trigger of his 30.06. I told him to quit fooling around, and he pulled his hand suddenly away from the stock and smiled guiltily and said he just wanted to know what it felt like having that power over someone. Then his trigger finger rose up and touched the gummy white scar that split his eyebrow. "I say we fuck with them a little."

I shook my head no.

Gordon said, "Just a little—to scare them."

"They've got guns," I said, and he said, "So we'll come back tonight."

Later, after an early dinner of beef jerky and trail mix and Gatorade, I happened upon a four-point stag nibbling on some bean grass, and I rested my rifle on a stump and shot it, and it stumbled backwards and collapsed with a rose blooming from behind its shoulder where the heart was hidden. Gordon came running, and we stood around the deer and smoked a few cigarettes, watching the thick arterial blood run from its mouth. Then we took out our knives and got to work. I cut around the anus, cutting away the penis and testes, and then ran the knife along the belly, unzipping the hide to reveal the delicate pink flesh and greenish vessels into which our hands disappeared.

The blood steamed in the cold mountain air, and when we finished— when we'd skinned the deer and hacked at its joints and cut out its back strap and boned out its shoulders and hips, its neck and ribs, making chops, roasts, steaks, quartering the meat so we could bundle it into our insulated saddlebags—Gordon picked up the deer head by the antlers and held it before his own. Blood from its neck made a pattering sound on the ground, and in the half-light of early evening Gordon began to do a little dance, bending his knees and stomping his feet.

"I think I've got an idea," he said, and he pretended to charge at me with the antlers. I pushed him away and he said, "Don't pussy out on me, Josh." I was exhausted and reeked of gore, but I could appreciate the need for revenge. "Just to scare them, right, Gordo?" I said.

"Right."

We lugged our meat back to camp, and Gordon brought the deer hide. He slit a hole in its middle and poked his head through so the hide hung off him loosely, a hairy sack, and I helped him smear mud and blood across his face. Then, with his Leatherman, he sawed off the antlers and held them in each hand and slashed at the air as if they were claws.

Night had come on, and the moon hung over the Cascades, grayly lighting our way as we crept through the forest imagining ourselves in enemy territory, with tripwires and guard towers and snarling dogs around every corner. From behind the boulder that overlooked their campsite, we observed our enemies as they swapped hunting stories and joked about Jessica Robertson's big-ass titties and passed around a bottle of whiskey and drank to excess and finally pissed on the fire to extinguish it. When they retired to their tents we waited an hour before making our way down the hill with such care that it took us another hour before we were upon them. Somewhere an owl hooted, its noise barely noticeable over the chorus of snores that rose from their tents. Seth's Bronco was parked nearby—the license plate read SMAN—and all their rifles lay in its cab. I collected the guns, slinging them over my shoulder, then I eased my knife into each of Seth's tires.

I still had my knife out when we were standing beside Seth's tent, and when a cloud scudded over the moon and made the meadow fully dark I stabbed the nylon and in one quick jerk opened up a slit. Gordon rushed in, his antler-claws slashing. I could see nothing but shadows, but I could hear Seth scream the scream of a little girl as Gordon raked at him with the antlers and hissed and howled like some cave creature hungry for man-flesh. When the tents around us came alive with confused voices, Gordon re-emerged with a horrible smile on his face, and I followed him up the hillside, crashing through the undergrowth, leaving Seth to make sense of the nightmare that had descended upon him without warning.

Winter came. Snow fell, and we threw on our coveralls and wrenched on our studded tires and drove our dirt bikes to Hole in the Ground, dragging our sleds behind us with towropes. Our engines filled the white silence of the afternoon. Our back tires kicked up plumes of powder and on sharp turns slipped out beneath us, and we lay there in the middle of the road bleeding, laughing, unafraid.

Earlier, for lunch, we had cooked a pound of bacon with a stick of butter. The grease, which hardened into a white waxy pool, we used as polish, buffing it into the bottoms of our sleds. Speed was what we wanted at Hole in the Ground. We descended the steepest section of the crater into its heart, three hundred feet below us. We followed each other in the same track, ironing down the snow to create a chute, blue-hued and frictionless, that would allow us to travel at a speed equivalent to free fall. Our eyeballs glazed with frost, our ears roared with wind, and our stomachs rose into our throats as we rocketed down and felt as if we were five again—and then we began the slow climb back the way we came and felt fifty.

We wore crampons and ascended in a zigzagging series of switchbacks. It took nearly an hour. The air had begun to go purple with evening when we stood again at the lip of the crater, sweating in our coveralls, taking in the view through the fog of our breath. Gordon packed a snowball. I said, "You better not hit me with that." He cocked his arm threateningly and smiled, then dropped to his knees to roll the snowball into something bigger. He rolled it until it grew to the size of a large man curled into the fetal position. From the back of his bike he took the piece of garden hose he used to siphon gas from fancy foreign cars and he worked it into his tank, sucking at its end until gas flowed.

He doused the giant snowball as if he hoped it would sprout. It didn't melt—he'd packed it tight enough—but it puckered slightly and appeared leaden, and when Gordon withdrew his Zippo, sparked it, and held it toward the ball, the fumes caught flame and the whole thing erupted with a gasping noise that sent me staggering back a few steps.

Gordon rushed forward and kicked the ball of fire, sending it rolling, tumbling down the crater, down our chute like a meteor, and the snow beneath it instantly melted only to freeze again a moment later, making a slick blue ribbon. When we sledded it, we went so fast our minds emptied and we felt a sensation at once like flying and falling.

On the news Iraqi insurgents fired their assault rifles. On the news a car bomb in Baghdad blew up seven American soldiers at a traffic checkpoint. On the news the president said he did not think it was wise to provide a time frame for troop withdrawal. I checked my e-mail before breakfast and found nothing but spam.

Gordon and I fought in the snow wearing snow boots. We fought so much our wounds never got a chance to heal, and our faces took on a permanent look of decay. Our wrists felt swollen, our knees ached, our joints felt full of tiny dry wasps. We fought until fighting hurt too much, and we took up drinking instead. Weekends, we drove our dirt bikes to Bend, twenty miles away, and bought beer and took it to Hole in the Ground and drank there until a bright line of sunlight appeared on the horizon and illuminated the snow-blanketed desert. Nobody asked for our IDs, and when we held up our empty bottles and stared at our reflections in the glass, warped and ghostly, we knew why. And we weren't alone. Black bags grew beneath the eyes of the sons and daughters and wives of Crow, their shoulders stooped, wrinkles enclosing their mouths like parentheses.

Our fathers haunted us. They were everywhere: in the grocery store when we spotted a thirty-pack of Coors on sale for ten bucks; on the highway when we passed a jacked-up Dodge with a dozen hay bales stacked in its bed; in the sky when a jet roared by, reminding us of faraway places. And now, as our bodies thickened with muscle, as we stopped shaving and grew patchy beards, we saw our fathers even in the mirror. We began to look like them. Our fathers, who had been taken from us, were everywhere, at every turn, imprisoning us.

Seth Johnson's father was a staff sergeant. Like his son, he was a big man but not big enough. Just before Christmas he stepped on a cluster bomb. A U.S. warplane dropped it and the sand camouflaged it and he stepped on it and it tore him into many meaty pieces. When Dave Lightener climbed up the front porch with a black armband and a somber expression, Mrs. Johnson, who was cooking a honeyed ham at the time, collapsed on the kitchen floor. Seth pushed his way out the door and punched Dave in the face, breaking his nose before he could utter the words *I regret to inform you . . .*

Hearing about this, we felt bad for all of ten seconds. Then we felt good because it was his father and not ours. And then we felt bad again, and on Christmas Eve we drove to Seth's house and laid down on his porch the rifles we had stolen, along with a six-pack of Coors, and then, just as we were about to leave, Gordon dug in his back pocket and removed his wallet and placed under the six-pack all the money he had—a few fives, some ones. "Fucking Christmas," he said.

We got braver and went to the bars—the Golden Nugget, the Weary Traveler, the Pine Tavern—where we square-danced with older women wearing purple eye shadow and sparkly dream-catcher earrings and push-up bras and clattery high heels. We told them we were Marines back from a six-month deployment, and they said, "Really?" and we said, "Yes, ma'am," and when they asked for our names we gave them the names of our fathers. Then we bought them drinks and they drank them in a gulping way and breathed hotly in our faces and we brought our mouths against theirs and they tasted like menthol cigarettes, like burnt detergent. And then we went home with them, to their trailers, to their waterbeds, where among their stuffed animals we fucked them.

Midafternoon and it was already full dark. On our way to the Weary Traveler we stopped by my house to bum some money off my grandfather, only to find Dave Lightener waiting for us. He must have just gotten there—he was halfway up the porch steps—when our headlights cast an anemic glow over him, and he turned to face us with a scrunched-up expression, as if trying to figure out who we were. He wore the black band around his arm and, over his nose, a white-bandaged splint.

We did not turn off our engines. Instead we sat in the driveway, idling, the exhaust from our bikes and the breath from our mouths clouding the air. Above us a star hissed across the moonlit sky, vaguely bright like a light turned on in a day-lit room. Then Dave began down the steps and we leapt off our bikes to meet him. Before he could speak I brought my fist to his diaphragm, knocking the breath from his body. He looked like a gun-shot actor in a Western, clutching his belly with both hands, doubled over, his face making a nice target for Gordon's knee. A snap sound preceded Dave falling on his back with blood coming from his already broken nose.

He put up his hands, and we hit our way through them. I punched him once, twice, in the ribs while Gordon kicked him in the spine and stomach and then we stood around gulping air and allowed him to struggle to his feet. When he righted himself, he wiped his face with his hand, and blood dripped from his fingers. I moved in and roundhoused with my right and then my left, my fists knocking his head loose on its hinges. Again he collapsed, a bloody bag of a man. His eyes walled and turned up, trying to see the animal bodies looming over him. He opened his mouth to speak, and I pointed a finger at him and said, with enough hatred in my voice to break a back, "Don't say a word. Don't you dare. Not one word."

He closed his mouth and tried to crawl away, and I brought a boot down on the back of his skull and left it there a moment, grinding his face into the ground so that when he lifted his head the snow held a red impression of his face. Gordon went inside and returned a moment later with a roll of duct tape, and we held Dave down and bound his wrists and ankles and threw him on a sled and taped him to it many times over and then tied the sled to the back of Gordon's bike and drove at a perilous speed to Hole in the Ground.

The moon shone down and the snow glowed with pale blue light as we smoked cigarettes, looking down into the crater, with Dave at our feet. There was something childish about the way our breath puffed from our mouths in tiny clouds. It was as if we were imitating choo-choo trains. And for a moment, just a moment, we were kids again. Just a couple of stupid kids. Gordon must have felt this, too, because he said, "My mom wouldn't even let me play with toy guns when I was little." And he sighed heavily as if he couldn't understand how he, how we, had ended up here.

Then, with a sudden lurch, Dave began struggling and yelling at us in a slurred voice and my face hardened with anger and I put my hands on him and pushed him slowly to the lip of the crater and he grew silent. For a moment I forgot myself, staring off into the dark oblivion. It was beautiful and horrifying. "I could shove you right now," I said. "And if I did, you'd be dead."

"Please don't," he said, his voice cracking. He began to cry. "Oh fuck. Don't. Please." Hearing his great shuddering sobs didn't bring me the satisfaction I had hoped for. If anything, I felt as I did that day, so long ago, when we taunted him in the Mountain View Mall parking lot—shameful, false.

"Ready?" I said. "One!" I inched him a little closer to the edge. "Two!" I moved him a little closer still, and as I did I felt unwieldly, at once wild and exhausted, my body seeming to take on another twenty, thirty, forty years. When I finally said "*Three*," my voice was barely a whisper.

We left Dave there, sobbing at the brink of the crater. We got on our bikes and we drove to Bend and we drove so fast I imagined catching fire like a meteor, burning up in a flash, howling as my heat consumed me, as we made our way to the U.S. Marine Recruiting Office, where we would at last answer the fierce alarm of war and put our pens to paper and make our fathers proud.

6

Smorgasbord

TOBIAS WOLFF

Tobias Wolff, a celebrated writer of short stories, memoirs, and novels, was born in Birmingham, Alabama, in 1945. His mother and father divorced when he was a young boy and the remainder of his childhood was turbulent; he relocated with his mother several times before settling in Washington State, where she married an abusive second husband. Wolff later drew from those experiences of domestic abuse and itinerancy in his memoir *This Boy's Life* (1989). After graduating high school and failing out of a prestigious prep school, Wolff enlisted and served in the U.S. Army (1964–68), including a tour of duty in Vietnam. After completing his military service, he enrolled at Oxford University, where he earned a BA and MA in English in 1972 and 1975, respectively. Wolff published his first novel, *Ugly Rumours*, in 1975 and was also awarded a Stegner writing fellowship at Stanford University, where he later earned a second MA in 1978. In 1980, Wolff began teaching writing and literature at Syracuse University, a tenure that lasted 17 years, during which he established himself as a leading figure in American letters—publishing four short story collections, two memoirs, and two novels. Since 1997, he has served as the Ward W. and Priscilla B. Woods Professor at Stanford University. He is the recipient of many honors, including two National Endowment Fellowships in 1978 and 1985; the O. Henry Award in 1980, 1981, and 1985; a Guggenheim Fellowship in 1982; and the PEN/Faulkner Award in 1985.

"A prep school in March is like a ship in the doldrums." Our history master said this, as if to himself, while we were waiting for the bell to ring after class. He stood by the window and tapped the glass with his ring in a dreamy, abstracted way meant to make us think he'd forgotten we were there. We were supposed to get the impression that when we weren't around he turned into someone interesting, someone witty and profound, who uttered impromptu bons mots and had a poetic vision of life.

The bell rang.

I went to lunch. The dining hall was almost empty, because it was a free weekend and most of the boys in school had gone to New York, or home, or to their friends' homes, as soon as their last class let out. About the only ones left were foreigners and scholarship students like me and a few other untouchables of various stripes. The school had laid on a nice lunch for us, cheese soufflé, but the portions were small and I went back to my room still hungry. I was always hungry.

Snow and rain fell past my window. The snow on the quad looked grimy; it had melted above the underground heating pipes, exposing long brown lines of mud.

I couldn't get to work. On the next floor down someone kept playing "Mack the Knife." That one song incessantly repeating itself made the dorm seem not just empty but abandoned, as if those who had left were never coming back. I cleaned my room. I tried to read. I looked out the window. I sat down at my desk and studied the new picture my girlfriend had sent me, unable to imagine her from it; I had to close my eyes to do that, and then I could see her, see her solemn eyes and the heavy white breasts she would gravely let me hold sometimes, but not kiss . . . not yet, anyway. But I had a promise. That summer, as soon as I got home, we were going to become lovers. "Become lovers." That was how she'd said it, very deliberately, listening to the words as she spoke them. All year I had repeated them to myself to take the edge off my loneliness and the fits of lust that made me want to scream and drive my fists through walls. We were going to become lovers that summer, and we were going to be lovers all through college, true to each other even if we ended up thousands of miles apart again, and after college we were going to marry and join the Peace Corps and then do something together that would help people. This was our plan. Back in September, the night before I left for school, we wrote it all down along with a lot of other specifics concerning our future: number of children (six), their names, the kinds of dogs we would own, a sketch of our perfect house. We sealed the paper in a bottle and buried it in her backyard. On our golden anniversary we were going to dig it up again and show it to our children and grandchildren to prove that dreams can come true.

I was writing her a letter when Crosley came to my room. Crosley was a science whiz. He won the science prize every year and spent his summers working as an intern in different laboratories. He was also a fanatical weight lifter. His arms were so knotty that he had to hold them out from his sides as he walked, as if he were carrying buckets. Even his features seemed muscular. His face was red. Crosley lived down the hall by himself in one of the only singles in the school. He was said to be a thief; that supposedly was the reason he'd ended up without a roommate. I didn't know if it was true, and I tried to avoid forming an opinion on the matter, but whenever we passed each other I felt embarrassed and dropped my eyes.

Crosley leaned in the door and asked me how things were.

I said okay.

He stepped inside and looked around the room, tilting his head to read my roommate's pennants and the titles of our books. I was uneasy. I said, "So what can I do for you," not meaning to sound as cold as I did but not exactly regretting it either.

He caught my tone and smiled. It was the kind of smile you put on when you pass a group of people you suspect are talking about you. It was his usual expression.

He said, "You know Garcia, right?"

"Garcia? Sure. I think so."

"You know him," Crosley said. "He runs around with Hidalgo and those guys. He's the tall one."

"Sure," I said. "I know who Garcia is."

"Well, his stepmother is in New York for a fashion show or something, and she's going to drive up and take him out to dinner tonight. She told him to bring along some friends.. You want to come?"

"What about Hidalgo and the rest of them?"

"They're at some kind of polo deal in Maryland. Buying horses. Or po-nies, I guess it would be."

The notion of someone my age buying ponies to play a game with was so unexpected that I couldn't quite take it in. "Jesus," I said.

Crosley said, "How about it. You want to come?"

I'd never even spoken to Garcia. He was the nephew of a famous dicta-tor, and all his friends were nephews and cousins of other dictators. They lived as they pleased here. Most of them kept cars a few blocks from the campus, though it was completely against the rules, and I'd heard that some of them kept women as well. They were cocky and prankish and charming. They moved everywhere in a body with sunglasses pushed up on their heads and jackets slung over their shoulders, twittering all at once like birds, *chinga* this and *chinga* that. The headmaster was completely buffaloed. After Christmas vacation a bunch of them came down with gonorrhea, and all he did was call them in and advise them that they should not be in too great a hurry to lose their innocence. It became a school joke. All you had to do was say the word "innocence" and everyone would crack up.

"I don't know," I said.

"Come on," Crosley said.

"But I don't even know the guy."

"So what? I don't either."

"Then why did he ask you?"

"I was sitting next to him at lunch."

"Terrific," I said. "That explains you. What about me? How come he asked me?"

"He didn't. He told me to bring someone else."

"What, just anybody? Just whoever happened to present himself to your attention?"

Crosley shrugged.

I laughed. Crosley gave me a look to make sure I wasn't laughing at him, then he laughed, too. "Sounds great," I said. "Sounds like a recipe for a really memorable evening."

"You got something better to do?" Crosley asked.

"No," I said.

The limousine picked us up under the awning of the headmaster's house. The driver, an old man, got out slowly and then slowly adjusted his cap before opening the door for us. Garcia slid in beside the woman in back. Crosley and I sat across from them on seats that pulled down. I caught her scent immediately. For some years afterward I bought perfume for women, and I was never able to find that one.

Garcia erupted into Spanish as soon as the driver closed the door behind me. He sounded angry, spitting words at the woman and gesticulating violently. She rocked back a little, then let loose a burst of her own. I stared openly at her. Her skin was very white. She wore a black cape over a black dress cut just low enough to show her pale throat and the bones at the base of her throat. Her mouth was red. There was a spot of rouge high on each cheek, not rubbed in to look like real color but left there carelessly, or carefully, to make you think again how white her skin was. Her teeth were small and sharp looking, and she bared them in concert with certain gestures and inflections. As she talked, her little pointed tongue flicked in and out.

She wasn't a lot older than we were. Twenty-five at the most. Maybe younger.

She said something definitive and cut her hand through the air. Garcia began to answer her, but she said "No!" and chopped the air again. Then she turned and smiled at Crosley and me. It was a completely false smile.

She said, "Where would you fellows like to eat?" Her voice sounded lower in English, even a little harsh, though the harshness could have come from her accent. She called us *fallows.*

"Anywhere is fine with me," I said.

"Anywhere," she repeated. She narrowed her big black eyes and pushed her lips together. I could see that my answer disappointed her. She looked at Crosley.

"There's supposed to be a good French restaurant in Newbury," Crosley said. "Also an Italian place. It depends on what you want."

"No," she said. "It depends on what you want. I am not so hungry."

If Garcia had a preference, he kept it to himself. He sulked in the corner, his round shoulders slumped and his hands between his knees. He seemed to be trying to make a point of some kind.

"There's also a smorgasbord," Crosley said. "If you like smorgasbords."

"Smorgasbord," she said. She repeated the word to Garcia. He frowned, then answered her in a sullen monotone.

I couldn't believe Crosley had suggested the smorgasbord. It was an egregiously uncouth suggestion. The smorgasbord was where the local fatties went to binge. Football coaches brought whole teams there to bulk up. The food was good enough, and God knows there was plenty of it, all you could eat, actually, but the atmosphere was brutally matter-of-fact. The food was good, though. Big platters of shrimp on crushed ice. Barons of beef. Smoked turkey. No end of food, really.

She was smiling. Obviously the concept was new to her. "You—do you like smorgasbords?" she asked Crosley.

"Yes," he said.

"And you?" she said to me.

I nodded. Then, not to seem wishy-washy, I said, "You bet."

"Smorgasbord," she said. She laughed and clapped her hands. "Smorgasbord!"

Crosley gave directions to the driver, and we drove slowly away from the school. She said something to Garcia. He nodded at each of us in turn and gave our names, then looked away again, out the window, where the snowy fields were turning dark. His face was long, his eyes sorrowful as a hound's. He had barely talked to us while we were waiting for the limousine. I didn't know why he was mad at his stepmother, or why he wouldn't talk to us, or why he'd even asked us along, but by now I didn't really care. By now my sentiments were, basically, Fuck him.

She studied us and repeated our names skeptically. "No," she said. She pointed at Crosley and said, "El Blanco." She pointed to me and said, "El Negro." Then she pointed at herself and said, "I am Linda."

"Leen-da," Crosley said. He really overdid it, but she showed her sharp little teeth and said, *"Exactamente."*

Then she settled back against the seat and pulled her cape close around her shoulders. It soon fell open again. She was restless. She sat forward and leaned back, crossed and recrossed her legs, swung her feet impatiently. She had on black high heels fastened by a thin strap; I could see almost her entire foot. I heard the silky rub of her stockings against each other, and breathed in a fresh breath of her perfume every time she moved. That perfume had a certain effect on me. It didn't reach me as just a smell; it was personal, it seemed to issue from her very privacy. It made the hair bristle on my arms. It entered my veins like fine, tingling wires, widening my eyes, tightening my spine, sending faint chills across my shoulders and the backs of my knees. Every time she moved I felt a little tug, and followed her motion with some slight motion of my own.

When we arrived at the smorgasbord—Swenson's, I believe it was, or maybe Hansen's, some such honest Swede of a name—Garcia refused to get out of the limousine. Linda tried to persuade him, but he shrank back into his corner and would not answer or even look at her. She threw up her hands. "Ah!" she said, and turned away. Crosley and I followed her across the parking lot toward the big red barn. Her dress rustled as she walked. Her heels clicked on the cement.

You could say one thing for the smorgasbord; it wasn't pretentious. It was in a real barn, not some quaint fantasy of a barn with butter-churn lamps and little brass ornaments nailed to the walls on strips of leather. At one end of the barn was the kitchen. The rest of it had been left open and filled with picnic tables. Blazing light bulbs hung from the rafters. In the middle of the barn stood what my English master would have called the groaning board—a great table heaped with food, every kind of food you could think of, and more. I had been there several times, and it always gave me a small, pleasant shock to see how much food there was.

Girls wearing dirndls hustled around the barn, cleaning up messes, changing tablecloths, bringing fresh platters of food from the kitchen.

We stood blinking in the sudden light. Linda paid up, then we followed one of the waitresses across the floor. Linda walked slowly, gazing around like a tourist. Several men looked up from their food as she passed. I was behind her, and I looked forbiddingly back at them so they would think she was my wife.

We were lucky; we got a table to ourselves. On crowded nights they usually doubled you up with another party, and that could be an extremely unromantic experience. Linda shrugged off her cape and waved us toward the food. "Go on," she said. She sat down and opened her purse. When I looked back she was lighting a cigarette.

"You're pretty quiet tonight," Crosley said as we filled our plates. "You pissed off about something?"

I shook my head. "Maybe I'm just quiet, Crosley, you know?"

He speared a slice of meat and said, "When she called you El Negro, that didn't mean she thought you were a Negro. She just said that because your hair is dark. Mine is light, that's how come she called me El Blanco."

"I know that, Crosley, Jesus. You think I couldn't figure that out? Give me some credit, okay?" Then, as we moved around the table, I said, "You speak Spanish?"

"*Un poco.* Actually more like *un poquito.*"

"What's Garcia mad about?"

"Money. Something about money."

"Like what?"

He shook his head. "That's all I could get. But it's definitely about money."

I'd meant to start off slow but by the time I reached the end of the table my plate was full. Potato salad, ham, jumbo shrimp, toast, barbecued beef, eggs Benny. Crosley's was full, too. We walked back toward Linda, who was leaning forward on her elbows and looking around the barn. She took a long drag off her cigarette, lifted her chin, and blew a stream of smoke up toward the rafters. I sat down across from her. "Scoot down," Crosley said, and settled in beside me.

She watched us eat for a while.

"So," she said, "El Blanco. Are you from New York?"

Crosley looked up in surprise. "No, ma'am," he said. "I'm from Virginia."

Linda stabbed out her cigarette. She had long fingernails painted the same deep red as the lipstick smears on her cigarette butt. She said, "I just came from New York, and I can tell you that is one crazy place. Just incredible. Listen to this. I am in a taxicab, you know, and we are stopping in this traffic jam for a long time and there is a taxicab next to us with this fellow in it who stares at me. Like this, you know." She made her eyes go round. "Of course I ignore him. So guess what, my door opens and he gets into my cab. 'Excuse me,' he says, 'I want to marry you.' 'That's nice,' I say. 'Ask my husband.' 'I don't care about your husband,' he says. 'Your husband is history. So is my wife.' Of course I had to laugh. 'Okay,' he says. 'You think that's funny? How about this. Then he says—"Linda looked sharply at each of us. She sniffed and made a face. "He says things you would never believe. Never. He wants to do this and he wants to do that. Well, I act like I am about to scream. I open my mouth like this. 'Hey,' he says, 'okay, okay. Relax.' Then he gets out and goes back to his taxicab. We are still sitting there for a long time again, and you know what he is doing? He is reading the newspaper. With his hat on. Go ahead, eat," she said to us, and nodded toward the food.

A tall, blond girl was carving slices of roast beef onto a platter. She smiled at us. She was hale and bosomy—I could see the laces on her bodice straining. Her cheeks glowed. Her bare arms and shoulders were ruddy with exertion. Crosley raised his eyebrows at me. I raised mine back but my heart wasn't in it. She was a Viking dream, pure gemütlichkeit, but I was drunk on Garcia's stepmother, and in that condition you don't want a glass of milk, you want more of what's making you stumble and fall.

Crosley and I filled our plates again and headed back.

"I'm always hungry," he said.

"I know what you mean," I told him.

Linda smoked another cigarette while we ate. She watched the other tables as if she were at a movie. I tried to eat with a little finesse and so did Crosley, dabbing his lips with a napkin between every bulging mouthful, but some of the people around us had completely slipped their moorings. They ducked their heads low to receive their food, and while they chewed it up they looked around suspiciously and kept their forearms close to their plates. A big family to our left was the worst. There was something competitive and desperate about them; they seemed to be eating their way toward a condition where they would never have to eat again. You would have thought that they were refugees from a great hunger, that outside these walls the land was afflicted with drought and barrenness. I felt a kind of desperation myself; I felt as if I were growing emptier with every bite I took.

There was a din in the air, a steady roar like that of a waterfall.

Linda looked around her with a pleased expression. She bore no likeness to anyone here, but she seemed completely at home. She sent us back for another plate, then dessert and coffee, and while we were finishing up she asked El Blanco if he had a girlfriend.

"No, ma'am," Crosley said. "We broke up," he added, and his red face turned purple. It was clear that he was lying.

"You. How about you?"

I nodded.

"Ha!" she said. "El Negro is the one! So. What's her name?"

"Jane."

"Jaaane," Linda drawled. "Okay, let's hear about Jaaane."

"Jane," I said again.

Linda smiled.

I told her everything. I told her how my girlfriend and I had met and what she looked like and what our plans were. I told her more than everything, because I gave certain coy but definite suggestions about the extremes to which our passion had already driven us. I meant to impress her with my potency, to inflame her, to wipe that smile off her face, but the more I told her the more wolfishly she smiled and the more her eyes laughed at me.

Laughing eyes—now there's a cliché my English master would have eaten me alive for. "How exactly did these eyes laugh?" he would have asked, looking up from my paper while my classmates snorted around me. "Did they titter, or did they merely chortle? Did they give a great guffaw? Did they, perhaps, *scream* with laughter?"

I am here to tell you that eyes can scream with laughter. Linda's did. As I played big hombre for her I could see exactly how complete my failure was, I could hear her saying, *Okay, El Negro, go on, talk about your little gorlfren, how pretty she is and so on, but we know what you want, don't we?—you want to suck on my tongue and slobber on my titties and lick my belly and bury your face in me. That's what you want.*

Crosley interrupted me. "Ma'am . . ." he said, and nodded toward the door. Garcia was leaning there with his arms crossed and an expression of fury on his face. When she looked at him he turned and walked out the door.

Her eyes went flat. She sat there for a moment. She began to take a cigarette from her case, then put it back and stood up. "Let's go," she said.

Garcia was waiting in the car, rigid and silent. He said nothing on the drive back. Linda swung her foot and stared out the window at the passing houses and bright, moonlit fields. Just before we reached the school, Garcia leaned forward and began speaking to her in a low voice. She listened impassively and did not answer. He was still talking when the limousine stopped in front of the headmaster's house. The driver opened the door.

Garcia fixed his eyes on her. Still impassive, she took her pocketbook out of her purse. She opened it and looked inside. She meditated over the contents, then withdrew a bill and offered it to Garcia. It was a one-hundred-dollar bill. "Boolshit!" he said, and sat back angrily. With no change of expression she turned and held the bill out to me. I didn't know what else to do but take it. She got another one from her pocket and presented it to Crosley, who hesitated even less than I did. Then she gave us the same false smile she had greeted us with, and said, "Good night, it was a pleasure to meet you. Good night, good night," she said to Garcia.

The three of us got out of the limousine. I went a few steps and then slowed down, and began to look back.

"Keep walking!" Crosley hissed.

Garcia let off a string of words as the driver closed the door. I faced around again and walked with Crosley across the quad. As we approached our dorm he quickened his pace. "I don't believe it," he whispered. "A hundred bucks." When we were inside the door he stopped and shouted, "A hundred bucks! A hundred fucking dollars!"

"Pipe down," someone called.

"All right, all right. Fuck you!" he added.

We went up the stairs to our floor, laughing and banging into each other. "Do you fucking believe it?" he said.

I shook my head. We were standing outside my door.

"No, really now, listen." He put his hands on my shoulders and looked into my eyes. He said, "Do you fucking *believe* it?"

I told him I didn't.

"Well, neither do I. I don't fucking believe it."

There didn't seem to be much to say after that. I would have invited Crosley in, but to tell the truth I still thought of him as a thief. We laughed a few more times and said good night.

My room was cold. I took the bill out of my pocket and looked at it. It was new and stiff, the kind of bill you associate with kidnappings. The picture of Franklin was surprisingly lifelike. I looked at it for a while. A hundred dollars was a lot of money then. I had never had a hundred dollars before, not in one chunk like this. To be on the safe side I taped it to a page in *Profiles in Courage*—page 100, so I wouldn't forget where it was.

I had trouble getting to sleep. The food I had eaten sat like a stone in me, and I was miserable about the things I had said. I understood that I had been a liar and a fool. I kept shifting under the covers, then I sat up and turned on my reading lamp. I picked up the new picture my girlfriend had sent me, and closed my eyes, and when I had some peace of mind I renewed my promises to her.

We broke up a month after I got home. Her parents were away one night, and we seized the opportunity to make love in their canopied bed. This was the fifth time that we had made love. She got up immediately afterward and started putting her clothes on. When I asked her what the problem was, she wouldn't answer me. I thought, *Oh Christ, what now.* "Come on," I said. "What's the problem?"

She was tying her shoes. She looked up and said, "You don't love me."

It surprised me to hear this, not because she said it but because it was true. Before this moment I hadn't known it was true, but it was—I didn't love her.

For a long time afterward I told myself that I had never really loved her, but this was a lie.

We're supposed to smile at the passions of the young, and at what we recall of our own passions, as if they were no more than a series of sweet frauds we had fooled ourselves with and then wised up to. Not only the passion of boys and girls for each other but the others, too—passion for justice, for doing right, for turning the world around—all these come in their time under our wintry smiles. But there was nothing foolish about what we felt. Nothing merely young. I just wasn't up to it. I let the light go out.

Sometime later I heard a soft knock at my door. I was still wide awake. "Yeah," I said.

Crosley stepped inside. He was wearing a blue dressing gown of some silky material that shimmered in the dim light of the hallway. He said, "Have you got any Tums or anything?"

"No. I wish I did."

"You too, huh?" He closed the door and sat on my roommate's bunk. "Do you feel as bad as I do?"

"How bad do you feel?"

"Like I'm dying. I think there was something wrong with the shrimp."

"Come on, Crosley. You ate everything but the barn."

"So did you."

"That's right. That's why I'm not complaining."

He moaned and rocked back and forth on the bed. I could hear real pain in his voice. I sat up. "Crosley, are you okay?"

"I guess," he said.

"You want me to call the nurse?"

"God," he said. "No. That's all right." He kept rocking. Then, in a carefully offhand way, he said. "Look, is it okay if I just stay here for a while?"

I almost said no, then I caught myself. "Sure," I told him. "Make yourself at home."

He must have heard my hesitation. "Forget it," he said bitterly. "Sorry I asked." But he made no move to go.

I felt confused, tender toward Crosley because he was in pain, repelled because of what I had heard about him. But maybe what I had heard about him wasn't true. I wanted to be fair, so I said, "Hey, Crosley, do you mind if I ask you a question?"

"That depends."

I sat up. Crosley was watching me. In the moonlight his dressing gown was iridescent as oil. He had his arms crossed over his stomach. "Is it true that you got caught stealing?"

"You fucker," he said. He looked down at the floor.

I waited.

He said, "You want to hear about it, just ask someone. Everybody knows all about it, right?"

"I don't."

"That's right, you don't." He raised his head. "You don't know shit about it and neither does anyone else." He tried to smile. His teeth appeared almost luminous in the cold silver light. "The really hilarious part is, I didn't actually get caught stealing it, I got caught putting it back. Not to make excuses. I stole the fucker, all right."

"Stole what?"

"The coat," he said. "Robinson's overcoat. Don't tell me you didn't know that."

I shook my head.

"Then you must have been living in a cave or something. You know Robinson, right? Robinson was my roommate. He had this camel's hair overcoat, this really just beautiful overcoat. I kind of got obsessed with it. I thought about it all the time. Whenever he went somewhere without it I would put it on and stand in front of the mirror. Then one day I just took the fucker. I stuck it in my locker over at the gym. Robinson was really upset. He'd go to his closet ten, twenty times a day, like he thought the coat had just gone for a walk or something. So anyway, I brought it back. He came into the room while I was hanging it up." Crosley bent forward suddenly, then leaned back.

"You're lucky they didn't kick you out."

"I wish they had," he said. "The dean wanted to play Jesus. He got all choked up over the fact that I had brought it back." Crosley rubbed his arms. "Man, did I want that coat. It was ridiculous how much I wanted that coat. You know?" He looked right at me. "Do you know what I'm talking about?"

I nodded.

"Really?"

"Yes."

"Good." Crosley lay back against the pillow, then lifted his feet onto the bed. "Say," he said, "I think I figured out how come Garcia invited me."

"Yeah? How come?"

"He was mad at his stepmother, right? He wanted to punish her."

"So?"

"So I'm the punishment. He probably heard I was the biggest asshole in the school, and figured whoever came with me would have to be an asshole, too. That's my theory, anyway."

I started laughing. It hurt my stomach, but I couldn't stop. Crosley said, "Come on, man, don't make me laugh," then he started laughing and moaning at the same time.

We lay without talking for a time. Crosley said, "El Negro."

"Yeah."

"What are you going to do with your C-note?"

"I don't know. What are you going to do?"

"Buy a woman."

"Buy a woman?"

"I haven't gotten laid in a really long time. In fact," he said. "I've never gotten laid."

"Me either."

I thought about his words. *Buy a woman.* He could actually do it. I could do it myself. I didn't have to wait. I didn't have to burn like this for month after month until Jane decided she was ready to give me relief. Three months was a long time to wait. It was an unreasonable time to wait for anything if you had no good reason to wait, if you could just buy what you needed. And to think that you could buy this—buy a mouth for your mouth, and arms and legs to wrap you tight. I had never considered this before. I thought of the money in my book. I could almost feel it there. Pure possibility.

Jane would never know. It wouldn't hurt her at all, and in a certain way it might help, because it was going to be very awkward at first if neither of us had any experience. As a man, I should know what I was doing. It would be a lot better that way.

I told Crosley that I liked his idea. "The time has come to lose our innocence," I said.

"*Exactamente*," he said.

And so we sat up and took counsel, leaning toward each other from the beds, holding our swollen bellies, whispering back and forth about how this thing might be done, and where, and when.

Shifting Identities

7

How to Date a Brown Girl (black girl, white girl, or halfie)

JUNOT DÍAZ

Junot Díaz was born in 1968 in Santo Domingo, Dominican Republic, where he lived until age six, when he immigrated with his family to New Jersey. Drawing from his experiences as an immigrant raised in a working-class family in a poor urban community, Díaz gives readers insight into a double immigrant consciousness in his fiction. He earned his BA in English at Rutgers University in 1992 and his MFA in creative writing at Cornell University in 1995. After placing short stories in *Story*, *The New Yorker*, *The Paris Review*, and other publications, Díaz published *Drown* (1996), a collection of short stories. He spent the ensuing decade teaching writing at MIT and working on his novel *The Brief Wondrous Life of Oscar Wao* (2007), which earned him the 2008 Pulitzer Prize, the John Sargent, Sr. First Novel Prize, the National Book Critics Circle Award, the Anisfield-Wolf Book Award, and the Dayton Literary Peace Prize. His fiction has also appeared in *African Voices*, *Best American Short Stories* (1996, 1997, 1999, 2000), in *The Pushcart Prize XXII* and in *The PEN/O. Henry Prize Stories 2009*. A distinguishing feature in all of Díaz's fiction is the absence of quotations around dialogue; he attributes that stylistic decision to his desire to more accurately present the way that people, especially men, remember and repeat things. Díaz also attributes his lack of quotations to the influence of Cormac McCarthy.

Wait until your brother, your sisters, and your mother leave the apartment. You've already told them that you were feeling too sick to go to Union City to visit that *tía* who likes to squeeze your nuts. (He's gotten big, she'll say.) And even though your moms knew you weren't sick you stuck to your story until finally she said, Go ahead and stay, *malcriado*.

Clear the government cheese from the refrigerator. If the girl's from the Terrace, stack the boxes in the crisper. If she's from the Park or Society Hill, then hide the cheese in the cabinet above the oven, where she'll never see it. Leave a reminder under your pillow to get out the cheese before morning or your moms will kick your ass. Take down any embarrassing photos of your family in the *campo*, especially that one with the half-naked kids dragging a goat on a rope. Hide the picture of yourself with an Afro. Make sure the bathroom is presentable. Since your toilet can't flush toilet paper, put the bucket with all the crapped-on toilet paper under the sink. Spray the bucket with Lysol, then close the lid.

Shower, comb, dress. Sit on the couch and watch TV. If she's an outsider her father will bring her, maybe her mother. Her parents won't want her seeing a boy from the Terrace—people get stabbed in the Terrace—but she's strong-headed and this time will get her way. If she's a white girl, you're sure you'll at least get a hand job.

The directions you gave her were in your best handwriting, so her parents won't think you're an idiot. Get up from the couch and check the parking lot. Nothing. If the girl's local, don't sweat. She'll flow over when she's good and ready. Sometimes she'll run into her friends and a whole crowd will show up, and even though that means that you ain't getting shit it will be fun anyway and you'll wish these people would come over more often. Sometimes the girl won't flow over at all and the next day in school she'll say, Sorry, and smile, and you'll believe her and be stupid enough to ask her out again.

You wait, and after an hour you go out to your corner. The neighborhood is full of traffic—commuters now cut through the neighborhood—making it hard on the kids and the *viejas*, who are used to empty streets. Give one of your friends a shout and when he says, Still waiting on that bitch? say, Hell, yeah.

Get back inside. Call her house and when her father picks up ask if she's there. If he sounds like a principal or a police chief, a dude with a big neck, someone who never has to watch his back, then hang up. Sit and wait. And wait. Until finally, just as your stomach is about to give out on you, a Honda, or maybe a Cherokee, will pull in and out she'll come.

Hey, she'll say.

Come on in, you'll say.

Look, she'll say. My mom wants to meet you. She's got herself all worried about nothing.

Don't panic. Say, Hey, no problem. Run a hand through your hair like the white boys do, even though the only thing that runs easily through your hair is Africa. She will look good. White girls are the ones you want most, aren't they? But the out-of-towners are usually black—black girls who grew up with ballet and Girl Scouts, and have three cars in their driveway. If she's a halfie don't be surprised that her mother is the white one. Say, Hi. She'll say, Hi, and you'll see that you don't scare her, not really. She will say that she needs easier directions to get out, and even though she already has the best directions on her lap, give her new ones. Make her happy.

If the girl's from the Terrace, none of this will happen.

You have choices. If the girl's from around the way, take her to El Cibao for dinner. Order everything in your busted-up Spanish. Amaze her if she's black, let her correct you if she's Latina. If she's not from around the way, Wendy's will do. As you walk to the restaurant, talk about school. A local girl won't need stories about the neighborhood, but the others might. Tell her about the *pendejo* who stored canisters of Army tear gas in his basement for years until one day they all cracked and the neighborhood got a dose of military-strength stuff. Don't tell her that your moms knew right away what it was, that she recognized the smell from the year the United States invaded your island.

Hope that you don't run into your nemesis, Howie, the Puerto Rican kid with the two killer mutts. He walks them all over the neighborhood, and every now and then the mutts corner a cat and tear it to shreds, as Howie laughs and the cat flips up in the air, its neck twisted around like an owl's, red meat showing through the soft fur. And if his dogs haven't cornered a cat, then he'll be behind you, asking, Is that your new fuck-buddy?

Let him talk. Howie weighs two hundred pounds and could eat you if he wanted. But at the field he'll turn away. He has new sneakers and doesn't want them muddy. If the girl's an outsider, that's when she'll hiss, What a fucking asshole. A homegirl would have been yelling back at him the whole time, unless she was shy. Either way, don't feel bad that you didn't do anything. Never lose a fight on a first date.

Dinner will be tense. You are not good at talking to people you don't know.

A halfie will tell you that her parents met in the Movement. Back then, she'll say, people thought it was a radical thing to do. It will sound like something her parents made her memorize. Your brother heard that one, too, and said, Sounds like a whole lot of Uncle Tomming to me. Don't repeat this.

Put down your hamburger and say, It must have been hard.

It was, she will say.

She'll appreciate your interest. She'll tell you more. Black people, she will say, treat me real bad. That's why I don't like them. You'll wonder how she feels about Dominicans. Don't ask. Let her speak on it and when you've finished eating, walk back through the neighborhood. The skies will be magnificent. Pollutants have made Jersey sunsets one of the wonders of the world. Point it out. Touch her shoulder and say, Isn't that nice?

Get serious. Watch TV, but stay alert. Sip some of the Bermudez your father left in the cabinet, which nobody touches. She'll drink enough to make her brave. A local girl will have hips and a nice ass but won't be quick about letting you touch her. She has to live in the same neighborhood as you do. She might just chill with you and then go home. She might kiss you and then leave. Or she might, if she's reckless, give it up, but that's rare. Kissing will suffice. A white girl might give it up right then. Don't stop her. She'll take her gum out of her mouth, stick it to the plastic sofa covers, and then move close to you. You have nice eyes, she might say.

Tell her that you love her hair, her skin, her lips, because, in truth, you love them more than you love your own.

She'll say, I like Spanish guys, and even though you've never been to Spain, say, I like you. You'll sound smooth.

You'll be with her until about eight-thirty, and then she'll want to wash up. In the bathroom, she'll hum a song from the radio and her waist will keep the beat against the lip of the sink. Think of her old lady coming to get her, and imagine what she would say if she knew that her daughter had just lain under you and blown your name into your ear. While she's in the bathroom, you might call one of your boys and say, *Ya lo hice, cabrón.* Or sit back on the couch and smile.

But usually it won't work this way. Be prepared. She will not want to kiss you. Just cool it, she'll say. The halfie might lean back and push you away. She will cross her arms and say, I hate my tits. Pretend to watch the TV, and then turn to her to stroke her hair, even though you know she'll pull away again. I don't like anybody to touch my hair, she will say. She will act like somebody you don't know. In school, she is known for her attention-grabbing laugh, high and far-ranging like a gull's, but here she will worry you. You will not know what to say.

You're the only kind of guy who asks me out, she will say. Your neighbors will start their hyena calls, now that the alcohol is in them. She will say, You and the black boys.

You want to say, Who do you want to ask you out? But you already know. Let her button her shirt and comb her hair, the sound of it like a crackling fire between you. When her father pulls in and beeps, let her go without too much of a goodbye. She won't want it. During the next hour, the phone will ring. You will be tempted to pick it up. Don't. Watch the shows you want to watch, without a family around to argue with you. Don't go downstairs. Don't fall asleep. It won't help. Put the government cheese back in its place before your moms kills you.

8

In the Cemetery Where Al Jolson Is Buried

AMY HEMPEL

Amy Hempel is a rare example of a writer who established her fictional voice writing solely short stories. She was born in Chicago, Illinois, in 1951 and grew up in Denver and later the San Francisco Bay Area. Her late teens and early twenties were beset with tragedy. When Hempel was 19, her mother committed suicide; shortly thereafter her sister also killed herself. In the years that followed, Hempel was in two major car accidents, but fortunately for American letters, she found a way to channel her acute understanding of tragedy and grief into her writing. The story featured in this collection, "In the Cemetery Where Al Jolson Is Buried," is Hempel's first published short story, which appeared in *TriQuarterly* in 1983. In 1985, she published her first story collection, *Reasons to Live*, which won the Commonwealth Club of California Silver Medal. She has also published *At the Gates of the Animal Kingdom* (1990), *Tumble Home* (1997), and *The Dog of the Marriage* (2005). Her short stories have appeared in *GQ, Playboy, Vanity Fair, Harper's, The Quarterly, The Yale Review,* and several anthologies, including *The Norton Anthology of Short Fiction.* She has won several prestigious literary awards for her work, including the Hobson Award and a Guggenheim Fellowship.

"Tell me things I won't mind forgetting," she said. "Make it useless stuff or skip it."

I began. I told her insects fly through rain, missing every drop, never getting wet. I told her no one in America owned a tape recorder before Bing Crosby did. I told her the shape of the moon is like a banana—you see it looking full, you're seeing it end-on.

The camera made me self-conscious and I stopped. It was trained on us from a ceiling mount—the kind of camera banks use to photograph robbers. It played us to the nurses down the hall in Intensive Care.

"Go on, girl," she said. "You get used to it."

I had my audience. I went on. Did she know that Tammy Wynette had changed her tune? Really. That now she sings "Stand by Your *Friends*"? That Paul Anka did it, too, I said. Does "You're Having *Our* Baby." That he got sick of all that feminist bitching.

"What else?" she said. "Have you got something else?"

Oh, yes.

For her I would always have something else.

"Did you know that when they taught the first chimp to talk, it lied? That when they asked her who did it on the desk, she signed back the name of the janitor. And that when they pressed her, she said she was sorry, that it was really the project director. But she was a mother, so I guess she had her reasons."

"Oh, that's good," she said. "A parable."

"There's more about the chimp," I said. "But it will break your heart."

"No, thanks," she says, and scratches at her mask.

We look like good-guy outlaws: Good or bad, I am not used to the mask yet. I keep touching the warm spot where my breath, thank God, comes out. She is used to hers. She only ties the strings on top. The other ones— a pro by now—she lets hang loose.

We call this place the Marcus Welby Hospital. It's the white one with the palm trees under the opening credits of all those shows. A Hollywood hospital, though in fact it is several miles west. Off camera, there is a beach across the street.

She introduces me to a nurse as the Best Friend. The impersonal article is more intimate. It tells me that *they* are intimate, the nurse and my friend.

"I was telling her we used to drink Canada Dry ginger ale and pretend we were in Canada."

"That's how dumb we were," I say.

"You could be sisters," the nurse says.

So how come, I'll bet they are wondering, it took me so long to get to such a glamorous place? But do they ask?

They do not ask.

Two months, and how long is the drive?

The best I can explain it is this—I have a friend who worked one summer in mortuary. He used to tell me stories. The one that really got to me was not the grisliest, but it's the one that did. A man wrecked his car on 101 going south. He did not lose consciousness. But his arm was taken down to the wet bone—and when he looked at it—it scared him to death.

I mean, he died.

So I hadn't dared to look any closer. But now I'm doing it—and hoping that I will live through it.

She shakes out a summer-weight blanket, showing a leg you did not want to see. Except for that, you look at her and understand the law that requires *two* people to be with the body at all times.

"I thought of something," she says. "I thought of it last night. I think there is a real and present need here. You know," she says, "like for someone to do it for you when you can't do it yourself. You call then up whenever you want—like when push comes to shove."

She grabs the bedside phone and loops the cord around her neck.

"Hey," she says, "the end o' the line."

She keeps on, giddy with something. But I don't know with what.

"I can't remember," she says. "What does Kübler-Ross say comes after Denial?"

It seems to me Anger must be next. Then Bargaining, Depression, and so on and so forth. But I keep my guesses to myself.

"The only thing is," she says, "is where's Resurrection? God knows, I want to do it by the book. But she left out Resurrection."

She laughs, and I cling to the sound the way someone dangling above a ravine holds fast to the thrown rope.

"Tell me," she says, "about that chimp with the talking hands. What do they do when the thing ends and the chimp says, 'I don't want to go back to the zoo'?"

When I don't say anything, she says, "Okay—then tell me another animal story. I like animal stories. But not a sick one—I don't want to know about all the seeing-eye dogs going blind."

No, I would not tell her a sick one.

"How about the hearing-ear dogs?" I say. "They're not going deaf, but they are getting very judgmental. For instance, there's this golden retriever in New Jersey, he wakes up the deaf mother and drags her into the daughter's room because the kid has got a flashlight and is reading under the covers."

"Oh, you're killing me," she says. "Yes, you're definitely killing me."

"They say the smart dog obeys, but the smarter dog knows when to disobey."

"Yes," she says, "the smarter anything knows when to disobey. Now, for example."

She is flirting with the Good Doctor, who has just appeared. Unlike the Bad Doctor, who checks the IV drip before saying good morning, the Good Doctor says things like "God didn't give epileptics a fair shake." The Good Doctor awards himself points for the cripples he could have hit in the parking lot. Because the Good Doctor is a little in love with her, he says maybe a year. He pulls a chair up to her bed and suggests I might like to spend an hour on the beach.

"Bring me something back," she says. "Anything from the beach. Or the gift shop. Taste is no object."

He draws the curtain around her bed.

"Wait!" she cries.

I look in at her.

"Anything," she says, "except a magazine subscription."

The doctor turns away.

I watch her mouth laugh.

What seems dangerous often is not—black snakes, for example, or clear-air turbulence. While things that just lie there, like this beach, are loaded with jeopardy. A yellow dust rising from the ground, the heat that ripens melons overnight—this is earthquake weather. You can sit here braiding the fringe on your towel and the sand will all of a sudden suck down like an hourglass. The air roars. In the cheap apartment on-shore, bathtubs fill themselves and gardens roll up and over like green waves. If nothing happens, the dust will drift and the heat deepen till fear turns to desire. Nerves like that are only bought off by catastrophe.

"It never happens when you're thinking about it," she once observed. "Earthquake, earthquake, earthquake," she said.

"Earthquake, earthquake, earthquake," I said.

Like the aviaphobe who keeps the plane aloft with prayer, we keep it up until an aftershock cracked the ceiling.

That was after the big one in '72. We were in college; our dormitory was five miles from the epicenter. When the ride was over and my jabbering pulse began to slow, she served five parts champagne to one part orange juice, and joked about living in Ocean View, Kansas. I offered to drive her to Hawaii on the new world psychics predicted would surface the next time, or the next.

I could not say that now—next.

Whose next? she could ask.

Was I the only one who noticed that the experts had stopped saying *if* and now spoke of *when*? Of course not; the fearful ran to thousands. We watched the traffic of Japanese beetles for deviation. Deviation might mean more natural violence.

I wanted her to be afraid with me. But she said, "I don't know. I'm just not."

She was afraid of nothing, not even of flying.

I have this dream before a flight where we buckle in and the plane moves down the runway. It takes off at thirty-five miles an hour, and then we're airborne, skimming the tree tops. Still, we arrive in New York on time.

It is so pleasant.

One night I flew to Moscow this way.

She flew with me once. That time she flew with me she ate macadamia nuts while the wings bounced. She knows the wing tips can bend thirty feet up and thirty feet down without coming off. She believes it. She trusts the laws of aerodynamics. My mind stampedes. I can almost accept that a battleship floats when everybody knows steel sinks.

I see fear in her now, and am not going to try to talk her out of it. She is right to be afraid.

After a quake, the six o'clock news airs a film clip of first-graders yelling at the broken playground per their teacher's instructions.

"*Bad* earth!" they shout, because anger is stronger than fear.

But the beach is standing still today. Everyone on it is tranquilized, numb, or asleep. Teenaged girls rub coconut oil on each other's hard-to-reach places. They smell like macaroons. They pry open compacts like clamshells; mirrors catch the sun and throw a spray of white rays across glazed shoulders. The girls arrange their wet hair with silk flowers the way they learned in *Seventeen*. They pose.

A formation of low-riders pulls over to watch with a six-pack. They get vocal when the girls check their tan lines. When the beer is gone, so are they—flexing their cars on up the boulevard.

Above this aggressive health are the twin wrought-iron terraces, painted flamingo pink, of the Palm Royale. Someone dies there every time the sheets are changed. There's an ambulance in the driveway, so the remaining residents line the balconies, rocking and not talking, one-upped.

The ocean they stare at is dangerous, and not just the undertow. You can almost see the slapping tails of sand sharks keeping cruising bodies alive.

If she looked, she could see this, some of it, from her window. She would be the first to say how little it takes to make a thing all wrong.

There was a second bed in the room when I got back to it!

For two beats I didn't get it. Then it hit me like an open coffin.

She wants every minute, I thought. She wants my life.

"You missed Gussie," she said.

Gussie is her parents' three-hundred-pound narcoleptic maid. Her attacks often come at the ironing board. The pillowcases in that family are all bordered with scorch.

"It's a hard trip for her," I said. "How is she?"

"Well, she didn't fall asleep, if that's what you mean. Gussie's great—you know what she said? She said, 'Darlin', stop this worriation. Just keep prayin', down on your knees'—me, who can't even get out of bed."

She shrugged. "What am I missing?"

"It's earthquake weather," I told her.

"The best thing to do about earthquakes," she said, "is not to live in California."

"That's useful," I said. "You sound like Reverend Ike—'The best thing to do for the poor is not to be one of them.'"

We're crazy about Reverend Ike.

I noticed her face was bloated.

"You know," she said. "I feel like hell. I'm about to stop having fun."

"The ancients have a saying," I said. "'There are times when the wolves are silent; there are times when the moon howls.'"

"What's that, Navaho?"

"Palm Royale lobby graffiti," I said. "I bought a paper there. I'll read you something."

"Even though I care about nothing?"

I turned to the page with the trivia column. I said, "Did you know the more shrimp flamingo birds eat, the pinker their feathers get?" I said, "Did you know that Eskimos need refrigerators? Do you know why Eskimos need refrigerators? Did you know that Eskimos need refrigerators because how else would they keep their food from freezing?"

I turned to page three, to a UPI filler datelined Mexico City. I read her MAN ROBS BANK WITH CHICKEN, about a man who bought a barbecued chicken at a stand down the block from a bank. Passing the bank, he got the idea. He walked in and approached a teller. He pointed the brown paper bag at her and she handed over the day's receipts. It was the smell of barbecue sauce that eventually led to his capture.

The story had made her hungry, she said—so I took the elevator down six floors to the cafeteria, and brought back all the ice cream she wanted. We lay side by side, adjustable beds cranked up for optimal TV-viewing, littering the sheets with Good Humor wrappers, picking toasted almonds out of the gauze. We were Lucy and Ethel, Mary and Rhoda in extremis. The blinds were closed to keep light off the screen.

We watched a movie starring men we used to think we wanted to sleep with. Hers was a tough cop out to stop mine, a vicious rapist who went after cocktail waitresses.

"This is a good movie," she said when snipers felled them both.

I missed her already.

A Filipino nurse tiptoed in and gave her an injection. The nurse removed the pile of Popsicle sticks from the nightstand—enough to splint a small animal.

The injection made us both sleepy. We slept.

I dreamed she was a decorator, come to furnish my house. She worked in secret, singing to herself. When she finished, she guided me proudly to the door. "How do you like it?" she asked, easing me inside.

Every beam and sill and shelf and knob was draped in gay bunting, with streamers of pastel crepe looped around bright mirrors.

"I have to go home," I said when she woke up.

She thought I meant home to her house in the canyon, and I had to say No, *home* home. I twisted my hands in the time-honored fashion of people in pain. I was supposed to offer something. The Best Friend. I could not even offer to come back.

I felt weak and small and failed.

Also exhilarated.

I had a convertible in the parking lot. Once out of that room, I would drive it too fast down the Coast highway through the crab-smelling air. A stop in Malibu for sangria. The music in the place would be sexy and loud.

They'd serve papaya and shrimp and watermelon ice. After dinner I would shimmer with lust, buzz with heat, vibrate with life, and stay up all night.

Without a word, she yanked off her mask and threw it on the floor. She kicked at the blankets and moved to the door. She must have hated having to pause for breath and balance before slamming out of Isolation, and out of the second room, the one where you scrub and tie on the white masks.

A voice shouted her name in alarm, and people ran down the corridor. The Good Doctor was paged over the intercom. I opened the door and the nurses at the station stared hard, as if this flight had been my idea.

"Where is she?" I asked, and they nodded to the supply closet.

I looked in. Two nurses were kneeling beside her on the floor, talking to her in low voices. One held a mask over her nose and mouth, the other rubbed her back in slow circles. The nurses glanced up to see if I was the doctor—and when I wasn't, they went back to what they were doing.

"There, there, honey," they cooed.

On the morning she was moved to the cemetery, the one where Al Jolson is buried, I enrolled in a "Fear of Flying" class. "What is your worst fear?" the instructor asked, and I answered, "That I will finish this course and still be afraid."

I sleep with a glass of water on the nightstand so I can see by its level if the coastal earth is trembling or if the shaking is still me.

What do I remember?

I remember only the useless things I hear—that Bob Dylan's mother invented Wite-Out, that twenty-three people must be in a room before there is a fifty-fifty chance two will have the same birthday. Who cares whether or not it's true? In my head there are bath towels swaddling this stuff. Nothing else seeps through.

I review those things that will figure in the retelling: a kiss through surgical gauze, the pale hand correcting the position of the wig. I noted these gestures as they happened, not in any retrospect—though I don't know why looking back should show us more than looking *at*.

It is just possible I will say I stayed the night.

And who is there that can say that I did not?

I think of the chimp, the one with the talking hands.

In the course of the experiment, that chimp had a baby. Imagine how her trainers must have thrilled when the mother, without prompting, began to sign to her newborn.

Baby, drink milk.

Baby, play ball.

And when the baby died, the mother stood over the body, her wrinkled hands moving with animal grace, forming again and again the words: Baby, come hug, Baby, come hug, fluent now in the language of grief.

for Jessica Wolfson

9

Metamorphosis

JOHN UPDIKE

Born in 1932 in Reading, Pennsylvania, John Updike chronicled the workaday struggles, urges, and desires of middle-class New Englanders as one of the premier styl-
ists in American letters for more than fifty years. He earned his BA in English at
Harvard University in 1954; that same year he published a short story and a poem
in *The New Yorker*. Those early successes put Updike on a publishing trajectory
that, over his lifetime, would lead to more than 50 books, several hundred short
stories, and a large body of poetry and essays. He served as a staff writer for *The
New Yorker* for two years (1955–1957), a relatively short period, but he would con-
sistently contribute to the magazine throughout his career. Updike is perhaps most
famous for his Rabbit series, which chronicles the life and times of Harry "Rabbit"
Angstrom, the series protagonist. Two of the novels from that series, *Rabbit Is Rich*
and *Rabbit At Rest*, earned Updike Pulitzer prizes for fiction in 1982 and 1991, respectively. Updike's novels also garnered him the National Book Award, the National Book Critics Circle Award, the Rosenthal Award, and the Howells Medal. He
died in January 2009.

Anderson, something of an idler and a playboy, had spent much time in the
sun; these sunny hours, as his years on earth passed fifty, came back to him
in the form of skin cancers, on his face and elsewhere tender and overex-
posed. His ophthalmologist, a conscientious man with a Brooklyn accent,
was troubled by a keratosis near the tear duct of his right eye—"If it invades,
you'll be crying for lack of tears"—and sent him to a facial plastic surgeon, a
Dr. Kim, who turned out to be a woman, a surprisingly young Korean-
American who even in her baggy lab coat evinced considerably loveliness.
She was relatively tall, nearly as tall as Anderson, yet with the low waist and
sturdy bow legs and rounded calves of Asian women. She moved with a
kind of suppressed athleticism, her gestures a little swifter and larger than
the moment demanded, so that her lab coat parted and the white halves of

it swung. She spoke a perfectly natural, assimilated American English, except that there was a soft, level insistence to it; the image came to him of a moon buggy, determinedly proceeding across uneroded terrain, in conditions of weak gravity. Her face was lean, widest at the cheekbones, and in color a matte pallor, a tinged ivory, of a smoothness that made him ruefully conscious of his own spotted, blotched, scarred visage. Yet she was a doctor, he need not be embarrassed. He could repose in her examination as an infant does within a mother's doting gaze.

She examined him first with her naked eyes, then with a loupe, and lastly with an elaborate mechanism in which he rested his chin while lenses clicked in and out and arcs and spots of light overlaid his half-eclipsed view of her face, posed inches from his in a darkened room. Finally she pushed the apparatus between them away and announced that, yes, she would operate, and saw no major difficulty. There were several types of lesion, actually, in that inner part of his socket and along his lower lid, but they could be excised without complication. "It looks as though you have at least a millimetre of unaffected tissue between the basal-cell carcinoma and the tear duct."

He was still seeing spots and fireflies. "What about the other eye?" he asked, less out of curiosity than a desire to hear her talk some more. There was a curious drone underlying her enunciation, a minor undertone that faintly persisted when the sentence was concluded.

"The other eye seems fine. No problems." *Problemmmss.*

"Isn't that odd, that one eye would and the other wouldn't, after being exposed to the same amount of sun? Or do you think I always scrunched up one eye, like Popeye?"

She smiled at so unscientific a query, and did not deign to reply. Instead she filled out a number of slips, which she gave Anderson as he left. When he stood beside her, he took pleasure in the inch or two that he was taller than she. Her black hair was parted in the middle and gathered behind into a pinned-up ponytail, like a handle to an exquisite jug.

"The front desk will make the appointment for the surgery," she said. "Only a light breakfast that morning, and not too much liquid. It will take a total of two hours." *Hourrsss.* She left the room ahead of him, hurrying to the next appointment, in another examining chamber, with that flighty, gliding walk of hers, her round calves gleaming below the lab coat.

He could hardly wait—the carcinoma was marching toward the tear duct, for one thing—but the quickest appointment the front desk could give him was ten weeks away. "Dr. Kim is a very busy girl," the middle-aged receptionist told Anderson, having read his infatuation at a glance. She was the clinic's treasure, Anderson saw, as priceless a part of it as their fortieth-story view, this sparkling morning, of the East River and the innocent low boroughs beyond.

Dr. Kim was pregnant. This fact had been utterly invisible to him during their consultation, and even ten weeks later it had to be drawn to his attention, by one of the attending nurses in the operating room. "I must say, Doctor," the nurse said, while Anderson's face was being prepped with Betadine and framed in antiseptic paper, "nobody would *dream* you were in your thirty-third week. When I was that far along, I felt like a bumper car. I was a *house*."

There were two nurses, and the three women talked over Anderson's head as if it were a centerpiece of wax fruit. "The first one was like this, too," the doctor said, with her thrilling offhand thrum. "Nothing showing, and then bang." *Bannggg.*

Anderson tried to raise his head, to see Dr. Kim's belly, but she was behind him, upside down in his vision, a glinting syringe in her hand. "It is very important," she told him, "that you keep your head still. Do you mind having your arms strapped down?"

"I don't think so. Let's try it."

"Some people panic," she explained.

Anderson had had facial surgery before, but not stretched out on an operating table. He had sat in a padded chair that tipped back to allow a preppy young man, wearing a white shirt and necktie as if boasting how small a role blood played in his procedures, to carve away at this or that small keratosis. The only pain came with the injection of the painkiller, especially in the upper lip or the bridge of the nose. The tear ducts would overflow. But Dr. Kim's needle, preceded by a swab smelling of cloves or cinnamon, slipped in imperceptibly. A nurse buckled light straps across his chest, and he relaxed into a bliss of secure helplessness.

The three women rotated around him; one of the nurses periodically took his pulse and inflated the blood-pressure cuff, while the other fed instruments to the surgeon. Dr. Kim's bulging belly, now that he was aware of it, rubbed against the top of his head, or one of his ears, as she bent over and confidently broke his skin with tools he could scarcely imagine, since they approached his face along the periphery of his vision. There was a knife shaped as acutely as a sharpened pencil, but also a kind of exquisite corer, whose cut he experienced as a gentle punch, and a cauterizer, producing passing hisses and whiffs of smoke. The touch of her fingers in their latex gloves felt like fairy feet shod in slippers sewn from the skins of baby moles. There were fits of dabbing, to stanch the flow of blood, and sometimes a pinch of pressure and a tugging as the stitches in their several sizes, colors, and degrees of solubility were inserted, pulled taut, and closed with a knot that involved a rapid, mesmerizing twirling of the angled forceps.

Conversational topics came and went among the women—Mayor Giuliani's uptightness, President Clinton's slipperiness, Hugh Grant in "Four Weddings and a Funeral," Julia Roberts in "My Best Friend's Wedding"—and at moments Anderson attempted to insert, from within his wimple of sterile paper, his own opinion. "Too skinny," he said of Julia Roberts. "And he stammers too much."

"When you talk," Dr. Kim observed, "it makes all the muscles of your face move."

"I couldn't believe," the instrument-handling nurse said, "when I was taking anatomy, how many muscles the face has. Eighty-four, I think the professor said, depending on what you count. I mean, the throat and eye ones."

Anderson felt the surgeon's hands and tools move to the lower lid, a ticklish, twitchy area.

The nurse handling his pulse and blood pressure asked above his head, "Are you tired, Doctor? It would kill me, standing this long on my feet in your condition."

"I never get tired operating," came the surprising avowal. "I totally forget myself." *Mysselff.* "I could go all night."

"Couldn't you sit on a stool?" Anderson asked gallantly, trying not to move his lips, like a ventriloquist.

"It never works for me," she deigned to answer. "I need to stand, to feel free in my arms." Her round, smooth *armmms.*

"Most barbers feel the same way," he said. "Standing with their hands up in the air all day, it would kill me."

"A bit more lidocaine," Dr. Kim said in a perceptibly sterner voice. "Don't move or say even a single word." She was playing with him, Anderson thought. They were beginning to learn to play with each other.

When they parted, he with flesh-color bandages dotting his eye socket and she, despite her protestations, wearing shadows of fatigue below her eyes, he wished her well with her accouchement. *Accouchement*: he prolonged the French nasal. She warned him he would have a black eye for a week and asked him to make appointments at the front desk for the removal of the stitches in a week, and for a six-month checkup. The East River, broken into fragments by intervening Manhattan skyscrapers, glistened below; a barge full of orange scrap iron was being nudged toward the sea by two tugs, and its slow black wake was overlaid with the rapidly fanning white one of a police launch. Next to his tear duct, little prickles of pain were beginning.

Nearly a year passed before he saw Dr. Kim again. She was still on leave with her baby when his checkup appointment came due, and in a kind of sulk he put off making another. His surgery had been slower to heal than he had expected, oozing for weeks, and an odd bump of gristly tissue on one side of the bridge of his nose was irritated for months by the nosepiece of his reading glasses. When the wounds finally settled, and the red spots blended into his face's patchwork of pink, there was still a new wrinkle—not exactly a wrinkle but a sort of raised tendon, a parenthesis of flesh near his tear duct. Anderson's girlfriend, one of a long and querulous series, thought it made him look slightly evil. When he pointed out this little abnormality to a newly slender Dr. Kim, she reached forward and gently prodded it, not once but several times. "You should have massaged," she said. "But now it may be too late."

"Too late?"

She smiled and reached out again, touching the offending bit of anatomy, and firmly caressed it with a small circling motion. "Like that," she said "Two, three times a day for thirty seconds."

Her touch numbed his brain, but he clung to reason. "I can't believe that will do much good."

"Try it for six months. Be patient."

"Can't you fix it surgically?"

"It troubles you so? Cosmetically it is very minor, but the operation to change it would not be simple or certain of success." *Success.* It was as if her voice were not quite hers, projected from an ideal world elsewhere.

Anderson edged forward in the examining chair, as when fitting himself to the metal chin rest. "I'd like to try it," he said, "if you're willing."

"The insurance—"

"I have a very generous medical plan," he assured her. He imagined the operation—the fitful pressure of her sheathed fingers, like dancing fairy shoes; the painless sizzle of the cauterizing instrument; the blithe topical chatter of the attending nurses; the rustle of the antiseptic paper on his face as he attempted to join in; the rub of her bulging stomach on his skull. The experience, when it at last came on its scheduled day, was not quite as he had imagined it. She was not pregnant, the operating room was smaller, and there was only one nurse, who wandered in and out. The procedure this time involved more strenuous tugging and a series of stitches that extended to the verge of the anesthetic wearing off. But the verity and intensity of the contact were undiluted. This time, he felt freer to use his eyes, and boldly watched her eyes, upside down in his vision. They appeared to brim from the chalices of her upper lids, underlined by the thin black smiles of her eyebrows. Elongate amber flecks like needles in an emulsion gave her irises a rayed, starry depth as her attention poured through the black apertures of her contracted pupils, holes through which the world in all its brilliance passed. Whenever she blinked, the action seemed monstrous, like a crab's mouth.

When it was over, and she lowered the pale-green paper mask, her mouth seemed pleased. She pulled off her mushroom-shaped scrub cap and shook her head so that her hair tumbled free, its thick body squirming with waxy gleams. "It went very well," she said "It is not easy, to persuade slack tissue to re-conform." *Reconforrrmmm*—the "r"s were so throaty and the "m"s so prolonged that he wondered if she was teasing him. But the professional manner she resumed was impeccable and impervious—solemn instructions to go with the prescriptions she wrote, a carefully spelled-out prediction as to the course of his healing. "This time, be sure to massage." She demonstrated little circles on the side of her own flawless, straight, taut, matte nose. As she moved, with her low-slung, hurried gait, through the motions of post-op routine, her unbound hair continued to hang and glisten down her back, still releasing, like muscles slowly relaxing, the shape of its coils. "The stitches will dissolve," she said. "Come back in six months."

By then, the East River was edged with ice and smoking with mid-January cold. He surreptitiously examined her for signs of pregnancy, and was unable to detect any beneath the baggy lab coat. She reached out and touched the nearly invisible scar near his tear duct. "Snug," she said. "Symmetrical."

"Congratulations."

"Did you massage?"

"Faithfully. But I notice now that the thin skin under that eye has a crease I don't have on the other side. And both my upper lids are sagging. In the morning they feel like they're resting on my eyelashes, and in the mirror I can *see* them sitting there in more or less random folds, like pieces of wet laundry."

She studied him intently, and rested her fingers on the skin there, pressing through the lid onto his eyeball, so that his vision distorted and doubled. "You could do with a tuck," she admitted, "but it is not strictly necessary. You still have undisturbed function." She continued to finger his lids, so that he spoke in spaced accents, like a man under torture.

"It disturbs *me*," he brought out, "that they are rumpling up like that. I want something that may be too difficult for you."

Her touch changed quality, became tentative. "What would that be?"

"I want my lids to look like yours."

Her fingertips, resting on the inner corners of his eyes, stayed there. He thought he detected a slight tremor. "With an epicanthus?" she asked.

"If possible."

"It would be as you say difficult. A graft—it would have to come from a very sensitive area. The body has few sites where the skin is so delicate. The inside of the thigh, the—The color match is never perfect."

"Couldn't you somehow tug the skin that *is* there into a fold? I feel like a rhinoceros lately, with heaps of extra skin. When I bend over, I can feel my face fall away from the bone. And all that under the chin—couldn't that be tightened up?"

Her fingers thoughtfully moved to his jaw, making moleskin-soft adjustments. "It is commonly done," she said, "but it is not as easy as cutting cloth. There is musculature beneath, and nerves and capillaries. It would be a long and strenuous operation." She settled back, her hands folded, palm up, in her lap in a lotus pose. He saw her face not only as a glowing oval but as a piece of seamless tailoring, layers of dermis fitted without tension to cheekbone and jaw hinge and gelatinous eye-white.

"It could be several operations," Anderson suggested.

Little frown lines flitted into the smooth space between her eyebrows, and were quickly erased. "It is better for you if it is done all at once. One session, one recovery."

"I can take it if you can," he said, in the lowered, virtually hostile tone in which, with another woman, in other circumstances, he would make his move.

Dr. Kim straightened in her chair, looked him in the eyes with her liquid, opaque own, and spoke more deliberately than ever. "I want to do it. If you want it done to you. Be aware," she said, "that there can sometimes be loss in sensitivity, even a certain stiffness of expression."

"I'll risk it," Anderson responded. "I hate my face the way it is." He had come to hate, though he did not want to scar their pure relation with such a

confession, the daily facts of life: shaving his face, combing his hair and ar-
ranging for a haircut, putting himself into pajamas and bed at night and getting himself out of them, rumpled and sweated, in the morning. He was
weary of the way whiffs of staleness arose to him from his nether regions,
and of the way his crowned and much-patched teeth harbored pockets of
suddenly tastable decay, as if all the deaths in the newspapers and all the
years he had put behind him had been miniaturized and lodged in the cran-
nies of his slimy mouth.

The operation was, as Dr. Kim had predicted, arduous—for six hours she
stood on her feet, cutting and tugging, injecting this and that section of his
face as she moved to it, like a farmer planting her fields. She wore magnify-
ing spectacles above the green paper mask; his face felt tranquil and lunar
under her attentions. Even the work on his eyelids seemed to take place at a
great anesthetic distance, though he had rather dreaded it. No graft was
necessary; she found as much spare skin around his nose as a puppy has at
the back of his neck. When it was over, the two nurses gathered around her
as if to save her from fainting. He stayed the night.

In the morning, from within his bandages, he smiled, stiffly, to see the
patients in the waiting room start at the mummylike menace he presented.
Through slits like those of Eskimo sunglasses he saw the East River far below, its black skin broken by the passage of a brimming garbage barge and,
at a faster clip, a tourist cruise boat, circling the island. The blue-green Cit-
ibank Building, the only skyscraper in Queens, thrust up like a crocus. It
was spring, the trees were in bud but still transparent, their leafing-out and
casting-off of leaves seemed a process as inevitable and graciously gradual
as his own healing and emergence into beauty.

There were several visits weeks apart, during which she removed her
brocade of stitches—more painful, oddly, than their insertion—and then a
two-month follow-up. As if they had shared a rapture too keen to be soon
repeated, these appointments were prophylactically cursory, hurried: she
was always running late, and the traffic of patients at the clinic approached
gridlock. Anderson's bruised and swollen face horrified him in the mirror.
His new girlfriend's reassurances that he was looking better and better every day meant nothing to him; they were the rote and predictable outcome
of female flattery, its customary irritating strategems. Only Dr. Kim could
be trusted to supply him with the truth.

In his eight-month visit, she studied him thoughtfully, from an arm's distance, and pronounced, "It came out well. Your canthi still show, but the

lids are very taut. The yellow bruising on the jaw will diminish"—*di-min-ish*, three even syllables, like a doll talking—"over time, as will the vertical red scars in front of your ears." She leaned forward and lightly stroked them, with bare fingertips. The halves of her lab coat parted, and he saw that she was pregnant again. She handed him a heavy plastic hand mirror, and said, "You look. You tell me what you see still to be improved. I will go out of the room."

Her rapid rolling gait, in low black heels rather than the universal, deplorable white running shoes of hospital habit, took her out the door, her lab coat floating, her pinned-up hair from behind glistening like a twist of black silk. It was Christmas season, and a little one-piece crèche unexpectedly stood on her desk. In the mirror he saw a face Oriental in its smoothness and impassive expression, its smooth, hardened surface marred only by a few lingering welts. The faded blue eyes were the wrong color, and his gray hair was gauzily receding, but otherwise he saw little to improve. She was a genius.

He had never been left alone in her office before. He got out of the examining chair, with its bothersome folding footrest, and walked to her desk. The crèche was of plastic, but rather lovingly designed, with identical startled expressions on the baby, Mary, Joseph, the sheep, the ox, and the shepherds. Next to it stood tinted photographs of a toddler and a kindergarten-age child—a boy and a girl, both of mixed race—and an old man. Not old, exactly, probably younger than Anderson by some years, but craggy, Caucasian, grinning, big-nosed, rather monstrously bumpy and creased.

"Oh!" Dr. Kim's voice behind him sounded girlish in her surprise at finding him at her desk. She regained her level, professional, rather murmurous pitch. "That is my husband." *Husbannnd*, deliciously prolonged, the very concept come from some far and perfect world. Keeping his back turned—how foolish he must look!—Anderson touched his right tear duct, grateful that it was still there.

10

Think

DAVID FOSTER WALLACE

David Foster Wallace's writings made his name synonymous with postmodern prose. He was born in Ithaca, New York, in 1962 and earned his BA at Amherst College in 1985, double majoring in English and philosophy. He went on to earn his MFA in creative writing from the University of Arizona in 1987, the same year he published his novel *The Broom of the System*. In 1989, Wallace published a collection of short stories, *Girl with Curious Hair*. He spent the next seven years writing his most heralded work, *Infinite Jest* (1996), the 1000-plus-page novel that established him as one of the most influential postmodern writers. Wallace went on to publish two subsequent short story collections: *Brief Interviews with Hideous Men* (1999), which contains the two-page story "Think," included in this collection, and *Oblivion* (2004). Wallace also produced a considerable body of literary journalism and essays on topics ranging from hip hop to politics to animal cruelty. His essay collections include *A Supposedly Fun Thing I'll Never Do Again* (1997), *Everything and More: A Compact History of Infinity* (2003), and *Consider the Lobster* (2005). Wallace received numerous prizes, including a Whiting Writers' Award (1987), a Lannan Award for fiction (1996), a MacArthur Fellowship (1997), a *Paris Review* prize for humor (1988), and an O. Henry Award (2002). Wallace committed suicide on September 12, 2008, after suffering from acute depression for more than 20 years.

Her brassiere's snaps are in the front. His own forehead snaps clear. He thinks to kneel. But he knows what she might think if he kneels. What cleared his forehead's lines was a type of revelation. Her breasts have come free. He imagines his wife and son. Her breasts are unconfined now. The bed's comforter has a tulle hem, like a ballerina's little hem. This is the younger sister of his wife's college roommate. Everyone else has gone to the mall, some to shop, some to see a movie at the mall's multiplex. The sister with breasts by the bed has a level gaze and a slight smile, slight and smoky, media-taught. She sees his color heighten and forehead go smooth in a kind of revelation—why she'd begged off the mall, the meaning of certain comments, looks, distended moments over the weekend he'd thought were his vanity, imagination. We see these things a dozen times a day in entertainment but imagine we ourselves, our own imaginations, are mad. A different man might have said what he'd seen was her hand moved to her bra and *freed* her breasts. His legs might slightly tremble when she asks what he thinks. Her expression is from Page 18 of the Victoria's Secret catalogue. She is, he thinks, the sort of woman who'd keep her heels on if he asked her to. Even if she'd never kept heels on before she'd give him a knowing, smoky smile, Page 18. In quick profile as she turns to close the door her breast is a half-globe at the bottom, a ski-jump curve above. The languid half-turn and push of the door are tumid with some kind of significance; he realizes she's replaying a scene from some movie she loves. In his imagination's tableau his wife's hand is on his small son's shoulder in an almost fatherly way.

It's not even that he decides to kneel—he simply finds he feels weight against his knees. His position might make her think he wants her underwear off. His face is at the height of her underwear as she walks toward him. He can feel the weave of his slacks' fabric, the texture of the carpet below that, over that, against his knees. Her expression is a combination of seductive and aroused, with an overlay of slight amusement meant to convey sophistication, the loss of all illusions long ago. It's the sort of expression that looks devastating in a photograph but becomes awkward when it's maintained over real time. When he clasps his hands in front of his chest it's now clear he is kneeling to pray. There can now be no mistaking what he's doing. His color is very high. Her breasts stop their slight tremble and sway when she stops. She's now on the same side of the bed but not yet right up against him. His gaze at the room's ceiling is supplicatory. His lips are soundlessly moving. She stands confused. Her awareness of her own nudity becomes a different kind of awareness. She's not sure how to stand or look while he's gazing so intently upward. His eyes are not closed. Her sister and her husband and kids and the man's wife and tiny son have taken the man's Voyager minivan to the mall. She crosses her arms and looks briefly behind her: the door, her blouse and brassiere, the wife's antique dresser stippled with sunlight through the window's leaves. She could try, for just a moment, to imagine what is happening in his head. A bathroom scale barely peeking out from below the foot of the bed, beneath the gauzy hem of the comforter. Even for an instant, to try putting herself in his place.

The question she asks makes his forehead pucker as he winces. She has crossed her arms. It's a three-word question.

'It's not what you think,' he says. His eyes never leave the middle distance between the ceiling and themselves. She's now aware of just how she's standing, how silly it might look through a window. It's not excitement that's hardened her nipples. Her own forehead forms a puzzled line.

He says, 'It's not what you think I'm afraid of.'

And what if she joined him on the floor, just like this, clasped in supplication: just this way.

Locations and Dislocations

11

Expensive Trips Nowhere

TOM BISSELL

Tom Bissell was born in the port city of Escanaba, Michigan, in 1974. After earning his BA at Michigan State University, Bissell applied to a number of creative writing MFA programs, and after failing to find acceptance in any of them, he volunteered to go to Uzbekistan with the Peace Corps in 1996. His experiences abroad would greatly influence much of his subsequent writing. His first nonfiction book, *Chasing the Sea: Lost Among the Ghosts of Empire in Central Asia*, was published in 2003; during the same year, he published *Speak, Commentary*, coauthored with Jeff Alexander. Bissell's collection of short stories, *God Lives in St. Petersburg: and Other Stories*, was published in 2005. He also wrote a memoir, *The Father of All Things: A Marine, His Son, and the Legacy of Vietnam* (2007). Bissell's short fiction and journalism has been anthologized in *The Best American Short Stories*, *The Best American Travel Writing*, and *The Best American Science Writing*.

Jayne breaks the morning's long silence: "I have a rock in my boot, I think."

Viktor and Douglas do not look at each other as Jayne hunkers into a lotus and with one pull dissolves an impressive knot of signal-orange laces. She removes her boot, turns it upside down, and gives it an irate ketchup-bottle shake. An incisor-shaped pebble plinks off her thigh.

When they continue on, it seems to Douglas that the silence has an entirely new implication. It reminds him of the equally unanswerable silence he and Jayne once shared, walking side by side to Lenox Hill Hospital after he'd accidentally broken her arm playing touch football with friends in Central Park. To speak, then as now, struck him as absurd.

A moraine-pocked valley sprawls before him beneath the cloudy dimmer of a huge gray sky. A powerless yellow blur is the only indication that the sun continues to exist. Jayne is ahead of him now, moving up the valley's gentle slope, hopping from boulder to boulder, her little brown ponytail bouncing. Viktor is in the lead. Far in the lead. Too far, Douglas thinks, popping an herbal cough drop. The valley and surrounding mountains are so quiet that the accumulated jingle of their equipment has the startling tonality of a triangle tapped over and over again. When Douglas closes his eyes, his skull filling with peppermint, he thinks of the *tink* of silverware at wordless meals spent with his parents and of childhood carriage rides through a powdery Central Park. But his lids lift and he is back on the steppe, moving across the world's empty center.

By leaping from rock to rock to rock in their quest to reach the valley's other side, Douglas understands that he and Jayne and Viktor are engaged in what is known as *bouldering,* a term that strikes Douglas as one rich with effortful coinage. He has bouldered before; this is their second boulder field of the day. They came upon their first early this morning, long before their run-in with the bandits, passing through a talus-littered cleft to find themselves at the base of a forbidding muskeg pitted with rocky islets, the unrisen sun a pink smear along the horizon. Some boulders were Volkswagen-sized, others no bigger than an ottoman. They lay fixed in the valley's spring-thawed soil and stretched for nearly a mile, forming by some glacial fluke a workable path. Viktor had been quick to provide navigational pointers

Keep your feet in center of any rock you step on. Otherwise you roll rock and turn your ankle. Step only on rocks with fur.

Douglas and Jayne had exchanged glances. *Lichens, you mean?*

Da, da, Lichens. Old rocks, he'd said. *Most secure.*

When Viktor finished, his indifferent powder-blue eyes locked on Douglas's. *Ponimayete?* he asked him. Understand? Douglas had nodded, irritated by Viktor's insistence on addressing him in Russian before the clarifying English switch-over. There is something malevolent about this, Douglas decides now.

Douglas watches Jayne maneuver along the rocks, wondering in a distracted way exactly what anatomical principle causes her rear end to double in size when she bends over. Jayne, it seems, has taken Viktor's instruction to heart; any time her feet wander out to a boulder's periphery, they spark immediately back to the center. Standing there, features scrunched, fussing with her backpack straps, her ponytail stilled, she spends the same amount of time settling on her next boulder as she does selecting fruit at the market. When she moves, though, she moves with beautiful simian grace, and only now can Douglas picture Jayne as the freckly, tree-climbing tomboy she claims to have once been. Some inner perversity moves Douglas to venture only to those boulders Jayne has dismissed. Once aboard a particularly chancy reject—a wobbly-looking anvil-shaped rock naked of any lichens whatsoever—Douglas, emboldened by transgression, pushes his waffled black boot sole right to the boulder's edge.

When Douglas cries out, Viktor calmly takes a seat and smokes an Okhotnichny cigarette. Jayne, perhaps twenty meters away, squats on a large rock with one hand pressed across her mouth. Through a mesh of fingers she asks her husband if he is all right.

The man pulls off his backpack and muddy, thickly sopping boot and sits down, rubbing his woolen foot. "Ankle," he tells her, grimacing. Then, quickly, he calls to Viktor, "I'm all right," and waves, once, as though forcefully wiping something from a blackboard. The idiot has turned his ankle. Of course. Viktor had decided long before the bandits that he does not much like this Douglas. He rarely respects his clients, though he often comes to tolerate them. For two hundred dollars a day, Viktor has found, most people can be tolerated quite easily. But not this Douglas. A large, soft, American oaf.

"Doug, honey," the woman says, shooting Viktor a quick look before turning back to her husband. It is the first conversation they have had, as far as Viktor knows, since the bandits. "Can you walk?"

The man is now holding his ankle with two hands, as though strangling it. He looks up at her, his cheeks lit with a burgundy glow. Sweat plasters his clipped black bangs to his forehead. His eyes are watery blurs, as though he has eaten something tiny, red, and hot. He is in some pain, obviously. "I can walk. Just—just give me a second."

The woman nods and looks back at Viktor. She stands, hugging herself. Her head is small and egg-shaped, her brown eyebrows as dense as hedges. Her face has the taut, squinty intensity Viktor knows well: the look of a worried American woman trying very hard to appear that she has seen it all. Jayne is short and, Viktor thinks, disappointing. Hard stocky legs. Medium-length camel-brown hair. Small muscular arms, like a *kishlak* boy's. Viktor can only imagine what taking such a tiny powerful thing might be like. Disappointing, he thinks. It is all very disappointing.

"Do you think they'll come back?" she asks Viktor.

Viktor stubs out his cigarette and deposits its accordioned husk into the breast pocket of his khaki vest. He shrugs. "Is difficult to say."

"They're not coming back," Douglas says. He is no longer holding his ankle but simply sitting there, his long inert legs hanging off the boulder's edge and his yellow marshmallowy Gore-Tex vest unzipped. Beneath his vest is a shadow-blue T-shirt affixed with a plain black Batman logo. ("The *old* Batman logo, from the forties," Douglas had been careful to point out to

Viktor, when Viktor asked about it, which feels to Viktor like a very long time ago.) Douglas's head is tipped back to the sunless sky, his eyes are closed, and his temples pulse as he pulverizes another cough drop.

Jayne looks back at her husband and sighs through her nose. Beneath her pack, her shoulders sag and her spinal column wishbones outward, as though respiration and posture had some complicated association. "Doug—"

"They're *not*." The second word is as propulsive as a round. Jayne rocks back a little, so stunned she is nearly smiling. Instantly Douglas shakes his head, an apology he seems to recognize is too impersonal to mean anything.

Jayne turns away, trolling her eyes across a motionless sea of rock. She has spent the last four days in such constant close contact with Douglas that intimacy's pleasant burden now feels more like a millstone. The twenty-four-hour flight from JFK to Frankfurt to Almaty. The two days they'd spent sightseeing in Almaty, trying valiantly to pretend that Almaty had two days' worth of sights to see. They'd bused from their hotel to the world's largest-ice rink at Medeo and skated beside ex-Soviet hockey stars. They'd traipsed through Panfilov Park and watched dozens of solemn old Kazakhs play chess in the murky sunshine. They'd scratched Zenkov Cathedral—which claimed to be the tallest wooden building in the world—from their pitiful itinerary. They drank fermented mare's milk in a fast-food restaurant shaped like a yurt, ate blocky tomato sandwiches and apples as big as softballs at the Zelyony Bazaar, and wandered back to their room, killing time with the BBC as they waited for the Hotel Kazakhstan's sixty minutes of hot-water service, which commenced at the supremely inconvenient hour of 5 p.m.

·   They are here for no real reason. Two years ago, Jayne found herself with Douglas ducking her way inside something called Glowworm Cave in Waitomo, New Zealand. Last year she'd had her photograph taken beside Hadrian's Arch in Jarash, Jordan. Both were what Douglas called Expensive Trips Nowhere, the rubric beneath which this current junket also falls. Douglas first conceived of the Expensive Trip Nowhere after his parents were blindsided on the New Jersey Turnpike by an Atlantic City–bound tour bus whose driver had suffered a stroke at the wheel. Douglas and Jayne had been married a little shy of a year when it happened. Jayne had stabilized into a teeth-clenched toleration of Douglas's parents, Park-and-Seventieth gentry who never understood why their son had settled for "some mousy midwestern girl." This was the phrase Douglas had once quoted—his ill-advised attempt at honesty—in trying to provide Jayne with some understandable frame for his parents' animosity.

Douglas did not seem surprised that his parents had ceded their estate to a number of New York charitable organizations rather than to him. His parents had, however, arranged for a *dipositive provision*—thus began Jayne's education in the phraseology of bequeathment—which ensured that a portion of their trust's income and dividends would be paid out monthly to Douglas, a "sum certain" to the tune of $8,000. Beyond that not a cent belonged to him, except in cases of "extreme need," and only then in "reasonable amounts," along with other similar caveats that kept the world in suspended litigation.

The monthly windfall was large enough to encourage carelessness yet modest enough to make frugality seem picayune. Months after the accident, in bed one night, at some namelessly late hour, neither of them sleeping, both of them knowing it, her back discreetly to him, Douglas proposed the Expensive Trip Nowhere, a journey to no place, for no reason, with no plan. Just to go. Just to leave. He spoke with such irreproachable sadness that Jayne rolled over to find his eyes pooled. She'd agreed, instantly. She knew that Douglas's wealthy Manhattan upbringing had been far too serious a matter to allow for even the suggestion of a childhood; rather like a sexually timid girl turning incandescent atop a boy she finally trusts, the death of his parents now allowed Douglas the consort of some unfamiliar, someday self he'd always been denied.

Three months ago, Douglas had burst into their apartment blabbing about Kazakhstan, from which one of his uniformly affluent students' parents had just returned. Jayne, whose purse had been stolen in New Zealand and who had been extravagantly ill in Jordan (or, as she called it, *Giardian*), stood there in their kitchen, holding a stack of DoubleStuf Oreos that she had spent a good part of the day stevedoring into her mouth, staring at Douglas with a slipping, ugly expression she hated him for not heeding.

The next day Douglas came home with a muddy fax from something called the Adventure Mountain Company in Almaty, Kazakhstan's largest city. It offered two- or four-day package tours of hiking, rock climbing, rafting, and other communions with the natural world of which Douglas knew nothing. She read over the fax, numb. "Come on," he'd wheedled. And suddenly he was Douglas again, her rescuer from Manhattan starving artistry. "You're a Midwesterner, Jayney. Aren't you supposed to *like* this stuff?"

Douglas was never embarrassed to be an American, never hesitant to reveal his monolingual helplessness. Wherever he found himself, he pumped hands with street vendors and enjoyed an incorruptible digestive system. Travel scraped him away to reveal not some dulled surface but bright new layers of personality. But Jayne is thirty years old. She wishes to learn nothing new about the man she married. That time is gone. It has been months since she has even attempted a sculpture, a career that has earned her a reliable five-figure salary, provided that one counted past the decimal points. This was her joke for the cocktail-party circuit.

Jayne now studies the plain, awful hurt on Douglas's face. It is a large lumpy face above which a periwig would not seem at all improper. The bluish beginnings of a spotty, erratic beard gleam upon his cheeks and chin like an unfinished tattoo. His boot is beside him, encased in a cracked shell of mud. She catches herself thinking, *Ruined. The boots I bought for him are ruined.* And she knows that for one horrible moment she has forgotten that he is hurt, or does not care, which is the same thing. This is marriage, she thinks, with a whelm of heartsick apathy. This is what happens. Its intimacy is such that you—

"God," Jayne says suddenly, paddling her hands in front of her face. Some of Viktor's cigarette smoke has, in the motionless air, drifted to her nostrils and given her lungs a toxic baptism. She looks over at Viktor. "What on *earth* are you smoking?"

Viktor flashes a horselike smile. He has a pure Slavic face that allows Jayne to grasp what *Caucasian* really means. The arches of his cheeks look as hard as whetstones. His hair is stalky and yellow, like wheat. It occurs to her that only Caucasian follicles pigment their yield with something other than humanity's standard-issue black.

"Death in swamp," Viktor answers her. "Very strong. Very bad taste. Is what we call them."

Jayne obliges him. "We?"

"Afghantsi," he says.

Jayne nods blithely and looks back to Douglas, who is staring at Viktor with huge confounded eyes.

"Afghantsi?" Douglas says, his tone one of vague challenge.

Viktor nods sharply, then stands. "*Da.* Come. Replace your boot. We walk again."

"What," Jayne asks Douglas after Viktor has forged out ahead, "is an Afghantsi?"

Douglas reaches out to Jayne and she pulls him onto her boulder, releasing his hand the moment he is balanced. Douglas's ankle feels vulcanized, though he has tied his laces so tightly he cannot quite claim that it hurts. He shrugs at Jayne. "That means he's a veteran."

Jayne stares into some middle distance, her chest heaved out. Stray coils of premature gray wisp around her small shell-like ears. "A veteran of what?"

"The Soviet war in Afghanistan."

They both look at Viktor. He has stopped ten boulders up and waits for them with a lavishly dour face and his arms in a tight cross-chest plait. Jayne stares at him, her lips scarcely moving as she speaks. "And these Afghantsi all smoke the same awful cigarettes?"

"Looks that way."

"Great," she says, leaping to the next rock

"Your coat," Viktor asks Jayne. "How much you pay?"

They are walking across a greenish hillock, pingo mounds squishing beneath their boots. The boulder field is an hour's walk behind them. The clouds have broken, and sunlight falls upon the steppe in huge warm rhomboids. The lower slopes of the Tien Shan Mountains are smoky with the vapor of spring-melted snow, and their white saw-toothed upper slopes and horns glitter like pyrite. Jayne walks beside Viktor, while Douglas has dropped back.

Jayne looks down at her orange jacket. It is a Patagonia Puffball jacket, space-agey and shiny, tricked out with Polarguard HV insulation, a ripstop nylon shell, and water-resistant coating. She purchased it and her Patagonia Capalene underwear, her Dana Design Glacier backpack, her Limmer hiking boots, her Helly Hansen rain pants, and her EMS Traverse sleeping bag at Paragon on Eighteenth and Broadway a few weeks after they booked their flight on Kazair. She can't remember what the jacket had set her back specifically, but remembers quite well the $1,200 dent the excursion bashed into her checking account. She feigns recollection. "Fifty dollars?"

Viktor eyes her suspiciously, a Grand Inquisitor of sportswear. "I ask another American about her coat. Same color. Patagonia. She tells that she pay three hundred dollars."

"It was on sale," Jayne says quietly, then stops to wait for Douglas.

Viktor smirks as he fishes the half-smoked cigarette from his breast pocket. As he lights up the remnant, he remembers his schoolboy days as group leader of his Oktyabryata youth group, back when he wore his bright red Young Pioneer scarf nightly to bed, still glowing from the A he'd re-

ceived in Scientific Communism for his critique of bourgeois individualism at School Number 3. This was before he knew of such things as
Patagonia jackets. Before, as a private in the Signal Corps stationed near
Kandahar, he went out on patrol as a demonstrably Soviet soldier and returned equipped with the battlefield tackle of half the planet's nations. After
scavenging the bodies of dead *mujahideen,* his platoon's medics threw away
their Soviet-made syringes, rendered magically sterile by a thin paper wrapping, and stocked up on Japanese disposable syringes whose plungers never
clogged. Their Soviet plasma containers, half-liter glass bottles that shattered constantly, were exchanged for captured Italian-made polyethylene
liter blood bags so rupture-resistant one could stomp on them in field boots
to no effect. Their Soviet flak jackets were so heavy many soldiers could
hardly lift them. Upon seizing their first American flak jacket, Viktor's mys-
tified platoon found that this vestment, which lacked a single metal part,
could not be penetrated at point-blank range with a Makarov pistol. He did
not know, then, that when the war began the *muj* were armed only with
cheap Maxim rifles you could not fire for long without scorching your
guide hand. He did not know of the CIA and ISI airlifts and border sanctu-
aries the *muj* were then making use of. His schoolboy critique of bourgeois
individualism did not foresee such contingencies any more than the Americans who would one day pay him to safeguard their leisure. But he feels little pleasure in having shamed the woman over her jacket. He lied to her
about knowing its true price. He has several such jackets at home, which he
wears only around the cafés of Almaty for the status their indiscreet labels
supply.

"Hey," Douglas says, as he falls in beside Jayne.

"Hey," Jayne returns.

Douglas's mouth goes tight, his mustache of sweat sparkling. "Are we
there yet?"

She motions toward his foot. "How's that ankle?"

"Okay. It just hurts. That's good, though, right? When it stops hurting is
when you're in trouble."

A small, toothless smile. "That's frostbite."

"Well. The good news then is that I don't have frostbite."

Jayne digs into her jacket's marsupial pocket and removes a cling-
wrapped piece of crumbly halvah. She holds it out to Douglas, who shakes
his head. Jayne takes a bite, several hundred sesame seeds instantly install-
ing themselves between her teeth. She looks across the steppe, a sweep of
land so huge and empty she wonders if a place can be haunted by an *absence*

of ghosts. She has never seen a sky so big. So big, in fact, it makes her own pathetic smallness somehow gigantic—as though to contemplate one's place in the nothingness of the universe can only set free some stoned homunculus of monomania.

"Walking here," she tells Douglas suddenly, "I can't get something out of my mind. It just repeats itself over and over again. What's weird is that it's a poem."

"That's not weird." His tone hovers just above annoyance.

She looks over at him, noting the new crease in his forehead. "Not if you're an English teacher. Normal people don't walk around with poems in their heads."

"What's the poem?" His tone is curt, satisfied, as though he has just prevailed in some internal argument of which he neglected to make her a part.

She ignores this, finding the loop in her mind and giving it voice: "'Two roads diverged in a yellow wood, / And sorry I could not travel both / And be one traveler, long I stood / And looked down one as far as I could / To where it bent in the undergrowth.'"

"Frost?" he says. "That's even less weird. He's as catchy as a pop song."

"I had to memorize it in fourth grade. If I've thought about it three times since then I'd be surprised."

Douglas stares at his boots and says, almost meditatively, "'Love and forgetting might have carried them / A little further up the mountainside / With night so near, but not much further up.'"

They walk silently for a while, strides synchronized. Jayne finishes her halvah and kisses the honey from her fingertips. "That's . . . really lovely," she says at last.

"Frost again," Douglas says.

She walks out ahead of him, shaking her head in affected wonder. "I've hiked in a lot of places, but never anywhere so big."

"Kazakhstan is five times the size of France."

"'That's what I mean. And it's so *empty*."

Douglas nods. "During Stalin, Kazakhstan was repopulated with Ukrainians and Russians, so much so that they soon outnumbered the Kazakhs. Rather than see their livestock collectivized, the Kazakhs slaughtered something like twenty million sheep and goats, five million cattle, and three million horses."

"Someone's been reading his guidebook."

"Kazakhstan also happened to be the Soviet Union's atomic playground. From the fifties to the early nineties, fifteen atom bombs a year were exploded over and under Semipalatinsk, which is"—he stops, gets his dubious bearings, and points—"I think about six hundred miles that way. So. You do the math, and it turns out that this place endured over eight hundred nuclear blasts in all. Enough to destroy the entire planet several times over. We haven't avoided a nuclear holocaust as much as localized it in one very unlucky place."

"Which explains perfectly why you're lecturing *me*."

The bleakness of her tone stops him dead. "I'm—" He can't get a word out; his throat is lined with thorns. He breathes until the pent sentence finally bursts free. "I'm *not* lecturing you. I can't *believe* you think I'm lecturing you." But now, of course, he is.

Jayne is walking fast now, as upright as a sea horse. "I'd like to thank you again for bringing me here," Douglas hears her say.

And then he is walking by himself, just as Jayne is, just as Viktor is. Three strangers on the steppe. Douglas feels the special bitter pleasure that comes with being angry and righteous and alone. She could leave him. He knows that. It is one of the many things he knows. He knows that he is a teacher because he enjoys the attention of children more than that of adults, and he knows there is something egotistical and sinister and frightened in this enjoyment. He knows that once, when he was haunting Lower Manhattan bookstores in the wake of his lawschool washout, Jayne had found him irresistible and strange but now finds him something else but has not yet fully figured out what, he doesn't think. He knows poetry, all about poetry—Frost, Auden, Stevens—and had—briefly!—tried to write it, but he knows he is no good, and this does not bother him, much. He knows nothing about IPOs and 401(k)s. He also knows he is in possession of no special gift, no appreciable talent, a peasant in the New Economy's fiefdom, and that his parents, whose living disapproval had once made this condition acceptable, are dead. And he knows, too, that he is a coward.

Viktor and Jayne have stopped at a small hill twenty yards ahead. They are turned toward him and stand in rugged colored silhouette against scalloped mountains and an icy blue sky. Douglas looks up, toward the sun. The morning's earlier cumulus ceiling has now fully dissipated, and thin lenticular saucer clouds float across the atmosphere. He trudges up the hill and, once he has joined them, hears a gush as thick as applause coming from its opposite side.

"A river," Jayne says. For some reason, she smiles. He looks to Viktor and wonders what they were talking about but does not really wish to know.

"Oh," Douglas says. "Okay." He casts his eyes to the base of the hill and sees the river, a rush of silver topped with turbulent foam.

"Doesn't look so bad," Jayne offers mildly.

"Rivers," Viktor intones. "Very dangerous. We cross!" He charges down the hill. Jayne watches Viktor with pallid awe. His movements have a thoughtless, animal anticipation, seemingly privy to the terrain's every secret. Viktor transfers his weight from one foot to the other so smoothly that gravity seems to pull him forward rather than down. Although it is spring and the steppe is still cold, Viktor wears dirty canvas shorts. This allows Jayne to note his grenadelike calves and the long pythonic muscles on the backs of his thighs. Jayne remembers, abruptly, that Russian men are famed ballet dancers.

"Once more into the breach," Douglas mutters, galloping down the hill himself. Jayne feels something uncomfortably close to disappointment that Douglas makes it to the bottom without stumbling. She ventures down the hill herself, slowly and sideways, like a crab.

After a moment of double-check reconnoitering, Viktor leads them along the river's bank. It is edged with rocks and mucky soil and vaguely pubic gray-green vegetation and not a speck of evidence that human beings had ever before walked this path. Long white phalanges of snow lie in every shady furrow. "We must find widest part," Viktor tells them.

Douglas shouts over the rage of the river, "Why don't we just cross right now?"

Viktor turns to answer, but Jayne beats him to it. "Wherever the river is widest is also where the current is slowest." She finds a stick marooned between two rocks at river's edge and, to illustrate her point, heaves it into the water. The stick is caught and swept away more quickly than even she was expecting.

Douglas shakes his head, either angry he is wrong or angry she has made him so. He calls to Viktor, "You knew the river was here, though, right? Why didn't you lead us . . . *around* it?"

"Once, river small," he responds, without turning around. "Now river big."

Douglas laughs, a cosmically empty laugh. "What does *that* mean?"

Viktor stops, head darkly tipped forward, then turns to confront him. His face has a clear unwrinkled menace. His mouth is open but he says nothing, his tongue dry and gray in its hollow. It is as though whole paragraphs of choice, partially translated reproaches are cycling through his Russian brain.

Suddenly Jayne is wedging herself between them. "The snow, you mean? The snow melted and ran down from the mountains?"

Viktor blinks. His mouth closes and stretches into a grin that doesn't seem to end. He claps, once, joylessly, and sets off again, all marching-past-the-Kremlin energy.

"You two are certainly hitting it off," Douglas tells her when Viktor is out of earshot. The words do not hang between them for long before he feels a cold tremor of regret. Amazing, he thinks: He really could not have said anything worse. He tries to launder the statement with a joke, softly elbowing her and hating the falseness of the smile tearing his lips away from his teeth. "Should I worry about going back home alone?"

Jayne takes a long time to respond, a silence in which Douglas hears her die to him three, four, five times. "I wonder if you *would* worry about that."

Douglas puts up a monitory hand. "Okay. Let's stop now." He walks for a while, kicking every bit of rock not bolted down by erosion into the river. "It would worry me. It would kill me. You know that."

Jayne says nothing. Douglas listens to her breathe, inhales the thin unpleasant scent coming off her unwashed body. She did not use to smell like this, not even after spending a whole day in bed with him. He wonders at what age it is exactly that women exchange their scent of talc for that of faint decay. Just as he begins to hold this against her, Douglas winces, his ankle knocking like a pinched blood vessel. The only thing that keeps him from stopping to tighten his bootlaces is the certainty that Jayne will not wait for him if he does.

Viktor drops his pack and turns to them. "We cross," he announces gravely.

"This doesn't look any wider," Douglas mutters to no one, bending down to redo his laces. When he is finished he looks at the river and sees that, actually, it *is* a bit wider here. On top of that, a dozen well-placed rocks make a broken span from one side of the river to the other. There is probably not a better place to cross a river in the entire former Soviet Union.

Viktor stands next to his huge torso-sized pack, contemplating the river. Jayne unloads her much smaller pack and sets it beside Viktor's. Viktor's pack is as gray and beaten as Almaty concrete; it appears better suited to haul potatoes than carry gear. Jayne's pack, Douglas notes, is offensively new and colored in laboratory hues of yellow and red and orange. When Jayne squats beside Viktor, her thighs spreading like thick flanks of beef, Douglas turns away.

He walks over to the river's edge and ponders the radioactivity that in all likelihood lurks along this riverbed's freezing silt. He imagines all of Kazakhstan's rivers as great glowing veins carrying their ghastly chemotherapy to the nation's every corner. That there is something catastrophically wrong right before his eyes, something he can do nothing to alleviate or worsen, fills him with almost holy relief.

Jayne stares at her pack, condemned by its newness. She feels Viktor's cold Russian eyes on her. "Please don't look at me," Jayne says softly, pulling the elastic cinch from the back of her head. Her ponytail comes apart, pungent oily hair falling into her downturned face. She blinks away the strands that catch in the barbed wire of her eyelashes.

Viktor nudges her pack with his boot, knocking his hands together in cryptic anticipation. She turns. His hands are eye-level, huge and chalky and cracked, his knuckles like rivets. "Steppe makes strong what is strong," Viktor says. "Makes weak what is weak."

She shakes her head. "Viktor, please. Spare me." When she looks back at him he is gone, leaping across the river.

Douglas wanders over to Jayne, still squatting by her pack. "More boulders, huh?" Jayne's eyebrows raise with crushing politeness. Douglas looks at Viktor and squints. "What's he doing?"

"Making sure it's safe?"

Douglas snorts and stares at a newfound rock. "Well, bully for him."

"You're having fun." Jayne is still looking away, toward the river's unimaginable headwaters. Fifty yards upstream is a miniature waterfall, the river pouring itself from one level to another in a clean glass-white arc that appears solid enough to walk upon.

He looks down at her. "I don't know what I'm supposed to say about this morning."

Her expression does not change. "You don't have to say anything, Doug."

Quickly he squats beside her. "You know that if they did *anything* to you—"

She nods in hard, quick countermeasure, her eyes awash with unhappiness. "I know. I don't want to talk about it."

Douglas looks over to see Viktor returning. His above-the-knee shorts are fringed with a dark watermark and his leather hiking boots have the soaked, deep-brown look of living cowflesh. His legs glisten hairlessly. "*Tak*," he says, approaching them. "Very important. You keep pack loose when you cross, *da*?"

"Loose?" Jayne says.

Viktor lifts his pack with one hand, as though it were no heavier than a stole. He threads his arms through its straps and buckles his waist belt and sternum strap. Then, in moron-befitting slow motion, he unbuckles his waist belt and sternum strap and lets them dangle meaningfully from his body. "Understand? No straps. Very dangerous."

"No straps," Douglas says, struggling beneath his pack to rise.

"You fall in, you leave pack."

"Right," Douglas says. "I get it."

"No straps."

Douglas's face fills with heat, as though he is leaning into a cleansing steam of dishwasher waft. "Drowning being what we're avoiding here."

Viktor regards Douglas with a vinegary expression, then shakes his head and stalks off toward the river.

"I'm not an idiot, you know," Douglas calls after him.

Viktor slows but does not turn and then continues on.

Jayne is standing now, angrily working her way into her pack. Each word from her mouth seems to sizzle. "Is it a good idea to make an enemy of the one guy who can lead us out of here?"

Douglas looks at her, serenely undoing his straps. "The helicopter picks us up tomorrow. In fifteen hours we'll never see him again."

Viktor gazelles across the river in eight confident bounds. Viktor has that, Douglas thinks: perfect confidence. All thoroughly second-rate people had it. Only once, on the very first rock, was Viktor forced to break stride. Douglas has noted that hesitation and stands on that rock now. Four—possibly five—feet lie between it and the next rock. Douglas grinds his boot waffle against stone, aware that Jayne is waiting behind him, on the bank, as impassive as one of the sculptures in her studio. He is not afraid—the river does not look all that deep; the current *does* seem to let up here—but he knows he cannot fail. He cannot. To do so will allow Viktor to believe any number of things about Douglas, many of which Douglas would ordinarily concede as true. But he is more than the steppe. He is more than this morning. Moments mean nothing. Spume collects on Douglas's face. Viktor now waits on the other side of the river. He sits Indian-style, gallingly oblivious, forearms draped across his knees, a cigarette dangling from his lip like an icicle. Bastard, Douglas thinks. Insolent bastard.

"Doug?" Jayne says.

He half turns. "I didn't say anything while I was waiting for you on those fucking boulders."

Douglas jumps before she can say anything else. His feet come down on rock, blessedly solid. The next few are as simple as walking, and he takes them with Christlike calm. He hops off the last rock, relishing the crunch of his boots in the pebbly ford, and saunters right up to where Viktor is sitting. In oppressive silence Douglas towers above Viktor, cloaking him with his shadow.

Viktor's eyes flick irritably from Douglas to the river to Douglas and then Viktor is standing. He throws his cigarette aside like a dart. Douglas's fists transform into mallets and he struggles free from his pack. But Viktor rushes past him, toward the river. Douglas turns. Splashing. Water in the air. Suddenly Viktor is standing next to Jayne, his hands cupping her small shoulders with unseemly intimacy. Jayne is sopping wet, every limb, every fiber, every part of her. Her waterlogged jacket looks so heavy it seems capable of foundering both of them. Her hair falls around her face in thick buds. She is crying, explaining something, pointing toward the bank and then at the rock and now she is slapping at the water, which is deep, up to her waist at least, and it is fast. Viktor has braced himself against the river's force, the water churning whitely at his thighs. Viktor lifts Jayne's backpack from the river, water pouring from its innumerable pockets. Jayne's teeth chatter as harshly as dice in a wooden box. She is still speaking when Viktor scoops her up and carries her toward the shore, her wet, frightened face pressed against his chest. Douglas stands at the bank, arms out, waiting for a delivery that never arrives, uselessly conscious of the play of a thousand rainbows on the water and in the air.

In monastic silence they set up camp on a hill a few kilometers from the river, unrolling the downy logs of their sleeping bags and pounding their tent pegs into the taiga. Jayne hangs her wool socks and pants and orange jacket around their glowing portable Daewoo stove, which, here on the treeless steppe, must serve as a campfire. She ducks into their tent and emerges wearing her black rain pants, Douglas's Green Lantern T-shirt, and a yellow windbreaker. She sits down across from Douglas, expressionless. Viktor putters around the camp's edges, as patient as a vulture, then unearths their dinner from his gear. They eat sardines and crackers and sip cognac. After a while they find themselves, still hungry, beneath a bright, freakishly starry sky. For close to an hour Douglas stares at them stare into the stove, then stands. His tent's zipper howls like a moonstruck animal.

Some time later, Douglas hears low, furtive voices. In the vast darkness, the Daewoo throws off a surprising amount of light, and the tent's walls are a molten orange. On one wall Viktor and Jayne's huge golem shadows glower. Douglas is in his sleeping bag, a shiny silver sleeve pleated with cushiony squares. The sleeping bag is said to offer protection up to −40 degrees Fahrenheit. Barring intergalactic travel, he cannot imagine why such protection is necessary. Tomorrow is their last morning on the steppe, he thinks. Tomorrow they will awaken for the last time in the sub-Saharan humidity of this tent's womb. Tomorrow they will rendezvous with the helicopter and for $300 an hour they will be ferried back to Almaty, board a plane, and fly home. Douglas thinks about tomorrow, his awareness crumbling, his eyes gliding shut. Outside, he hears Viktor and Jayne's voices rise a little, his mind suspended in the sandy place between sleep and lucidity.

"What animal are you talking about?" Jayne asks.

"It is bird," Viktor says. "Very . . . beautiful bird. I have seen pictures, photographs of such bird. So beautiful. Is American bird. Its feathers green, and . . . *kak, oranzhivye?*"

"Orange?"

"*Da.* O-range. Red. Yellow. Very beautiful. I want very badly to see this bird fly. I think about this bird much. In Russian we call this bird *utka.* I wonder what word in English must this bird be called. And then I learn that in American you call this bird *duck.* You laugh at me now."

"No, no. I'm just—I've never thought of it that way, I guess. Your English is . . . very good, Viktor."

"*Nyet.* My English is . . . *uzhasny.* Very bad. Idiot English."

Douglas is closer to sleep now, brain waves prenatally flattened. He finds himself cast backward, to this morning, minutes after clearing their first boulder field. He is looking up at a gunmetal overcast sky, wondering if it will rain. Jayne is beside him, talking, though he is listening only enough to offer appropriate grunted interjections. Suddenly he feels Jayne's fingers stab into his wrist, above his watch. His eyes drop.

Viktor is standing fifteen feet ahead of them, frozen. Three men are approaching. Two are not men at all but teenagers. The man is wearing a knockoff Adidas tracksuit and carrying a small antiquated pistol, three of his fingers wrapped around the stock and the fourth extended, casually perpendicular to the breech. One of the boys carries a large curved knife. His face is dirty in the permanent way that suggests poverty, not circumstance. On his long-sleeved sweatshirt is a version of the Chicago Bulls logo so completely mistaken Douglas feels almost sorry for the boy. In Almaty's bazaars he had seen similarly ludicrous permutations: New York Yankees T-shirts which somehow incorporated into their design the Empire State Building, Dallas Cowboy knit hats emblazoned with a single red star, sweatshirts for nonexistent clubs like the Las Vegas Braves and Illinois Champions. All stitched from careless memory and a deep nameless want—the least cynical piracy he has ever seen. The man with the pistol lifts his empty hand, and the boys come to a militaristic halt several feet behind him. From the trio's black hair and papyrus-colored skin and almond eyes Douglas knows they are Kazakh. They are smiling.

"What was it like," Jayne asks Viktor outside Douglas's tent, "when you got back?"

"I had to sell my sunglasses! This in Tashkent. *Demobilizatsiya* were sent there, after. No instructions. You understand. Our photos were destroyed. Our letters destroyed. We could not talk about Afghanistan. Illegal, *tak?*"

"Yes. Illegal."

"I had to sell my sunglasses for ticket to Alma-Ata. Now Almaty, then Alma-Ata. I was private, only. Signal Corps. Brute with iron fist! That is what our sergeant say to us. If we do not yell back same loud enough, we are given hole training."

"Hole training."

"*Da.* This is very interesting. You yell into dirty toilet with sergeant behind you. If you don't yell back same loud enough, he push in your face. I ask my mother in Alma-Ata soon to buy me small dog and name it Sergeant so I can strangle small dog when I get home. You laugh at me another time."

"I'm sorry. That's a little funny, though."

"So I wait at train station in Tashkent, and I watch pretty girls in blouses and short skirts. I drink vodka so cold it is like cream. I think of Pavel, my friend, when he wakes up to see his leg cut off by doctors. His face like little girl's, all pink and white. I think of donkeys in Kandahar, how they sit down during shelling, then rise and walk away when shelling stop. That is what I think of Afghanistan then and now. Here. More cognac. Drink."

Viktor greets the Kazakhs in a friendly voice. Douglas looks over at Jayne. Her face is impassive, though her fingers have taloned even deeper into Douglas's wrist. Douglas does not believe Viktor is speaking Russian to them—these harsh, gargly syllables sound nothing like Russian—and this seems to Douglas a cunning tactic indeed. Yes. That's good, isn't it? Enrage them on their home court. He notices that Viktor keeps stepping between them and the man with the pistol. He does this casually, artfully, and the man seems simultaneously disinterested and utterly intent on getting a look at them.

One of the teenagers steps away from his comrades, to his left, a large comical cartoonlike step, and peeks around Viktor's shoulder at Douglas. Half a decade logged in classrooms triggers the Pavlovian workings of Douglas's face: he smiles. The boy instantly breaks into Viktor and the man's conversation, chattering and pointing at Douglas. Douglas's chin lifts, his chest expands. He will not give them the comfort of terror, even as his stomach distends with what feels like ice cream and razor blades. But no. The boy is not pointing at Douglas, he realizes. He is pointing at Jayne.

"When bullet hits man," Viktor tells Jayne, "you hear it. Very strange sound. Like slap. You fall down in sand and you look over at your friend and you see the cigarette you gave him three minute ago is still in his teeth."

"I can't imagine that. I can't imagine *any* of this."

"What I remember most is little boy, little *muj*, running at our APC with Molotov cocktail. With our guns we turn him into nothing. Nothing."

"That's—how did that make you feel?"

"I never had problem. Dying is hard. Killing much easier, even for three rubles a month. Tell me why as twenty-year-old I can kill and now I cannot? Children have no pity. That is reason why. Think of their fairy tales. Many death in fairy tales. Baba Yaga cooks little girls in her oven, and children never frightened. They don't cry."

"Fairy tales used to scare me to death. I cried. I cried all the time."

"After little *muj*, my friend buys urine from medics. Urine with . . . hepatitis, *tak*? He drinks urine, he get sick, he go home. Back to Georgia. Very smart friend. War make good men better, and I think make bad men much worse."

Zhoq, Viktor tells them, as the boy points at Jayne and the man with the pistol nods and nods. *Zhoq, zhoq*. Douglas suspects that in Kazakh this means *No* and hopes deeply that he is correct. For the first time, Viktor sounds angry. The man sneers and taps his pistol against his tracksuited leg. Viktor steps close to the man and says something, something hard and final, then looks at the ground. This is a ploy, and Douglas knows it: Viktor's mind throws off a sudden telepathic thunder. They are silent, all of them, for half a minute. Viktor then sighs and digs into his vest pocket for his cigarettes. He offers the man one. The man takes it. Oddly, the man does not light up but gives the cigarette to one of the boys, who pockets it.

Douglas has no conception of what is being said, for what reason, to what end. A black geyser of frustration pushes its way out of him. Before he can stop himself, Douglas calls out to Viktor: *What do they want?* Jayne's other hand whips around, and now both are clamped around Douglas's wrist.

Viktor turns to Douglas, his face the astonished white of a lanced blister. *Shut up,* he says softly. It sounds to Douglas like *shtup.* At this, the man with the pistol points at himself, furiously, then thrusts his arms out at Douglas. Douglas finds himself studying the flailing pistol. It is fixed on him, now the sky, now the ground, him again. Then the rant is finished. The pistol drops. The man spits at Viktor's feet. The boys laugh. Douglas finds himself thinking of music, of poetry, of themes and motifs building to sensible effect. But life is not like that. Life is chaos. People are horrifyingly alive and unknowable. As if personally escorting this realization from the stable of Douglas's mind, the man walks over to Douglas, shrugging off Viktor's feeble attempt to get in his way. Douglas's knees fill with gelatin. As the man advances, he raises his pistol with almost threatless firing-range composure and points it at Douglas again. The man stops, his wet lips pushed out in curiosity. The pistol's tiny black aperture is twenty inches from Douglas's forehead, and without thought or intention Douglas takes hold of Jayne's shoulders and pushes her in front of him.

Jayne gasps, her face buried in her jacket's shoulder. Douglas lets go of her instantly and steps forward, halving the distance between his forehead and the pistol. His eyes squeeze shut. He does not know where Jayne is. The boys are laughing again. When Douglas opens his eyes he sees that Viktor has materialized next to the man, and he whispers indulgently into his ear. The boy with the knife polishes its curved blade along his thigh.

"Is never the same, after. Never. Many Afghantsi go on killing. Gangsters. Criminals. Hooligans who beat up rock-and-rollers at concerts. I throw my medals into Balkhash after war."

"Do you ever talk to anyone about it?"

"Sometimes I see Afghantsi in Gorky Park. No legs, no arms, and I know them. I say nothing. Soviet Army Day, twenty-three February, they carry flowers and wear their medals and walk through Alma-Ata. That day, only that day, I go to cemetery. We are not buried in military cemetery because we did not fight in war. We fulfilled our international duty. That is what every red tombstone say: DIED IN EXECUTION OF HIS INTERNATIONAL DUTY. But beneath that are other messages, from Mama and Papa and sweethearts. 'Sun and moon extinguished without you, dearest son.' That is on tombstone of my friend Alek Ladutko. Nineteen years old. And on tombstone of

Boris Zilfigarov, my friend shot with my cigarette, his sweetheart writes, 'The earth is a desert without you.' I drink to him now."

Viktor has calmed the man. He lowers his pistol, then scratches his temple with its long needlelike barrel. He rubs his chin. He enjoys a series of frowns. At what seems to Douglas precisely the right moment, Viktor's arm finds its way around the man's shoulder and, gently, he guides him away from Douglas and Jayne. When their backs are to them, Douglas does not look at Jayne, nor she at him.

The Kazakhs leave. Agreeably. Suddenly. Saluting Viktor, Viktor saluting back. The three of them trudge off in the direction from which they appeared, and Viktor turns to Jayne and Douglas, one eye squinted shut in the sun.

"Why are you looking at me like that?" Jayne asks Viktor now. "Stop looking at me like that."

"You are very beautiful," Viktor tells her. "I do not have beautiful things in my life."

"I'm not beautiful. I'm awful."

"You say that because your husband is in his tent, listening to us. If he not there, you would not be awful. You would only be beautiful."

"You're awful. You're being awful to me right now. I don't even know if anything you've told me is true."

"The earth is a desert without you. . . ."

"Stop it."

"You sleep with me in my tent tonight. Your oaf is asleep. He will not know. He fails you. Over and over today he fails you. He does not deserve—"

"Have you ever thought, Viktor, that whatever a man says to you, no matter what it is, at some level whatever he's saying to you is just so fucking . . . *poisonous*?"

"I don't understand."

"Of course you don't. I've had too much to drink. Oh, I don't want to sleep. I've had too—"

"I got to tent now. You can join me. Your choose. I could make you. I could kill your oaf now, in his bed. I think maybe he would not mind so much. But I won't do this. Where you sleep is your choose."

Who were they? Jayne had asked.

Bandits, Viktor said, shrugging. On the steppe, such things happen. What could one do? *Bad men.*

What did they want? Douglas had asked, again.

Viktor had looked at him, not unkindly. *I think you no want to know.*

Douglas's eyes flicker open, his mind half conscious of the sudden, growing silence outside his tent. No, he thinks. No, I don't want to know. Not this, not that. Nothing. Nothing and not anything not ever again.

12

Near-Extinct Birds of the Central Cordillera

BEN FOUNTAIN

Ben Fountain's short stories have appeared in *Harper's*, *The Paris Review*, and *Zoetrope: All-Story*, and he has twice been awarded both the O. Henry Award and the Pushcart Prize. He was born in 1958 in Chapel Hill, North Carolina. He earned a BA in English from the University of North Carolina at Chapel Hill in 1980 and a law degree from the Duke University School of Law in 1984. Fountain worked as a lawyer for only a short period before changing course, to devote his life to writing. His collection of short stories, *Brief Encounters With Che Guevara*, earned him the PEN/ Hemingway Foundation Award for a distinguished first book of fiction, and a Whiting Writers' Award. Fountain is currently working on his forthcoming debut novel, *The Texas Itch*.

"I extended to the comandante the opportunity to walk the floor of the exchange with me, and he seemed reasonably intrigued."
— Richard Grasso, Chairman, New York Stock Exchange
Bogotá, Colombia, June 26, 1999

No way Blair insisted to anyone who asked, no self-respecting bunch of extortionist rebels would ever want to kidnap him. He was the poorest of the poor, poorer even than the hardscrabble campesinos pounding the mountains into dead slag heaps—John Blair, graduate assistant slave and aspiring Ph.D, whose idea of big money was a twenty-dollar bill. In case of trouble he had letters of introduction from Duke University, the Humboldt Institute, and the Instituto Geográpica in Bogotá, whose director was known to have contacts in the Movimiento Unido de Revolucionarios de Colombia, the MURC, which controlled unconscionable swaths of the southwest cordilleras. For three weeks Blair would hike through the remnant cloud forest, then go back to Duke and scratch together enough grants to spend the following year in the Huila district, where he would study the effects of habitat fragmentation on rare local species of parrotlets.

It could be done; it would be done; it had to be done. Even before he'd first published in a peer-reviewed journal—at age seventeen, in *Auk,* "Field Notes on the Breeding and Diet of the Tovi Parakeet"—Blair had known his was likely the last generation that would witness scores of these species in the wild, which fueled a core urgency in his boyhood passion—obsession, his bewildered parents would have said—for anything avian. Full speed ahead, and damn the politics; as it happened they grabbed him near Popayán, a brutally efficient bunch in jungle fatigues who rousted all the livestock and people off the bus. Blair hunched over, trying to blend in with the compact Indians, but a tall skinny gringo with a big backpack might as well have had a turban on his head.

"You," said the *comandante* in a cool voice, "you're coming with us."

Blair started to explain that he was a scholar, thus worthless in any monetary sense—he'd been counting on his formidable language skills to walk him through this very sort of situation—but one of the rebels was into his backpack now, spilling the notebooks and Zeiss-Jena binoculars into the road, then the Leica with the cannon-barrel 200× zoom. Blair's most valuable possessions, worth more than his car.

"He's a spy," announced the rebel.

"No, no," Blair politely corrected. *"Soy ornithologo. Estudiante."*

"You're a spy," declared the *comandante,* poking Blair's notebooks with the tip of his gun. "In the name of the Secretariat I'm arresting you."

When Blair protested they hit him fairly hard in the stomach, and that was the moment he knew that his life had changed. They called him *la merca,* the merchandise, and for the next four days he slogged through the mountains eating cold *arepas* and sardines and taking endless taunts about firing squads, although he did, thanks to an eighty-mile-a-week running habit, hold up better than the oil executives and mining engineers the rebels were used to bringing in. The first day he simply put down his head and marched, enduring the hardship only because he had to, but as the column moved deeper into the mountains a sense of possibility began to assert itself, a signal too faint to call an idea. To the east the cordillera was scorched and spent, rubbled by decades of desperate agriculture. The few mingy scraps of surviving forest were eerily silent, but once they crossed the borders of the MURC-controlled zone the vegetation closed around them with the density of a cave. At night Blair registered a deep suck and gurgle, the engine of the forest's vast plumbing system; every morning they woke to piha birds screaming like pigs, and then the mixed-species flocks kicked in with their contrapuntal yammerings and groks and crees that made the forest sound like a construction site. In three days on the trail Blair reliably saw fourteen species on the CITES endangered species list, as well as an exceedingly rare *Hapalopsittaca* perched in a fern the size of a minivan. He was amazed, and said as much to the young *comandante*, who eyed him a moment in a thoughtful way.

"Yes," the rebel answered, "ecology is important to the revolution. As a scholar"—he gave a faint, possibly ironic smile—"you can appreciate this," and he made a little speech about the environment, how the *firmeza revolucionaria* had banned the multinational logging and mining "mafias" from all liberated zones.

The column reached base camp on the fourth day, trudging into the fortified MURC compound through a soiling rain. They hauled Blair straight to the Office of Complaints and Claims, where he sat for two hours in a damp hallway staring at posters of Lenin and Che, wondering if the rebels planned to shoot him at once. When at last they led him into the main office, Comandante Alberto's first words were:

"You don't look like a spy."

A number of Blair's possessions lay on the desk: binoculars, camera, maps, and compass, the notebooks with their microscopic Blairian scribble. Seven or eight *subcomandantes* were seated along the wall, while Alberto, the *comandante maximo*, studied Blair with the calm of someone blowing smoke rings. He resembled a late-period Jerry Garcia in fatigues, a heavy man with steel-rim glasses, double bags under his eyes, and a dense Brillo bush of graying hair.

"I'm not a spy," Blair answered in his wired, earnest way. "I'm an ornithologist. I study birds."

"However," Alberto continued, "if they wanted to send a spy they wouldn't send somebody who looked like a spy. So the fact that you don't look like a spy makes me think you're a spy."

Blair considered. "And what if I did look like a spy?"

"Then I'd think you were a spy."

The *subcomandates* hawed like drunks rolling around in the mud. So was it all a big joke, Blair wanted to know, or was his life really at stake? Or both, thus a means of driving him mad? "I'm an ornithologist," he said a little breathlessly, "I don't know how many ways I can tell you that, but it's true. I came to study the birds."

Alberto's jaws made a twisted, munching motion, like he was trying to eat his tongue. "That is for the Secretariat to decide, all cases of spying go to the Secretariat. And even if you are what you say you are, you will have to stay with us while your release is arranged."

"My 'release,'" Blair echoed bitterly. "You know kidnapping is a crime in most countries. Not to mention a violation of human rights."

"This isn't a kidnapping, this is a *retención* in the sociopolitical context of the war. We merely hold you until a fee is paid for your release."

"What's the difference?" Blair cried, and when Alberto wouldn't answer he came slightly unglued. "Listen," he said, "I don't have any money, I'm a student, okay? In fact I'm worse than worthless, I owe twenty thousand dollars in student loans. And if I'm not back at Duke in two weeks," he went on, his voice cracking with the wrongness and rage of it all, "they're going to give my teaching-assistant slot to somebody else. So would you please save us all a lot of trouble and let me go?"

They scanned his passport photo instead, then posted it on their Web site with a $5 million ransom demand, which even the hard-core insurgents knew was a stretch. "Sixth Front gets the Exxon guys," Subcomandante Lauro bitched, "and we get the scientist with the holes in his boots." He became known around camp as "John Blair," always the two names together, *Johnblair,* but *John* got mangled in the depths of their throats so that it came out as the even more ridiculous *Joan.* In any case they couldn't seem to speak his name without smiling; thirty years of low-intensity warfare had given the rebels a heightened sense of the absurd, and Blair's presence was just too fertile to ignore, a gringo so thick, so monumentally oblivious that he'd walked into the middle of a war to study a bunch of birds.

"So tell me, Joan Blair," one of the *subcomandantes* might say, pointing to a manakin spouting trills and rubatos or the tanagers that streaked about like meteor showers, "what is the name of that species, please?"

He knew they were testing him, nominally probing for chinks in his cover, but more than that they were indulging in the fatuous running joke that seemed to follow him everywhere. Which he handled by coming right back at them, rattling off the Latin and English names and often as not the Spanish, along with genus and all the natural history he could muster before the rebel waved his arms and retreated. But an implacable sense of mission was rising in Blair. He eyed the cloud forest lapping the compound's walls and knew that something momentous was waiting for him.

"If you let me do my work," he told Comandante Alberto, "I'll prove to you I'm not a spy."

"Well," Alberto answered, "perhaps." A man of impressive silences and ponderous speech, who wore his gravitas like a pair of heavy boots, he had a habit of studying his hands while he spoke, slowly turning them back and forth while he declaimed Marxist rhetoric in the deep rolling voice of a river flowing past giant boulders. "First the Secretariat must review your case."

Always the Secretariat, MURC's great and powerful Oz. In the evenings the officers gathered on the steps of their quarters to listen to the radio and drink *aromática* tea. Blair gradually insinuated himself onto the bottom step, and after a couple of weeks of Radio Nacional newscasts he understood that Colombia was busily ripping itself to shreds. Gargantuan car bombs rocked the cities each week; judges and journalists were assassinated in droves; various gangs, militias, and guerrillas fought the Army and the cops, while the drug lords and revanchists sponsored paramilitary *autodefensa* squads which seemed to specialize in massacring unarmed peasants. In their own area Blair could hear shooting at night, and the distant thud of helicopters during the day. Rebel patrols brought in bodies and bloody *autodefensa* prisoners, while U.S. Air Force planes gridded the sky overhead, reconnoitering the local coca crop.

"Where," Blair asked during a commercial break, "is this Zone of Disarmament they're always talking about?"

"You're in it," Subcomandante Tono answered, to which Lauro added with a sarcastic snarl, *"You mean you couldn't tell?"*

Some evenings Alberto joined them, usually when one of his interviews was being broadcast; he'd settle onto the steps with a mug of tea and listen to himself lecturing the country on historical inevitability and the Bolivarian struggle and the venemous strategies of the World Bank. After one such broadcast he turned to Blair.

"So, Joan Blair, what do you think of our position?"

"Well, Blair said in his most formal Spanish, "of course I support these things as general principles—an end to poverty, an equable education system, elections where everyone is free to participate." The officers murmured patronizingly and winked at each other; amid the strenuous effort of articulating himself Blair barely took notice. "But frankly I think you're being too timid in your approach. If you really want to change society you're going to have to start thinking in more radical terms."

Everyone endured several moments of intense silence, until Alberto cleared his throat. "For example, Joan Blair?"

"Well, you're always going on about agrarian reform, but face it, you're just evading the real issue. If you really want to solve the land problem you're going to have to get away from the cow. They're too big, they overload the entire ecosystem. What we have to do is forget the cow and switch over to a diet of mushrooms and insects."

"Mushrooms and insects?" Lauro retched. "You think I'm risking my ass out here for mushrooms and insects?"

But Alberto was laughing. "Shut up Lauro, he gave an honest answer. I like this guy, he doesn't bullshit around—with a hundred guys like him I could take Bogotá in about two weeks."

During the day Blair was free to wander around the compound; for all their talk of his being a spy the rebels didn't seem to mind him watching their drills, though at night they put him in a storage hut and handcuffed him to a bare plank bed. His beard grew in a dull sienna color, and thanks to the high-starch, amoeba-enriched diet he began to drop weight from his already aerodynamic frame, a process helped along by the chronic giardia that felt like screws chewing through his gut. But these afflictions were mild compared to the awesome loneliness, and like all prisoners he spent countless vacant hours savoring the lost, now-clarified sweetness of ordinary days. The people in his life seemed so precious to him now—*I love you all!* he wanted to tell them, his parents and siblings, the Biology Department secretaries, his collegial though self-absorbed and deeply flawed professors. He missed books, and long weekend runs with his buddies; he missed women so badly that he wanted to gnaw his arm. To keep his mind from rotting in this gulag-style sump he asked for one of his blank notebooks back. Alberto agreed, more to see what the gringo would do than out of any humane impulse; within days Blair had extensive notes on countersinging among Scaled Fruiteaters and agnostic displays in Wood-rails, along with a detailed gloss of Haffer's theory of speciation.

Alberto fell into the habit of chatting with Blair whenever they happened to cross paths in the compound. He would inquire about his research, admire the sketches in his notebook and generally smile on Blair like a benevolent uncle. It came out that Alberto was a former banker, a *burgués* city kid with advanced degrees; he'd chucked it all twenty years ago to join the MURC. "It was false, that bourgeois life," he confided to Blair. "I was your typical social parasite." But no matter how warm or frank these personal exchanges Blair couldn't shake the sense that Alberto was teasing him, holding back some essential part of himself.

"You know," Alberto said one day, "my grandmother was also very devoted to birds. She was a saint, this woman—when she walked into her garden and held out her arms the birds would fly down and perch on her hands."

"Amazing," said Blair.

"Of course I was just a kid, I thought everyone's grandmother could do this trick. But it was because she truly loved them, I know that now. She said the reason we were put here on earth was to admire the beauty which God created."

"Ah."

Alberto's lips pooched out in a sad, nostalgic smile. "Beauty, you know, I think it's nice, but it's just for pleasure. I believe that men should apply their lives to useful things."

"Who says beauty and pleasure aren't useful?" Blair shot back, sensing that Alberto was messing with his mind again. "Isn't that what revolutions are ultimately about, beauty and pleasure for everyone?"

"Well," the *comandante* laughed, "maybe. I'll have to think about that."

So much depended on the rebels' goodwill—whether they lived by the ideals they so solemnly sloganized. Blair knew from the beginning that their honor was the best guarantee of his life, and with time he began to hope that he'd found a group of people with a passion, a sense of mission, that was equal to his. They seemed to be authentic *concientizados,* fiercely committed to the struggle; they were also, to Blair's initial and recurring confusion, loaded with cash. They had the latest in laptops and satellite phones, fancy uniforms, flashy SUVs, and a potent array of high-tech weapons— not to mention Walkmen and VCRs—all financed, according to the radio news, by ill-gotten gains from the cocaine trade.

"It's a tax!" the rebels screamed whenever a government spokesman started going on about the "narcoguerrillas" of the MURC. "We tax coca just like any other crop!" A tax which brought in $600 million a year, according to the radio, a sum that gave Blair a wifty, out-of-body feeling. On the other hand there were the literacy classes and crop-rotation seminars, which the rebels sponsored for the local campesinos, who looked, however, just as scrawny here as in the nonliberated areas. So was it a revolution *a conciencia,* or just a beautifully fronted trafficking operation? Or something of both—Blair conceived that the ratio roughly mirrored his own odds of coming out alive.

The notebook became his means of staying clued to reality, of ordering time, which seemed to be standing still or maybe even running backwards. The only thing the guerrillas would say about his ransom negotiations was that Ross Perot might pay for his release, which Blair guessed—though he could never be sure—was some kind of joke. A group of the younger rebels took to hazing him, *los punketos*, ruthless kids from the city *comunas* who jittered the safeties of their guns whenever Blair walked by, the rapid *click-click-click* cascading in his wake like the prelude to a piranha feed. Sometimes he woke at night totally disoriented, unsure of where or even who he was; other nights it seemed that he never really slept, sinking instead into an oozing, submetabolic trance that left him vague and cranky in the morning. One night he was drifting in just such a haze when a *punketo* burst into the shed, announcing through riffs of soft hysterical laughter that he was going to blow Blair's head off.

"I wouldn't recommend it," Blair said flatly. The kid was giggling and twitching around, literally vibrating—hopped up on *basuco* was Blair's guess. He'd probably been smoking for hours.

"Go fuck yourself," said the kid, jamming his gun into the notch behind Blair's left ear. "I'll kill you if I want."

"It'll be thrilling for a minute, just after you pull the trigger." Blair was winging it, making it up as he went along; the main thing, he sensed, was to keep talking. "Then it'll be like having a hangover the rest of your life."

"Shut up you cocksucker, just shut the fuck up. Shut up so I can kill you."

"But it's true. I know what I'm talking about."

"*You*? You never killed anybody in your life."

"Are you kidding? The United States is an extremely violent country. You must have seen the movies, right? *Rambo? Die Hard?* Where I come from makes this place look like a nursery school."

"You're a liar," the kid said, though less certainly.

"Why do you think I'm here? I have so much innocent blood on my hands, I was ready to kill myself I was so miserable. Then it came to me in a dream, the Virgin came to me in a dream," he amended, remembering how the rebels fell to their knees and groveled whenever the Spanish priest came to say mass, and the *punketos* were always the worst, weeping and slobbering on the padre's ring as he walked among them. "'Follow the birds and you'll have peace,' that's what she told me in the dream. 'Follow the birds and your soul will know peace.'"

And Blair talked on in the most hypnotic, droning voice imaginable, cataloguing the wonders of Colombian avifauna until the *punketo* finally staggered off into the night, either stupified or transcendent, it was hard to say which. But when dawn broke and Blair was still alive a weird peacefulness came over him, along with the imperatives of an irresistible conviction. As soon as the cuffs came off he strode across the yard to Complaints and Claims, brushed past the guard and walked into Alberto's office without so much as a knock. Alberto and Tono were spreading maps across the *jefe's* big desk; when the door flew open they went for their holsters, a reflex that nearly got Blair's head blown off.

"Go on," he dared them, stepping up to the desk. "Either let me do my work, or shoot me."

There was a heat, a grim fury about Blair that most people would associate with madmen and fanatics. The *comandantes* eyed the gringo at a wary slant, and it occurred to Blair that, for the moment at least, they were actually scared of him.

"Well," said Alberto in a cautious voice, "what do you think, Tono?"

Tono blinked. "I think he's a good man, Comandante. And ecology is important to the revolution."

"Yes," Alberto agreed, "ecology is important to the revolution." He tried to smile, to inject some irony into the situation, but his mouth looked more like a fluttery open wound.

"Okay, Joan Blair, it will be as you wish. I give you permission to study your birds."

Blair was twelve the first time it happened, on a trip to the zoo—he came on the aviary's teeming mosh pit of cockatoos and macaws and Purple-naped Lories and it was as if an electric arc had shot through him. And he'd felt it every time since, this jolt, the precision stab in the heart whenever he saw Psittacidae—he kept expecting it to stop but it never did, the impossibly vivid colors like some primal force that stoked the warm liquid center of your soul.

He'd known a miracle was in these mountains, he'd felt it in his bones. For five rainy days he tramped ever-widening circles out from the base, traversing ridges and saddles and moiling through valleys while the armed guard followed him every step of the way. Hernan, Blair guessed, was another of the *comandantes'* jokes, a slight mestizo youth with catlike looks and a manner as blank and flaky as cooled ashes. By now Blair knew a killer when he saw one; Hernan would as soon shoot a man as pinch off a hangnail, but as they trudged through the gelatinous drizzle together Blair began to get the subtext of the *comandantes'* choice.

"So how long have you been with the MURC?" he asked.

"Always," Hernan replied in a dreamy voice.

"Always?"

"That other boy," Hernan said in a gaseous hum, "that other boy died. I have been a *revolucionario* my whole life."

Blair studied the youth, then went back to scanning the canopy. Alberto had returned the binoculars but not the camera.

"So I guess you've been in a lot of battles?"

"Yes," Hernan said in his humming voice, and he seemed to reflect. "Yes, many," he added.

"What's it like?" Blair asked rudely, but the kid's catatonia was driving him nuts.

"Oh, it's not so bad. Once the shooting starts everything's okay."

Which Blair took for a genuine answer; five days through some of the most beautiful, rugged country in the world and the youth showed all the emotion of a turtle. It might not matter what you hit him with—a firefight, a bowl of stew, a trip to Disneyland—Hernan would confront each one with the same erased stare, but when Blair passed him the binoculars on the fifth day, pointing down a valley at a grove of wax palms and the birds wheeling around like loose sprockets, Hernan focused and gazed in silence for a time, then burst out laughing.

"They're so silly!" he cried.

And they were, Blair agreed, they were delightful, this remnant colony of Crimson-capped parrots whose flock notes gave the impression of a successful cocktail party. There'd been no sightings of the Crimson since 1973, when Tetzlaff et al. spotted a single breeding pair in Pichincha, Ecuador. CITES listed the species as critically endangered, though the more pessimistic literature assumed extinction; that first day Blair counted sixty-one birds, a gregarious, vocal group with flaming crowns and chunky emerald-green bodies, their coverts flecked with blues and reds like glossy M&Ms. Sixty-one birds meant that God was good: not only was there a decent chance of saving the species, but if he lived and made it home with his data intact Blair was going to knock the ornithological world on its ass. He and Hernan built a blind of bunchgrass and palm fronds, and Blair settled into the grind-it-out fieldwork mode. He charted the foraging grounds, the potential nest holes, the roosts and flyways across the valley; he identified the mated pairs within the flock and noted the species' strong affinity for wax palms—*Ceroxylon andiculum*, itself endangered—and surmised a trophic relationship. They talked constantly, with complex repertoires of sounds, chattering in an offhand, sociable way as they clambered about the canopy or sputtered from tree to tree, their short shallow wing beats batting the air with the noisy ruction of windup toys.

Within weeks Blair had a basic ethological profile. In exchange for the privilege of fieldwork he had to do camp chores every afternoon, which was nothing—three years of graduate school had inured him to slave labor and subsistence living. In some ways this was better than school: he got room and board, worked with minimal interruptions, and was furnished a local guide-bodyguard free of charge. Hernan proved adept at tracking the birds on their feeding rounds, leading Blair through the forest as they listened for debris tumbling through the leaves, then the fuddles and coos that meant Crimsons were overhead. At the blind he usually lay back on the grass and dozed, rousing from time to time to say amazing things about himself.

"I had a girlfriend," he once confessed to Blair in a sleepy voice. "She wouldn't let me kiss her, but she'd bite me on the ear."

In the same vacant drone he told all manner of terrible stories: battles he'd fought, prisoners he'd executed, patrols where his column had come across peasants burned to death or babies nailed to planks. The stories were so patently nightmarish that Blair wondered if Hernan was talking in his sleep, channeling the dreams that rose like swamp gas out of his wounded subconscious. His own family had been killed when he was twelve, their village wiped out by *autodefensas* for electing a former insurgent as mayor.

"Sometimes I see them," Hernan murmured in a half-doze, one arm thrown over his eyes, feet crossed at the ankles. "Sometimes I'm lying on my cot at night, and I look up and all my family's standing there. And it's like I'm lying in a coffin, you know? My family's alive and I'm the one who's really dead, and they've come to my funeral to tell me good-bye."

Blair was so horrified that he had to write it all down, the baroque, spiraling cycles of murder and revenge mixed with his notes on allopreening among the mated Crimsons and the courtship dances of the unattached males, the way they minced around like fops doing a French quadrille. *Sickness* he wrote in the margin of his notes, *there's a sickness in the world*, along with *parrots the most intelligent and beautiful of birds, also the most threatened—a clue to the nature of things (?)*. He wrote it all because it all seemed bound together in some screamingly obvious way that he couldn't quite get. Tramping through the woods, he and Hernan kept coming across giant cocaine labs, the thuggish workers warning them off with drawn machetes. The coca fields around the camp kept expanding; radio reports of the fledgling peace talks took on a spectral air, with the MURC insisting on prenegotiation of themes which might be substantively negotiated at a later time. Every few weeks Hernan would go off on a mission, and after three or four days he'd drag in with the other survivors, skinnier, with corpse-like shadows under his eyes but otherwise the same—the next dawn he and Blair would be at the blind, watching the birds greet the day with gurgling chatter. In March the males began to hold territory, and when the females developed brood patches Hernan offered to climb the trees for a look at the nests, a job they both knew was beyond Blair. After a year in the mountains he was a rashy stick figure of his former self, prone to fevers and random dizzy spells that made his head feel like a vigorously shaken snow globe. Sometimes he coughed so hard that his nose bled; his bowels were papier-mâché, his gums ached, and the sturdiest thing about him seemed to be his beard, which looked positively rabbinical.

"Go for it," Blair answered, and in a flash Hernan was seventy feet up the tree, relaying information while Blair wrote. Clutch, two; eggs, white; nest, about the size of a Guambiano water jar. Hernan had left his rifle propped against a nearby tree; Blair eyed it while allowing an escape fantasy to float through his head, a minivacation from the knowledge that if he ran they'd catch him before the day was out. Still, the rifle raised a nagging question: how could he leave, now, in the middle of his research, even if he got the chance? But not to leave might be a slow form of suicide. Sooner or later something would get him, either sickness, a swacked-out *punketo* or an *autodefensa* raid, or maybe the Secretariat would decide to make a point at his expense. The hard line had lately crept back into the MURC's rhetoric, which Blair guessed was part posturing for the peace talks, part exasperation at the trend of the times. The Soviet Union had imploded, the Berlin Wall was gravel, and the Cuban adventure was on life support, and yet the MURC insisted it would soldier on.

"Some say the end of history has come," Alberto intoned to the journalists. "We can all have different interpretations about what's happening in the world during these very complex years, but the fact of the matter is that most things haven't changed. Hunger, injustice, poverty, all of the issues which led the guerrilla of the MURC to take up arms are still with us."

True, thought Blair. He wanted to believe in the Revolution, in its infinite capacity for reason and justice, but the Revolution wouldn't return his camera for one day. All of his research would be deemed hypothetical unless supported by a photo or specimen. No photo, no dissertation, and he'd sooner burn every page of his notes than take a specimen.

"I could steal the camera back for you," Hernan offered. "I think I know where he's keeping your stuff."

"What would happen if they caught us?"

Hernan reflected. "To me, nothing—I can just disappear. To you?" He shrugged. "They'd probably cut off your fingers and send them to your family."

Blair considered for a second, then shook his head. Not yet. He wasn't that desperate yet.

When the chicks hatched Hernan went up again, checking out the nests while the parents and auxiliaries seethed around his head like a swarm of belligerent box kites. One egg would hatch, then the second a few days later; Blair knew the second hatchlings were insurance, doomed to die unless their older siblings died first, and he sketched out a program for taking the second chicks and raising them in captivity.

The Crimsons had saved him, in a way; maybe he'd save them in turn, but he had to know everything about them first. "There's something wrong with us," he told Hernan one day. He was watching the nest holes for the soon-to-fledge chicks and thinking about the news, the latest massacres and estimates of coca acreage. The U.S. had pledged Colombia $1.6 billion in aid—advisers, weapons, helicopters, the whole bit—which made Blair wonder if his countrymen had lost their minds. There was a fire raging in Columbia, and the U.S. planned to hose it down with gasoline.

"Who?" Hernan answered, cracking open one eye.

"Us. People. The human race."

Hernan lunked up on one elbow and looked around, then subsided to the grass and closed his eyes. "People are devils," he said sleepily. "The only *persona decente* who ever lived was Jesus Christ. And the Virgin. And my mother," he added.

"Tell me this, Hernan—would you shoot me if they told you to?"

"Anh." Hernan didn't bother to open his eyes. "They'd never ask me."

"They wouldn't?" Blair felt an unfamiliar surge of hope.

"Of course not. They always put the new guys on the firing squads, to toughen them up. Guys like me they never bug for stuff like that."

Over the next few days seven chicks came wobbling out of the nests, and Blair set himself the task of tracking the flock as it educated the youngsters. Back in the shed he had notebooks and loose papers crammed with data, along with feathers, eggshell fragments, and stool samples, also a large collection of seeds with beak-shaped chunks gnarled out of them. Occasionally Alberto would trek up the mountain to the blind, checking in on Blair and the latest developments with "the children," as he'd taken to calling the parrots. He seemed relaxed and jolly during these visits, though his essential caginess remained; he would smile and murmur noncommittally when

Blair lobbied to start his captive-breeding program. "Get with it, Alberto," Blair pressed one day. "It would be a huge PR coup for you guys if the MURC rescued an endangered species. I could help you across the board with that, like as an environmental consultant. You know we're really on the same side."

Alberto started to speak, then broke off laughing as he studied the wild gringo in front of him. Blair was dressed in scruffy jungle fatigues—his civilian clothes had worn out long ago—and with his gaunt, weathered face and feral beard he looked as hardened as any of the guerrillas. New recruits to the camp generally assumed that he was a zealot from the mythical suicide squad.

"Joan Blair, you remind me of a man I once knew. A man of conviction, a real hero, this guy. Of course he died in Bolivia many years ago."

"Doing what?"

"Fighting for the revolution, of course!"

Blair winced, then shook off the spasm of dread. "So what about my captive-breeding program?"

Alberto chuckled and patted Blair's shoulder. "Patience, Joan Blair, you must learn patience. The revolution is a lot more complicated than you think."

"They're negotiating you," Hernan said a few weeks later. "Some big shot's supposed to be coming soon."

"Bullshit," Blair said. The camp was a simmering cesspool of rumors, but nothing ever happened.

"It's true, Joan Blair, I think you're going home."

"Maybe I'll stay," Blair said, testing the idea on himself. "There isn't an ornithologist in the world who's doing the work I'm doing here."

"No, Joan, I think you should go. You can come back after we've won the war."

"What, when I'm eighty?" Blair chewed a blade of grass and reflected for a moment. "I still don't have my photo. I'm not going anywhere until I get that."

The rumors persisted, gradually branched into elaborate subrumors. Just to be safe Blair got all his data in order, but it was still a shock to see the helicopters come squalling out of the sky one day, cutting across the slopes at a sassy angle and heading for camp. Blair and Hernan were walking back for afternoon chores, and if there was ever any doubt about Blair's intentions his legs resolved it for him, carrying him down the trail at a dead sprint. At camp the helicopters were parked on the soccer field, two U.S. surplus Hueys with the sky-blue Peace Commission seal on their hulls. Campesinos and guerrillas were streaming into the compound; Blair had to scrum his way through the crowd to get a view of Complaints and Claims, where some kind of official moment was taking place on the steps. Several distinct factions were grouped around a microphone: Alberto and the *subcomandantes* were on one side, along with some senior *comandantes* whom Blair didn't recognize, while to their right stood a sleek delegation of civilians, Colombians with careful haircuts and tasteful gold chains. Blair spotted the American delegation at once—their smooth, milky skin was the giveaway, along with their khaki soft-adventure wear and identical expressions of informed concern. Everyone was raked toward the microphone, where a Colombian was saying something about the stalled peace talks.

Why didn't you tell me? Blair almost screamed. A Tele-Nacional crew was filming the ceremony; photographers scuttled around like dogs chasing table scraps. *What about me?* he wanted to shriek, *say something about me!* He tried in vain to make eye contact with the Americans, who'd arranged themselves into two distinct pairs. The two middle-aged men stood farthest from the action, robust, toned, country-club types; the other two Americans stood close to the center, a tall, older gentleman with a shrinking hairline and sharp Adam's apple, then the sturdy young woman who was glued to his side, short of stature, hyperalert, firecracker cute. *The international community's show of support*, said the speaker. *A message of hope from U.S financial circles.* Blair felt one of his dizzy spells coming on, his eyes clouding over in a spangly haze. He slumped and let the crowd hold him up; Hernan had vanished somewhere along the trail. When the delegation began to move inside Blair watched them disappearing as if in a dream, then roused himself at the last moment.

"Hey!" he yelped in English, "I'm American! Hey you guys, I'm an American!"

Only the woman seemed to hear, flashing a quick, startled look over her shoulder, then continuing inside. Blair started to follow but a guard blocked his way.

"*Alto*, Joan Blair. Only the big shots go in there."

"Who are those people?" Blair asked, craning for a look through the door. Which abruptly shut.

"Well," the guard said, assuming the manner of someone schooling a particularly dense child, "there is Señor Rocamora, the Peace Commissioner, and there is Señor Gonzalo, the Finance Minister—"

"But the Americans, who are they?"

"How the hell should I know? *Peces gordos*, I guess."

Blair didn't dare leave, not for a second, though he could feel the sun baking all the juices out of him. The crowd in the compound absently shuffled about, disappointed without really knowing why. *Fritanguera* ladies set up their grills and started frying dough; a King Vulture scraped lazy circles in the sky. After a while the American woman stepped outside and walked down the gallery to speak to the reporters. Blair brushed past the guard and was up in a second, intercepting the woman as she walked back to the door. Out of instinct she started to dodge him; he looked wild with his castaway's beard and grimy jungle fatigues, but his blue eyes beaming through the wreckage brought her up short.

"Oh. You must be John Blair!"

He could have wept with gratitude. "Yes, I'm John Blair! You know who I am!"

"Of course, State briefed us on your situation. I'm Kara Coleman, with the—" A scissoring blast of syllables shot off her lips. "Wow," she continued, eyeing him up and down, "you look like"—*hell*, she barely avoided saying—"you've been here awhile."

"Fifteen months and six days," Blair instantly replied. "You're with the State Department?"

"No, I'm with the—" She made that scissoring sound again. "I'm Thomas Spasso's assistant, he's leading our group. Thomas *Spasso*," she repeated in a firm voice, and Blair realized that he was supposed to know the name. "Chairman of the Nisex," she continued, almost irritated, but still Blair didn't have a clue. "The *Nisex*," she said as if speaking to a dunce, "the New York *Stock* Exchange."

Blair was confused, but quite as capable as anyone of rationalizing his confusion—he knew that fifteen months in the Andes might have turned his American frame of reference to mush. So maybe it wasn't so strange that the king of Wall Street would turn up here, in the jungly heart of MURC territory. Blair's impression of the stock market, admittedly vague, was of a quasi-governmental institution anyway.

"Right," he said, straining to put it all together. The unfamiliar English felt like paste on his tongue. "Sure, I understand. But who, I mean what, uh—why exactly are you here?"

"We're here to deliver a message from the financial community of its support for the current peace initiative. Foreign investment could do so much for this country, we felt the MURC might be more flexible if they knew the opportunities we could offer them. And Mr. Spasso has a special interest in Colombia. You know he's close personal friends with Ambassador Moreno."

Blair shut his eyes and wondered if he'd lost his mind. "You mean," he said in a shattered whisper, "this doesn't have anything to do with me?"

"Well, no, we came chiefly with the peace process in mind. I'm sorry"— she realized the effect she was having—"I'm truly sorry, I can see how insensitive that must seem to you right now."

Blair was sagging; all of a sudden he felt very, very tired. "Isn't there something you can do for me?" he softly wailed. "Anything?" Kara touched his arm and gave him a mournful look; she wasn't heartless, Blair could see, but rather the kind of person who might cry in movies, or toss bites of her bagel to stray dogs.

"Mr. Spasso might have some ideas," she said. "Come inside, I'll try to get you a few minutes with him."

She led Blair through the door, down a short hallway and into the big concrete room where the *comandantes* mediated peasant disputes every Tuesday and Thursday. The delegates were sitting in the center of the room, their chairs drawn in a circle as if for a group therapy session. Thomas Spasso was speaking through an interpreter, and in seconds Blair formed an impression of the chairman as a ticky, nervous guy, the kind of intractable motormouth who said the exact same thing no matter where he was. "Peace will bring you huge benefits from global investors," the chairman told the *comandantes*. "The capital markets are lining up for you, they want to be your partner in making Colombia an integral part of the Americas' economic bloc." He rattled on about markets and foreign investment, the importance of strong ratings from Moody's bond-risk service—the rebels sat there in their combat fatigues and Castro-style hats smiling and nodding at the chairman's words, but Blair could see they were barely containing themselves. It was so close that they didn't dare look at each other, but the real challenge came when the chairman invited them to visit Wall Street. "I personally extend to each and every one of you an invitation to walk the floor of the exchange with me," Spasso said, his voice thrumming with heartfelt vibrato. He clearly thought he was offering them the thrill of their lives, but Blair could picture the rebels howling on the steps tonight—*Oooo, that we should have this big honor, to walk the floor of the bourgeois exchange with him.* Even now the *comandantes'* eyes were bugging out, their jaws quivering with the strain of holding it in, and it was only by virtue of supreme discipline that they didn't fall out of their chairs laughing.

Spasso, ingratiating yet oblivious, talked on. "He's very passionate," Kara whispered to Blair, who was thinking how certain systems functioned best when they denied the existence of adverse realities. After awhile the Peace Commissioner got to say some words, then the Finance Minister, and then Alberto, who limited his comments to an acknowledgment of the usefulness of market mechanisms, "so long as social justice for the masses is achieved." Then some aides circulated a proposed joint statement, and the meeting dissolved into eddies and swirls as each group reviewed the language.

Kara waited until Spasso stood to stretch his legs. "Mr. Spasso," she called, hustling Blair over, "this is John Blair."

Spasso turned, saw Blair, and seemed to lose his power of speech.

"The hostage," Kara said helpfully, "he's in your briefing kit. The guy from Duke."

"Oh yes, yes, of course, the gentleman from Duke. How are you, so very nice to see you."

Nice to see you? Fifteen months in hell and *nice to see you?* For Blair it was like a curtain coming down.

"Sir, John and I were discussing his situation, and while he understands the limited scope of our visit he was also wondering if we could do anything with regard to facilitating his return home. At some possible future point."

"Well," Spasso said, "as you know we're here in the spirit of a private-sector exchange. Though your name did come up at the embassy this morning." He paused as one of the other Americans approached, a fellow with silver-blond hair and a keen, confident look. "Working the final numbers," he told Spasso, waving a legal pad at the chairman. "Then we're good to go. Thanks so much for setting this up, Tom."

Spasso nodded and glanced at his watch as the American moved off. People were milling about the big room, talking and bumping shoulders.

"Uhhh—"

"John Blair," Kara prompted.

"Mr. Blair, absolutely. I'm afraid your situation is rather problematic. There are laws"—he looked to Kara for confirmation—"apparently there are laws here in Colombia which prohibit private citizens from engaging in kidnap negotiations. Am I correct on that, Kara?"

"Unfortunately yes, sir."

"'Aiding and abetting a kidnap negotiation,' I believe those are the words. We're to avoid any action that could be construed as aiding and abetting a kidnap negotiation, those are our strict instructions from the State Department. Which I know must seem rather harsh to you—"

Blair had groaned.

"—but I'm sure you can appreciate the bind this puts us in. Much as we'd like to help, our hands are tied."

Blair wanted to hit this fool, or at least shake him hard enough that some air got to his brain. "Look," he said in his most determined voice, "they're threatening to kill me, they've accused me of being a spy. They could take me out and shoot me as soon as you leave."

"I'm certainly aware of the seriousness of your situation." *Señor Spasso,* someone called from across the room. "Believe me, I am most sympathetic. But any goodwill we foster here today will redound to your future benefit, I'm sure."

Señor Spasso, we're ready.

"Be right there! People are working for your release, I can assure you. Top people, extremely capable people. So hang in there, and God bless."

Spasso joined the general push of people toward the door. "I am so, so sorry," Kara said. She reached into her satchel and pulled out a handful of Power Bars. "Here, take these," she said, passing them to Blair. "I'll talk to you before we leave."

Kara melted into the crowd. Blair allowed the flow to carry him out to the gallery, where he leaned against a column and closed his eyes. He could not comprehend what was happening to him, but it had something to do with the casual cruelty of people who'd never missed a meal or had a gun stuck to their heads. Out in the yard the press was forming ranks for another photo op. Spasso and company gathered around the microphone; while they made the same speeches as two hours ago Blair ate his Power Bars and discretely wept, though in time he pulled himself together and resolved to make one last plea for help. He scanned the yard and gallery for Kara, then entered the building, where he found her in the big concrete room. She and the other two Americans were sitting with Alberto and one of the senior *comandantes.* They were speaking in quiet, reasoned tones, their chairs so close that their knees almost touched. Blair was struck by their visible ease with each other, the intimate air which enclosed the little group.

"Oh, John!" Kara cried. "Maybe John can help," she said to the others, waving Blair over. "John, we're having some trouble with the language here, maybe you can help us out."

The blond American stood with his legal pad. "All those years of high school Spanish," he chuckled, "and I don't remember a thing."

"John's American," said Kara. "He's in graduate school at Duke."

"Super!" The man pulled Blair close. "Listen, we're trying to work out the numbers here and we can't seem to get on the same page. I'm offering thirty-five hundred per fifty unit, fifty thousand board feet in other words. Think you could put that into Spanish for me?"

Blair eyed the scribble of numbers on the pad. "Thirty-five hundred . . ."

"Dollars, U.S."

Blair kept scanning the pad, the numbers teasing him; it seemed important to make sense of the mess. "Board feet . . ."

"It's the standard unit in the industry. One square foot by one inch thick."

"Of board," Blair said. "You're talking about lumber."

"You bet."

"Who are you?"

The man stuck out his hand. "Ruck Hunley, Weyerhauser precious woods division."

"You're going to log this area?"

"That's the plan, if we can close this thing."

Blair turned to Alberto, who gave him a squirrelly, sullen look. The honks and woofs of the press conference drifted through the door, and that, Blair realized, was simply a show, a concoction of smiles and talking heads. Whereas the deal was happening right here in this room.

"Alberto," he cried in bitter, lancing Spanish, "how could you? How could you even think of doing such a thing?"

Alberto shrugged, then turned away as if he smelled something bad. "Running an army is expensive, Joan Blair. The revolution doesn't survive on air, you know."

"Christ, look at all the coca out there, how much money could you possibly need? You're going to wipe out the parrots if you log up here."

"We have to save the country, Joan Blair."

"What, so you can turn it over to these guys?"

"Enough."

"You think there'll be something to save when they're done with it?"

"Enough, Joan Blair, I mean it." Alberto flicked his hand as if shooing a fly. "Get out of here, I'm tired of listening to you. Beat it. Where are those son-of-a-whore guards—"

But Blair had rounded on Hunley. "There's a parrot up here," he said in very fast English, "an extremely rare species, these are probably the last birds of their kind in the world. If you guys come in here logging it's a pretty sure thing you're going to wipe them out."

"Whoa, that's news to me." Hunley and his partner exchanged dire looks; Hunley turned to Alberto. "Comandante, I can tell you right now if we get bogged down in any environmental issues then we're outta here. We don't have time to mess around that stuff."

"Is not a problem," Alberto said, emitting the gruff sort of English that a bear might speak.

"Well according to your interpreter it is."

"Not a problem, no, for sure, no bird problems here. Forget the birds."

"I won't stand for this," Blair stated flatly. "I don't accept it. You people can't do this."

Alberto's lips cramped inward, holding back a smile, though Blair could see it surface in his eyes well enough, the near-lethal mix of pity and contempt. "Okay, Joan Blair, why don't you stop us," he mocked, but something skittish and shamed began to leak into his eyes, a grey, mizzly vapor that snuffed out all the light. Alberto tried to stare him down but couldn't, and at the moment he turned away Blair knew: the revolution had reached that classic mature stage where it existed only to serve itself.

"Okay," Alberto said, reaching for Hunley's legal pad, "I think we can make the deal." He circled a number on the pad and handed it back to Hunley. "For that, okay? For this price we make the deal, but one more thing. You have to take this guy with you."

"No way," Blair said, "forget it. You aren't getting rid of me. "

"Yes, yes, you are going. We are tired of feeding you, you have to go home now."

"Go to hell Alberto, I'm staying right here."

Alberto paused, then turned to the Americans. "This man," he said stiffly, pointing to Blair, "is a spy. As a gesture of goodwill, for the peace process, I am giving him to you, you may please take him home. And if you don't take him home, today, now, he will be shot. Because that is what we do to spies."

Kara gasped, but the worldly lumber executives just laughed. "Well, son," said Hunley, turning to Blair, "I guess you better come with us."

Blair wouldn't look at them, Spasso, Kara, the others, he wouldn't acknowledge the smiling people in the seats around him. He kept his face turned toward the helicopter's open door, watching the dust explode as the engines powered up, the crowd waving through the storm of rotor wash. The chopper throbbed, shuddered, shyly wicked off the ground, and as it rose Blair glimpsed Hernan in the crowd, the kid dancing like a boxer as he waved good-bye. In the chaos of loading he'd slipped through the muddled security cordon and shoved a plastic capsule into Blair's hand—film, Blair had known without looking at it, a thirty-five-millimeter cartridge. The film was tucked into Blair's pants pocket now, while he clutched to his lap the backpack with its bundles of data and artifacts: the first, and very likely the last, comprehensive study of the Crimson-capped Parrot. He hung on as the Huey accelerated, trapdooring his stomach into empty space as it slammed into a sheer vertical climb. The world fell away like a ball dropped overboard, the torque and coil of the jungle slopes diminishing to finely pebbled sweeps of green. The craft pivoted as it climbed, nose swinging to the east, the Crimsons' valley with its fragile matchstick palms sliding past the door like a sealed tableau—from this height Blair could see how easy it would be, nothing at all to rub out the faint cilia of trees. Easy. The sheltering birds just so much incidental dust.

How does it feel? Spasso was shouting in his ear. *How does it feel to be free?* They were rising, rising, they might never stop—Blair closed his eyes and let his head roll back, surrendering to the awful weightlessness. Like dying, he wanted to tell them, like death, and how grieved and utterly lost you'd feel as everything precious faded out. That ultimate grief which everyone saves for the end, Blair was spending it, burning through all his reserves as the helicopter bore him away.

13

Shiloh

BOBBIE ANN MASON

Bobbie Ann Mason was born in 1940 and raised on her family's dairy farm in May-field, Kentucky. She earned her BA from the University of Kentucky, her MA from the State University of New York at Binghamton, and her PhD from the University of Connecticut. Her first publications were literary criticism, *Nabokov's Garden: A Nature Guide to 'Ada'* (1974) and *The Girl Sleuth: A Feminist Guide to the Bobbsey Twins, Nancy Drew, and Their Sisters* (1975). Mason then turned her attention to short fiction and published stories in such publications as *The New Yorker* and *The Atlantic Monthly*. Those successes made way for her to publish her first collection of short stories, *Shiloh and Other Stories* (1982), which earned her the PEN/Hemingway Foundation Award. She went on to publish three other short story collections—*Love Life* (1989), *Midnight Magic* (1998), and *Zigzagging Down a Wide Trail* (2001), and three novels—*Spence + Lila* (1988), *Feather Crowns* (1993), and *In Country* (1985). *In Country* was adapted into a major motion picture.

Leroy Moffitt's wife, Norma Jean, is working on her pectorals. She lifts three-pound dumbbells to warm up, then progresses to a twenty-pound barbell. Standing with her legs apart, she reminds Leroy of Wonder Woman.

"I'd give anything if I could just get these muscles to where they're real hard," says Norma Jean. "Feel this arm. It's not as hard as the other one."

"That's 'cause you're right-handed," says Leroy, dodging as she swings the barbell in an arc.

"Do you think so?"

"Sure."

Leroy is a truck driver. He injured his leg in a highway accident four months ago, and his physical therapy, which involves weights and a pulley, prompted Norma Jean to try building herself up. Now she is attending a body-building class. Leroy has been collecting temporary disability since his tractor-trailer jackknifed in Missouri, badly twisting his left leg in its socket. He has a steel pin in his hip. He will probably not be able to drive his rig again. It sits in the back yard, like a gigantic bird that has flown home to roost. Leroy has been home in Kentucky for three months, and his leg is almost healed, but the accident frightened him and he does not want to drive any more long hauls. He is not sure what to do next. In the meantime, he makes things from craft kits. He started by building a miniature log cabin from notched Popsicle sticks. He varnished it and placed it on the TV set, where it remains. It reminds him of a rustic Nativity scene. Then he tried string art (sailing ships on black velvet), a macrame owl kit, a snap-together B-17 Flying Fortress, and a lamp made out of a model truck with a light fixture screwed in the top of the cab. At first the kits were diversions, something to kill time, but now he is thinking about building a full-scale log house from a kit. It would be considerably cheaper than building a regular house, and besides, Leroy has grown to appreciate how things are put together. He has begun to realize that in all the years he was on the road he never took time to examine anything. He was always flying past scenery.

"They won't let you build a log cabin in any of the new subdivisions," Norma Jean tells him.

"They will if I tell them it's for you," he says, teasing her. Ever since they were married, he has promised Norma Jean he would build her a new home one day. They have always rented, and the house they live in is small and nondescript. It does not even feel like a home, Leroy realizes now.

Norma Jean works at the Rexall drugstore, and she has acquired an amazing amount of information about cosmetics. When she explains to Leroy the three stages of complexion care, involving creams, toners, and moisturizers, he thinks happily of other petroleum products—axle grease, diesel fuel. This is a connection between himself and Norma Jean. Since he has been home, he has felt unusually tender about his wife and guilty over his long absences. But he can't tell what she feels about him. Norma Jean has never complained about his travelling; she has never made hurt remarks, like calling his truck a "widow-maker." He is reasonably certain she has been faithful to him, but he wishes she would celebrate his permanent homecoming more happily. Norma Jean is often startled to find Leroy at home, and he thinks she seems a little disappointed about it. Perhaps he reminds her too much of the early days of their marriage, before he went on the road. They had a child who died as an infant, years ago. They never speak about their memories of Randy, which have almost faded, but now that Leroy is home all the time they sometimes feel awkward around each other, and Leroy wonders if one of them should mention the child. He has the feeling that they are waking up out of a dream together—that they must create a new marriage, start afresh. They are lucky they are still married. Leroy has read that for most people losing a child destroys the marriage—or else he heard this on "Donahue." He can't always remember where he learns things anymore.

At Christmas, Leroy bought an electric organ for Norma Jean. She used to play the piano when she was in high school. "It don't leave you," she told him once. "It's like riding a bicycle."

The new instrument had so many keys and buttons that she was bewildered by it at first. She touched the keys tentatively, pushed some buttons, then pecked out "Chopsticks." It came out in an amplified foxtrot rhythm, with marimba sounds.

"It's an orchestra!" she cried.

The organ had a pecan-look finish and eighteen pre-set chords, with optional flute, violin, trumpet, clarinet, and banjo accompaniments. Norma Jean mastered the organ almost immediately. At first she played Christmas songs. Then she bought "The Sixties Songbook" and learned every tune in it, adding variations to each with the rows of brightly colored buttons.

"I didn't like these old songs back then," she said. "But I have this crazy feeling I missed something."

"You didn't miss a thing," said Leroy.

Leroy likes to lie on the couch and smoke a joint and listen to Norma Jean play "Can't Take My Eyes Off You" and "I'll Be Back." He is back again. After fifteen years on the road, he is finally settling down with the woman he loves. She is still pretty. Her skin is flawless. Her frosted curls resemble pencil trimmings.

Now that Leroy has come home to stay, he notices how much the town has changed. Subdivisions are spreading across western Kentucky like an oil slick. The sign at the edge of town says "Pop: 10,500"—only seven hundred more than it said twenty years ago. Leroy can't figure out who is living in all the new houses. The farmers who used to gather around the courthouse square on Saturday afternoons to play checkers and spit tobacco juice have gone. It has been years since Leroy has thought about the farmers, and they have disappeared without his noticing.

Leroy meets a kid named Stevie Hamilton in the parking lot at the new shopping center. While they pretend to be strangers meeting over a stalled car, Stevie tosses an ounce of marijuana under the front seat of Leroy's car.

Stevie is wearing orange jogging shoes and a T-shirt that says "CHATTA-
HOOCHEE SUPER-RAT." His father is a prominent doctor who lives in one of
the expensive subdivisions in a new white-columned brick house that looks
like a funeral parlor. In the phone book under his name there is a separate
number, with the listing "Teenagers."

"Where do you get this stuff?" asks Leroy. "From your pappy?"

"That's for me to know and you to find out," Stevie says. He is slit-eyed
and skinny.

"What else you got?"

"What you interested in?"

"Nothing special. Just wondered."

Leroy used to take speed on the road. Now he has to go slowly. He needs
to be mellow. He leans back against the car and says, "I'm aiming to build
me a log house, soon as I get time. My wife, though, I don't think she likes
the idea."

"Well, let me know when you want me again," Stevie says. He has a cigarette in his cupped palm, as though sheltering it from the wind. He takes a
long drag, then stomps it on the asphalt and slouches away.

Stevie's father was two years ahead of Leroy in high school. Leroy is
thirty-four. He married Norma Jean when they were both eighteen, and
their child Randy was born a few months later, but he died at the age of
four months and three days. He would be about Stevie's age now. Norma
Jean and Leroy were at the drive-in, watching a double feature ("Dr.
Strangelove" and "Lover Come Back"), and the baby was sleeping in the
back seat. When the first movie ended, the baby was dead. It was the sud-
den-infant-death syndrome. Leroy remembers handing Randy to a nurse at
the emergency room, as though he were offering her a large doll as a present. A dead baby feels like a sack of flour. "It just happens sometimes," said
the doctor, in what Leroy always recalls as a nonchalant tone. Leroy can
hardly remember the child anymore, but he still sees vividly a scene from
"Dr. Strangelove" in which the President of the United States was talking in
a folksy voice on the hot line to the Soviet Premier about the bombers accidentally headed toward Russia. He was in the War Room, and the world
map was lit up. Leroy remembers Norma Jean standing catatonically beside
him in the hospital and himself thinking, Who is this strange girl? He had
forgotten who she was. Now scientists are saying that crib death is caused
by a virus. Nobody knows anything, Leroy thinks. The answers are always
changing.

When Leroy gets home from the shopping center, Norma Jean's mother,

Mabel Beasley, is there. Until this year, Leroy has not realized how much time she spends with Norma Jean. When she visits, she inspects the closets and then the plants, informing Norma Jean when a plant is droopy or yellow. Mabel calls the plants "flowers," although there are never any blooms. She always notices if Norma Jean's laundry is piling up. Mabel is a short, overweight woman whose tight, brown-dyed curls look more like a wig than the actual wig she sometimes wears. Today she has brought Norma Jean an off-white dust ruffle she made for the bed; Mabel works in a custom-upholstery shop.

"This is the tenth one I made this year," Mabel says. "I got started and couldn't stop."

"It's real pretty," says Norma Jean.

"Now we can hide things under the bed," says Leroy, who gets along with his mother-in-law primarily by joking with her. Mabel has never really forgiven him for disgracing her by getting Norma Jean pregnant. When the baby died, she said that fate was mocking her.

"What's that thing?" Mabel says to Leroy in a loud voice, pointing to a tangle of yarn on a piece of canvas.

Leroy holds it up for Mabel to see. "It's my needlepoint," he explains. "This is a 'Star Trek' pillow cover."

"That's what a woman would do," says Mabel. "Great day in the morning!"

"All the big football players on TV do it," he says.

"Why, Leroy, you're always trying to fool me. I don't believe you for one minute. You don't know what to do with yourself—that's the whole trouble. Sewing!"

"I'm aiming to build us a log house," says Leroy. "Soon as my plans come."

"Like *heck* you are," says Norma Jean. She takes Leroy's needlepoint and shoves it into a drawer. "You have to find a job first. Nobody can afford to build now anyway."

Mabel straightens her girdle and says, "I still think before you get tied down y'all ought to take a little run to Shiloh."

"One of these days, Mama," Norma Jean says impatiently.

Mabel is talking about Shiloh, Tennessee. For the past few years, she has been urging Leroy and Norma Jean to visit the Civil War battleground there. Mabel went there on her honeymoon—the only real trip she ever took. Her husband died of a perforated ulcer when Norma Jean was ten, but Mabel, who was accepted into the United Daughters of the Confederacy in 1975, is still preoccupied with going back to Shiloh.

"I've been to kingdom come and back in that truck out yonder," Leroy says to Mabel, "but we never yet set foot in that battleground. Ain't that something? How did I miss it?"

"It's not even that far," Mabel says.

After Mabel leaves, Norma Jean reads to Leroy from a list she has made. "Things you could do," she announces. "You could get a job as a guard at Union Carbide, where they'd let you set on a stool. You could get on at the lumberyard. You could do a little carpenter work, if you want to build so bad. You could—"

"I can't do something where I'd have to stand up all day."

"You ought to try standing up all day behind a cosmetics counter. It's amazing that I have strong feet, coming from two parents that never had strong feet at all." At the moment, Norma Jean is holding on to the kitchen counter, raising her knees one at a time as she talks. She is wearing two-pound ankle weights.

"Don't worry," says Leroy "I'll do something."

"You could truck calves to slaughter for somebody. You wouldn't have to drive any big old truck for that."

"I'm going to build you this house," says Leroy. "I want to make you a real home."

"I don't want to live in any log cabin."

"It's not a cabin. It's a house."

"I don't care. It looks like a cabin."

"You and me together could lift those logs. It's just like lifting weights."

Norma Jean doesn't answer. Under her breath, she is counting. Now she is marching through the kitchen. She is doing goose steps.

Before his accident, when Leroy came home he used to stay in the house with Norma Jean, watching TV in bed and playing cards. She would cook fried chicken, picnic ham, chocolate pie—all his favorites. Now he is home alone much of the time. In the mornings, Norma Jean disappears, leaving a cooling place in the bed. She eats a cereal called Body Buddies, and she leaves the bowl on the table, with the soggy tan balls floating in a milk puddle. He sees things about Norma Jean that he never realized before. When she chops onions, she stares off into a corner, as if she can't bear to look. She puts on her house slippers almost precisely at nine o'clock every evening and nudges her jogging shoes under the couch. She saves bread heels for the birds. Leroy watches the birds at the feeder. He notices the peculiar way goldfinches fly past the window. They close their wings, then fall, then spread their wings to catch and lift themselves. He wonders if they close their eyes when they fall. Norma Jean closes her eyes when they are in bed. She wants the lights turned out. Even then, he is sure she closes her eyes.

He goes for long drives around town. He tends to drive a car rather carelessly. Power steering and an automatic shift make a car feel so small and inconsequential that his body is hardly involved in the driving process. His injured leg stretches out comfortably. Once or twice he has almost hit something, but even the prospect of an accident seems minor in a car. He cruises the new subdivisions, feeling like a criminal rehearsing for a robbery. Norma Jean is probably right about a log house being inappropriate here in the new subdivisions. All the houses look grand and complicated. They depress him.

One day when Leroy comes home from a drive he finds Norma Jean in tears. She is in the kitchen making a potato and mushroom-soup casserole, with grated-cheese topping. She is crying because her mother caught her smoking.

"I didn't hear her coming. I was standing here puffing away pretty as you please," Norma Jean says, wiping her eyes.

"I knew it would happen sooner or later," says Leroy, putting his arm around her.

"She don't know the meaning of the word 'knock,'" says Norma Jean. "It's a wonder she hadn't caught me years ago."

"Think of it this way," Leroy says. "What if she caught me with a joint?"

"You better not let her!" Norma Jean shrieks. "I'm warning you, Leroy Moffitt!"

"I'm just kidding. Here, play me a tune. That'll help you relax."

Norma Jean puts the casserole in the oven and sets the timer. Then she plays a ragtime tune, with horns and banjo, as Leroy lights up a joint and lies on the couch, laughing to himself about Mabel's catching him at it. He thinks of Stevie Hamilton—a doctor's son pushing grass. Everything is funny. The whole town seems crazy and small. He is reminded of Virgil Mathis, a boastful policeman Leroy used to shoot pool with. Virgil recently led a drug bust in a back room at a bowling alley, where he seized ten thousand dollars' worth of marijuana. The newspaper had a picture of him holding up the bags of grass and grinning widely. Right now, Leroy can imagine Virgil breaking down the door and arresting him with a lungful of smoke. Virgil would probably have been alerted to the scene because of all the racket Norma Jean is making. Now she sounds like a hard-rock band. Norma Jean is terrific. When she switches to a Latin-rhythm version of "Sunshine Superman," Leroy hums along. Norma Jean's foot goes up and down, up and down.

"Well, what do you think?" Leroy says, when Norma Jean pauses to search through her music.

"What do I think about what?"

His mind has gone blank. Then he says, "I'll sell my rig and build us a house." That wasn't what he wanted to say. He wanted to know what she thought—what she *really* thought—about them.

"Don't start in on that again," says Norma Jean. She begins playing "Who'll Be the Next in Line?"

Leroy used to tell hitchhikers his whole life story—about his travels, his home town, the baby. He would end with a question: "Well, what do you think?" It was just a rhetorical question. In time, he had the feeling that he'd been telling the same story over and over to the same hitchhikers. He quit talking to hitchhikers when he realized how his voice sounded—whining and self-pitying, like some teen-age-tragedy song. Now Leroy has the sudden impulse to tell Norma Jean about himself, as if he had just met her. They have known each other so long they have forgotten a lot about each other. They could become reacquainted. But when the oven timer goes off and she runs to the kitchen, he forgets why he wants to do this.

The next day, Mabel drops by. It is Saturday and Norma Jean is cleaning. Leroy is studying the plans of his log house, which have finally come in the mail. He has them spread out on the table—big sheets of stiff blue paper, with diagrams and numbers printed in white. While Norma Jean runs the vacuum, Mabel drinks coffee. She sets her coffee cup on a blueprint.

"I'm just waiting for time to pass," she says to Leroy, drumming her fingers on the table.

As soon as Norma Jean switches off the vacuum, Mabel says in a loud voice, "Did you hear about the datsun dog that killed the baby?"

Norma Jean says, "The word is 'dachsund.'"

"They put the dog on trial. It chewed the baby's legs off. The mother was in the next room all the time." She raises her voice. "They thought it was neglect."

Norma Jean is holding her ears. Leroy manages to open the refrigerator and get some Diet Pepsi to offer Mabel. Mabel still has some coffee and she waves away the Pepsi.

"Datsuns are like that," Mabel says. "They're jealous dogs. They'll tear a place to pieces if you don't keep an eye on them."

"You better watch out what you're saying, Mabel," says Leroy.

"Well, facts is facts."

Leroy looks out the window at his rig. It is like a huge piece of furniture gathering dust in the back yard. Pretty soon it will be an antique. He hears the vacuum cleaner. Norma Jean seems to be cleaning the living-room rug again.

Later, she says to Leroy, "She just said that about the baby because she caught me smoking. She's trying to pay me back."

"What are you talking about?" Leroy says, nervously shuffling blueprints.

"You know good and well," Norma Jean says. She is sitting in a kitchen chair with her feet up and her arms wrapped around her knees. She looks small and helpless. She says, "The very idea, her bringing up a subject like that! Saying it was neglect."

"She didn't mean that," Leroy says.

"She might not have *thought* she meant it. She always says things like that. You don't know how she goes on."

"But she didn't really mean it. She was just talking."

Leroy opens a king-sized bottle of beer and pours it into two glasses, dividing it carefully. He hands a glass to Norma Jean and she takes it from him mechanically. For a long time, they sit by the kitchen window watching the birds at the feeder.

Something is happening. Norma Jean is going to night school. She has graduated from her six-week body-building course and now she is taking an adult-education course in composition at Paducah Community College. She spends her evenings outlining paragraphs.

"First you have a topic sentence," she explains to Leroy. "Then you divide it up. Your secondary topic has to be connected to your primary topic."

To Leroy, this sounds intimidating. "I never was any good in English," he says.

"It makes a lot of sense."

"What are you doing this for anyhow?"

She shrugs. "It's something to do." She stands up and lifts her dumbbells a few times.

"Driving a rig, nobody cared about my English."

"I'm not criticizing your English."

Norma Jean used to say, "If I lose ten minutes' sleep, I just drag all day." Now she stays up late, writing compositions. She got a B on her first paper—a how-to theme on soup-based casseroles. Recently Norma Jean has been cooking unusual foods—tacos, lasagna, Bombay duck. She doesn't play the organ anymore, though her second paper was called "Why Music Is Important to Me." She sits at the kitchen table, concentrating on her outlines while Leroy plays with his log-house plans, practicing with a set of Lincoln Logs. The thought of getting a truckload of notched, numbered logs scares him, and he wants to be prepared. As he and Norma Jean work together at the kitchen table, Leroy has the hopeful thought that they are sharing something, but he knows he is a fool to think this. Norma Jean is miles away. He knows he is going to lose her. Like Mabel, he is just waiting for time to pass.

One day Mabel is there before Norma Jean gets home from work, and Leroy finds himself confiding in her. Mabel, he realizes, must know Norma Jean better than he does.

"I don't know what's got into that girl," Mabel says. "She used to go to bed with the chickens. Now you say she's up all hours. Plus her a-smoking. I like to died."

"I want to make her this beautiful home," Leroy says, indicating the Lincoln Logs. "I don't think she even wants it. Maybe she was happier with me gone."

"She don't know what to make of you, coming home like this."

"Is that it?"

Mabel takes the roof off his Lincoln Log cabin. "You couldn't get *me* in a log cabin," she says. "I was raised in one. It's no picnic, let me tell you."

"They're different now," says Leroy.

"I tell you what," Mabel says, smiling oddly at Leroy.

"What?"

"Take her on down to Shiloh. Y'all need to get out together, stir a little. Her brain's all balled up over them books."

Leroy can see traces of Norma Jean's features in her mother's face. Mabel's worn face has the texture of crinkled cotton, but suddenly she looks pretty. It occurs to Leroy that Mabel has been hinting all along that she wants them to take her with them to Shiloh.

"Let's all go to Shiloh," he says. "You and me and her. Come Sunday."

Mabel throws up her hands in protest. "Oh, no, not me. Young folks want to be by theirselves."

When Norma Jean comes in with groceries, Leroy says excitedly, "Your mama here's been dying to go to Shiloh for thirty-five years. It's about time we went, don't you think?"

"I'm not going to butt in on anybody's second honeymoon," Mabel says.

"Who's going on a honeymoon, for Christ's sake?" Norma Jean says loudly.

"I never raised no daughter of mine to talk that-a-way," Mabel says.

"You ain't seen nothing yet," says Norma Jean. She starts putting away boxes and cans, slamming cabinet doors.

"There a log cabin at Shiloh," Mabel says. "It was there during the battle. There's bullet holes in it."

"When are you going to *shut up* about Shiloh, Mama?" asks Norma Jean.

"I always thought Shiloh was the prettiest place, so full of history," Mabel goes on. "I just hoped y'all could see it once before I die, so you could tell me about it." Later, she whispers to Leroy, "You do what I said. A little change is what she needs."

"Your name means 'the king,'" Norma Jean says to Leroy that evening. He is trying to get her to go to Shiloh, and she is reading a book about another century.

"Well, I reckon I ought to be right proud."

"I guess so."

"Am I still king around here?"

Norma Jean flexes her biceps and feels them for hardness. "I'm not fooling around with anybody, if that's what you mean," she says.

"Would you tell me if you were?"

"I don't know."

"What does *your* name mean?"

"It was Marilyn Monroe's real name."

"No kidding!"

"Norma comes from the Normans. They were invaders," she says. She closes her book and looks hard at Leroy. "I'll go to Shiloh with you if you'll stop staring at me."

On Sunday, Norma Jean packs a picnic and they go to Shiloh. To Leroy's relief, Mabel says she does not want to come with them. Norma Jean drives, and Leroy, sitting beside her, feels like some boring hitchhiker she has picked up. He tries some conversation, but she answers him in monosyllables. At Shiloh, she drives aimlessly through the park, past bluffs and trails and steep ravines. Shiloh is an immense place, and Leroy cannot see it as a battleground. It is not what he expected. He thought it would look like a golf course. Monuments are everywhere, showing through the thick clusters of trees. Norma Jean passes the log cabin Mabel mentioned. It is surrounded by tourists looking for bullet holes.

"That's not the kind of log house I've got in mind," says Leroy apologetically.

"I know *that*."

"This is a pretty place. Your mama was right."

"It's O.K.," says Norma Jean. "Well, we've seen it. I hope she's satisfied."

They burst out laughing together.

At the park museum, a movie on Shiloh is shown every half hour, but they decide that they don't want to see it. They buy a souvenir Confederate flag for Mabel, and then they find a picnic spot near the cemetery. Norma Jean has brought a Styrofoam cooler, with pimiento sandwiches, soft drinks, and Yodels. Leroy eats a sandwich and then smokes a joint, hiding it behind the picnic cooler. Norma Jean has quit smoking altogether. She is picking cake crumbs from the cellophane wrapper, like a fussy bird.

Leroy says, "So the boys in gray ended up in Corinth. The Union soldiers zapped 'em finally. April 7, 1862."

They both know that he doesn't know any history; he is just talking about some of the historical plaques they have read. He feels awkward, like a boy on a date with an older girl. They are still just making conversation.

"Corinth is where Mama eloped to," says Norma Jean.

They sit in silence and stare at the cemetery for the Union dead and, beyond, at a tall cluster of trees. Campers are parked nearby bumper to bumper, and small children in bright clothing are cavorting and squealing. Norma Jean wads up the cake wrapper and squeezes it tightly in her hand. Without looking at Leroy, she says, "I want to leave you."

Leroy takes a bottle of Coke out of the cooler and flips off the cap. He holds the bottle poised near his mouth but cannot remember to take a drink. Finally he says, "No, you don't."

"Yes, I do."

"I won't let you."

"You can't stop me."

"Don't do me that way."

Leroy knows Norma Jean will have her own way. "Didn't I promise to be home from now on?" he says.

"In some ways, a woman prefers a man who wanders," says Norma Jean. "That sounds crazy, I know"

"You're not crazy."

Leroy remembers to drink from his Coke. Then he says, "Yes, you *are* crazy. You and me could start all over again. Right back at the beginning."

"We *have* started all over again," says Norma Jean. "And this is how it turned out."

"What did I do wrong?"

"Nothing."

"Is this one of those women's-lib things?" Leroy asks.

"Don't be funny."

The cemetery, a green slope dotted with white markers, looks like a subdivision site. Leroy is trying to comprehend that his marriage is breaking up, but for some reason he is wondering about white slabs in a graveyard.

"Everything was fine till Mama caught me smoking," says Norma Jean, standing up. "That set something off."

"What are you talking about?"

"*She* won't leave me alone—*you* won't leave me alone." Norma Jean seems to be crying, but she is looking away from him. "I feel eighteen again. I can't face that all over again." She starts walking away. "No, it *wasn't* fine. I don't know what I'm saying. Forget it."

Leroy takes a lungful of smoke and closes his eyes as Norma Jean's words sink in. He tries to focus on the fact that thirty-five hundred soldiers died on the grounds around him. He can only think of that war as a board game with plastic soldiers. Leroy almost smiles, as he compares the Confederates' daring attack on the Union camps and Virgil Mathis's raid on the bowling alley. General Grant, drunk and furious, shoved the Southerners back to Corinth, where Mabel and Jet Beasley were married years later, when Mabel was still thin and good-looking. The next day, Mabel and Jet visited the battleground, and then Norma Jean was born, and then she married Leroy and they had a baby, which they lost, and now Leroy and Norma Jean are here at the same battleground. Leroy knows he is leaving out a lot. He is leaving out the insides of history. History was always just names and dates to him. It occurs to him that building a house out of logs is similarly empty—too simple. And the real inner workings of a marriage, like most of history, have escaped him. Now he sees that building a log house is the dumbest idea he could have had. It was clumsy of him to think Norma Jean would want a log house. It was a crazy idea. He'll have to think of something else, quickly. He will wad the blueprints into tight balls and fling them into the lake. Then he'll get moving again. He opens his eyes. Norma Jean has moved away and is walking through the cemetery, following a serpentine brick path.

Leroy gets up to follow his wife, but his good leg is asleep and his bad leg still hurts him. Norma Jean is far away, walking rapidly toward the bluff by the river, and he tries to hobble toward her. Some children run past him, screaming noisily. Norma Jean has reached the bluff, and she is looking out over the Tennessee River. Now she turns toward Leroy and waves her arms. Is she beckoning to him? She seems to be doing an exercise for her chest muscles. The sky is unusually pale—the color of the dust ruffle Mabel made for their bed.

14

COMMCOMM

GEORGE SAUNDERS

George Saunders was born in Amarillo, Texas, in 1958, but he spent his formative years growing up on the South Side of Chicago. He earned his BS in geophysical engineering from the Colorado School of Mines in 1981 and then undertook a string of itinerant and eclectic jobs that included working as an oil prospector in Sumatra, a doorman in Beverly Hills, a roofer in Chicago, a convenience store clerk, a guitarist in a Texas country and western band, and a knuckle-puller in a West Texas slaughterhouse. Saunders ultimately settled into a position at Radian International, an environmental engineering firm, where he served as a technical writer and geophysical engineer until he hired on as an assistant professor at Syracuse University in 1997. Saunders has published three story collections, *CivilWarLand in Bad Decline* (1996), *Pastoralia* (2000), and *In Persuasion Nation* (2006), as well as a novella, *The Brief and Frightening Reign of Phil* (2005). A children's book, *The Very Persistent Gappers of Frip*, was published in 2000, and a collection of essays, *The Braindead Megaphone*, in 2007. His fiction and essays have appeared in *The New Yorker, Story, McSweeney's, Harper's, GQ*, and *The Guardian*. Saunders's science-fiction-infused burlesques of consumerism, corporate America, and bureaucracy have earned him considerable acclaim. He won the National Magazine Award for Fiction in 1994, 1996, 2000, 2004, and 2010, and second prize in the O. Henry Awards in 1997. In 2006, he was awarded a MacArthur Fellowship and a Guggenheim Fellowship.

Tuesday morning, Jillian from Disasters calls. Apparently an airman named Loolerton has poisoned a shitload of beavers. I say we don't kill beavers, we harvest them, because otherwise they nibble through our Pollution Control Devices (P.C.D.s) and polluted water flows out of our Retention Area and into the Eisenhower Memorial Wetland, killing beavers.

"That makes sense," Jillian says, and hangs up.

The press has a field day. "AIR FORCE KILLS BEAVERS TO SAVE BEAVERS," says one headline. "MURDERED BEAVERS SPEAK OF AIR FORCE CRUELTY," says another.

"We may want to PIDS this," Mr. Rimney says.

I check the files: There's a circa-1984 tortoise-related PIDS from a base in Oklahoma. There's a wild-horse-related PIDS from North Dakota. Also useful is a Clinton-era PIDS concerning the inadvertent destruction of a dove breeding ground.

From these I glean an approach: I *admit* we harvested the beavers. I *concede* the innocence and creativity of beavers. I *explain* the harvesting as a regrettable part of an ongoing effort to prevent Pollution Events from impacting the Ottowattamie. Finally I *pledge* we'll find a way to preserve our P.C.D.s without, in the future, harming beavers. We are, I say, considering transplanting the beaver population to an innovative Beaver Habitat, to be installed upstream of the Retention Area.

I put it into PowerPoint. Rimney comes back from break and reads it.

"Innovative Beaver Habitat?" he says.

"I say we're considering," I say.

"All hail to the king of PIDS," he says.

I call Ed at the paper; Jason, Heather, and Randall at NewsTen, Action-Seven, and NewsTeamTwo, respectively; then Larry from Facilities. I have him reserve the Farragut Auditorium for Wednesday night, and just like that I've got a fully executable PIDS and can go joyfully home to my wife and our crazy energized loving kids.

Just kidding.

I wish.

I walk between Mom and Dad into the kitchen, make those frozen mini-steaks called SmallCows. You microwave them or pull out their ThermoTab. When you pull the ThermoTab, something chemical happens and the SmallCows heat up. I microwave. Unfortunately, the ThermoTab erupts and when I take the SmallCows out they're coated with a green, fibrous liquid. So I make ramen.

"You don't hate the Latvians, do you?" Dad says to me.

"It was not all Latvians done it," Mom says.

I turn on Tape 9, "Omission/Partial Omission." When sadness-inducing events occur, the guy says, invoke your Designated Substitute Thought-stream. Your D.S.T. might be a man falling off a cliff but being caught by a group of good friends. It might be a bowl of steaming soup, if one likes soup. It might be something as distractive/mechanical as walking along a row of cans, kicking them down.

"And don't even hate them two," Mom says. "They was just babies."

"They did not do that because they was Latvian," says Dad. "They did it because of they had poverty and anger."

"What the hell," says Mom. "Everything turned out good."

My D.S.T. is tapping a thin rock wall with a hammer. When that wall cracks, there's another underneath. When that wall cracks, there's another underneath.

"You hungry?" Mom says to Dad.

"Never hungry anymore," he says.

"Me too," she says. "Plus I never pee."

"Something's off but I don't know what," Dad says.

When that wall cracks, there's another underneath.

"Almost time," Mom says to me, her voice suddenly nervous. "Go upstairs."

I go to my room, watch some World Series, practice my PIDS in front of the mirror.

What's going on down there I don't watch anymore: Mom's on the landing in her pajamas, calling Dad's name, a little testy. Then she takes a bullet in the neck, her hands fly up, she rolls the rest of the way down, my poor round Ma. Dad comes up from the basement in his gimpy comic trot, concerned, takes a bullet in the chest, drops to his knees, takes one in the head, and that's that.

Then they do it again, over and over, all night long.

Finally it's morning. I go down, have a bagel.

Our house has this turret you can't get into from inside. You have to go outside and use a ladder. There's nothing up there but bird droppings and a Nixon-era plastic Santa with a peace sign scratched into his toy bag. That's where they go during the day. I climbed up there once, then never again: jaws hanging open, blank stares, the two of them sitting against the wall, insulation in their hair, holding hands.

"Have a good one," I shout at the turret as I leave for work.

Which I know is dumb, but still.

When I get to work, Elliot Giff from Safety's standing in the Outer Hall. Giff's a GS-9 with pink glasses and an immense underchin that makes up a good third of the length of his face.

"Got this smell-related call?" he says.

We step in. There's definitely a smell. Like a mildew/dirt/decomposition thing.

"We have a ventilation problem," Rimney says stiffly.

"No lie," Giff says. "Smells like something crawled inside the wall and died. That happened to my aunt."

"Your aunt crawled inside a wall and died," Rimney says.

"No, a rat," says Giff. "Finally she had to hire a Puerto Rican fellow to drill a hole in her wall. Maybe you should do that."

"Hire a Puerto Rican fellow to drill a hole in your aunt's wall," Rimney says.

"I like how you're funny," Giff says. "There's joy in that."

Giff's in the ChristLife Reënactors. During the reënactments, they eat only dates and drink only grape juice out of period-authentic flasks. He says that this weekend's reënactment was on the hill determined to be the most topographically similar to Calvary in the entire Northeast. I ask who he did. He says the guy who lent Christ his mule on Palm Sunday. Rimney says it's just like Giff to let an unemployed Jew borrow his ass.

"You're certainly not hurting me with that kind of talk," Giff says.

"I suppose I'm hurting Christ," says Rimney.

"Not hardly," says Giff.

On Rimney's desk is a photo of Mrs. Rimney before the stroke: braless in a tank top, hair to her waist, holding a walking stick. In the photo, Rimney's wearing a bandanna, pretending to toke something. Since the stroke, he works his nine or ten, gets groceries, goes home, cooks, bathes Val, does the dishes, goes to bed.

My feeling is, no wonder he's mean.

Giff starts to leave, then doubles back.

"You and your wife are in the prayers of me and our church," he says to Rimney. "Despite of what you may think of me."

"You're in my prayers, too," says Rimney. "I'm always praying you stop being so sanctimonious and miraculously get less full of shit."

Giff leaves, not doubling back this time.

Rimney hasn't liked Giff since the day he suggested that Rimney could cure Mrs. Rimney if only he'd elevate his prayerfulness.

"All right," Rimney says. "Who called him?"

Mrs. Gregg bursts into tears and runs to the ladies'.

"I don't get why all the drama," says Rimney.

"Hello, the base is closing in six months," says Jonkins.

"Older individuals like Mrs. G. are less amenable to quick abrupt changes," says Verblin.

When Closure was announced, I found Mrs. G. crying in the Outer Hall. What about Little Bill? she said. Little Bill had just bought a house. What about Amber, pregnant with twins, and her husband, Goose, drunk every night at the Twit? What about Nancy and Vendra? What about Jonkins and Al? There's not a job to be had in town, she said. Where are all these sweet people supposed to go?

I've sent out more than thirty résumés, been store to store, chatted up Dad's old friends. Even our grocery's half-closed. What used to be Produce is walled off with plywood. On the plywood is a sign: "If We Don't Have It, Sorry."

CommComm's been offered a group transfer to NAIVAC Omaha. But Mom and Dad aren't allowed into the yard, much less to Omaha. And when I'm not around they get agitated. I went to Albany last March for a seminar and they basically trashed the place. Which couldn't have been easy. To even disturb a drape for them is a big deal. I walked in and Mom was trying to tip over the coffee table by flying through it on her knees and Dad was inside the couch, trying to weaken the springs via repetitive fast spinning. They didn't mean to but were compelled. Even as they were flying/spinning they were apologizing profusely.

"Plus it really does stink in here," Little Bill says.

"Who all is getting a headache, raise your hand," says Jonkins.

"Oh, all right," Rimney says, then goes into my cubicle and calls Odors. He asks why they can't get over immediately. How many odors do they have exactly? Has the entire base suddenly gone smelly?

I walk in and he's not talking into the phone, just tapping it against his leg.

He winks at me and asks loudly how Odors would like to try coördinating Community Communications while developing a splitting headache in a room that smells like ass.

All afternoon it stinks. At five, Rimney says let's hope for the best overnight and wear scuba gear in tomorrow, except for Jonkins, who, as far as Jonkins, they probably don't make scuba gear that humongous.

"I cannot believe you just said that," says Jonkins.

"Learn to take a joke," Rimney says, and slams into his office.

I walk out with Jonkins and Mrs. Gregg. The big flag over the Dirksen excavation is snapping in the wind, bright-yellow leaves zipping past as if weighted.

"I hate him," says Jonkins.

"I feel so bad for his wife," says Mrs. Gregg.

"First you have to live with him, then you have a stroke?" says Jonkins.

"And then you still have to live with him?" says Mrs. Gregg.

The Dirksen Center for Terror is the town's great hope. If transferred to the Dirksen, you keep your benefits and years accrued and your salary goes up, because you're Homeland Security instead of Air Force. We've all submitted our Requests for Transfer and our Self-Assessment Worksheets and now we're just waiting to hear.

Except Rimney. Rimney heard right away. Rimney knows somebody who knows somebody. He was immediately certified Highly Proficient and is Dirksen-bound, which, possibly, is another reason everybody hates him.

My feeling is, good for him. If he went to Omaha, imagine the work. He and Val have a routine here, contacts, a special van, a custom mechanical bed. Imagine having to pick up and start over somewhere else.

"Home, home, home," says Mrs. Gregg.

"PIDS, PIDS, PIDS," I say.

"Oh, you poor thing," says Mrs. Gregg.

"If I had to stand up in front of all those people," says Jonkins, "I'd put a bullet in my head." Then there's a long silence.

"Shit, man, sorry," he says to me.

The Farragut's full. I *admit, concede, explain,* and *pledge.* During the Q. & A., somebody says if the base is closing, why spend big bucks on a Beaver Habitat? I say because the Air Force is committed to insuring that, postClosure, all Air Force sites remain environmentally viable, prioritizing both species health and a diverse life-form mix.

Afterward Rimney's back by the snacks. He says is there anything I can't PIDS? I say probably not. I've PIDSed sexual-harassment cases, a cracked hazardous-waste incinerator, half a dozen jet-fuel spills. I PIDSed it when General Lemaster admitted being gay, retracted his admission, then retracted his retraction, all in the same day, before vanishing for a week with one of his high-school daughter's girlfriends.

"You might have noticed earlier that I was not actually calling Odors," Rimney says.

"I did notice that," I say.

"Thing I like about you, you're a guy who understands life gets complicated," he says. "Got a minute? I need to show you something."

I follow him back to CommComm. Which still stinks. I follow him into the copier closet, which stinks even worse.

In the closet is something big, in bubble wrap.

"Note to self," he says. "Bubble wrap? Not smell-preventing."

He slits open the bubble wrap. Inside is this giant dirt clod. Sticking out of the clod is a shoe. In the shoe is a foot, a rotted foot, in a rotted sock.

"I don't get it," I say.

"Found down in the Dirksen excavation," he says. "Thought I could stash them in here a few days, but phew. Can you believe it?"

He slits open a second bubble-wrap package. There's another guy, not enclodded, cringed up, in shredded pants, looking like he's been dipped in mustard. This one's small, like a jockey.

"They look old-timey to me," Rimney says.

They do look old-timey. Their shoes are big crude shoes with big crude nails.

"So you see our issue," he says. "Dirksen-wise."

I don't. But then I do.

The Racquetball Facility was scrapped due to someone found an Oneida nose-ring portion on the site. Likewise the proposed Motor Pool Improvement, on account of a shard of Colonial crockery.

If a pottery shard or partial nose ring can scrap a project, think what a couple of Potentially Historical corpses/mummies will do.

"Who else knows?" I say.

"The contractor," Rimney says. "Rick Granis. You know Rick?"

I've known Rick since kindergarten. I remember how mad he'd get if anyone called his blanket anything but his binkie. Now he's got an Escalade and a summer house on Otissic Lake.

"But Rick's cool with it," he says. "He'll do whatever."

He shows me Rick's Daily Historical-Resource Assessment Worksheet. Under "Non-Historical Detritus," Rick's written, "Two contemp soda bottles, one contemp flange." Under "Evidence of Pre-Existing Historical/Cultural Presence," he's written, "Not that I know of."

Rimney says that a guy like me, master of the public-presentation aspect, could be a great fit at the Dirksen. As I may know, he knows somebody who knows somebody. Do I find the idea of Terror work at all compelling?

I say sure, yes, of course.

He says, thing is, they're just bodies. The earth is full of bodies. Under every building in the world, if you dig deep enough, is probably a body. From the looks of it, someone just dumped these poor guys into a mass grave. They're not dressed up, no coffins, no dusty flower remains, no prayer cards.

I say I'm not sure I totally follow.

He says he's thinking a respectful reburial, somewhere they won't be found, that won't fuck up the Dirksen.

"And tell the truth," he says, "I could use some help."

I think of Tape 4, "Living the Now." What is the Now Situation? How can I pull the pearl from the burning oyster? How can the "drowning boy" be saved? I do an Actual Harm Analysis. Who would a reburial hurt? The mummy guys? They're past hurt. Who would it help? Rimney, Val Rimney, all future Dirksen employees.

Me.

Mom, Dad.

Dad worked thirty years at Gallup Chain, with his dad. Then they discontinued Automotive. Only Bike remained. A week after his layoff, Grandpa died. Day of the wake, Dad got laid off too. Month later, we found out Jean was sick. Jean was my sister, who died at eight. Her last wish was Disneyland. But money was tight. Toward the end, Dad borrowed money from Leo, the brother he hated. But Jean was too sick to travel. So Dad had an Army friend from Barstow film all of Disney on a Super-8. The guy walked the whole place. Jean watched it and watched it. Dad was one of these auto-optimists. To hear him tell it, we'd won an incredible last-minute victory. Hadn't we? Wasn't it something, that we could give Jeanie such a wonderful opportunity?

But Jean had been distilled down to like pure honesty.

"I do wish I could have gone, though," she said.

"Well, we practically did," Dad said, looking panicked.

"No, but I wish we really did," she said.

After Jean died, we kept her room intact, did a birthday thing for her every year, started constantly expecting the worst. I'd come home from a high-school party and Mom would be sitting there with her rosary, mumbling, praying for my safe return. Even a dropped shopping bag, a broken jar of Prego, would send them into a funk, like: Doom, doom, of course, isn't this the way it always goes for us?

Eight years later came the night of the Latvians.

So a little decent luck for Mom and Dad doesn't seem like too much to ask.

"About this job thing," I say.

"I will absolutely make it happen," he says.

The way we do it is we carry them one at a time out to his special van. He's got a lift in there for Val. Not that we need the lift. These guys are super-light. Then we drive out to the forest behind Missions. We dig a hole, which is not easy, due to roots. I go in, he hands them down very gentle. They're so stiff and dry it's hard to believe they can still smell.

We backfill, kick some leaves around, drag over a small fallen tree.

"You O.K.?" he says. "You look a little freaked."

I ask should we maybe say a prayer.

"Go ahead," he says. "My feeling is, these guys have been gone so long they're either with Him or not. If there even is a Him. Might be real, might not. To me? What's real? Val. When I get home tonight, there she'll be, waiting. Hasn't eaten yet, needs her bath. Been by herself the whole day. That, to me? Is real."

I say a prayer, lift my head when done.

"I thank you, Val thanks you," he says.

In the van, I do a Bad Feelings Acknowledgment re the reburial. I visualize my Useless Guilt as a pack of black dogs. I open the gate, throw out the Acknowledgment Meat. Pursuing the Meat, the black dogs disappear over a cliff, turning into crows (i.e., Neutral/Non-Guilty Energy), which then fly away, feeling Assuaged.

Back at CommComm, we wash off the shovels, Pine-Sol the copier closet, throw open the windows, check e-mail while the place airs out.

Next morning, the stink is gone. The office just smells massively like Pine-Sol. Giff comes in around eleven, big bandage on his humongous under-chin.

"Hey, smells super in here today," he says. "Praise the Lord for that, right? And all things."

"What happened to your chin?" says Rimney. "Zonk it on a pew while speaking in tongues?"

"We don't speak in tongues," says Giff. "I was just shaving."

"Interesting," Rimney says. "Goodbye."

"Not goodbye," says Giff. "I have to do my Situational Follow-Up. What in your view is the reason for the discontinued nature of that crappo smell you all previously had?"

"A miracle," says Rimney. "Christ came down with some Pine-Sol."

"I don't really go for that kind of talk," says Giff.

"Why not pray I stop?" says Rimney. "See if it works."

"Let me tell you a like parable," Giff says. "This one girl in our church? Had this like perma-smile? Due to something? And her husband, who was non-church, was always having to explain that she wasn't really super-happy, it was just her malady. It was like the happier she looked, the madder he got. Then he came to our church, guess what happened?"

"She was miraculously cured and he was miraculously suddenly not angry," says Rimney. "God reached down and fixed them both, while all over the world people who didn't come to your church remained in misery, weeping."

"Well, no," says Giff.

"And that's not technically a parable," says Verblin.

"See, but you're what happens when man stays merely on his own plane," says Giff. "Man is made bitter. Look, I'm not claiming I'm not human and don't struggle. Heck, I'm as human as you. Only I struggle, when I struggle, with the help of Him that knows no struggle. Which is why sometimes I maybe seem so composed or, you might say, together. Everyone in our church has that same calm. It's not just me. It's just Him, is how we say it."

"How calm would you stay if I broke your neck?" says Rimney.

"Ron, honestly," Jonkins says.

"Quiet, Tim," Rimney says to Jonkins. "If we listen closely, we may hear the call of the North American extremist loony."

"Maybe you're the extremist due to you think you somehow created your own self," says Giff.

"Enough, this is a place of business," says Rimney.

Then Milton Gelton comes in. Gelton's a GS-5 in Manual Site Aesthetics Improvement. He roams the base picking up trash with a sharp stick. When he finds a dead animal, he calls Animals. When he finds a car battery, he calls Environmental.

"Want to see something freaky?" he says, holding out his bucket. "Found behind Missions?"

In the bucket is a yellow-black human hand.

"Is that a real actual hand of someone?" says Amber.

"At first I thought glove," Gelton says. "But no. See? No hand-hole. Just solid."

He pokes the hand with a pen to demonstrate the absence of a hand-hole.

"You know what else I'm noting. as weird?" Giff says. "In terms of that former smell? I can all of a sudden smell it again."

He sniffs his way down to the bucket.

"Yoinks, similar," he says.

"I doubt this is a Safety issue," says Rimney.

"I disagree," says Giff. "This hand seems like it might be the key to our Possible Source of your Negative Odor. Milton, can you show me the exact locale where you found this at?"

Out they go. Rimney calls me in. How the hell did we drop that fucker? Jesus, what else did we drop? This is not funny, he says, do I realize we could go to jail for this? We knowingly altered a Probable Historical Site. At the very least, we'll catch hell in the press. As for the Dirksen, this gets out, goodbye Dirksen.

I eat lunch in the Eating Area. Little Bill's telling about his trip to Omaha. He stayed at a MinTel. The rooms are closet-size. They like slide you in. You're allowed two slide-outs a night. After that it's three dollars a slide-out.

Rimney comes out, says he's got to run home. Val's having leg cramps. When she has leg cramps, the only thing that works is hot washrags. He's got a special pasta pot and two sets of washrags, one blue, one white. One set goes on her legs, while the other set heats.

With Rimney gone, discipline erodes. Out the window I see Verblin sort of mincing to his car. A yardstick slides out of his pants. When he stoops to get the yardstick, a print cartridge drops out of his coat. When he bends to pick up the cartridge, his hat falls off, revealing a box of staples.

At three, Ms. Durrell from Environmental calls. Do we have any more of those dioxin coloring books? Do I know what she means? It's not a new spill, just reawakened concern over an old spill. I know what she means. She means "Donnie Dioxin: Badly Misunderstood But Actually Quite Useful Under Correct Usage Conditions."

I'm in Storage looking for the books when my cell rings.

"Glad I caught you," Rimney says stiffly. "Can you come out to Missions? I swung by on the way back and, boy, oh boy, did Elliot ever find something amazing."

"Is he standing right there?" I say.

"O.K., see you soon," he says, and hangs up.

I park by the Sputnik-era jet-on-apedestal. The fake pilot's head is facing backward and a twig's been driven up his nose. Across the fuselage some kid's painted, "This thing looks like my pennis if my pennis has wings."

It starts to flurry. Giff's been at the grave with a shovel. So far, it's just the top of the jockey's head sticking out, and part of the enclodded guy's foot.

"Wow," I say.

"Wow is correct," Rimney says.

"Thanks be to Scouts," Giff says. "See? Footprints galore. Plus tire tracks. To me? It's like a mystery or one of those deals where there's more than meeting the eyes. Because where did these fellows come from? Who put them here? Why did your office smell so bad, in an off way similar to that gross way that hand smelled? In my logic? I ask, Where locally is somewhere deep that's recently been unearthed or dug into? What I realized? The Dirksen. That is deep, that is new. What do you think? I'll get with Historical tomorrow, see what used to be where the Dirksen is at now."

I helped Rimney get Val home from the hospital after the stroke, watched the two of them burst into tears at the sight of her mechanical bed.

He looks worse than that now.

"Fuck it. I'm going to tell him, trust him. What do you think?" he says.

My feeling is no, no, no. Giff's not exactly the King of Sense of Humor. Last year, I was the only non-church person at his Christmas party. The big issue was, somebody on Giff's wife's side had sent their baby a stuffed DevilChild from Hell from the cartoon "HellHood." The DevilChild starts each episode as a kindly angel with a lisp. Then something makes him mad and he morphs into a demon and starts speaking with an Eastern European accent while running around stabbing uptight people in the butt with a red-hot prod.

"As for me and my house, this little guy has no place here," Giff had said. "Although Cyndi apparently feels otherwise."

Cyndi I would describe as pretty but flinchy.

"Andy doesn't see it as the Devil," she said. "He just likes it."

"Well, I do see it as the Devil," Giff said. "And I don't like it. And here in this house a certain book tells us the role of the father/husband. Am I right?"

"I guess so," she said.

"You guessing so, like Pastor Mike says, is sypromatic of your having an imperfect understanding of what the Lord has in mind for our family, though," he said. "Right? Right, Pastor Mike?"

"Well, it's certainly true that a family can only have one head," said a guy in a Snoopy sweater who I guessed was Pastor Mike.

"O.K., tough guy," Cyndi said to Giff, and stomped off, ringing the tree ornaments.

I can see Giff's wheels turning. Or trying to. He's not the brightest. I once watched him spend ten minutes trying to make a copy on a copier in the Outer Hall which was unplugged and ready for Disposal.

"Wait, are you saying you guys did this?" he says.

Rimney says Giff has a wife, Giff has a baby—would a transfer to the Dirksen be of interest? Maybe Giff's aware that he, Rimney, knows somebody who knows somebody?

"Oh, my gosh, you guys did do it," Giff says.

He lets the shovel fall and walks toward the woods, as if so shocked he has to seek relief in the beauty of nature. Out in the woods are three crushed toilets. Every tenth bush or so has a red tag on it, I have no idea why.

"All's I can say is wow," Giff says.

"They're dead, man," Rimney says. "What do you care?"

"Yes, but who was it shaped these fellows?" says Giff. "You? Me? Look, I'm going to speak frank. I think I see what's going on here. Both you guys took recent hard hits. One had a wife with a stroke, the other a great tragic loss of their parents. So you got confused, made a bad call. But He redeemeth, if only we open our hearts. Know how I know? It happened to me. I also took a hard hit this year. Because guess what? In terms of my wife? I'm just going to say it. Our baby is not my baby. Cyndi had a slipup with this friend of ours, Kyle. I found out just before Christmas, which was why I was such a fart at our party. That put me in a total funk—we were like match and gas. I was so mad there was a darkness upon me. Poor thing had bruises all up her arms, due to I started pinching her. In her sleep, or sometimes I would get so mad and just come up quick and do it. Then, January tenth, I'd had enough, and I prayed, I said, 'Lord, I am way too small, please take me up into You, I don't want to do this anymore.' And He did it. I dropped as if shot. And when I woke? My heart was changed. All glory goes to Him. I mean, it was a literal release in my chest. All my hate about the baby was gone and all of a sudden Andy was just my son for real."

"Nice story," says Rimney.

"It's not a story. It happened to me for real in my life," says Giff. "Point is? I had it in me to grow. We all do! I'm not all good, but there's a good part of me. My fire may be tiny, but it's a fire just the same. See what I mean? Same like you. Do you know that good part? Have you met it, that part of you that is all about Truth, that is called, in how we would say it, your Christ-portion? My Christ-portion knew that pinching was wrong. How does your Christ-portion feel about this sneaky burial thingy? I mean honestly. In a perfect world, is that what you would have chose to do?"

This catches me a little off guard.

"Is this where I go into a seizure and you heal me by stroking my dick?" Rimney says.

Giff blinks at this, turns to me.

"Think these things up in your heart," he says softly. "Treasure them around. See what it is. Then be in touch, come to our church, if you want. I am hopeful that you will come to your Truth."

Suddenly my eyes tear up.

And I don't even know why.

"This is about my wife, jackass," says Rimney.

"'Do what's right, come what may,'" Giff says. "That's what it says on all our softball sweatshirts, and I believe it. And on the back? 'Say no thanks to Mr. Mere Expedience.' Good words for you, friend."

Rimney's big. Once when mad he smacked the overhang on the way to Vending and there's still a handprint up there. Once he picked up one end of the photocopier so Mrs. Gregg could find her earring, and a call came in and he had this big long conversation with Benefits while still holding up the copier.

"Cross me on this, you'll regret it," he says.

"Get thee behind me," says Giff.

So, a little tense.

My phone rings. Ms. Durrell again. She's got a small vocal outraged group coming at four to eat her alive. Where the hell am I? Those dioxin books? Had something to do with a donkey, "Donkey Dioxin, Who Got the Job Done"? Or it was possibly an ape or possum or some such shit? She remembers a scene at the end with some grateful villagers, where the ape/possum/donkey/whatever gave the kids a ride, and also the thing came with a CD?

"Go," Rimney says. "Elliot and I will work this out."

By the time I get the books out of Storage and over to Environmental it's after five.

I clock out, race home through our wincing little town. Some drunks outside the Twit are heaving slushballs up at the laughing neon Twit. Blockbuster has a new program of identifying all videos as either Artsy or Regular. Two beautiful girls in heels struggle down to the banks of the Ottowattamie, holding each other up. Why are they going down there? It's dusk and that part of the river's just mud and an old barge.

I wish I could ask them but I don't have time. When I'm late Mom and Dad race around shouting, "Where? Where? Where?" It always ends in this bitter mutual crying. It's just one of their things. Like when it rains, they go up to the ceiling and lie there facing up. Like when feeling affectionate, they run full speed toward each other and pass through, moaning/laughing.

The night of the Latvians I was out with Cleo from Vehicles. We went parking, watched some visiting Warthogs practice their night-firing. Things heated up. She had a room on the side of a house, wobbly wooden stairs leading up. Did I call, say I'd be late, say I might not be back at all? No, I did not. Next morning I came home, found the house taped off. For the body locations, the cops didn't use chalk. There was just a piece of loose-leaf on the stairs labelled "Deceased Female" and one on the kitchen floor labelled "Deceased Male."

I tell myself, If I'd been home, I'd be dead, too. The Latvians had guns. They came in quick, on crack, so whacked out they forgot to even steal anything.

Still. Mom's sciatica was acting up. She'd just had two teeth pulled. At the end, on the steps, on her back, she kept calling my name, as in, Where is he? Did they get him too? Next day, on the landing, I found the little cotton swab the dentist had left in her mouth.

So if they want me home right after work I'm home right after work.

They're standing at the kitchen window, looking out at the old ballbearing plant. All my childhood, discarded imperfect ball bearings rolled down the hill into our yard. When the plant closed, a lathe came sliding down, like a foot a day, until it hit an oak.

"Snowing like a mother," Dad says.

"Pretty, but we can't go out," says Mom.

"Too old, I guess," Dad says sadly.

"Or something," says Mom.

I set three places. They spend the whole dinner, as usual, trying to pick up their forks. Afterward they crowd under the floor lamp, the best part of their night. When they stand in direct heat, it doesn't make them warmer, just makes them vividly remember their childhoods.

"Smell of melted caramel," Mom says.

"The way I felt first time I seen a Dodger uniform in color," says Dad.

Dad asks me to turn up the dimmer. I do, and the info starts coming too fast for grammar.

"Working with beets purple hands Mother finds that funny," says Mom.

"Noting my boner against ticking car, Mr. Klemm gives look of you-are-rubbing-your-boner, mixed sense of shame/pride, rained so hard flooded gutters, rat wound up in the dog bowl," says Dad.

They step out of the light, shake it off.

"He's always talking about boners," says Mom.

"Having a boner is a great privilege," says Dad.

"You had your share," says Mom.

"I should say so," says Dad. "And will continue to, I hope, until the day I die."

Having said "die," Dad blinks. Whenever we see a murder on TV, they cover their eyes. Whenever a car backfires, I have to coax them out from under the couch. Once a bird died on the sill and they spent the entire day in the pantry.

"Until the day you die," Mom says, as if trying to figure out what the words mean.

Before they can ask any questions, I go outside and shovel.

From all over town comes the sound of snowplows, the scraping plus the beeping they do when reversing. The moon's up, full, with halo. My phone rings in my parka pocket.

"We have a situation," Rimney says. "Can you step outside?"

"I am outside," I say.

"Oh, there you are," he says.

The special van's coming slowly up the street.

"New plan," he says, still on the phone, parking now. "What's done is done. We can save the Dirksen or lose it. Minimize the damage or maximize."

He gets out, leads me around to the sliding door.

You didn't, I think. You did not dig those poor guys up again. Does he think Historical is stupid? Does he think Historical, getting a report of mummies, finding only a recently filled hole, is going to think, Oh, Giff, very funny, you crack us up?

"Not the mummies," I say.

"I wish," he says, and throws open the door.

Lying there is Giff, fingers clenched like he's trying to cling to a ledge, poor pink glasses hanging off one ear.

I take a step back, trip on the curb, sit in a drift.

"We took a walk, things got out of hand," he says. "Shit, shit, shit. I tried to reason with him, but he started giving me all his Christian crap. Something snapped, honestly. It just got away from me. You've probably had that happen?"

"You killed him?" I say.

"An unfortunate thing transpired, after which he died, yes," Rimney says.

Thrown in there with Giff is a big rock, partly wrapped in bloody paper towels.

I ask did he call the police. He says if he planned on calling the police, would he have thrown Giff in back of the freaking van? He says we've got to think pragmatic. He did it, he fucked up, he knows that. He'll be paying for it the rest of his life, but no way is Val paying for it. If he goes to jail, what happens to Val? A state home? No, no, no, he says. Dead is dead, he can't change that. Why kill Val as well?

"What do we do with this guy?" he says. "Think, think."

"We?" I say. "You."

"Oh God, oh shit," he says. "I can't believe I killed somebody. Me, I did it. Jesus, wow. O.K. O.K."

Snow's blowing in over Giff, melting on his glasses, clumping up between his pants and bare leg.

"You know Val, you like Val, right?" Rimney says.

I do like Val. I remember her at Mom and Dad's funeral, in her wheelchair. She had Rimney lift one of her hands to my arm, did this sad little pat pat pat.

"Because here's the thing," Rimney says. "Dirksen-wise? You're all set. I submitted my rec. It's in the system. Right? Why not take it? Prosper, get a little something for yourself, find a wife, make some babies. The world's shit on you enough, right? You did not do this, I did. I shouldn't have come here. How about pretend I didn't?"

I stand up, start to do a Moral Benefit Eval, then think, No, no way, do not even think about doing that stupid shit now.

The bandage on Giff's underchin flips up, showing his shaving scar.

"Because who was he?" says Rimney. "Who was he really? Was he worth a Val? Was he even a person? He, to me, was just a dumb-idea factory. That's it."

Poor Giff, I think. Poor Giff's wife, poor Giff's baby.

Poor Val.

Poor everybody.

"Don't fuck me on this," Rimney says. "Are you going to fuck me on this? You are, aren't you? Fine. Fine, then."

He turns away, slams the van door shut, emits this weird little throat-sound, like he can't live with what he's done and would like to end it all, only can't, because ending it all would make him even more of a shit.

"I feel I'm in a nightmare," he says.

Then he crashes the Giff-rock into my head. I can't believe it. Down I go. He swung so hard he's sitting down too. For a second we both sit there, like playing cards or something. I push off against his face, crawl across the yard, get inside, bolt the door.

"I don't like that," says Dad, all frantic. "I did not like seeing that."

"People should not," Mom says. "That is not a proper way."

When terrified, they do this thing where they flicker from Point A to Point B with no interim movement. Mom's in the foyer, then in the kitchen, then at the top of the stairs.

"You better get to the hospital," Dad says.

"Take this poor kid with you," Mom says.

"He just suddenly showed up," Dad says.

Somebody's on the couch. It takes me a second to recognize him. Giff.

Or something like Giff: fish-pale, naked, bloody dent in his head, squinting, holding his glasses in one hand.

"Whoa," he says. "Is this ever not how I expected it would be like."

"What what would be like?" says Dad.

"Death and all?" he says.

Dad flickers on and off: smiling in his chair, running in place, kneeling near the magazine rack.

"You ain't dead, pal, you're just naked," says Dad.

"Naked, plus somebody blammed you in the head," says Mom.

"Do they not know?" Giff says.

I give him a look, like, Please don't. We're just enjoying a little extra time. I'm listening to their childhood stories, playing records from their courtship days, staring at them when they're not looking, telling them how good they were with me and Jean, how safe we always felt.

"Don't you love them?" Giff says.

I remember them outside the funeral home the day we buried Jean, Mom holding Dad up, Dad trying to sit on a hydrant, wearing his lapel button, his lapel photo-button of little smiling Jean.

"Then better tell them," Giff says. "Before it's too late. Because watch."

He stands, kind of shaky, hobbles over, breathes in my face.

Turns out when the recently dead breathe in your face they show you the future.

I see Mom and Dad trapped here forever, reënacting their deaths night after night, more agitated every year, finally to the point of insanity, until, in their insanity, all they can do is rip continually at each other's flesh, like angry birds, for all eternity.

I tell them.

"Very funny," says Mom.

"Cut it out," Dad says.

"We're a little sad sometimes," says Mom. "But we definitely ain't dead."

"Are we?" Dad says.

Then they get quiet.

"Holy crap," Dad says.

Suddenly they seem to be hearing something from far away.

"Jeez, that's better," Dad says.

"Feels super," Mom says.

"Like you had a terrible crick and then it went away," Dad says.

"Like your dirty dress you had on for the big party all of a sudden got clean," says Mom.

They smile, step through the wall, vanish in two little sudden blurps of light.

Giff's pale and bent, glowing/shimmering, taller than in life, a weird breeze in his hair that seems to be coming from many directions at once.

"There is a glory, but not like how I thought," he says. "I had it all wrong. Mostly wrong. Like my mind was this little basket, big flood pouring in, but all I got was this hint of greater water?"

"You were always a nice person," I say.

"No, I was not," he says. "Forced my little mini-views down everybody's throat. Pinched my wife! And now it's so sad. Because know what he did? Rimney? Typed her a note, like it was from me, saying I was leaving, due to I didn't love her, due to that Kyle thing. But that is so not true! I loved her all through that. But now, rest of her life, she's going to be thinking that of me, that I left her and the baby, when we were just getting over that pinching thing."

His eyes fill with tears and his hair stops blowing and he crushes his pink glasses in his hand.

"Go see her," I say. "Tell her the truth."

"Can't," he says. "You just get one."

"One what?" I say.

"Visitation or whatever?" he says.

I think, So why'd you come here?

He just smiles, kind of sad.

Then the front window implodes and Rimney climbs through with a tire iron.

"It's going to happen now," Giff says.

And it does. It takes two swings. It doesn't hurt, really, but it's scary, because it's happening to me, me, me, me, the good boy in school, the boy who felt lilacs were his special flower, the boy who, when poor Jean was going, used to sneak off to cry in the closet.

As I go, there's an explosion of what I can only call truth/energy flood. I can't exactly convey it, because you're still in that living/limited state, so lucky/unlucky, capable of smelling rain, rubbing palm against palm, having some new recently met someone suddenly brighten upon seeing you.

Rimney staggers to the door, unbolts it, stands looking out.

I pass through him and see that even now all his thoughts are of Val, desperate loving frightened thoughts of how best to keep her safe.

Giff and I cross the yard hand in hand, although like fifteen feet apart. Where are we going? I have no idea. But we're going there fast, so fast we're basically skimming along Trowman Street, getting simultaneously bigger/ lighter, and then we're flying, over Kmart/Costco Plaza, over the width of Wand Lake, over the entire hilly area north of town.

Below us now is Giff's house: snow on the roof, all the lights on, pond behind it, moon in the pond.

Giff says/thinks, Will you?

And I say/think, I will.

She's at the table doing bills, red-eyed, the note at her feet, on the floor. She sees me and drops her pen. Am I naked, am I pale, is my hair blowing? Yes and yes and yes. I put one bare foot on the note.

A lie, I say. Elliot's dead, sends his love. Rimney did it. Rimney. Say it.

Rimney, she says.

That's all the chance I get. The thing that keeps us flying sucks me out of the house. But as I go I see her face.

Rejoining Giff on high I show him her face. He is glad, and now can go.

We both can go.

We go.

Snow passes through us, gulls pass through us. Tens of towns, hundreds of towns stream by below, and we hear their prayers, grievances, their million signals of loss. Secret doubts shoot up like tracers, we sample them as we fly through: a woman with a too-big nose, a man who hasn't closed a sale in months, a kid who's worn the same stained shirt three days straight, two sisters worried about a third who keeps saying she wants to die. All this time we grow in size, in love, the distinction between Giff and me diminishing, and my last thought before we join something I can only describe as Nothing-Is-Excluded is, Giff, Giff, please explain, what made you come back for me?

He doesn't have to speak, I just know, his math emanating from inside me now: Not coming back, he would only have saved himself. Coming back, he saved Mom, Dad, me. Going to see Cyndi, I saved him.

And, in this way, more were freed.

That is why I came back. I was wrong in life, limited, shrank everything down to my size, and yet, in the end, there was something light-craving within me, which sent me back, and saved me.

15

Mines

SUSAN STRAIGHT

Susan Straight's fiction draws from her experiences growing up in poly-ethnic communities in California's Inland Empire, where she taught refugees, gang members and high school dropouts with the Inland Empire Job Corps. She was born in Riverside, California, in 1960 and earned her BA at the University of Southern California in 1981 and her MFA in creative writing at the University of Massachusetts at Amherst in 1984. She published *Aquaboogie: A Novel in Stories*, in 1990, and won the Milkweed National Fiction Prize. Straight has since published five novels: *I Been in Sorrow's Kitchen and Licked Out All the Pots* (1993), *Blacker than a Thousand Midnights* (1995), *The Gettin' Place* (1997), *Highwire Moon* (2001), and *A Million Nightingales* (2006). She has also published essays on issues of race, gender, and parenthood. Straight's short story "Mines," included in this collection, was included in *The Best American Short Stories 2003*. She has also received a Lannan Literary Award for Fiction (2007) and an Edgar Allan Poe Award (2008). Since 1988, she has taught creative writing at the University of California Master of Fine Arts in Creative Writing & Writing for the Performing Arts program at the Riverside campus.

They can't shave their heads every day like they wish they could, so their tattoos show through stubble. Little black hairs like iron filings stuck on magnets. Big roundhead fool magnets.

The Chicano fools have gang names on the sides of their skulls. The white fools have swastikas. The Vietnamese fools have writing I can't read. And the black fools—if they're too dark, they can't have anything on their heads. Maybe on the lighter skin at their chest, or the inside of the arm.

Where I sit for the morning shift at my window, I can see my nephew in his line, heading to the library. Square-head light-skinned fool like my brother. Little dragon on his skull. Nothing in his skull. Told me it was cause he could breathe fire if he had to. ALFONSO tattooed on his arm.

"What, he too gotdamn stupid to remember his own name?" my godfather said when he saw it. "Gotta look down by his elbow every few minutes to check?"

Two names on his collarbone: twins. Girls. EGYPT and MOROCCO. Seventeen and he's got kids. He's in here for eight years. Riding in the car when somebody did a drive-by. Backseat. Law say same as pulling the trigger.

Ten o'clock. They line up for shift between classes and voc ed. Dark blue backs like fool dominoes. Shuffling boots. Fred and I stand in the doorway, hands on our belts, watching. From here, seeing all those heads with all those blue-green marks like bruises, looks like everybody got beat up big time. Reyes and Michaels and the other officers lead their lines past the central guard station, and when the wards get closer, you can see all the other tattoos. Names over their eyebrows, teardrops on their cheeks, words on their necks, letters on their fingers.

One Chicano kid has PERDÓNEME MI ABUELITA in fancy cursive on the back of his neck. Sorry my little grandma. I bet that makes her feel much better.

When my nephew shuffles by, he grins and says softly, "Hey, Auntie Clarette."

I want to slap the dragon off the side of his stupid skull.

Fred says, "How's your fine friend Tika? The one with green eyes?"

I roll my brown eyes. "Contacts, okay?"

I didn't tell him I saw Tika last night, at Lincoln Elementary. "How can you work at the youth prison? All those young brothers incarcerated by the system?" That's what Tika said to me at Back-to-School Night. "Doesn't it hurt you to be there?"

"Y'all went to college together, right?" Fred says.

"Mmm-hmm." Except she's teaching African-American studies there now, and I married Ray. He quit football and started drywalling with his uncle.

"Ray went with y'all, too, didn't he? Played ball till he blew out his knee?"

The wind's been steady for three days now, hot fall blowing all the tumbleweeds across the empty fields out here, piling them up against the chain-link until it looks like hundreds of heads to me. Big-ass naturals from the seventies, when I squint and look toward the east. Two wards come around the building and I'm up. "Where you going?"

The Chicano kid grins. "TB test."

"Pass."

He flashes it, and I see the nurse's signature. The blister on his forearm looks like a quarter somebody slid under the skin. Whole place has TB so bad we gotta get tested every week. My forearm's dotted with marks like I'm a junkie.

I lift up my chin. I feel like a guy when I do it, but it's easier than talking sometimes. I don't want to open my mouth. "Go ahead," Fred calls out to them.

"Like you got up and looked."

Fred lifts his eyebrows at me. "Okay, Miss Thang."

It's like a piece of hot link burning in my throat. "Shut the fuck up, Fred." That's what Michaels and Reyes always say to him. I hear it come out like that, and I close my eyes. When I get home now, and the kids start their homework, I have to stand at the sink and wash my hands and change my mouth. My spit, everything, I think. Not a prayer. More like when you cool down after you run. I watch the water on my knuckles and think: No TB, no cussing, no meds. Because a couple months after I started at Youth Authority, I would holler at the kids, "Take your meds."

Flintstones, Mama, Danae would say.

Fred looks up at the security videos. "Tika still single, huh?"

"Yeah."

She has a gallery downtown, and she was at the school to show African art. She said to me, "Doesn't it hurt your soul? How can you stand it?"

I didn't say anything at first. I was watching Ray Jr. talk to his teacher. He's tall now, fourth grade, and he smells different to me when he wakes up in the morning.

I told Tika, "I work seven to three. I'm home when the kids get off the bus. I have bennies."

She just looked at me.

"Benefits." I didn't say the rest. Most of the time now Ray stays at his cousin Lafayette's house. He hasn't worked for a year. He and Lafayette say construction is way down, and when somebody is building, Mexican drywallers get all the business in Rio Seco.

When I got this job, Ray got funny. He broke dishes, washing them. He wrecked clothes, washing them. He said, "That ain't a man—that's a man's job." He started staying out with Lafayette.

Tika said, "Doesn't it hurt you inside to see the young brothers?"

For my New Year's resolution I told myself: Silence is golden. At work, cause me talking just reminds them I'm a woman. With Ray and my mother and everyone else except my kids. I looked at Tika's lipstick, and I shouted in my head: I make thirty-five grand a year! I've got bennies now! Ray never had health care, and Danae's got asthma. I don't get to worry about big stuff like you do, cause I'm worrying about big stuff like I do. Pay the bills, put gas in the van, buy groceries. Ray Jr. eats three boxes of Cheerios every week, okay?

"Fred Harris works there. And J.C. and Marcus and Beverly."

Tika says, "Prison is the biggest growth industry in California. They're determined to put everyone of color behind a wall."

Five days a week, I was thinking, I drive past the chain-link fence and past J.C. at the guard gate. Then Danae ran up to me with a book. They had a book sale at Back-to-School Night. Danae wanted an *American Girl* story. $4.95.

Tika walked away. I went to the cash register. Five days a week, I park my van and walk into the walls. But they're fences with barbed wire and us watching. Everything. Every face.

"Nobody in the laundry?" I ask, and Fred shakes his head. Laundry is where they've been fighting this week. Black kid got his head busted open Friday in there, and we're supposed to watch the screens. The bell rings, and we get up to stand in the courtyard for period change. We can hear them coming from the classrooms, doors slamming and all those boots thumping on the asphalt. The wind moving their stiff pants around their ankles, it's so hard right now. I watch their heads. Every day it's a scuffle out here, and we're supposed to listen to who's yelling, or worse, talking that quiet shit that sets it off.

All the damn heads look the same to me, when I'm out here with my stick down by my side. Light ones like Alfonso and the Chicano kids and the Vietnamese, all golden brown. Dark little guys, some Filipino, even, and then the white kids, almost green they're so pale. But all the tattoos like scabs. Numbers over their eyebrows and FUCK YOU inside their lips when they pull them down like clowns.

The wind whips through them and they all squint but don't move. My head is hurting at the temples, from the dust and wind and no sleep. Laundry. The wards stay in formation, stop and wait, boots shining like dark foreheads. I hear muttering and answers and shit-talking in the back, but nobody starts punching. Then the bell rings and they march off.

"Youngblood. Stop the mouth," Fred calls from behind me. He talks to the wards all the time. Old school. Luther Vandross-loving and hair fading back like the tide at the beach—only forty-two, but acts like he's a grandpa from the South. "Son, if you'da thought about what you were doing last year, you wouldn't be stepping past me this year." They look at him like they want to spit in his face. "Son, sometimes what the old people say is the gospel truth, but you wasn't in church to hear." They would knock him in the head if they could. "Son, you're only sixteen, but you're gonna have to go across the street before you know it, you keep up that attitude."

Across the street is Chino. Men's Correctional Facility. The wards laugh and sing back to Fred like they're Snoop Doggy Dogg: "I'm on my way to Chino, I see no, reason to cry . . ."

He says, "Lord knows Mr. Dogg ain't gonna be there when you are."

The Chicano kids talk Spanish to Reyes, and he looks back at them like a statue wearing shades. The big guy, Michaels, used to play football with Ray. He has never looked into my face since I got here. My nephew knows who he is. He says, "Come on, Michaels, show a brotha love, Michaels. Lemme have a cigarette. You can't do that for a brotha, man? Brothaman?"

Alfonso thinks this is a big joke. A vacation. Training for life. His country club.

I don't say a damn thing when he winks at me. I watch them walk domino lines to class and to the kitchen and the laundry and the field. SLEEPY and SPOOKY and DRE DOG and SCOOBY and G DOG and MONSTER all tattooed on their arms and heads and necks. Like a damn kennel. Nazis with spiderwebs on their elbows, which is supposed to mean they killed somebody dark. Asians with spidery writing on their arms, and I don't know what that means.

"I'ma get mines, all I gotta say, Auntie Clarette," my nephew always said when he was ten or eleven. "I ain't working all my life for some shitty car and a house. I'ma get mines now."

I can't help it. Not supposed to look out for him, but when they change, when they're in the cafeteria, I watch him. I don't say anything to him. But I keep seeing my brother in his fool forehead, my brother and his girlfriend in their apartment, nothing but a couch and a TV. Always got something to drink, though, and plenty weed.

Swear Alfonso might think he's better off here. Three hots and a cot, the boys say.

We watch the laundry screens, the classrooms, and I don't say anything to Fred for a long time. I keep thinking about Danae's reading tonight, takes twenty minutes, and then I can wash a load of jeans and pay the bills.

"Chow time, baby," Fred says, pushing it. Walking behind me when we line everybody up. They all mumbling, like a hundred little air conditioners, talking shit to each other. Alfonso's lined up with his new homeys, lips moving steady as a cartoon. I know the words are brushing the back of the heads in line, the Chicano kids from the other side of Rio Seco, and I walk over with my stick. "Move," I say, and the sweaty foreheads go shining past like windshields in a traffic jam.

"Keep moving," I say louder.

Alfonso grins. My brother said, Take care my boy, Clarette. It's on you.

No, I want to holler back at him. You had seventeen years to take care of him. Why I gotta do your job? How am I supposed to make sure he don't get killed? I feel all the feet pounding the asphalt around me and I stand in the shade next to Fred, tell him "Shut up" real soft, soft as Alfonso still talking yang in the line.

I have a buzzing in my head. Since I got up at five to do two loads of laundry and make a hot breakfast and get the kids ready for school. When I get home, I start folding the towels and see the bus stop at the corner. I wait for the kids to come busting in, but all the voices fade away down the street like little radios. Where are these kids? I go out on the porch and the sidewalk's empty, and my throat fills up again like that spicy meat's caught. Ray Jr. knows to meet Danae at her classroom. The teacher's supposed to make sure they're on the bus. Where the hell are they?

I get back in the van and head toward the school, and on Palm Avenue I swear I see Danae standing outside the barbershop, waving at me when I'm stopped at the light.

"Mama!" she calls, holding a cone from the Dairy Queen next door. "Mama!"

The smell of aftershave coats my teeth. And Ray Jr.'s in the chair, his hair's on the tile floor like rain clouds.

My son. His head naked, a little nick on the back of his skull, when he sees me and ducks down. Where someone hit him with a rock last year in third grade. The barber rubs his palms over Ray Jr.'s skin and it shines.

"Wax him up, man," Ray says, and I move on him fast. His hair under my feet, too, I see now, lighter and straighter. Brown clouds. The ones with no rain.

"How could you?" I try to whisper, but I can't whisper. Not after all day of hollering, not stepping on all that hair.

The barber, old guy I remember from football games, said, "Mmm-mmm-mmm."

"The look, baby. Everybody wants the look. You always working on Danae's hair, and Ray-Ray's was looking ragged." Ray lifts both hands, fingers out, like he always does. Like it's a damn sports movie and he's the ref. Exaggerated. "Hey, I thought I was helping you out."

I heard the laughing in his mouth. "Like Mike, baby. Like Ice Cube. The look. He said some punks was messin with him at school."

I go outside and look at Ray Jr.'s head through the grimy glass. I can't touch his skull. Naked. How did it get that naked means tough? Naked like when they were born. When I was laying there, his head laced with blood and wax.

My head pounding when I put it against the glass, and I feel Danae's sticky fingers on my elbow. "Mama, I got another book at school today. *Sheep in a Jeep.*"

When we were done reading, she fell asleep. My head hurt like a tight swim cap. I went into Ray Jr.'s room and felt the slickness of the wax.

In the morning I'm so tired my hands are shaking when I comb Danae's hair. "Pocahontas braids," she says, and I feel my thumbs stiff when I twist the ties on the ends. I stare at my own forehead, all the new hair growing out, little explosions at my temples. Bald. Ray's bald now. We do braids and curls or Bone Strait and half the day in the salon, and they don't even comb theirs? Big boulder heads and dents all in the bone, and that's supposed to look good?

I gotta watch all these wards dressed in dark blue work outfits, baggy-ass pants, big old shirts, and then get home and all the kids in the neighborhood are wearing dark blue Dickies; Ray is wearing dark blue Dickies and a Big Dog shirt.

Like my friend Saronn says, "They wear that, and I'm supposed to wear stretch pants and a sports bra and high heels? Give me a break."

Buzzing in my head. Grandmere said we all got the pressure, inherited. Says I can't have salt or coffee, but she doesn't have to eat lunch here or stay awake looking at screens. Get my braids done this weekend, feels like my scalp has stubbles and they're turned inside poking my brain.

Here sits Fred across from me, still combs his hair even though it looks like a black cap pushed way too far back on his head. He's telling me I need to come out to the Old School club with him and J.C. and Beverly sometime. They play Cameo and the Bar-Kays. "Your Love Is Like the Holy Ghost."

"What you do for Veterans Day? Kids had the day off, right?" he says.

"I worked an extra shift. My grandmere took the kids to the cemetery." I drink my coffee. Metal like the pot. Not like my grandmere's coffee, creole style with chicory. She took the kids to see her husband's grave, in the military cemetery. She told Danae about World War II and all the men that died, and Danae came home crying about all the bodies under the ground where they'd walked.

Six—they cry over everything. Everything is scary. I worked the extra shift to pay off my dishwasher. Four hundred dollars at Circuit City. Plus installation.

I told Ray Jr., "Oh, yeah, you gonna load this thing. Knives go in like this. Plates like this."

He said, "Why you yelling, Mama? I see how to do it. I did it at Grandmere's before. Ain't no big thing. I like the way they get loaded in exactly the same every time. I just don't let Daddy know."

He grinned. I wanted to cry.

"Used piano in the paper cost $500. Upright."

"What the hell is that?" Ray said on the phone. Hadn't come by since the barber.

I tried to think. "The kind against the wall, I guess. Baby grand is real high."

"For you?"

"For Ray Jr. Fooled around on the piano at school, and now he wants to play like his grandpere did in Baton Rouge."

Ray's voice got loud. "Uh-uh. You on your own there. Punks hear he play the piano, they gon kick his ass. Damn, Clarette."

I can get louder now, since YA. "Oh, yeah. He looks like Ice Cube, nobody's gonna mess with him. All better, right? Damn you, Ray."

I slam the phone down so hard the back cracks. Cheap purple Target cordless. $15.99.

Next day I open the classifieds on the desk across from Fred and start looking. Uprights. Finish my iron coffee. Then I hear one of the wards singing, "Three strikes you're out, tell me what you gonna do?"

Nate Dogg. That song. "Never Leave Me Alone."

This ward has a shaved black head like a bowling ball, a voice like church. "Tell my son all about me, tell him his daddy's sorry . . ."

Shows us his pass at the door. "Yeah, you sorry all right," Fred says.

The ward's face changes all up. "Not really, man. Not really."

Mamere used to say, "Old days, the men go off to the army. Hard time, let me tell you. They go off to die, or they come back. But if they die, we get some money from the army. If they come back, they get a job on the base. Now them little boys, they go off to the prison just like the army. Like they have to. To be a man. They go off to die, or come back. But they ain't got nothin. Nothin either way."

Wards in formation now. The wind is still pushing, school papers cart-wheeling across the courtyard past the boots. I check Alfonso, in the back again, like every day, like a big damn Candyland game with Danae and it's never over cause we keep picking the same damn cards over and over cause it's only two of us playing.

I breathe in all the dust from the fields. Hay fields all dry and turned when I drive past, the dirt skimming over my windshield. Two more hours today. Wards go back to class. Alfonso lifts his chin at me, and I stare him down. Fred humming something. What is it?

"If this world were mine, I'd make you my queen . . ." Old Luther songs. "Shut up, Fred," I tell him. I don't know if he's trying to rap or not. He keeps asking me about Ray.

"All them braids look like a crown," he says, smiling like a player.

"A bun," I say. He knows we have to wear our hair tight back for security. And Esther just did my braids Sunday. That's gotta be why my temples ache now.

"They went at it in the laundry room again Sunday," Fred says, looking at the screens.

I stare at the prison laundry, the huge washers and dryers like an old cemetery my grandmere took me to in Louisiana once, when I was a kid. All those dead people in white stone chambers, with white stone doors. I see the wards sorting laundry and talking, see J.C. in there with them.

"Can't keep them out of there," I say, staring at their hands on the white T-shirts. "Cause everybody's gotta have clean clothes."

At home I stand in front of my washer, dropping in Danae's pink T-shirt, her Old Navy capris. One trip to Old Navy in spring, one in fall all I can afford. And her legs getting longer. Jeans and jeans. Sometimes they take so long to dry I just sit down on the floor in front of the dryer and read the paper, cause I'm too tired to go back out to the couch. If I sit down on something soft, I'll fall asleep, and the jeans will be all wrinkled in the morning.

Even the wards have pressed jeans.

In the morning, my forehead feels like it's full of hot sand. Gotta be the flu. I don't have time for this shit. I do my hair first, before I wake up Danae and Ray Jr. I pull the braids back and it hurts, so I put a softer scrunchie around the bun.

Seen a woman at Esther's Sunday. She says, "You got all that pretty hair, why you scrape it back so sharp?"

"Where I work."

"You cookin somewhere?"

"Nope. Sittin. Lookin at fools."

She pinched up her eyes. "At the jail?"

"YA."

Then she pulls in her chin. "They got my son. Two years. He wasn't even doin nothin. Wrong place, wrong time."

"YA wrong place, sure."

She get up and spit off Esther's porch. "I come back later, Esther."

Esther says, "Don't trip on Sisia. She always mad at somebody."

Shouldn't be mad at me. "I didn't got her son. I'm just tryin to make sure he comes home. Whenever."

Esther nodded and pulled those tittle hairs at my temple. I always touch that part when I'm at work. The body is thy temple. My temple. Where the blood pound when something goes wrong.

The laundry's like people landed from a tornado. Jean legs and shirt sleeves all tangled up on my bed.

"You foldin?" I say. Ray Jr. pulling out his jeans and lay them in a pile like logs. Then he slaps them down with his big hand.

"They my clothes."

"Don't tell your daddy."

"I don't tell him much."

His hair growing back on his skull. Not like iron-filings. Like curly feathers. Still soft.

Next day Fred put his comb away and say, "Give a brotha some time."

"I gave him three years."

"That's all Ray get? He goin through some changes, right?"

"We have to eat. Kids got field trips and books to buy."

Three years. The laundry piled on my bed like a mound over a grave. On the side where Ray used to sleep. The homework. Now piano lessons.

Fred says, "So you done?"

"With Ray?" I look right at him. "Nope. I'm just done."

"Oh, come on, Clarette. You ain't but thirty-five. You ain't done."

"You ain't Miss Cleo."

"You need to come out to the Comedy Club. No, now, I ain't sayin with me. We could meet up there. Listen to some Earth, Wind and Fire. Elements of life, girl."

Water. They missed water. Elements of life: bottled water cause I don't want the kids drinking tap. Water pouring out the washing machine. Water inside the new dishwasher—I can hear it sloshing around in there.

I look out at the courtyard. Rogue tumbleweed, a small one, rolling across the black.

"Know what, Clarette? You just need to get yours. I know I get mines. I have me some fun, after workin here all day. Have a drink, talk to some people, meet a fine lady. Like you."

"Shut up, Fred. Here they come."

Reyes leading in his line and I see two boys go down, start punching. I run into the courtyard with my stick out and can't get to them, cause their crews are working now. The noise—it's like the crows in the pecan grove by Grandmere's, all the yelling, but not lifting up to the sky. All around me. I pull off shirts, Reyes next to me throwing kids out to Michaels and Fred. Shoving them back, and one shoves me hard in the side. I feel elbows and hands. Got to get to the kid down, and I push with my stick

Alfonso. His face bobbing over them like a puppet. "Get out of here!" I yell at him, and he's grinning. I swear. I reach down and the Chicago kid is on top, black kid under him, and I see a boot. I pull the top kid and hear Reyes hollering next to me, voice deep as a car stereo in my ear.

Circle's opening now. Chicano kid is down, he's thin, bony wrists green-laced with writing. The black kid is softer, neck shining, and he rolls over. But then he throws himself at the Chicano kid again, and I catch him with my boot. Both down. Reyes kicks the Chicano kid over onto his belly and holds him. I have to do the same thing. His lip split like a pomegranate. Oozing red. Some mother's son. It's hard not to feel the sting in my belly. Reyes's boy yelling at me in Spanish. I kick him one more time, in the side.

I bend down to turn mine over, get out my cuffs, and one braid pulls loose. Falls by my eyes. Bead silver like a raindrop. I see a dark hand reach for it, feel spit spray my forehead. Bitch. My hair pulled from my temple. My temple.

My stick. Blood on my stick. Michaels and Reyes take the wards. I keep my face away from all the rest, and a bubble of air or blood or something throbs next to my eyebrow. Where my skin pulled from my skull, for a minute. Burning now, but I know it's gon turn black like a scab, underneath my hair. I have to stand up. The sky turns black, then gray, like always. They're all heading to lockdown. I make sure they all see me spit on the cement before I go back inside. Fred stands outside talking to the shift supervisor, Williams, and I know he's coming in here in a minute, so I open the classifieds again and put my finger on Upright.

Across Divides

16

Skinless

AIMEE BENDER

Aimee Bender's father was a psychiatrist and her mother was a choreographer and dance teacher—parental influences that she says contributed to her interest in unconscious subtexts, surreal imagery, and deeply psychological elements in her fiction. She was born in Los Angeles, California, in 1969 and she received her BA from the University of California, San Diego, and an MFA in creative writing from University of California, Irvine. She has published two collections of short stories, *The Girl in the Flammable Skirt* (1998) and *Willful Creatures* (2005), as well as two novels, *An Invisible Sign of My Own* (2000) and *The Particular Sadness of Lemon Cake: A Novel* (2010), and a novella, *The Third Elevator* (2009). Her short stories have appeared in *Granta, GQ, Harper's, Tin House, McSweeney's, The Paris Review*, and other print and online publications. The recipient of two Pushcart Prizes, Bender teaches creative writing at the University of Southern California's doctoral creative writing program.

Renny's phone privileges were revoked when they discovered a swastika carved into his bed board. He had been at Ocean House for three days. The staff, arguing in the Off-Limits Room with their hands warmed by white Styrofoam coffee cups, took an hour before they decided on this as a punishment. Jill Cohen, the activities director, went into his room while Renny was playing pool with Damon, the one who'd stabbed himself in the thigh, and turned the swastika into four boxes and then put a roof and a chimney on top. She wanted to make smoke coming out of the chimney, but the fork did not carve curls well, so she left the hearth cold.

Jill drove forty-five minutes every other day to run the evening activities for the group of runaway teenagers living at Ocean House. This was her first job out of college, and she had been thrilled when they accepted her. "The kids are supposed to be really troubled but really great," she'd told her college roommate, who was silently walking out the door with a banana box filled with books in her arms. "Good luck," they had said to each other, and then college was over. Jill had a new boyfriend named Matthew who liked to eat foods so spicy they made him cough. His body was covered with fair, shining hair, and in bed, with the side lamp on, he seemed to almost glow. When he held her while they made love, she would sometimes imagine scratching off his skin, scratching repeatedly with her nails until the layers peeled off and she discovered that beneath that sheath of flesh, he was made entirely out of pearl.

How? she'd splutter, and he'd laugh and kiss light into her mouth.

She often remembered the day she first grew breasts, how her usually olive skin was covered with red, crisscrossing stretch marks, like a newly revealed secret map to the treasures of her body.

Renny ran away from home because his older brother Jordan came to visit. Returning home from a friend's house one afternoon, Renny found Jordan's green truck parked crooked, taking over the driveway. Renny kept going as if he didn't even recognize the house. As he walked, he gathered a globule of spit in his mouth in case he saw anyone who looked, in any way, dark. He walked straight, over an hour, to the sagging framework of Ocean House because you only had to stay for a couple weeks, the food was supposed to be decent, and if you were lucky, he'd heard you might even meet other members of the Resistance there.

Jill hung up the phone with her mother, and looked searchingly at Matthew. He was sitting on the sofa, balancing the remote control on his knee. "You know," she said, "that if we had kids, they'd be rightfully Jewish. You know that, right?"

He nodded. His eyes were on the TV.

"I think it would be okay with me, as long as you don't think it's totally important to teach them all about Christ, do you? You don't believe in Christ, do you?"

"Not really, but Jill, we're not getting married."

"I know," she said, pulling on her earlobe, "but just in case?"

"Jill," he said, "we're not getting married."

But she couldn't get the wedding out of her head. There would be both a rabbi and a priest, and the priest would have no hairs on the backs of his hands, like a young boy. She walked over to Matthew, eyebrows pulling down. "If you know that for sure," she said, "then why are we going out?"

Matthew drew her onto his lap. "How long till you have to leave for work?"

"Half hour," she said, absently rubbing the top of his wrist. "Just in case," she said, "it's mainly a cultural thing."

"Half an hour is plenty of time," he said and he reached his hand up her shirt. "Shhh, Jill, sshh."

Renny's father was dead, but his brother was eight years older, in the army, and handsome. He wrote home once a month, one side of one page, from a country with unusual stamps. Jordan was well loved by women, and had three illegitimate children spread over the country. He never called them, met them, touched them.

At thirteen, Renny captured his brother's little black phone book in an effort to find information on these mothers. He carefully copied their names and numbers onto the inside of his closet door.

"Little shit," Jordan said to Renny when he found him frozen in the closet, phone book in lap, "what are you doing with my book?"

Renny leaned his back carefully against the door, hiding his writing. "Just looking at all the people you know," he said, half-holding his breath.

"Impressed?" Jordan asked, looking down and smiling.

"Oh yeah," Renny said, "lots of girls."

Jordan pulled his brother up and put one big hand on Renny's neck. "Just don't fuck with my stuff, little brother, okay? You ask first." He tightened his grip, then let go. "Nosy fuck."

Renny sank back to the floor. Jordan went into the backyard to smoke a cigarette. Renny waited until he heard the screen door slam, and then turned around to look at the numbers. They were smudged, but still readable. He leaned his forehead on the wood of the door frame and breathed in the bitter smell of the lacquer.

Jill's mother, in phase three of her career, was the owner of a Jewish dating service. She tried to meet at least three new Jews a day and convince them that she held their ticket to marital bliss. Often, she did. Her agency had something like a 75 percent success rate because it only accepted customers who were willing to work and commit, and who had abandoned their Prince Charming/Virgin–Whore fantasies. Jill worked there during summers and had met every available Jewish man in Los Angeles. She dated some, liked some, but was required by the agency to fill out a date report after each encounter. Her mother liked to supplement her daughter's questionnaire with new, handwritten inquiries, like: What do you appreciate in a good kiss, Jill? At first she answered these questions openly, believing it was part of that mother/daughter "we are now best friends" syndrome. But suddenly, her dates began to execute these perfect kisses, and the third time a man tipped up her chin gently before he laid his lips on hers, Jill ran, yelling, to her mother and quit the job. Her mother did not understand. But Jill remembered that the woman was, in fact, not her best friend but her mother, and proceeded to divulge the kissing facts only to her friends, telling her mother instead about her intricate opinions on all the recently released movies.

On Saturdays, when rates were lower, Renny called Boston, Atlanta and Hagerstown, Maryland. Often, the mothers were home taking care of their new babies, usually crying in the background.

"Hello, Mrs. Stevens," he said in his best older voice, "I'm calling from *Parents* magazine, may I have a few minutes of your time?" If they said no, he plowed ahead anyway. "Is your baby happy? How old is your baby? Would you describe your baby as a fun-loving baby or a serious baby? Does your baby more resemble you or the father?" Sometimes he slipped up and asked questions too personal, and the women began to fall suspect, and hang up. He called them, on average, every two months. Sometimes he was a contest man, asking them to send photos to a P.O. box and enter My Baby's the Cutest! contest. Maybe they would win $100,000! Sometimes he just pretended he'd gotten the wrong number. He liked to hear their voices. They sounded tired, but kind.

"We're drawing our dreams tonight," Jill announced to the group of seven teenagers in front of her.

"You must've been such a geek in high school," Trina said.

"No hostile comments," Jill said, smoothing down her red Gap T-shirt, "If you're mad about something, maybe you should tell the group."

"I don't think any of us want to be here for that long," Trina said. She smiled at Damon. "And it still wouldn't change you being a geek in high school."

Jill passed out pencils and papers. "I was not a geek," she said. "Do you want to do this or not?"

"Go ahead, Jill," said Damon, smiling. "Dreams. Cool. Trina's a geek too, she just doesn't want you to know."

"Oh, shut up, Damon." Trina rolled her foot into his lap. No sex was allowed at Ocean House, guests would be expelled. Damon circled her ankle quickly and gave it a squeeze. Trina pulled it out, and relaxed.

"Any crayons?" George asked. No one liked him. He smiled too much and made jokes about cyberspace that were either stupid or confusing. Jill pulled a 64 crayon box out of her huge, denim purse.

Renny watched her carefully rezip her purse. Then he leaned back and drew circles on his paper. He put the eraser end of his pencil in his stomach and pushed it in until it ached. He imagined Jill, emaciated and naked, her hair in strings, trying to speak to him in German, begging him for mercy.

"Did my drawing, Jilly," he said.

She looked it over. "You dream about bubbles?"

"Ha ha." He looked at the other residents who were, mostly, doodling. Damon was drawing a big eye.

Renny leaned over. "Eyes the color of sky . . . ?" he asked. He hadn't pegged Damon for the Resistance because he talked to Trina, the black girl, so much, but you never knew.

"You a poet?" Damon said, turning around to face Renny. "I never knew we had such a wonderful poet among us." Renny leaned back. No one here but him. He filled in the circles with black crayon.

"I dream about the insides of olives," he told Jill. "I dream about big black holes."

One mother sent a photograph to Renny's P.O. box. The baby was a girl, half black, dark, dark eyes and a serious face. Her arms reached toward the camera, wanting to play with the lens. "Nicole Shaw," it read on the back, "ten months old." Renny took the picture to the park with him and stared at his niece for an hour. He could feel her, how heavy she would be in his arms, how she would fall asleep and curl her head into his chest, enamored by the unfamiliar arms of a boy. Are you my daddy? she would ask. He looked into her eyes, and he could see in them, already, already, that death of loneliness, covering her like a thin gauze, impossible to remove. He picked up a twig and scraped at her face. The colors eased off, thin white stripes crossing through her tiny body. He erased Nicole and her arms and her eyes until she was just scratches on a piece of film.

Matthew broke up with Jill because she wouldn't go on the pill. She said she'd go on the pill only if he would move in with her, and he looked at her like she was crazy, and said he hated condoms, they had to have a change. I get bladder infections, she told him, I can't use a diaphragm. Let's wait a little while, and maybe I will go on the pill, if it seems like we're more serious. I'm not serious, he told her, I don't want a real relationship now. Maybe you do, but you're scared, she said. Maybe I'm not, he said back. I think we want different things. I have to go to work, she said. In a half hour. Go early, he said, maybe there's traffic.

"We're going to do trust exercises today," Jill stated.

"Fabulous," said Trina, glaring at Damon.

Jill cleared her throat and continued. "One of you is blindfolded, and the other leads the first person around the house and the backyard, being gentle and trustworthy, and then you switch. It's scary because you're used to using your eyes so much, but it's a nice way to learn about trusting each other. Okay, pick partners."

Trina and Damon were an obvious pair. The two cocaine addicts who giggled a lot and were pretty nice to Renny grabbed hands. George, the outcast, looked toward Renny who looked away, realizing there was an odd number; George was paired with Lana, the very quiet, beautiful one who moved in slow motion like she was underwater and never told anyone why she was there.

"Did your math wrong, Jilly," Renny said, kicking out his boots and running his palm over the smooth splinters of hair poking out of his skull.

"No, you'll be my partner, Renny," Jill said. He blanched.

"I don't want to do it," he said.

"It's tonight's activity," Jill said. Her eyes were tired from crying about Matthew. "Do you want to go first, or shall I?"

"You go. Get blindfolded," Renny said. She selected a blue bandanna from the stack. "Do you trust me, Jilly?" he asked.

"Yes," she said, tying the cloth at the back of her head and letting the triangles fall over most of her face. She stood directly in the middle of the room, arms straight down her sides. "Please don't call me Jilly, Renny. Lead me around. I trust you."

Her mother had taken her to lunch that day. Jill hadn't wanted to mention the breakup with Matthew.

"I forget, honey, is he cute?" her mother asked, bright eyes boring into her daughter. Jill had never brought Matthew home to be scrutinized.

"He's not blond," Jill said, "if that's what you mean."

"I don't know what you mean," her mother said, "I'm sure he's a very nice boy. His parents come from where, again?"

"I don't know." Jill wished she could lay her cheek down on her plate and just rest there with the cold porcelain. "Whatever. It's not serious." Her voice was fading.

"But do you want it to be?" Mrs. Cohen asked, a piece of French bread stilled in her hand.

"Doesn't really matter, does it, whether or not I want it to be. It's not."

"Well, it could always become serious, right?" She scooped up some white butter with her knife and spread it on the bread. "Does he talk about commitment?"

"We broke up yesterday, Mother," Jill said finally. "It's not an issue. We're broken up. Stop asking questions."

Jill's mother took a bite out of the bread and chewed for a moment. "Well, I'm sorry to hear that," she said, and smiled.

After he got the photo in the P.O. box, Renny painted the inside of his closet door with white paint. He painted slowly up, then down, until the numbers had vanished, and the paint would never flake away. He went into the bathroom and tried to throw up, but he couldn't. Grabbing the leftover paint, he walked down to the train station. There was an empty cave where his older brother used to fuck girls, or smoke pot, or whatever he did before he left for the army. Renny painted seventeen swastikas, one for each year of his life, all over the cave and then curled up underneath them and went to sleep. The swastikas looked like spider boomerangs that he could fling out into the world. They would clear a path, and then come back, to guide him to safety.

Renny led Jill through the kitchen.

"Counter's on your left, fridge on your right," he said.

"Thanks." She walked up the stairs and down the stairs and through the back door into the yard

"So do you like it here, Renny?" she asked.

"Yeah, it's okay," he said. "Step up. Just walk straight here." They reached the cliffs overlooking the beach, across the street from Ocean House. He could see the distant figures of the other residents, their tentative arms. He heard Trina laugh.

"Are we going too far?" Jill asked.

"We'll switch soon."

He stopped her at the edge of a cliff. The ground beneath them crumbled down for thirty feet, and then led into the sand, and then the water.

"We're at the edge of a cliff, Jill," Renny said, standing behind her, his hands cupping her shoulders.

"I'm trying to trust you here, Renny," she said. The wind blew her T-shirt to her skin. She watched the strange colors underneath her blindfold, and pictured Matthew's back growing smaller and smaller and how the world seemed to close in on her then.

"I hated what you did to my swastika," Renny said.

"Well I couldn't just leave it there," she said back. The palms of his hands were on her upper arms, warm. "I hate swastikas."

"See, Jill," Renny said, "it's eyes the color of sky, not of earth, that's what it's about, see, that's what we say. Eyes the color of sky, not of earth." He stared at her hair; it was dark and long and felt soft where it touched his hands.

"But Renny," she said, "your eyes are brown."

He gripped her shoulders. He wondered if by the time the two weeks were up, and he returned home, Jordan would be gone.

Jill pictured the wedding again. Except now the priest was nowhere to be found, the groom was nowhere to be found, and it was just herself and the rabbi. His arm was tan and thick with black hair. See our skin, the rabbi was telling her, this skin was made for the desert.

"It's a long way down," Renny said.

She imagined scratching at the skin on the rabbi's arm, scratching at her own arm, scratching them down, until underneath the thin layers of flesh she found out just what exactly they were made of.

"Are you scared?" Renny held her shoulders tightly.

"Should I be?"

Renny didn't answer. Jill shivered.

"Are you cold?" he asked.

"Yeah," she said, "a little."

He put his arms around her chest, and brought her closer to him. One thumb very gently: brushed against the side of her nipple, standing up from the chill. She was quiet.

"Is that okay?" he asked.

"Yeah," she said. She breathed out, and closed her eyes beneath the blindfold. Her skin was rising. I am made out of dirt, she thought.

"Do you want to switch?" Renny asked quietly. His hand was light against her breast.

I am made out of gold.

"No," she said, "do you?"

"No." He hugged her in closer and listened to the water rush at them from far away.

17

View from a Headlock

JONATHAN LETHEM

Jonathan Lethem was born into a working class and bohemian neighborhood in Brooklyn, New York in 1964. He would later draw from his upbringing in his novels *Motherless Brooklyn* and *The Fortress of Solitude*. After high school, Lethem enrolled at Bennington College as an arts student in 1982, but he dropped out the following year—a decision motivated in part by his desire to focus on writing rather than art. He spent the next decade in Berkeley, California, working at two of the city's renowned used bookstores, Pegasus Books and Moe's Books. In his spare time, Lethem worked on his writing. Although he considers himself fundamentally a novelist, Lethem's first publishing successes were with short stories. After completing his first novel, *Gun, With Occasional Music* (1994), Lethem devoted his energies entirely to writing. He has since published six other novels: *Amnesia Moon* (1995), *As She Climbed Across the Table* (1997), *Girl in Landscape* (1998), *Motherless Brooklyn* (1999), *The Fortress of Solitude* (2003), and *Chronic City* (2009). The short story "View From a Headlock," included in this collection, was initially published in *The New Yorker* but a version of the text is also part of *The Fortress of Solitude*. Lethem also published a collection of short stories, *The Wall of the Sky, The Wall of the Eye* (1996), and he regularly publishes essays and reviews. He was the recipient of a 2005 MacArthur Fellowship.

"Let me see it for a minute."

Let me see it: you saw a basketball or a pack of baseball cards or a plastic water gun by taking it into your hands, and what happened after that was in doubt. Ownership depended mostly on not letting anyone see anything. If you let a kid see a bottle of Yoo-hoo for a minute, he'd drink what was left of it.

"Let me see it, let me check it out. I only want to take it for a ride."

Dylan Ebdus gripped the handlebars. His father had pried off the train-

ing wheels the day before, and Dylan still wobbled, still scuffed with his
sneakers groping away from the pedals to steady and brake against the sidewalk. "Only if you stay on the block," Dylan said, miserably.

"You afraid I'm gonna take it? I just want a ride. You get it back after that,
you got it all day, man. Just let me go around the block."

It was a trap or a puzzle, the way Robert Woolfolk already knew to work
Dylan's guilt. And the empty block conspired to leave Dylan alone to solve
it. Robert Woolfolk was a kid who carried a vacuum around with him, or
revealed by his presence the vacuum on Dean Street, the expanse of moments when no one saw and no one knew what happened in plain sight,
when all of the block was shrouded in daylight.

Robert Woolfolk added his hands to the handlebars beside Dylan's and
tugged gently at the bike.

"Stay on the block."

"Around once, that's all."

"No, I mean stay in front of the house."

"What, you think I'm not coming back? Just around the block."

What came out of Robert Woolfolk's mouth was petition and chant, irresistible in its illogic. His eyes, meanwhile, were hard, a little bored.

"Just once around."

Robert Woolfolk's legs were too long to unfold in the span between seat
and pedals, so he rode with his knees doubled and knobbing up near the
handlebars, like a clown on a tricycle. Then he changed his approach, elevated his hips above the seat to stand on the pedals and pump side to side,
elbows flaring. The bike teetered, annexed to Robert Woolfolk's stretching
limbs. Like that, a vanishing pile of elbows, he took the bike around the
corner of Nevins.

How long did it take to go around the block?

How long was twice as long as that?

The tonguelike latch of Dylan's black ironwork gate rattled with the vi-
bration of a bus going by. Though there were no trees on the Nevins end of
Dean Street, red fallen leaves had blown into the gutter from somewhere.
The plastic milk cartons in front of the bodega claimed you could be fined
or go to jail for not returning them to May Creek Farm, Incorporated, a
fairly unlikely destination if you gave it any thought.

The afternoon withered like a balloon around Dylan on his stoop, waiting for Robert Woolfolk to return. The minutes accumulated, stacked up
indifferently on the distant face of the Williamsburg Savings Bank tower
clock. Nevins Street might as well have been a canyon into which Robert

Woolfolk had vanished like a cartoon coyote, wordlessly, trailing puffs of dust. It was pretty much as if there had never been a bike.

The last thing Dylan Ebdus's mother, Rachel, had taught him, before she left Dylan's father and vanished from their home, was the word "gentrification." They were walking home to Dean Street from Flatbush Avenue, on a rare jaunt past the slummy blocks east of Nevins. Rachel was trying, perhaps, to make him understand Brooklyn, the world into which she was about to abandon him.

There were two worlds, anyway. In one, his father paced upstairs, creaked chairs, painted, while his mother, downstairs, played records, ran water over dishes, laughed on the telephone, her voice trailing up the curve of the long stair. His mother's spaces—the parlor, full of her books and records, the kitchen, where she cooked and laughed and argued on the phone, her table littered with newspapers and cigarettes and wineglasses—were for Dylan full of unpredictability and unrest, like his mother herself. Dylan's solitude, which his father left unbruised, his mother burst like a grape. She might clutch him and, with fingers kneading his skull through his hair, say, "You're so beautiful, so beautiful, you're such a beautiful boy," or just as likely sit apart from him smoking a cigarette and say, "Where did you come from? Why are you here? Why am I here?" or "You know, precious child, that your father is insane." She was wild with information he couldn't yet use: Nixon was a criminal, the Dodgers moved to California, Chinese food gives you a headache, Muhammad Ali resisted the war and went to jail, Hitchcock's British films were better than his American ones, circumcision was unnecessary but women preferred it. Dylan worked Rachel's margins, dodging her main force to dip sidelong into what he could make sense of. He tiptoed close under the cover of Rachel's monologue, thinking it was another phone call, to find someone seated at her table instead, drinking iced tea, sharing Rachel's ashtray, laughing, listening, detecting Dylan's footfalls, which Rachel had ignored. Then Rachel would stir from her chair, cigarette in her fingers, and usher Dylan to the front door, point out the children playing on the sidewalk, insist that he join them. Rachel had a program, a plan. She had grown up a Brooklyn street kid and so would Dylan. And so she'd eject him from the first of his two worlds, the house, into the second. The outside, the block. Dean Street. Brooklyn.

"Gentrification" was a Nixon word, uncool. "If someone asks you, say you live in Gowanus," she said. "Don't be ashamed. Boerum Hill is pretentious bullshit." Rachel sprayed language as the hydrant opened by the

Puerto Rican kids around the corner on Nevins on the hottest days that year sprayed water, unstoppered, gushing. "Never let me hear you say the word 'nigger,'" she said, whispering it heavily, lusciously. "That's the only word you can't ever say, not even to yourself. In Brooklyn Heights they call them *animals*, they call the projects *a zoo*. Those uptight reactionaries deserve the break-ins. They ought to lose their quadraphonic stereos. We're here to live. Gowanus Canal, Gowanus Houses, Gowanus people. The Creature from the Gowanus Lagoon!" She inflated her cheeks and curled her fingers and attacked him. Her raven hair haloed in sunlight, her fingertips stained with nicotine or marijuana.

Brooklyn was actually simple compared with his mother.

"A gang from the Gowanus Houses picked up a fifth grader after school and took him into the park and they had a knife and they were daring each other and they *cut off his balls*," she told him. "He didn't fight or scream or anything. It's not too soon for you to know, my profound child, the world is nuttier than a fruitcake. Run if you can't fight, run and scream 'fire' or 'rape,' be wilder than they are, wear flames in you hair, that's my recommendation."

Rachel wasn't fully responsible for what she said, Dylan knew. She was afraid, too. Dylan's role was to unravel what she said and ignore ninety percent of it, to solve her.

"That beautiful black man who moved next door is Barrett Rude, Jr., he's a singer, he was in the Distinctions, he's got this amazing voice, he sounds just like Sam Cooke. I actually once saw them, opening for the Stones. His son is your age. He's going to be your new best friend before the end of the summer, that's my prediction."

It was the last of Rachel's setups. Her last chance to steer him into a Brooklyn future.

Dylan Ebdus, one-man integration unit.

"You like comics?" Mingus Rude said, the first day they met.

"Sure," Dylan said, unsure.

Mingus Rude excavated four comic books from his closet floor, *Daredevil #77, Ghost Rider #4, Doctor Strange #12, The Incredible Hulk #68*. They'd been tenderly handled to death, corners rounded, paper browned by hot, attentive breath, pages chewed by eyes. "MINGUS RUDE" was written in slanted ballpoint capitals on each first interior page.

Mingus read certain panels aloud, incanting them, shaping Dylan's attention, shaping his own. Dylan felt himself permeated by some ray of attention. He felt an uncanny warmth in the half of his chest that was turned toward Mingus.

"You know what they say now? Doctor Strange could take the Incredible Hulk by making some kind of mystical cage but he couldn't take Thor because Thor's a godlike figure, as long as he doesn't lose his hammer. If he loses his hammer dude's nothing better than a cripple."

"Who's Thor?"

"You'll see. You know where to buy comics?"

"Uh, yeah."

"Ever steal comics?"

"No."

"It's no big thing. You go to camp this year?"

"No." *No year*, Dylan almost said. He'd found an artifact on Mingus's dresser, a sort of tuning fork.

"That's a pick," said Mingus.

"Oh."

"Like a comb, for black hair. Want to see a gold record?"

Dylan nodded mutely, dropped the pick. Mingus Rude was a world, an exploding bomb of possibilities. Dylan was already jealous, wondering how long he'd be able to keep the new kid to himself.

They crept upstairs. Barrett Rude, Jr., had placed his bed opposite the heavily ornate marble mantelpiece, behind the shaded light of the tall windows, the showpiece windows meant for front parlors filled with pianos and upholstery, eighteenth-century Bibles on stands, who knew what else. Barrett Rude, Jr.'s bed, which lay on the floor there under the scrolled Dutch ceiling, was a wide flat bag filled, as Mingus Rude demonstrated in passing with a neat two-palmed shove, with actual *water*, an undulating sea trapped in slick sheets. The two gold records were, oddly, just what their name promised, gold records, 45s, glued to white matting and framed in stained aluminum, not up on the bare walls but propped on the crowded mantel beside balled dollar bills and empty packs of Kools.

Mingus led Dylan to the back yard, where they winged rocks into the sky, let them plop into the Puerto Ricans' yard. The air smelled like somebody's arm up close. You could hear the steady *ding* of a Mister Softee truck on Bergen Street, probably with a string of the usual kids hanging on it.

"I guess you know my mother's white," Mingus said.

"Sure."

"White women like black men, you heard that, right?"

"Uh, sure."

"My father don't talk to that lying bitch no more." He followed this with a sharp laugh of self-surprise. "He paid a million dollars for me. That's what he had to pay to get me back, a million *cold*. You can ask him if you think I'm lying."

"I believe you."

"I don't *care* if you believe me, it's true."

Dylan looked at Mingus Rude's lips and eyes, his exact brownness, took it in. Dylan wanted to read Mingus Rude like a language, wanted to know if the new kid had changed Dean Street or only changed Dylan himself by arriving here. Mingus Rude breathed through his mouth. The palms of his hands were as white as Dylan's. He wore corduroys. Anything was possible, really.

A million-dollar kid doesn't belong on Dean Street, Dylan wanted to say. The word "million," even.

Mingus Rude was a scant four months older than Dylan Ebdus, but those months hit the calendar such that Mingus was a grade ahead. He'd start sixth grade this year, at the Intermediate School 293 Annex, in the turf of the Gowanus Houses: no man's land. If Mingus were four months younger, then he and Dylan would have been heading to grade five at P.S. 38 together.

A grade of school was a bridge in mist. No way to picture where it touched land again, or who you'd be when it did.

You met zones everywhere. Th schoolyard was neighborhoods: black, black girl, Puerto Rican, basketball, handball, left behind. Black girls had a language of partial words, chants harder to learn than anything in class. The place was a cage for growing, nothing else. You couldn't be left back from fish sticks and sloppy joes.

There was a general noise at the edges you'd begun to detect, akin to indecipherable ballpoint desktop gougings. A scribbled voice. The first few times someone said, "Hey, white boy," it sounded like a mistake. You had to be guided into the new relation by the girls, the boys were actually a little shy about it.

Older kids bunched at the school entrances and in corners of the yard. Robert Woolfolk was among them, the lurkers. Even standing in one place, Woolfolk moved like a sprained knee, like he was forever angling a too-small bike around the corner of Nevins.

Dylan Ebdus and Mingus Rude: one crossing the street to dodge a clump of kids from the projects, keeping his white face hidden in a jacket hood, the other hanging in loose gangs of black kids after school, then walking alone to Dean Street. The two of them, a fifth grader and a sixth, stranded in zones, in selves. White kid, black kid, *Captain America* and *The Falcon, Luke Cage* and *Iron Fist*. Returning from different schools to the same block, two brownstones, two fathers, Abraham Ebdus and Barrett Rude, Jr., each wrinkling back foil edges on TV dinners to discover peas and carrots that had invaded the mashed potatoes and Salisbury steak, setting them on the table in dour silence. Dinner in silence or to the sound of the television drowned by the baying of sirens, Nevins Street a fire lane, a path of destruction, the projects flaring up again, an apartment on the eighteenth floor with a smoldering mattress pushed halfway out the window, stuck. The grid of zones, the huddled brownstone streets between prison and projects, Wyckoff Gardens, Gowanus Houses. The whores on Nevins and Pacific. The high-school kids pouring out of Sarah J. Hale all afternoon, black girls already bigger than *yo mama*, Third Avenue another no man's land, the empty lot where *they raped that girl*. The halfway house. It was all halfway, you walked out of your halfway school and tried to chart a course through your halfway neighborhood to make it back to your own halfway house, your half-empty house.

Afternoons after school, Dylan could hear the telephone ring from the kitchen while he sat out on his stoop, waiting, watching, afternoons sliding to twilight, as the traffic trickled down Nevins, mothers walked kindergartners home from the Y.W.C.A., buses drifted like humming loaves to the stoplight, waited, drifted on. It was a season of vanishing, of a silence like raw stupidity, like the unbearable ticking silence of a teacher expecting an answer from a kid everyone knew couldn't even say his own name right.

Let his father answer the phone, if he could even hear it. Let him say she's not here. Dylan's father lacked Rachel's street-readiness. His disapproval or his affection were usually aspects of a floating arrangement of father-notions, largely sonic: footsteps pacing overhead, a voice descending the stairs.

One or two afternoons a week Mingus would lope down the block and raise his hand in greeting. He carried his notebook and textbooks loose under his arm, no bag, and he'd clatter them on the stoop carelessly, expressing something less that utter disdain and more than total mastery. They never discussed fifth or sixth grade, stuff too basic and mysterious to mention. Instead they read comics, shoulders hunched to protect the flimsy covers from the wind, puzzling out the last dram, the last square inch of information, the credits, the letters page, the copyright, the Sea Monkeys ads, *the insult that made a man out of Mac.* Then, just when Dylan had thought he was alone, Dean Street came back to life, Mingus Rude knowing everyone, saying yo to a million different kids coming out of the Ramirez's store with a Yoo-hoo or a Pixy Stix, to Alberto fetching Schlitz and Marlboros for his older brother. Mothers calling kids inside, the bus lit inside now, fat ladies coming home from offices at the Board of Education, on Livingston Street, their weary shapes like black teeth inside the glowing mouth of the bus, the light fading, street lights buzzing as they lit, their arched poles decorated with boomeranged-up sneakers, and Mingus Rude saying, one dying afternoon, eyes never ungluing from a panel in *Marvel's Greatest Comics* in which Mr. Fantastic had balled himself into an orb the size of a baseball in order to be shot from a bazooka into the vulnerable mouth of an otherwise impervious fifty-foot-tall robot named Tomazooma, the Living Totem, "Your moms is still gone?"

"Yeah."

"Dang, man. That's fucked up."

Then, sixth grade. Intermediate School 293. As before, Mingus had leapfrogged from the sixth-grade annex building where Dylan now was to the main building, a block away, where the seventh and eighth graders were housed. This was the year of the headlock, the year of the *yoke*, Dylan's heat-flushed cheeks wedged into one or another black kid's elbow, book bag skidding to the gutter, pockets rapidly, easily frisked for lunch money or a bus pass. On Hoyt Street, on Bergen, on Wyckoff if he was stupid enough to walk on Wyckoff. On Dean Street, even, one block from home, before the dead eyes of the brownstones. Adults, teachers, they were remote, blind, indifferent. Dylan, he was a bug on a grid of slate, white boy walking.

"Yoke him, man," they'd say, exhorting. He was the object, the occasion, it was irrelevant what he overheard. "Yoke the white boy. *Do* it, nigger."

He might be yoked low, bent over, hugged to someone's hip then spun on release like a human top, legs buckling, crossing at the ankles. Or from behind, never sure by whom once the headlock popped loose and the three or four guys stood around, witnesses with hard eyes, shaking their heads at the sheer dumb luck of being white. It was as routine as laughter. Yoking erupted spontaneously, a joke of fear, a piece of kidding.

He was dismissed from it as from an episode of light street theatre. "Nobody hurt you, man. It ain't for real. You know we was just fooling with you, right?" They'd spring away, leave him tottering, hyperventilating, while they high-fived, more like amazed spectators than perpetrators. If Dylan choked or whined they were perplexed and slightly disappointed at the white boy's hysteria. On those occasions, they'd pick up his books or hat and press them on him, tuck him back together. A ghost of fondness lived in a head-lock's shadow. Yoker and yokee had forged a funny compact. You regularly promised your enemies that what you did together had no name.

Dylan leaked saliva, tears. On a cold day a nostril-path of snot. Once, pee. He'd bite his tongue and taste the seepage, the tang of humiliation swallowed back. They made faces, rolled eyes. Dylan was hopeless, stained with shame. They'd try to overlook it.

"Boy bleeds you touch him, dang."

"Nah, man, he all right. Let him alone, man."

"You ain't gonna say nothing, right? 'Cause you know we just messin' around. We wouldn't never *do* nothin' to you, man."

He'd nod, collect himself. Wait to be congratulated for gulping back a clog of tears, for exhibiting silence.

"See? You pretty cool, for a white boy. Get outta here now."

White boy was his name. He'd grown into it, crossed a line, become visible. He shined like free money. The price of the name was whatever was in his pockets at the time, fifty cents or a dollar.

"White boy, lemme talk to you for a minute." Head tipped sideways, too lazy to take hands from pockets to summon him. One black kid, two, three. Eyes rolled, laughing. The whole event a quotation of itself, a little boring.

If he ignored it, tried to keep walking: "Yo, *white boy*! I'm *talking* to you, man."

"What's the matter, you can't *hear*?"

No. Yes.

"You don't like me, man?"

Helpless.

The fact of it: he'd cross the street to have his pockets emptied.

"Just come here for a minute, man, I ain't gonna hurt you. What you gotta be afraid for? *Dang*, man. You think I'm gonna hurt you?"

No. Yes.

The logic was insane, except as a polyrhythm of fear and reassurance, a seduction. "What you afraid of? You a *racist*, man?"

"Who you looking for? Ain't nobody gonna help you, man."

"Nah, man, chill out. This white boy's all right, he's cool. You don't got to fuck with him."

"Fuck he starin' at me for, then? Yo, man, you a racist motherfucker? I might have to fuck up your stupid ass, just for that."

"Nah, man, shut up, he's cool. You cool, right, man? Hey, you got a dollar you could loan me?"

The distillation, the question at the core of the puzzle, asked a million times, a million ways:

"What you lookin' at?"

"*Fuck* you lookin' at, man?"

"Don't look at me, white boy. I'll slap you, motherfucker."

Here was what Robert Woolfolk had prepared him for. The bicycle thief had awarded Dylan the gift of his own shame, his mummy's silence, for use on a daily basis. Each encounter bore Robert's signature tilted logic, inter-rogations spinning nowhere, ritual assurance that nothing had actually hap-pened. And the guilt of Dylan's whiteness excusing everything, covering it all.

What

the

fuck

am

I

looking

at?

If Dylan ever lifted his eyes from the pavement he might have been cast-ing around for a grownup, or some older kid he knew to bail him out. Min-gus Rude, say, not that he was clear he'd want Mingus to see him this way, cowering at the prospect of a yoke, white boy with cheeks hate-red. And he never allowed himself to say what he thought a hundred times: Hey, I'm not a racist, my best friend is black! It wasn't halfway sayable. Besides, no-body had ever said who was whose best friend. Mingus Rude likely had a million of them, seventh graders, black, white, who knew. And Dylan could have said *black* aloud about as easily as *Fucking looking at motherfucking YOU, man!*

One afternoon, near the finish of that sixth-grade spring, Mingus Rude was waiting for Dylan at the bottom of his stoop. Mingus wore a military-green jacket though it was too warm for a jacket, and the jacket clanked, full of some metallic something that had been pushed through torn pockets to nestle in the lining. The jacket's back panel bore Mingus's tag, Dose, elabo-rately surrounded by asterisk-like stars and swooping punctuation. Dylan pushed his schoolbag just inside Mingus's basement door and they slouched their way together down Dean Street.

They crept wordlessly into Brooklyn Heights, away from Dean Street, putting the Gowanus Houses at their backs, skirting I.S. 293 entirely. They were invisible in the throngs on Montague Street, the three-o'clock flood of private-school kids from Packer Institute and Saint Ann's and Brooklyn Friends. The Heights kids clustered around the Burger King and the Baskin-Robbins in giddy crowds, boys mixed with girls, all in corduroys and Lacoste shirts, flutes and clarinets in leather cases heaped carelessly with their backpacks at their feet, their senses so bound up in a private cosmos of flirtation that Dylan and Mingus passed through them like an X-ray.

Then a blond girl with an intricate mouthful of braces stepped out of her posse of look-alikes and called them over. Eyes wild with her own daring, she showed a cigarette.

"Got a light?"

Her friends busted up at the self-conscious comedy of it, but Mingus didn't care. He dug in his jacket lining and pulled out a bright-blue lighter, like a Pez container that blurted a curl of fire. How she'd known he'd have it Dylan couldn't fathom. The tone of the scene switched again, the girl leaned in, eyes narrowed ferally now, thrilled and wary, tilted her head, scooped her hair around her ear to protect it from the flame. She turned her back the moment the cigarette was lit and Dylan and Mingus moved on, dismissed.

The Heights Promenade was a rim of park cantilevered over the shipyards, Brooklyn's sulky lip. Old men and women pecked forward like pigeons on cobblestone, or sat frozen with clutched newspapers on benches in the face of Manhattan's tedious spires, the skyline a channel no one watched that played anyway, like famous static. Dylan and Mingus were detectives, following clues. The trail was legible in gushy, streaked fonts on lamppost bases and mail-deposit boxes, fire-alarm poles, garage doors, finger-traced in dust on the panels of trucks.

"Roto I," "Bel I," "Deal," "Buster NSA," "SuperStrut," "FMD."

"Non Stop Action," translated Mingus. He was hushed by the knowledge, his eyes unfocussed. Tags and their invisible authors were the next Marvel superheroes, the hidden lore. "Flow Master Dancers."

Roto and Bel and Deal were in DMD Crew, a new outfit from Atlantic Terminals, a housing project across Flatbush. SuperStrut was old school. The style might look funny now, but you wouldn't disrespect it. The syllable "TOY" was written in mockery over certain tags, disrespect for a writer who was a toy.

Mingus fished in his lining for his El Marko, a Magic Marker consisting of a puglike glass bottle stoppered with a fat wick of felt. Purple ink sloshed inside the tiny screw-top bottle, staining the glass in curtains of color. Mingus drew out a safety pin and stuck the felt in a dozen places, until the ink bled so freely it stained the green cuff of his oversized jacket.

"Dose" went up on a lamppost, Mingus's hand moving in studied arcs.

A tag was a reply, a call to those who heard, like a dog's bark understood across fences. A reply in moist purple. The letters dripped and stunk thrillingly. Every time they went up, Mingus hustled Dylan away, the El Marko clanking back in his jacket lining against the blue lighter and whatever else. Their path was a zigzag sentence consisting of a single word, "Dose," written in blank spots found everywhere.

Under oblivious eyes, the invisible autographed the world.

The long path of the Promenade curled at the end in a small abandoned playground, two swings, a slide. Mingus took a minute to tag "Dose" on the heel-dented mercury sheen of the slide, a particularly juicy rendition with a dripping halo.

He offered Dylan the El Marko. The purple-fingerprinted bottle rolled like something ripe in Mingus's stained palm, a plum.

"Go ahead," he said, "Tag up. Hurry."

"How do I know what to write?"

"Don't you got a tag yet? Make one up."

Marvel Comics had it right, the world was all secret names, you only needed to uncover your own.

White Boy?

"Dillinger," Dylan said. He stared, not quite reaching for the El Marko.

"Too long man. Something like Dill 3, D-Lone."

A Filipino babysitter creaked a stroller into the playground. Mingus slipped the marker into his jacket, tilted his head.

"Let's go."

You could flee a woman who was four feet tall with a baby lashed into a stroller, scramble away giddy and hysterical. It was only real threat that froze you where you stood, your feet like bricks, to dig in your pocket and offer up your bills and change.

Mingus hoisted onto the fence surrounding the playground, swung a leg, dropped. Dylan, trying to follow, doubled himself on the fence. Mingus braced under Dylan's arms while Dylan scrabbled with his foot. They fell together like cartoon cats in a sack on the other side.

"Dang, son, get off me!"

Dylan found his glasses where they'd tumbled in the grass. Mingus brushed at his pants, his jacket, like James Brown checking his suit for imaginary lint. He was grinning, lit up. A shard of leaf in the coils of his hair.

"Get up, son, you're on the ground!" Mingus at his happiest called Dylan "son" in a booming voice, another quotation, half Redd Foxx, half Foghorn Leghorn.

He offered his hand, yanked Dylan to his feet. Dylan wanted to clear the leaf from Mingus's hair but left it alone.

They trudged down a grade to a hidden patch of land, a tilted triangle of desolate ailanthus and weeds, choked in exhaust at the edge of the Brook-lyn-Queens Expressway, cars whirring indifferent below. The patch was lit-tered with cigarette butts, forty-ounce bottles, shreds of tire—an oasis of neglect. Mingus leaned against the wall, and thumbed the blue lighter, held it sideways to the tip of a small, faucetlike chrome pipe, another surprise product of the green jacket's lining. Head titled, eyes squeezed in concen-tration, Mingus sipped at smoke, held it in with thin-pressed lips. Fumes leaked from his nose. He nodded his chin at Dylan, finally exhaled.

"You want some weed?"

"Nah." Dylan tried to keep it breezy, an incidental turndown that could have gone either way.

Below, trucks roared past, bearing their own graffiti markings from other parts of the city, alien communication spread by an indifferent carrier, like a virus.

"I took it from my pops. He keeps it in the freezer."

"Does he know?" Dylan asked.

Mingus shook his head. "He got so much, he won't even notice." He flicked the lighter again, th bowl of the pipe flaring orange, crackling faintly. Dylan worked not to tip his fascination.

"You ever smoke weed?"

"Sure," Dylan lied.

"It's no big thing."

"It's O.K., I did it before, I just don't want to right now."

"Before?"

"Sure," Dylan said. "My *mom's* a pothead." As it came from his mouth Dylan felt he'd betrayed Rachel, played her like a card he didn't mind losing.

"Yeah, well, speaking of which, my moms kicked my father out for smok-ing drugs," Mingus said. Having chipped in his own disaster, he went mute. Possibly mentioning anyone's moms out loud, even your own, was miscal-culation enough to blow an afternoon.

You were never ineligible for a screwup like that—say the unsayable word and watch it foul the sky. Then you were right back where you didn't want to be. Pinned to the grid.

A white boy with no moms, squirming in the glare.

Yoked.

Yo mama.

Mingus made the pipe disappear into his jacket. The two of them clambered back up the grade, scaled the fence easily, and in silence walked home, putting the Promenade behind them. Though Dylan was ready now to be offered the El Marko, ready to uncap the pinned-out purple-soaked felt and feel it flow under his own hand, to discover his own graffiti name and to plop it dripping on the sides of lampposts beside Mingus's "Dose," they tagged nothing. Mingus's hands remained buried in the pockets of the jacket, fists pushed into the lining to grip the lighter and the pipe and the El Marko so they didn't clank together as they bounced against his thighs. Leaf still in his hair.

The first day of seventh grade Dylan stood on the slate in front of Mingus Rude's stoop, waiting. If Mingus would walk with him up Dean Street to Court, walk through the doors of the school with him, side by side, everything might be different.

Women trudged little kids to kindergarten at the Y or moved alone up Nevins to the subway. A bunch of black girls swept up from the projects to high school. They shared a cigarette for breakfast, rumbled around the corner in a ball of smoke and laughter. It was the first day of school everywhere in the world, possibly.

Only one thing wrong with this picture, as the block cleared, the bus breathed past, a dog barked in a cycle like code: Dylan standing in long pants and with his backpack full of unruined binder pages and dumb pencils. He felt like an apple skinned for inspection, already souring in the sun. Those dogs could tell and probably anybody else, too: he stank of panic.

Dylan should have planned it with Mingus in advance, he saw now.

Up the stoop, he rang the bell.

He rang it again, shifting in his Keds, anxious, time ticking away, the day and the prospect of seventh grade rapidly spoiling with him in the sun.

Then, like an irrational puppet, panicked, he leaned on the doorbell and let it ring in a continuous trill. He was still ringing it when the door opened.

It wasn't Mingus but Barrett Rude, Jr., in a white bathrobe, naked underneath, unhidden to the street, arms braced in the door, looking down. Face clotted with sleep, he blinked in the slanted, scouring light. He lifted his arm to cover his eyes with shade, looking like he wanted to wave the day off as a bad idea, a passing mistake.

"Hell you doing, Little Dylan?"

Dylan took a step backward from the door.

"Don't *never* be ringing my doorbell seven in the morning, man."

"Mingus—"

"You'll see Mingus at the *got-damn* school." Barrett Rude was waking into his anger, his voice like a cloud of hammers. "Get out of here now."

It was entirely possible that one song could destroy your life. Yes, musical doom could fall on a lone human form and crush it like a bug. The song, *that song*, was sent from somewhere else to find you, to pick the scab of your whole existence. The song was your personal shitty fate, manifest as a throb of pop floating out of radios everywhere.

At the very least the song was the soundtrack to your destruction, the *theme*. Your days reduced to a montage cut to its cowbell beat, inexorable doubled bass line and raunch vocal, a sort of chanted sneer, surrounded by groans of pleasure. The stutter and blurt of what—a *tuba*? French horn? Rhythm guitar and trumpet, pitched to mockery. The singer might as well have held a gun to your head. How could it have been allowed to happen, how could it have been allowed on the *radio*? That song ought to be illegal. It wasn't racist—you'll never sort that one out, don't even start—so much as anti-*you*.

Yes they were dancing, and singing / and movin' to the goovin' / and just when it hit me / somebody turned around and shouted—

Every time your sneakers met the street, the end of that summer, somebody was hurling it at you head, *that song*.

September 4, 1976, the week Dylan Ebdus began seventh grade in the main building on Court Street and Butler, Wild Cherry's "Play That Funky Music" was the top song on the rhythm-and-blues charts. Fourteen days later it topped *Billboard's* pop charts. Your misery's anthem, No. 1 song in the nation.

Sing it through gritted teeth: *WHITE BOY!*

Lay down the boogie and play that funky music till you die.

Seventh grade was where it turned out that when Dylan Ebdus finally joined Mingus Rude in the main building Mingus Rude was never there. It was as if Mingus walked another Dean Street to school, had actually all this time gone to another I.S. 293 entirely. The only evidence he existed was the proliferation of Dose tags on lampposts and mailboxes, Mingus's handiwork spread in a nimbus with the school building at the center. Every few days, it seemed, produced a fresh supply. Dylan would covertly push a forefinger against the metal, wondering if he could measure in the tackiness of the ink the tag's vintage. If his finger stuck slightly Dylan imagined he'd followed Mingus by minutes to the spot, barely missed catching him in the act.

Seventh grade was sixth grade desublimated, uncorked. It was the "Lord of the Rings" trilogy to sixth grade's "The Hobbit," the real story at last, all the ominous foreshadowed stuff flushed from the margins and into view. It wasn't for children, seventh grade. You could read the stress of even entering the building in the postures of the teachers, the security guards. Nobody could relax in such a racial and hormonal disaster area.

Bodies ranged like ugly cartoons, as though someone without talent were scribbling in flesh.

Chinese kids had apparently gotten some warning well in advance, and had thoroughly disappeared. Puerto Rican or Dominican kids seemed to be tiptoeing away from the scene of everything. They decorated themselves differently and spoke more Spanish each passing hour. The scariest fights were between black girls.

There were just four other white kids in the school, three of them girls, with their own girl factors to work out. When Dylan Ebdus first spotted the fourth, Arthur Lomb, it was at a distance, across the schoolyard. It was like noticing the flight and fall of a bird across and expanse of leaf-blurred sky. It occurred at that moment after the bell had rung and the gym teachers who patrolled the yard had returned inside, ahead of the flood of students, and the yard became a lawless zone—that terrible sudden reframing of space which could happen anywhere, even inside the corridors of the school. Nevertheless it was a clumsy mistake for the boy now cringing on the ground to have been caught on the side of the yard so far from the entrance, a mistake Dylan felt he couldn't forgive. He wouldn't have forgiven it in himself.

Arthur Lomb fell to his knees and clutched his chest and keened. His words were briefly audible across the depopulating yard, each syllable riding a sharp insuck of air, "*I!*" Pause. "*Can't!*" Pause. "*Breathe!*"

Arthur Lomb was pretending asthma or some other weakness. It was an identifiable method: preëmptive suffering. Nobody could do much with a kid who was already crying. He had no spirit to crush and it was faintly disgusting, in poor taste. He might even be truly sick, fucked up, in pain, who knew? Your only option was to say, "Dang, white boy, what's your problem? I didn't even touch you." And move on.

Dylan admired the strategy, feeling at once a cool quiver of recognition and a hot bolt of shame. He felt that he was seeing his double, his stand-in. It was at least true that any punishment Arthur Lomb endured was likely otherwise to be Dylan's, or anyway that a gang of black kids couldn't knock Dylan to the pavement or put him in a yoke at the exact moment they were busy doing it to Arthur Lomb.

From that point on Arthur Lomb's reddish hair and hunched shoulders were easy to spot. He dressed in conspicuous striped polo shirts and wore soft brown shoes, and carried an enormous bright-blue backpack, an additional blight. All his schoolbooks must be inside, or maybe a couple of stone tablets. The bag glowed as a target, begged to be jerked downward, to crumple Arthur Lomb to the corridor floor to enact his shortness-of-breath routine. Dylan had seen it done five times already before he and Arthur Lomb ever spoke. Dylan had even heard kids chanting the song at Arthur Lomb as they slapped at his reddened neck or the top of his head while he squirmed on the floor. Play that *fucking* music, white boy! Stretching the last words to a groaning, derisive, Bugs Bunnyesque *whyyyyyyyboy!*

It was in the library that they finally spoke. Dylan and Arthur Lomb's two homerooms had been deposited there together for a period, the school librarian covering some unexplained absence of teachers. Below a poster advertising "A Hero Ain't Nothn' but a Sandwich," a book the library didn't actually offer, Dylan placed himself against a wall and flipped open issue No. 2 of the Marvel Comics adaptation of "Logan's Run." As the period ticked away glacially, Arthur Lomb buzzed him twice, squinting to see the title of the comic, then pursing his lips in false concentration as he mimed browsing the half-empty shelves nearby, before stepping close enough for Dylan to hear him speak in an angry, clenched whisper.

"That guy George Perez can't draw Farrah Fawcett to save his life."

It was a startling allusion to several bodies of knowledge simultaneously. Dylan could only glare, his curiosity mingled with the certainty that he and Arthur Lomb were more objectionable, more unpardonable, together than apart. Up close, Arthur Lomb had a blinky agitated quality to his features which made Dylan want to knock him down himself. His face seemed to reach for something, his features like a grasping hand. Dylan wondered if there might be a pair of glasses tucked in the background somewhere, perhaps in a side pocket of the monumental blue backpack.

"Seen it?"

"What?"

"'Logan's Run.'"

Fuck you looking at? Dylan wanted to shriek at Arthur Lomb, before it was too late, before he succumbed to his loneliness and allowed himself to meet Arthur, the other white boy.

"Not yet," Dylan said instead.

"Farrah Fawcett is a *fox.*"

Dylan didn't answer.

"Don't feel bad. I bought ten copies of *Logan's Run #1.*" Arthur Lomb spoke in a hurried whisper, showing some awareness of his surroundings, but compelled to spill what he had, to force Dylan to know him. "You *have* to buy No. 1s, it's an investment. I've got ten of *Eternals*, ten of *2001*, ten of *Omega*, ten of *Kobra*. And all those comics stink. No. 1's a No. 1, doesn't matter. You know *Fantastic Four #1* goes for four hundred dollars? Kobra might be an all-time record for the stupidest character ever. Doesn't matter. Put it in plastic and put it on the shelf, that's what I say. You use plastic, don't you?"

"Of course," Dylan said resentfully.

He understood every word Arthur Lomb said. Worse, he felt his sensibility colonized by Arthur's, his future interests coöpted.

The writing was on the wall. If Mingus didn't resurface, Dylan and Arthur were doomed to friendship.

A day later, Mingus did resurface. At three o'clock, the hour when the doors were thrown open and the school exploded onto the October-bright pavement, when Court Street shopkeepers stood arms-crossed in doorways, their jaws chewing gum or nothing at all, just chewing under narrowed eyes. Dylan tried to be lost in the flow of anonymous faces as he left the building, hoping to be carried a distance down Court Street disguised in a clot of anybodies before exposing himself as a solitary white boy. Today he stopped. Mingus sat cross-legged on the hump of a mailbox on the corner of Court and Butler, regarding the manic outflow of kids with a Buddha's calm, as though from an even greater height than the mailbox, another planet maybe. Dylan understood at once that not only hadn't Mingus been inside the school today, he hadn't crossed its doors since summer, since the start of his eighth-grade year.

"Yo, Dill-Man!" said Mingus, laughing. "I was looking for you, man. Where you been?"

Mingus unfolded his legs and slid off the mailbox, pulled Dylan sideways out of the crowd, like there was never a question they left school together, like they'd done it every day for three weeks. They crossed into Cobble Hill, Dylan hitching his backpack high on his shoulders and trotting to keep up. "I haven't seen you—" Dylan began.

"'Whenever you call me, I'll be there,'" Mingus sang, "'Whenever you need me, I'll be there—I been a-round!' Here." He crumpled a couple of dollars into Dylan's hands and nodded at the Arab newsstand on the corner of Clinton. "Get me a pack of Kools, Super-D." He tipped his head again. "I'll be over here."

"I can't buy cigaretters."

"Say it's for your mom, he'll sell it to you, don't worry. Better let me hold your backpack."

Dylan tried not to turn his head at the rack of comics as he stepped into the narrow, darkened space of the newsstand.

"Uh, pack of Kools. It's for my mother."

The operation unfolded precisely as scripted. The guy raised an eyebrow at the word "mother," then slid the Kools across the linoleum counter with nothing besides a grunt.

Mingus stashed both cigarettes and change in his jacket-of-mystery, then led Dylan back toward the small park on Amity Street.

"Dill-Man, D-Lone, Dillinger," Mingus chanted. "Diggity Dog, Deputy Dog, *Dillimatic*."

"I haven't seen you anywhere," Dylan said, unable to check the plaint in his voice.

"You all right, man?" Mingus asked. "Everything cool with you?"

Dylan knew precisely what *everything* Mingus meant—all of seventh grade, whatever went on or didn't inside the building that was apparently no longer Mingus's problem.

"Everything cool?" Mingus demanded.

Mingus Rude was unreachable, blurred, maybe high, Dylan saw now. There wasn't going to be any communing with his core, that vivid happy sadness which called out to Dylan's own.

Dylan shrugged, said, "Sure."

"That's all I want to know, man. You know you're my main man, Dillinger. D-Train."

As they slipped into the park, Mingus exaggerated his ordinary lope, raised a hand in dreamy salute. Arrayed at the concrete chessboard tables were three black teen-agers in assorted slung poses. One more chaotically slung than the others, a signature geometry of limbs that caused Dylan's heart to madly lurch. Nevertheless he strolled beside Mingus into the thick of it, accepted whatever was meant to unfold in the park from within his own sleepwalker's daze, which, perfected at the new school, covered even the appearance here of Robert Wookfolk, Bike Stealer. Yoker Prime.

"Yo," said Mingus Rude, lazily slapping at hands, humming swallowed syllables that might be names.

"What's goin' on, Gus?" said Woolfolk. When he saw Dylan he flinched with his whole face, his sour-lemon features hiding nothing, yet didn't alter the arrangement of his limbs an inch.

The party was full of little white kids with bowl haircuts, maybe second or third graders from Packer or Saint Ann's. They ran and screamed past the chessboard tables, dressed in Garanimals, arms loaded with plastic toys, G.I. Joes, water pistols, Wiffle balls. They might as well have been animated Disney bluebirds, twittering harmlessly around the head of the Wicked Witch as she coated an apple with poison.

"Shit," Robert Woolfolk said, and now he smiled. "You know this dude, G?"

"This my man *D-Lone*," Mingus said. "He's cool. We go back, he's my boy from around the block."

Robert looked at Dylan a long while before he spoke.

"I know your boy," he said. "I seen him from before you were even around, G." He flicked his eyes at Dylan. "What up, Dylan man? Don't say you don't remember me, because I know you do."

"Sure," Dylan said.

"Oh, yeah?" Mingus said, carefully blasé. "So you down, right? You cool with my man Dylan."

Robert Woolfolk laughed. "What you need me to say, man? You can hang with your white boy, don't mean shit to me."

At that, the moment was shattered in hilarity. The two other black teenagers snorted, slapped each other five for the words "white boy," as ever a transport to hear said aloud. "Ho, *snap*," one said, shaking his head in wonderment as if he'd just seen a good stunt in a movie, a car flipped over or a body crumpled in a hail of blood-spurting bullet *thwips*.

Dylan stood frozen in his stupid backpack and unpersuasive Keds in the innocent afternoon, his arms numb, blinking his eyes at Mingus.

"We going down to bomb some trains or we sit here all day taking 'bout this and that?" Woolfolk said.

"Let's go," Mingus said softly.

"You bringing your homeboy here?"

Suddenly a woman stepped into the thick of them. Out of nowhere she made herself present. It was as though she'd ruptured a force field Dylan hadn't thought was permeable, one where their talk, no matter how many times the word "fuck" was included, was sealed in a glaze of distant car horns and bird tweets and the younger kids' sweet yells.

The woman was a mom, surely, one of the running kids had to be hers. She was maybe twenty-five or thirty, with blond hair, matching bluejean jacket and bell-bottoms, and granny glasses. Dylan could imagine her at one of his mother's parties, waving a joint around, making some passionate digression about Altman or Szechuan, aggravating men accustomed to holding the floor. There were probably hundreds like her, false Rachels.

"You O.K., kid?"

She spoke to Dylan alone, there was no mistaking. The rest of them, Mingus included, were one thing in her eyes, Dylan another. Of all times, it would have to be now. Dylan had wished what felt like a million times for an adult to step up, for a teacher or a friend of his father's to turn a corner on Dean Street and collide with one of his unnameable disasters, to break it open with a simple question like "You O.K., kid?" But not now. This woman sealed his status as *white boy* forever, precisely when Mingus had been working to change it.

"Hey, kid? Something wrong?"

Dylan had turned to her, helpless, gaping. There was no way to tell her how right and wrong she was at once, no way to make her evaporate. All the worse that she was beautiful, gleaming like the cover of one of Rachel's *Ms.* magazines, which were still stacked up in the living room for Dylan's eventual guilty perusal of illustrated features on bralessness. She shouldn't have popped out of the other world, the Cobble Hill world of private-school kids, it was a misunderstanding.

"They're my friends," Dylan said feebly. As it was out of his mouth it occurred to him he'd failed another test, another where the correct answer was "Fuck you lookin' at?" That phrase, robustly applied, might have actually transported them all back in time to a moment before Robert Woolfolk had said the words "white boy." Dylan might have then been invited to trail the others to a transit yard or wherever else they were going in order to *bomb some trains*, a richly terrifying prospect. Dylan longed to bomb some trains as fiercely as if he'd been hearing that phrae for years instead of just once, moments ago.

No one else piped up to say, "Lady, mind your own fuckin' business," and Dylan saw that Robert Woolfolk and his two companions, Robert's laugh track, were missing. Gone. Dylan had slipped a gear in staring perplexedly at the blond woman, lost a moment in dreaming, and in that moment Robert Woolfolk had shunted away, out of the blithe park that seemed intended to contain anything but him. As though making a silent confession of whatever it was the woman suspected was going on. Only Mingus remained, and he stood apart from the table where the others had sat, and from Dylan.

"Do you want me to walk you home?" the woman asked. "Where do you live?"

"Yo, Dylan man, I'll check you later," Mingus said. He wasn't fearful, only uninterested in contending with the blond woman and anything she thought she knew. "Be cool," Mingus said. He held out his hand, waiting for Dylan to tap it with his fingertips. "I'll check you on the block, D."

With that, Mingus hunched his arms around his jacket pockets as though leaning into a strong wind and ambled into the sun-blobbed trees in the far corner of the park, toward the B.Q.E., the shipyards, wherever he was going where Dylan wasn't going to be swept along now.

That's my best friend, Dylan wanted to tell the blond woman, who the longer he didn't reply to her offer was more and more squinting at Dylan like she might have miscalculated, like he might be a thing spoiled by the company she'd found him in, a misfit, not a kid worth her rescue in the first place.

And that's what he wanted to be to her: spoiled, stained with blackness.

Racist bitch.

Where do I live? In his fantasy Dylan replied, I live in the housing project on Wyckoff Street, that's where. The Gowanus Houses. You know the ones, they're always on fire. If you want to walk me home, lady, let's go.

18

Brownies

ZZ PACKER

ZZ Packer's given name is Zuwena, which means "good" in Swahili. Over the years she grew tired of the difficulty others had pronouncing the name and decided to use the moniker ZZ. She was born in 1973 in Chicago and raised in Atlanta, Georgia, and Louisville, Kentucky. Packer was initially interested in becoming an electrical engineer but later changed course and pursued a writing career. She earned her BA from Yale and then went on to receive an MA at Johns Hopkins University and an MFA at the Iowa Writer's Workshop. Packer made her fictional debut in *The New Yorker* in 2000 with "Drinking Coffee Elsewhere," which would be the titular story in her collection of short stories published in 2003 to considerable acclaim. Her fiction has appeared in *The New Yorker*, *Harper's* and *Zoetrope*. She has also published essays in *New York Times Magazine*, *New York Times Book Review*, and *Salon*. She has received a Whiting Writers' Award, a Rona Jaffe Foundation Writers' Award and a Guggenheim Fellowship. Packer is currently working on her forthcoming novel, *The Thousands*.

By the end of our first day at Camp Crescendo, the girls in my Brownie troop had decided to kick the asses of each and every girl in Brownie Troop 909. Troop 909 was doomed from the first day of camp; they were white girls, their complexions like a blend of ice cream: strawberry, vanilla. They turtled out from their bus in pairs, their rolled-up sleeping bags chromatized with Disney characters—Sleeping Beauty, Snow White, Mickey Mouse—or the generic ones cheap parents bought—washed-out rainbows, unicorns, curley-eyelashed frogs. Some clutched Igloo coolers and still others held on to stuffed toys like pacifiers, looking all around them like tourists determined to be dazzled.

Our troop wended its way past their bus, past the ranger station, past the colorful trail guide drawn like a treasure map, locked behind glass.

"Man, did you smell them?" Arnetta said, giving the girls a slow once-over. "They smell like Chihuahuas. *Wet* Chihuahuas." Although we had passed their troop by yards, Arnetta raised her nose in the air and grimaced.

Arnetta said this from the very rear of the line, far away from Mrs. Margolin, who strung our troop behind her like a brood of obedient ducklings. Mrs. Margolin even looked like a mother duck—she had hair cropped close to a small ball of a head, almost no neck, and huge, miraculous breasts. She wore enormous belts that looked like the kind weight lifters wear, except hers were cheap metallic gold or rabbit fur or covered with gigantic fake sunflowers. Often these belts would become nature lessons in and of themselves. "See," Mrs. Margolin once said to us, pointing to her belt. "This one's made entirely from the feathers of baby pigeons."

The belt layered with feathers was uncanny enough, but I was more disturbed by the realization that I had never actually *seen* a baby pigeon. I searched for weeks for one, in vain—scampering after pigeons whenever I was downtown with my father.

But nature lessons were not Mrs. Margolin's top priority. She saw the position of troop leaders as an evangelical post. Back at the A.M.E. church where our Brownie meetings were held, she was especially fond of imparting religious aphorisms by mean of acrostics—Satan was the "Serpent Always Tempting And Noisome"; she'd refer to the Bible as "Basic Instructions Before Leaving Earth." Whenever she occasionally quizzed us on these at the beginning of the Brownie meeting, expecting to hear the acrostics parroted back to her, only Arnetta's correct replies soared over our vague mumblings. "Jesus?" Mrs. Margolin might ask expectantly, and Arnetta alone would dutifully answer, "Jehovah's Example, Saving Us Sinners."

Arnetta made a point of listening to Mrs. Margolin's religious talk and giving her what she wanted to hear. Because of this, Arnetta could have blared through a megaphone that the white girls of Troop 909 were "wet Chihuahuas" without arousing so much as a blink from Mrs. Margolin. Once Arnetta killed the troop goldfish by feeding it a french fry covered in ketchup, and when Mrs. Margolin demanded an explanation, Arnetta claimed that the goldfish had been eyeing her meal for *hours*, until—giving in to temptation—it had leapt up and snatched the whole golden fry from her fingertips.

"*Serious* Chihuahua," Octavia added—though neither Arnetta nor Octavia could *spell* "Chihuahua" or had ever *seen* a Chihuahua. Trisyllabic words had gained a sort of exoticism within our fourth-grade set at Woodrow Wilson Elementary. Arnetta and Octavia, compelled to outdo each other, would flip through the dictionary, determined to work the vulgar-sounding ones like "Djibouti!" and "asinine" into conversation.

"*Caucasian* Chihuahuas," Arnetta said.

That did it. Drema and Elise doubled up on each other like inextricably entwined kites; Octavia slapped the skim of her belly; Janice jumped straight up in the air, then did it again, just as hard, as if to slam-dunk her own head. No one had laughed so hard since a boy named Martez had stuck his pencil in the electric socket and spent the whole day with a strange grin on his face.

"Girls, girls," said our parent helper, Mrs. Hedy. Mrs. Hedy was Octavia's mother. She wagged her index finger perfunctorily, like a windshield wiper. "Stop it now. Be good." She said this loudly enough to be heard, but lazily, nasally, bereft of any feeling or indication that she meant to be obeyed, as though she would say these words again at the exact same pitch if a button somewhere on her were pressed.

But the girls didn't stop laughing; they only laughed louder. It was the word "Caucasian" that had got them all going. One day at school, about a month before the Brownie camping trip, Arnetta had turned to a boy wearing impossibly high-ankled floodwater jeans and said, "What are *you*? *Caucasian*?" The word took off from there, and soon everything was Caucasian. If you ate too fast, you ate like a Caucasian; if you ate too slow, you ate like a Caucasian. The biggest feat anyone at Woodrow Wilson could do was to jump off the swing in midair, at the highest point in its arc, and if you fell (like I had, more than once) instead of landing on your feet, knees bent Olympic-gymnast-style, Arnetta and Octavia were prepared to comment. They'd look at each other with the silence of passengers who'd narrowly escaped an accident, then nod their heads and whisper with solemn horror and haughtiness, "*Caucasian*."

Even the only white kid in our school, Dennis, got in on the Caucasian act. That time when Martez stuck the pencil in the socket, Dennis had pointed and yelled, "That was *so* Caucasian!"

Living in the south suburbs of Atlanta, it was easy to forget about whites. Whites were like those baby pigeons: real and existing, but rarely thought about. Everyone had been to Rich's to go clothes shopping, everyone had seen white girls and their mothers coo-cooing over dresses; everyone had gone to the downtown library and seen white businessmen swish by importantly, wrists flexed in front of them to check the time on their watches as though they would change from Clark Kent into Superman any second. But those images were as fleeting as cards shuffled in a deck, whereas the ten white girls behind us—*invaders*, Arnetta would later call them—were instantly real and memorable, with their long shampoo-commercial hair, straight as spaghetti from the box. This alone was reason for envy and hatred. The only black girl most of us had ever seen with hair that long was Octavia, whose hair hung past her butt like a Hawaiian hula dancer's. The sight of Octavia's mane prompted other girls to listen to her reverentially, as though whatever she had to say would somehow activate their own follicles. For example, when, one the first day of camp, Octavia made as if to speak, a silence began. "Nobody," Octavia said, "calls us niggers."

At the end of that first day, when half of our troop made its way back to the cabin after tag-team rest-room visits, Arnetta said she'd heard one of the girls in Troop 909 call Daphne a nigger. The other half of the girls and I were helping Mrs. Margolin clean up the pots and pans from the ravioli dinner. When we made our way to the rest rooms to wash up and brush our teeth, we met up with Arnetta midway.

"Man, I completely heard the girl," Arnetta reports. "Right, Daphne?"

Daphne hardly ever spoke, but when she did her voice was petite and tinkly, the voice one might expect from a shiny new earring. She'd written a poem once, for Langston Hughes Day, a poem brimming with the teacher-winning ingredients—trees and oceans, sunsets and moons—but what cinched the poem for the grown-ups, snatching the win from Octavia's musical ode to Grandmaster Flash and The Furious Five, were Daphne's last lines:

> Your are my father, the veteran
> When you cry in the dark
> It rains and rains and rains in my heart

She'd worn clean, though faded, jumpers and dresses when Chic jeans were the fashion, but when she went up to the dais to receive her prize journal, pages trimmed in gold, she wore a new dress with a velveteen bodice and a taffeta skirt as wide as an umbrella. All the kids clapped, though none of them understood the poem. I'd read encyclopedias the way others read comics, and I didn't get it. But those last lines pricked me, they were so eerie, and as my father and I ate cereal, I'd whisper over my Froot Loops, like a mantra, "*You are my father, the veteran. You are my father, the veteran, the veteran, the veteran*," until my father, who acted in plays as Caliban and Othello and was not a veteran, marched me up to my teacher one morning and said, "Can you tell me what the hell's wrong with this kid?"

I had thought Daphne and I might become friends, but she seemed to grow spooked by me whispering those lines to her, begging her to tell me what they meant, and I had soon understood that two quiet people like us were better off quiet alone.

"Daphne? Didn't you hear them call you a nigger?" Arnetta asked, giving Daphne a nudge.

The sun was setting through the trees, and their leafy tops formed a canopy of black lace for the flame of the sun to pass through. Daphne shrugged her shoulders at first, then slowly nodded her head when Arnetta gave her a hard look.

Twenty minutes later, when my rest-room group returned to the cabin, Arnetta was still talking about Troop 909. My rest-room group had passed by some of the 909 girls. For the most part, they had deferred to us, waving us into the rest rooms, letting us go even though they'd gotten there first.

We'd seen them, but from afar, never within their orbit enough to see whether their faces were the way all white girls appeared on TV—ponytailed and full of energy, bubbling over with love and money. All I could see was that some rapidly fanned their faces with their hands, though the heat of the day had long passed. A few seemed to be lolling their heads in slow circles, half-purposefully, as if exercising the muscles of their necks, half-ecstatically, rolling their heads about like Stevie Wonder.

"We can't let them get away with that," Arnetta said, dropping her voice to a laryngitic whisper. "We can't let them get away with calling us niggers. I say we teach them a lesson." She sat down cross-legged on a sleeping bag, an embittered Buddha, eyes glimmering acrylic-black. "We can't go telling Mrs. Margolin, either. Mrs. Margolin'll say something about doing unto others and the path of righteousness and all. Forget that shit." She let her eyes flutter irreverently till they half closed, as though ignoring an insult not worth returning. We could all hear Mrs. Margolin outside, gathering the last of the metal camp-ware.

Nobody said anything for a while. Arnetta's tone had an upholstered confidence that was somehow both regal and vulgar at once. It demanded a few moments of silence in its wake, like the ringing of a church bell or the playing of taps. Sometimes Octavia would ditto or dissent whatever Arnetta had said, and this was the signal that others could speak. But this time Octavia just swirled a long cord of hair into pretzel shapes.

"*Well?*" Arnetta said. She looked as if she had discerned the hidden severity of the situation and was waiting for the rest of us to catch up. Everyone looked from Arnetta to Daphne. It was, after all, Daphne who had supposedly been called the name, but Daphne sat on the bare cabin floor, flipping through the pages of the Girl Scout handbook, eyebrows arched in mock wonder, as if the handbook were a catalogue full of bright and startling foreign costumes. Janice broke the silence. She clapped her hands to broach her idea of a plan.

"They gone be sleeping," she whispered conspiratorially, "then we gone sneak into they cabin, then we gone put daddy longlegs in they sleeping bags. Then they'll wake up. Then we gone beat 'em up till they flat as frying pans!" She jammed her fist into the palm of her hand, then made a sizzling sound.

Janice's country accent was laughable, her looks homely, her jumpy acrobatics embarrassing to behold. Arnetta and Octavia volleyed amused, arrogant smiles whenever Janice opened her mouth, but Janice never caught the hint, spoke whenever she wanted, fluttered around Arnetta and Octavia futilely offering her opinions to their departing backs. Whenever Arnetta and Octavia shooed her away, Janice loitered until the two would finally sigh, "What is it, Miss Caucasoid? What do you want?"

"Oh shut up, Janice," Octavia said, letting a fingered loop of hair fall to her waist as though just the sound of Janice's voice had ruined the fun of her hair twisting.

"All right," Arnetta said, standing up. "We're going to have a secret meeting and talk about what we're going to do."

The word "secret" had a built-in importance. Everyone gravely nodded her head. The modifier form of the word had more clout than the noun. A secret meant nothing; it was like gossip: just a bit of unpleasant knowledge about someone who happened to be someone other than yourself. A secret *meeting*, or a secret *club*, was entirely different.

That was when Arnetta turned to me, as though she knew doing so was both a compliment and a charity.

"Snot, you're not going to be a bitch and tell Mrs. Margolin, are you?"

I had been called "Snot" ever since first grade, when I'd sneezed in class and two long ropes of mucus had splattered a nearby girl.

"Hey," I said. "Maybe you didn't hear them right—I mean—"

"Are you gonna tell on us or not?" was all Arnetta wanted to know, and by the time the question was asked, the rest of our Brownie troop looked at me as though they'd already decided their course of action, me being the only impediment. As though it were all a simple matter of patriotism.

Camp Crescendo used to double as a high school band and field hockey camp until an arching field hockey ball landed on the clasp of a girl's metal barrette, knifing a skull nerve, paralyzing the right side of her body. The camp closed down for a few years, and the girl's teammates built a memorial, filling the spot on which the girl fell with hockey balls, upon which they had painted—all in nail polish—get-well tidings, flowers, and hearts. The balls were still stacked there, like a shrine of ostrich eggs embedded in the ground.

On the second day of camp, Troop 909 was dancing around the mound of nail polish–decorated hockey balls, their limbs jangling awkwardly, their cries like the constant summer squeal of an amusement park. There was a stream that bordered the field hockey lawn, and the girls from my troop settled next to it, scarfing down the last of lunch: sandwiches made from salami and slices of tomato that had gotten waterlogged from the melting ice in the cooler. From the stream bank, Arnetta eyed the Troop 909 girls, scrutinizing their movements to glean inspiration for battle.

"Man," Arnetta said, "we could bum-rush them right now if that damn lady would *leave*."

The 909 troop leader was a white woman with the severe pageboy hairdo of an ancient Egyptian. She lay sprawled on a picnic blanket, Sphinx-like, eating a banana, sometimes holding it out in front of her like a microphone. Beside her sat a girl slowly flapping one hand like a bird with a broken wing. Occasionally, the leader would call out the names of girls who'd attempted leapfrogs and flips, or of girls who yelled too loudly or strayed far from the circle.

"I'm just glad Big Fat Mama's not following us here," Octavia said. "At least we don't have to worry about her." Mrs. Margolin, Octavia assured us, was having her Afternoon Devotional, shrouded in mosquito netting, in a clearing she'd found. Mrs. Hedy was cleaning mud from her espadrilles in the cabin.

"I handled them." Arnetta sucked on her teeth and proudly grinned. "I told her we was going to gather leaves."

"Gather leaves," Octavia said, nodding respectfully. "That's a good one. They're so mad-crazy about this camping thing." She looked from ground to sky, sky to ground. Her hair hung down her back in two braids like a squaw's. "I mean, I really don't know why it's even called *camping*—all we ever do with Nature is find some twigs and say something like, 'Wow, this fell from a tree.'" She then studied her sandwich. With two disdainful fingers, she picked out a slice of dripping tomato, the sections congealed with red slime. She pitched it into the stream embrowned with dead leaves and the murky effigies of other dead things, but in the opaque water a group of small silver-brown fish appeared. They surrounded the tomato and nibbled.

"Look!" Janice cried. "Fishes! Fishes!" As she scrambled to the edge of the stream to watch, a covey of insects threw up tantrums from the wheatgrass and nettle, a throng of tiny electric machines, all going at once. Octavia snuck up behind Janice as if to push her in. Daphne and I exchanged terrified looks. It seemed as though only we knew that Octavia was close enough—and bold enough—to actually push Janice into the stream. Janice turned around quickly, but Octavia was already staring serenely into the still water as though she were gathering some sort of courage from it. "What's so funny?" Janice said, eyeing them all suspiciously.

Elise began humming the tune to "Karma Chameleon," all the girls joining in, their hums light and facile. Janice began to hum, against everyone else, the high-octane opening chords of "Beat It."

"I love me some Michael Jackson," Janice said when she'd finished humming, smacking her lips as though Michael Jackson were a favorite meal. "I will marry Michael Jackson."

Before anyone had a chance to impress upon Janice the impossibility of this, Arnetta suddenly rose, made a sun visor of her hand, and watched Troop 909 leave the field hockey lawn.

"Dammit!" she said. "We've got to get them *alone*."

"They won't ever be alone," I said. All the rest of the girls looked at me. If I spoke even a word, I could count on someone calling me Snot, but everyone seemed to think that we could beat up these girls; no one entertained the thought that they might fight *back*. "The only time they'll be unsupervised is in the bathroom."

"Oh shut up, Snot," Octavia said.

But Arnetta slowly nodded her head. "The bathroom," she said. "The bathroom," she said, again and again. "The bathroom! The bathroom!" She cheered so blissfully that I thought for a moment she was joking.

According to Octavia's watch, it took us five minutes to hike to the rest rooms, which were midway between our cabin and Troop 909's. Inside, the mirrors above the sinks returned only the vaguest of reflections, as though someone had taken a scouring pad to their surfaces to obscure the shine. Pine needles, leaves, and dirty flattened wads of chewing gum covered the floor like a mosaic. Webs of hair matted the drain in the middle of the floor. Above the sinks and below the mirrors, stacks of folded white paper towels lay on a long metal counter. Shaggy white balls of paper towels sat on the sink tops in a line like corsages on display. A thread of floss snaked from a wad of tissues dotted with the faint red-pink of blood. One of those white girls, I thought, had just lost a tooth.

The rest room looked almost the same as it had the night before, but it somehow seemed stranger now. We had never noticed the wooden rafters before, coming together in great Vs. We were, it seemed, inside a whale, viewing the ribs of the roof of its mouth.

"Wow. It's a mess." Elise said.

"You can say that again."

Arnetta leaned against the door-jamb of a rest-room stall. "This is where they'll be again," she said. Just seeing the place, just having a plan, seemed to satisfy her. "We'll go in and talk to them. You know, 'How you doing? How long will you be here?' that sort of thing. Then Octavia and I are gonna tell them what happens when they call any one of us a nigger."

"I'm going to say something, too," Janice said.

Arnetta considered this. "Sure," she said. "Of course. Whatever you want."

Janice pointed her finger like a gun at Octavia and rehearsed the line she'd thought up, "'We're gonna teach you a *lesson.*' That's what I'm going to say." She narrowed her eyes like a TV mobster. "We're gonna teach you little girls a lesson!"

With the back of her hand, Octavia brushed Janice's finger away. "You couldn't teach me to shit in a toilet."

"But," I said, "what if they say, 'We didn't say that. We didn't call anyone a N-I-G-G-E-R'?"

"Snot," Arnetta sighed. "Don't think. Just fight. If you even know how."

Everyone laughed while Daphne stood there. Arnetta gently laid her hand on Daphne's shoulder. "Daphne. You don't have to fight. We're doing this for you."

Daphne walked to the counter, took a clean paper towel, and carefully unfolded it like a map. With this, she began to pick up the trash all around. Everyone watched.

"C'mon," Arnetta said to everyone. "Let's beat it." We all ambled toward the rest-room doorway, where the sunshine made one large white rectangle of light. We were immediately blinded and shielded our eyes with our hands, our forearms.

"Daphne?" Arnetta asked. "Are you coming?"

We all looked back at the girl, who was bending, the thin of her back hunched like a maid caught in stage limelight. Stray strands of her hair were lit nearly transparent, thin fiber-optic threads. She did not nod yes to the question, nor did she shake her head no. She abided, bent. Then she began again, picking up leaves, wads of paper, the cotton fluff innards from a torn stuffed toy. She did it so methodically, so exquisitely, so humbly, she must have been trained. I thought of those dresses she wore, faded and old, yet so pressed and clean; I then saw the poverty in them, I then could imagine her mother, cleaning the houses of others, returning home, weary.

"I guess she's not coming."

We left her, heading back to our cabin, over pine needles and leaves, taking the path full of shade.

"What about our secret meeting?" Elise asked.

Arnetta enunciated in a way that defied contradiction: "We just had it."

Just as we caught sight of our cabin, Arnetta violently swerved away from Octavia. "You farted," she said.

Octavia began to sashay, as if on a catwalk, then proclaimed, in a Hollywood-starlet voice, "My farts smell like perfume."

It was nearing our bedtime, but in the lengthening days of spring, the sun had not yet set.

"Hey, your mama's coming," Arnetta said to Octavia when she saw Mrs. Hedy walk toward the cabin, sniffing. When Octavia's mother wasn't giving bored, parochial orders, she sniffled continuously, mourning an imminent divorce from her husband. She might begin a sentence, "I don't know what Robert will do when Octavia and I are gone. Who'll buy him cigarettes?" and Octavia would hotly whisper "*Mama*" in a way that meant: Please don't talk about our problems in front of everyone. Please shut up.

But when Mrs. Hedy began talking about her husband, thinking about her husband, seeing clouds shaped like the head of her husband, she couldn't be quiet, and no one could ever dislodge her from the comfort of her own woe. Only one thing could perk her up—Brownie songs. If the rest of the girls were quiet, and Mrs. Hedy was in her dopey sorrowful mood, she would say, "Y'all know I like those songs, girls. Why don't you sing one?" Everyone would groan except me and Daphne. I, for one, liked some of the songs.

"C'mon everybody," Octavia said drearily. "She likes 'The Brownie Song' best."

We sang, loud enough to reach Mrs. Hedy:

> I've something in my pocket;
> It belongs across my face.
> And I keep it very close at hand in a most convenient place.
> I'm sure you couldn't guess it
> If you guessed a long, long while.
> So I'll take it out and put it on—
> It's a great big Brownie Smile!

"The Brownie Song" was supposed to be sung as though we were elves in a workshop, singing as we merrily cobbled shoes, but everyone except me hated the song and sang it like a maudlin record, played at the most sluggish of rpms.

"That was good," Mrs. Hedy said, closing the cabin door behind her. "Wasn't that nice, Linda?"

"Praise God," Mrs. Margolin answered without raising her head from the chore of counting out popsicle sticks for the next day's session of crafts.

"Sing another one," Mrs. Hedy said, with a sort of joyful aggression, like a drunk I'd once seen who'd refused to leave a Korean grocery.

"God, Mama, get over it," Octavia whispered in a voice meant only for Arnetta, but Mrs. Hedy heard it and started to leave the cabin.

"Don't go," Arnetta said. She ran after Mrs. Hedy and held her by the arm. "We haven't finished singing." She nudged us with a single look. "Let's sing 'The Friends Song.' For Mrs. Hedy."

Although I liked some of the songs, I hated this one:

> Make new friends
> But keep the o-old,
> One is silver
> And the other gold.

If most of the girls in my troop could be any type of metal, they'd be bunched-up wads of tinfoil maybe, or rusty iron nails you had to get tetanus shots for.

"No, no, no," Mrs. Margolin said before anyone could start in on "The Friends Song." "An uplifting song. Something to lift her up and take her mind off all these earthly burdens."

Arnetta and Octavia rolled their eyes. Everyone knew what song Mrs. Margolin was talking about, and no one, no one, wanted to sing it.

"Please, no," a voice called out. "Not 'The Doughnut Song.'"

"Please not 'The Doughnut Song,'" Octavia pleaded.

"I'll brush my teeth twice if I don't have to sing 'The Doughnut—'"

"Sing!" Mrs. Margolin demanded.

We sang:

> Life without Jesus is like a do-ough-nut!
> Like a do-ooough-nut!
> Like a do-ooough-nut!
> Life without Jesus is like a do-ough-nut!
> There's a hole in the middle of my soul!

There were other verses, involving other pastries, but we stopped after the first one and cast glances toward Mrs. Margolin to see if we could gain a reprieve. Mrs. Margolin's eyes fluttered blissfully, half-asleep.

"Awww," Mrs. Hedy said, as though giant Mrs. Margolin were a cute baby. "Mrs. Margolin's had a long day."

"Yes indeed," Mrs. Margolin answered. "If you don't mind, I might just go to the lodge where the beds are. I haven't been the same since the operation."

I had not heard of this operation, nor when it had occurred, since Mrs. Margolin had never missed the once-a-week Brownie meetings, but I could see from Daphne's face that she was concerned, and I could see that the other girls had decided that Mrs. Margolin's operation must have happened long ago in some remote time unconnected to our own. Nevertheless, they put on sad faces. We had all been taught that adulthood was full of sorrow and pain, taxes and bills, dreaded work and dealings with whites, sickness, and death.

"Go right ahead, Linda," Mrs. Hedy said. "I'll watch the girls." Mrs. Hedy seemed to forget about divorce for a moment; she looked at us with dewy eyes, as if we were mysterious, furry creatures. Meanwhile, Mrs. Margolin walked through the maze of sleeping bags until she found her own. She gathered a neat stack of clothes and pajamas slowly, as though doing so were almost painful. She took her toothbrush, her toothpaste, her pillow. "All right!" Mrs. Margolin said, addressing us all from the threshold of the cabin. "Be in bed by nine." She said it with a twinkle in her voice, as though she were letting us know she was allowing us to be naughty and stay up till 9:15.

"C'mon everybody," Arnetta said after Mrs. Margolin left. "Time for us to wash up."

Everyone watched Mrs. Hedy closely, wondering whether she would insist on coming with us since it was night, making a fight with Troop 909 nearly impossible. Troop 909 would soon be in the bathroom, washing their faces, brushing their teeth—completely unsuspecting of our ambush.

"We won't be long," Arnetta said. "We're old enough to go to the rest rooms by ourselves."

Mrs. Hedy pursed her lips at this dilemma. "Well, I guess you Brownies are almost Girl Scouts, right?"

"Right!"

"Just one more badge," Drema said.

"And about," Octavia droned, "a million more cookies to sell." Octavia looked at all of us. *Now's our chance,* her face seemed to say, but our chance to do *what* I didn't exactly know.

Finally, Mrs. Hedy walked to the doorway where Octavia stood, dutifully waiting to say goodbye and looking bored doing it. Mrs. Hedy held Octavia's chin. "You'll be good?"

"Yes, Mama."

"And remember to pray for me and your father? If I'm asleep when you get back?"

"Yes, Mama."

When the other girls had finished getting their toothbrushes and washcloths and flashlights for the group rest-room trip, I was drawing pictures of tiny birds with too many feathers. Daphne was sitting on her sleeping bag, reading.

"You're not going to come?" Octavia asked.

Daphne shook her head.

"I'm also gonna stay, too," I said. "I'll go to the rest room when Daphne and Mrs. Hedy go."

Arnetta leaned down toward me and whispered so that Mrs. Hedy, who had taken over Mrs. Margolin's task of counting popsicle sticks, couldn't hear. "No, Snot. If we get in trouble, you're going to get in trouble with the rest of us."

.   .   .

We made our way through the darkness by flashlight. The tree branches that had shaded us just hours earlier, along the same path, now looked like arms sprouting menacing hands. The stars sprinkled the sky like spilled salt. They seemed fastened to the darkness, high up and holy, their places fixed and definite as we stirred beneath them.

Some, like me, were quiet because we were afraid of the dark; others were talking like crazy for the same reason.

"Wow," Drema said, looking up. "Why are all the stars out here? I never see stars back on Oneida Street."

"It's a camping trip, that's why," Octavia said. "You're supposed to see stars on camping trips."

Janice said, "This place smells like the air freshener my mother uses."

"These woods are *pine*," Elise said. "Your mother probably uses pine air freshener."

Janice mouthed an exaggerated "Oh," nodding her head as though she just then understood one of the world's great secrets.

No one talked about fighting. Everyone was afraid enough just walking through the infinite deep of the woods. Even without seeing anyone's face, I could tell this wasn't about Daphne being called a nigger. The word that had started it all seemed melted now into some deeper, unnameable feeling. Even though I didn't want to fight, was afraid of fighting, I felt as though I were part of the rest of the troop, as though I were defending something. We trudged against the slight incline of the path, Arnetta leading the way. I wondered, looking at her back, what she could be thinking.

"You know," I said, "their leader will be there. Or they won't even be there. It's dark already. Last night the sun was still in the sky. I'm sure they're already finished."

"Whose flashlight is this?" Arnetta said, shaking the weakening beam of the light she was holding. "It's out of batteries."

Octavia handed Arnetta her flashlight. And that's when I saw it. The bathroom was just ahead.

But the girls were there. We could hear them before we could see them.

"Octavia and I will go in first so they'll think there's just two of us. Then wait till I say, "'We're gonna teach you a lesson,'" Arnetta said. "Then bust in. That'll surprise them."

"That's what I was supposed to say," Janice said.

Arnetta went inside, Octavia next to her. Janice followed, and the rest of us waited outside.

They were in there for what seemed like whole minutes, but something was wrong. Arnetta hadn't given the signal yet. I was with the girls outside when I heard one of the Troop 909 girls say "NO. That did NOT happen!"

That was to be expected, that they'd deny the whole thing. What I hadn't expected was *the voice* in which the denial was said. The girl sounded as though her tongue were caught in her mouth. "That's a BAD word!" the girl continued. "We don't say BAD words!"

"Let's go in," Elise said.

"No," Drema said. "I don't want to. What if we get beat up?"

"Snot?" Elise turned to me, her flashlight blinding. It was the first time anyone had asked my opinion, though I knew they were just asking because they were afraid.

"I say we go inside, just to see what's going on."

"But Arnetta didn't give us the signal," Drema said. "She's supposed to say, 'We're going to teach you a lesson' and I didn't hear her say it."

"C'mon," I said. "Let's just go in."

We went inside. There we found the white girls, but about five girls were huddled up next to one big girl. I instantly knew she was the owner of the voice we'd heard. Arnetta and Octavia inched toward us as soon as we entered.

"Where's Janice?" Elise asked, then we heard a flush. "Oh."

"I think," Octavia said, whispering to Elise, "they're retarded."

"We ARE NOT retarded!" the big girl said, though it was obvious that she was. That they all were. The girls around her began to whimper.

"They're just pretending," Arnetta said, trying to convince herself. "I know they are."

Octavia turned to Arnetta. "Arnetta. Let's just leave."

Janice came out of a stall, happy and relieved, then she suddenly remembered her line, pointed to the big girl, and said, "We're gonna teach you a lesson."

"Shut up, Janice," Octavia said, but her heart was not in it. Arnetta's face was set in a lost, deep scowl. Octavia turned to the big girl and said loudly, slowly, as if they were all deaf, "We're going to leave. It was nice meeting you, okay? You don't have to tell anyone that we were here. Okay?"

"Why not?" said the big girl, like a taunt. When she spoke, her lips did not meet, her mouth did not close. Her tongue grazed the roof of her mouth, like a little pink fish. "You'll get in trouble. I know. I know."

Arnetta got back her old cunning. "If you said anything, then you'd be a tattletale."

The girls looked sad for a moment, then perked up quickly. A flash of genius crossed her face: "I *like* tattletale."

"It's all right, girls. It's gonna be all right!" the 909 troop leader said. It was as though someone had instructed all of Troop 909 to cry at once. The troop leader had girls under her arm, and all the rest of the girls crowded about her. It reminded me of a hog I'd seen on a field trip, where all the little hogs would gather about the mother at feeding time, latching on to her teats. The 909 troop leader had come into the bathroom shortly after the big girl threatened to tell. Then the ranger came, then, once the ranger had radioed the station, Mrs. Margolin arrived with Daphne in tow.

The ranger had left the rest room area, but everyone else was huddled just outside, swatting mosquitoes.

"Oh. They *will* apologize," Mrs. Margolin said to the 909 troop leader, but Mrs. Margolin said this so angrily, I knew she was speaking more to us than to the other troop leader. "When their parents find out, every one a them will be on punishment."

"It's all right. It's all right," the 909 troop leader reassured Mrs. Margolin. Her voice lilted in the same way it had when addressing the girls. She smiled the whole time she talked. She was like one of those TV cooking show women who talk and dice onions and smile all at the same time.

"See. It could have happened. I'm not calling your girls fibbers or anything." She shook her head ferociously from side to side, her Egyptian-style pageboy flapping against her cheeks like heavy drapes. "It *could* have happened, see. Our girls are *not* retarded. They are *delayed* learners." She said this in a syrupy instructional voice, as though our troop might be delayed learners as well. "We're from the Decatur Children's Academy. Many of them just have special needs."

"Now we won't be able to walk to the bathroom by ourselves!" the big girl said.

"Yes you will," the troop leader said, "but maybe we'll wait till we get back to Decatur—"

"I don't want to wait!" the girl said. "I want my Independence patch!"

The girls in my troop were entirely speechless. Arnetta looked as though she were soon to be tortured but was determined not to appear weak. Mrs. Margolin pursed her lips solemnly and said, "Bless them, Lord. Bless them."

In contrast, the Troop 909 leader was full of words and energy. "Some of our girls are echolalic—" She smiled and happily presented one of the girls hanging on to her, but the girl widened her eyes in horror and violently withdrew herself from the center of attention, as though she sensed she were being sacrificed for the village sins. "Echolalic," the troop leader continued. "That means they will say whatever they hear, like an echo—that's where the word comes from. It comes from 'echo.'" She ducked her head apologetically. "I mean, not all of them have the most *progressive* of parents, so if they heard a bad word they might have repeated it. But I guarantee it would not have been *intentional.*"

Arnetta spoke. "I saw her say the word. I heard her." She pointed to a small girl, smaller than any of us, wearing an oversized T-shirt that read: "Eat Bertha's Mussels."

The troop leader shook her head and smiled. "That's impossible. She doesn't speak. She can, but she doesn't."

Arnetta furrowed her brow. "No. It wasn't her. That's right. It was *her.*"

The girl Arnetta pointed to grinned as though she'd been paid a compliment. She was the only one from either troop actually wearing a full uniform: the mocha-colored A-line shift, the orange ascot, the sash covered with patches, though all the same one—the Try-It patch. She took a few steps toward Arnetta and made a grand sweeping gesture toward the sash. "See," she said, full of self-importance, "I'm a Brownie." I had a hard time imagining this girl calling anyone a "nigger"; the girl looked perpetually delighted, as though she would have cuddled up with a grizzly if someone had let her.

On the fourth morning, we boarded the bus to go home.

The previous day had been spent building miniature churches from popsicle sticks. We hardly left the cabin. Mrs. Margolin and Mrs. Hedy guarded us so closely, almost no one talked for the entire day.

Even on the day of departure from Camp Crescendo, all was serious and silent. The bus ride began quietly enough. Arnetta had to sit beside Mrs. Margolin, Octavia had to sit beside her mother. I sat beside Daphne, who gave me her prize journal without a word of explanation.

"You don't want it?"

She shook her head no. It was empty.

Then Mrs. Hedy began to weep. "Octavia," Mrs. Hedy said to her daughter without looking at her, "I'm going to sit with Mrs. Margolin. All right?"

Arnetta exchanged seats with Mrs. Hedy. With the two women up front, Elise felt it safe to speak. "Hey," she said, then she set her face into a placid vacant stare, trying to imitate that of a Troop 909 girl. Emboldened, Arnetta made a gesture of mock pride toward an imaginary sash, the way the girl in full uniform had done. Then they all made a game of it, trying to do the most exaggerated imitations of the Troop 909 girls, all without speaking, all without laughing loud enough to catch the women's attention.

Daphne looked at her shoes, white with sneaker polish. I opened the journal she'd given me. I looked out the window, trying to decide what to write, searching for lines, but nothing could compare with the lines Daphne had written, "*My father, the veteran,*" my favorite line of all time. The line replayed itself in my head, and I gave up trying to write.

By then, it seemed as though the rest of the troop had given up making fun of the 909 girls. They were now quietly gossiping about who had passed notes to whom in school. For a moment the gossiping fell off, and all I heard was the hum of the bus as we sped down the road and the muffled sounds of Mrs. Hedy and Mrs. Margolin talking about serious things.

"You know," Octavia whispered, "why did *we* have to be stuck at a camp with retarded girls? You know?"

"*You* know why," Arnetta answered. She narrowed her eyes like a cat. "My mama and I were in the mall in Buckhead, and this white lady just kept looking at us. I mean, like we were foreign or something. Like we were from China."

"What did the woman say?" Elise asked.

"Nothing," Arnetta said. "She didn't say nothing."

A few girls quietly nodded their heads.

"There was this time," I said, "when my father and I were in the mall and—"

"Oh shut up, Snot," Octavia said.

I stared at Octavia, then rolled my eyes from her to the window. As I watched the trees blur, I wanted nothing more than to be through with it all: the bus ride, the troop, school—all of it. But we were going home. I'd see the same girls in school the next day. We were on a bus, and there was nowhere else to go.

"Go on, Laurel," Daphne said to me. It was the first time she'd spoken the whole trip, and she'd said my name. I turned to her and smiled weakly so as not to cry, hoping she'd remember when I'd tried to be her friend, thinking maybe that her gift of the journal was an invitation of friendship. But she didn't smile back. All she said was, "What happened?"

I studied the girls, waiting for Octavia to tell me to "shut up" again before I even had a chance to utter another word, but everyone was amazed that Daphne had spoken. I gathered my voice. "Well," I said. "My father and

I were in this mall, but I was the one doing the staring." I stopped and glanced from face to face. I continued. "There were these white people dressed like Puritans or something, but they weren't Puritans. They were Mennonites. They're these people who, if you ask them to do a favor, like paint your porch or something, they have to do it. It's in their rules."

"That sucks," someone said.

"C'mon," Arnetta said. "You're lying."

"I am not."

"How do you know that's not just some story someone made up?" Elise asked, her head cocked full of daring. "I mean, who's gonna do whatever you ask?"

"It's not made up. I know because when I was looking at them, my father said, 'See those people. If you ask them to do something, they'll do it. Anything you want.'"

No one would call anyone's father a liar. Then they'd have to fight the person, but Drema parsed her words carefully. "How does your *father* know that's not just some story? Huh?"

"Because," I said, "he went up to the man and asked him would he paint our porch, and the man said, 'Yes.' It's their religion."

"Man, I'm glad I'm a Baptist," Elise said, shaking her head in sympathy for the Mennonites.

"So did the guy do it?" Drema asked, scooting closer to hear if the story got juicy.

"Yeah," I said. "His whole family was with him. My dad drove them to our house. They all painted our porch. The woman and girl were in bonnets and long, long skirts with buttons up to their necks. They guy wore this weird hat and these huge suspenders."

"Why," Arnetta asked archly, as though she didn't believe a word, "would someone pick a *porch*? If they'll do anything, why not make them paint the whole *house*? Why not ask for a hundred bucks?"

I thought about it, and I remembered the words my father had said about them painting our porch, though I had never seemed to think about his words after he'd said them.

"He said," I began, only then understanding the words as they uncoiled from my mouth, "it was the only time he'd have a white man on his knees doing something for a black man for free."

I remembered the Mennonites bending like Daphne had bent, cleaning the rest room. I remembered the dark blue of their bonnets, the black of their shoes. They painted the porch as though scrubbing a floor. I was already trembling before Daphne asked quietly, "Did he thank them?"

I looked out the window. I could not tell which were the thoughts and which were the trees. "No," I said, and suddenly knew there was something mean in the world that I could not stop.

Arnetta laughed. "If I asked them to take off their long skirts and bonnets and put on some jeans, they would do it?"

And Daphne's voice—quiet, steady: "Maybe they would. Just to be nice."

19

Pie of the Month

JEAN THOMPSON

Jean Thompson, a prolific writer of short stories and novels, was born in Chicago, Illinois, and raised in Tennessee and Kentucky. She has published three short fiction collections: *Gasoline Wars* (1979), *Who Do You Love: Stories* (1999), *Throw Like a Girl* (2007), and *Do Not Deny Me* (2009). She has also published four novels: *My Wisdom* (1981), *The Woman Driver* (1985), *Wide Blue Yonder* (2002), and *City Boy* (2004) as well as a collection of children's stories, *Little Face and Other Stories* (1984). Thompson's short fiction has appeared in a national roster of magazines and has been anthologized in *The Best American Short Stories*. She is the recipient of Guggenheim and National Endowment for the Arts fellowships. A graduate of Bowling Green State University's creative writing MFA program, Thompson taught creative writing at the University of Illinois at Urbana-Champaign for more than 30 years. In a *Chicago Tribune* article, Thompson stated: "I'm much less interested in the glamorous, the extreme, the freakish. Fiction that features such characters often seems contrived to me. What intrigues me are the interior lives of anyone you might meet during the course of an unremarkable day, the possibilities for tragedy and drama that exist in any life."

So much of the world had changed and kept on changing. But you could count on the pie list to remain the same. January was always custard, February chocolate, March lemon meringue. There were no substitutions. The absoluteness of this was comforting, since there were, in general, many rules now, which were often superseded without warning by new, contradictory rules. In the matter of coconut cream (April) it was true that Mrs. Colley had persuaded Mrs. Pulliam to allow, if not a substitution, at least a little flexibility. There were people who had really violent feelings about coconut. Mrs. Pulliam was not inclined to humor them. She was an artist. There were aesthetics involved in the choice of pies, the harmonies of taste and weather. The cycle of seasons gave rise to the cycle of cravings, for tart or smooth or juicy. Mrs. Colley had to frame it as a question of allergies, and only then did Mrs. Pulliam relent and offer (on occasion, and by special request) a banana cream alternative. But it always set her to brooding, and Mrs. Colley had learned to walk wide of her at such times.

The Pie of the Month Club's motto was Easy as Pie! With an exclamation point in the shape, of a rolling pin. Pies were delivered to subscribers on the first or third Friday of the month. Although Hi Ho was not a large community, the reputation of the pies was such that the ladies had no lack of business. The crusts were perfect marriages of shortening and flour, so that each bite simultaneously resisted and gave way. The fillings were piled high and handsome. Of course only the best-quality ingredients were used. Nowadays, when there was so much concern about contamination (air, water, crops), a pie harkened back to simpler, more wholesome times. No one had yet cast any aspersions on pie. People in Hi Ho were sensible folks with their feet firmly on the ground, not inclined to sway with each new panic. Still, Mrs. Colley was afraid a day might come when even pie would turn up in one of those ominous newspaper articles, accused of causing some disease you never knew existed until then.

Mrs. Colley tried to avoid the news as much as possible. It was all so worrisome, and all so completely beyond your control. She much preferred the kind of magazines that had recipes instead of news, and television programs where people lived in nice houses and had glamorous problems. But sometimes the news seeped in anyway. She'd be settled in her chair, her front still faintly damp from the evening's dishes, her iced tea and Kleenex within reach, and instead of her program there would be a news bulletin you couldn't avoid. Usually it was about something blowing up. And since whatever blew up was in a place you'd never been, or sometimes never even heard of, you first thought what a terrible thing it was, followed by relief that it had nothing to do with you, really, followed by a vague guilt at feeling relieved.

It was all the fault of the War, or Wars. One ran into the other nowadays, Mrs. Colley couldn't keep them straight. Wars were different than they used to be. They were all fought in hot places, for one thing. The current War had begun back in October (pecan), and they were trying to get it wrapped up before summer, when the great parade of fruit pies (cherry, blueberry, peach) began. Fruit pie season was not a good time to be fighting a War in a hot place. The War news was always about how we were winning, but the enemy was refusing to admit it and was fighting back in dirty, underhanded ways, such as blowing things up or poisoning (or threatening to poison) some vital resource. How were you supposed to deal reasonably with people like that?

When the phone rang at a certain time of evening, it was always Mrs. Pulliam. Mrs. Colley pressed the mute button on the television remote so she could still follow her program as she conversed. Mrs. Pulliam said, "Tell me this rhubarb was meant as a joke."

"What's wrong with it?"

"Aside from being so woody you can whittle it, nothing."

When Mrs. Pulliam was in this particular mood, you had to let her run on for a time. Mrs. Colley murmured that people these days did not understand rhubarb as they used to. She thought this was true. Certain vegetables, peas for example, no longer got the respect they once had. Mrs. Pulliam sniffed in disdain, "The only thing to understand about rhubarb is you pick it before it gets old and tough. It's not rocket science."

Mrs. Colley's program required her attention just then. Something was being explained, some important part of the story that you wouldn't get if you couldn't hear. She clicked the volume up to the first level and said, trying to sound more concerned than she was, "It's what, just six pies tomorrow? Couldn't you mix them three-quarters strawberry, one-quarter rhubarb instead of half and half?"

"It's the rhubarb that gives it body," said Mrs. Pulliam, not ready to stop being irritable. "Without enough rhubarb, it's like jam."

"Well Joyce, why not let me make them? Then if they don't turn out, everybody can blame me."

"Absolutely not," said Mrs. Pulliam, just as Mrs. Colley had meant her to. "You know very well I always do May. It's my responsibility and I'll see to it, thank you very much."

After she put the phone down and got caught up with her program, Mrs. Colley thought, not for the first time, that Mrs. Pulliam made things more difficult than was necessary. She attributed this to Mrs. Pulliam's divorce and the fact that her only child, a boy, had a bad character and had gone off to live in Chicago. Mrs. Colley was a widow. Her daughter, Margery, lived right here in Hi Ho. Margery and her husband had two precious babies, well they were hardly babies anymore, four and six, but that was how she thought of them. Mrs. Colley's son John and his wife lived in Des Moines, which was too far away for Mrs. Colley's liking but at least in the same state. John and his wife did not have any children yet, even though Mrs. Colley dropped hints from time to time about how much she would love to have more grandbabies.

The news said that before they went to the War, some soldiers had stored their sperm in freezers, in case something chemical happened to them in battle. You were really better off not knowing a thing like that.

Mrs. Colley had grown accustomed to widowhood. It had been a terrible thing, of course, her husband's heart attack, and the anxious tug of hope while he lingered, and then the press of large and small events necessary to accomplish a man's death. Everything after that was slower. Slow march of hours and days, months and years. Nothing much changed, except she grew older and more settled into her leftover life.

She got by all right. Sometimes she turned on a football game so she would have a man's voice in the house. And sometimes, if she was shopping at the SuperStuff and found herself in the automotive or hardware or electrical aisle, surrounded by all the mysterious items men used to keep the world running, she missed her husband terribly. Then she would feel so down and blue, she would start thinking bad, crazy things, like what if her grandson, Ronnie, grew up and went to a War and they did something to his sperm? That multitude of little unformed pearls inside him, all doomed. Or what if something in Hi Ho were to blow up? The grain elevator, for instance, or the American Legion. Hi Ho would be the last place you'd expect something like that to happen, and that was exactly why it would be targeted.

At such times Mrs. Colley turned to the Rainbow pills her doctor had prescribed. Of course the pills had a longer, medical name, but they were advertised on television with rainbows. The commercial began with a gray, drippy cartoon sky, which gradually gave way to arcs of violet, red, yellow, green. Cartoon flowers sprouted and cartoon birds sang. While you understood that this was a commercial and was not meant as a literal representation—when it came to advertising one both resisted and succumbed, like pie crust—it was true that the pills made Mrs. Colley *feel* more rainbowlike. Peaceful and sort of glowing. And what was the harm in that, as long as your side effects (headache, nausea, gas, bloating, diarrhea or menstrual pain) were the exact same ones the commercial reassured you were normal?

Mrs. Colley went to Mrs. Pulliam's house in midafternoon, when the strawberry-rhubarb pies were scheduled to be done. Mrs. Pulliam had not disappointed. The six pies sat cooling on the kitchen table. The crusts were delicate brown with scroll-shaped cutouts that showed the deep jewel color of the filling. The pies smelled of May, of blossom and warm wind and sweetness. Mrs. Colley leaned over to drink in the smell. "Oh, heaven," she murmured.

Mrs. Pulliam stood at the sink, washing up. "That rhubarb gave me fits."

"Joyce, they turned out perfect."

"*Perfect,*" said Mrs. Pulliam, angling the spray hose to scald a glass, "is a word cheapened by overuse. In the course of a normal lifetime, I very much doubt if anyone encounters perfection."

Yet Mrs. Colley knew that her friend relied on her appreciation, even as she grudged and pushed it from her. Mrs. Pulliam's tall figure bent over to scour a cookie sheet. She wore a hairnet while baking and with her hair skinned back her profile was severe. If you were uncharitable, you might even say it was witchlike. Fretting had kept her thin over the years. Mrs. Colley didn't think that Mrs. Pulliam was unhappy, not in any active sense. More like she'd grown into the habit of mistrusting happiness and had to call it by other names.

A breeze ruffled Mrs. Pulliam's blue curtains. Outside the window a bumblebee lumbered in the white flowers of the spirea. The new grass bent and tossed like a herd of green ponies at play. One of the Mexican families who lived in the trailers across the field had put out a line of wash, children's small bright shirts and pants.

The Mexicans were something new. Hi Ho had been founded by industrious German and Swiss farmers, just the sort of people you would have chosen yourself to found a town, if you'd had any say in it. There were streets in Hi Ho named Hoffman and Schroeder. In the fall there was a Heritage Day when children were dressed up in dirndls and lederhosen and performed Tyrolean folk songs.

But in the last few years, a portion of town had come more to resemble Guadalajara. The Mexicans mostly worked in the meatpacking plants two towns over. Although they were from a hot country, we were not at War with them. There was a new Catholic church to accommodate them, an addition to the many flavors of Protestant. The Hi Ho Market now sold chilies and cans of hominy and packets of Mexican spices. Mrs. Colley did not know any Mexicans personally. She thought they were all right as long as they kept to themselves and didn't go jabbering Spanish at you when they knew you couldn't understand it. She was not the sort to be prejudiced about people just because they came from a hot country.

Mrs. Pulliam looked out the window, where two of the Mexican children had come outside and were kicking a ball around, soccer-style. "Those people won't ever be subscribers. They don't have a tradition of pie."

"We could take some pies by the Catholic church sometime. A free, introductory offer."

"I don't see them going for it, in a business way."

"It would be neighborly," said Mrs. Colley, but they let the idea pass. Being neighborly was a good thing, of course, except there was a sense in which the Mexicans were not real neighbors.

Mrs. Pulliam took her apron off and poured two cups of coffee. She set the cream jug in front of Mrs. Colley's chair, although she herself continued to stand. "Maybe it's just as well we don't add subscribers. Who knows how much longer I'll want to keep on with the baking."

Mrs. Colley tried not to show her alarm. In all of Mrs. Pulliam's history of complaint, she had never mentioned quitting the pies outright. "A long time, I hope. Otherwise, people would be so disappointed."

"Would they," said Mrs. Pulliam. She reached up to pull the hairnet off, though her hair stayed in the same crimped, hairnet shape. "Oh, I suppose. Yes, they would at first, sure. Then they'd adjust. It's only pie. I keep thinking that. All the fuss and bother for something people gobble down in a day or two."

Mrs. Colley knew better than to approach any issue with Mrs. Pulliam head-on. She said, "I saw the most interesting recipe in one of my magazines. Rustic plum tart."

"Gaaagh."

"I'm just saying. Maybe something different once in a while. Perk you right up. They had another one, peanut butter pie with an Oreo crust."

"If I'm going to start down that road, I might as well bake *cupcakes*. I make pies the way they're meant to be. I have to believe there's still an audience for that. Now you'd better get this batch around to people."

Mrs. Colley always handled the deliveries. She had certain people skills that Mrs. Pulliam, being an artist, lacked, and besides, she enjoyed getting out and about. She loaded the pies in their special baskets and set off in her old car, motoring carefully down the quiet streets. Tree shadow from the new leaves cast lace patterns on the pavement. There was a cloud at the edge of the beautiful day. For reasons of her own, or for no reason except temperament, Mrs. Pulliam might decide to end Pie of the Month. It no longer seemed to give her satisfaction to make pie for pie's sake. Mrs. Colley wished she could get Mrs. Pulliam to see how sociable a pie really was, how it brought people together, gave them something to look forward to, talk about, share.

The first delivery stop was Jeffy Johnson. He was out watering his grass seed when Mrs. Colley pulled up. "Hi Jeffy, how are you today?"

"Wonderful and blessed, Mrs. C., wonderful and blessed."

Jeffy always said that. There was a sense that you were meant to answer back, "Hallelujah," but Mrs. Colley never could bring herself to do so. Jeffy was short and round-bottomed and cheerful. Like all the other black people in Hi Ho, he went to the A.M.E. church. He drove an Oldsmobile Cutlass with a license plate that read PRAY MOR. He was a bachelor and the A.M.E. ladies were always trying to marry him off. Mrs. Colley thought that Jeffy enjoyed all the fuss and attention and would hold out as long as possible before he got himself a wife, and then he would say it was the Lord's plan. Mrs. Colley attended the Lutheran church and would have called herself religious, although not to the point where she thought religion made any actual difference in the world.

Jeffy set the pie basket on the porch and said that strawberry-rhubarb was his favorite pie. "Until you come along with next month's, that is." It was the joke he always made.

"Pray that there is a next month, Jeffy," said Mrs. Colley, trying to make it come out humorous instead of small and quavering, as it did. Jeffy clasped Mrs. Colley's hands in his big brown ones and when he bowed his head she felt obliged to do likewise. When Jeffy raised up again and said, "Amen," Mrs. Colley felt embarrassed, as if she'd taken advantage.

The last stop on the pie route was always her daughter Margery's, so that Mrs. Colley could visit with the grandbabies. Margery did not bake her own pies because she worked part-time, in addition to chasing after two kids whenever she was home and never having a minute to herself.

Mrs. Colley tried not to pass judgment on any of this, or on the state of Margery's house, which today as usual was at sixes and sevens. Cheerios floated in the kitchen sink. Every towel in the house seemed to have assembled on the bathroom floor. The television was on, although no one was watching it. The President was doing a commercial for the War. Ronnie and his little sister, Crystal, were playing chase. Ronnie had a potato peeler in his mouth and his arms spread out, airplane-style. He made *rat-tat-tat* noises as he tried to trap Crystal in a corner and divebomb her. "Look, darlings, Grandma's here! I brought you a strawberry-rhubarb pie!"

"I hate strawberry," said Ronnie, talking around the potato peeler.

"I hate rhubarb," Crystal chimed in, although she didn't really. She was just being cute.

Margery cleared a space for the pie on the kitchen counter but didn't go out of her way to act appreciative. Margery sometimes sneaked cigarettes. Mrs. Colley was not supposed to know about this but she did anyway. Margery still wore her red smock from work. She was a sales associate at Super-Stuff. Margery said, "They cut back my hours again."

"I'm sorry."

"Ronnie, knock it off," Margery called, but without energy. The thunder of feet kept shaking the house. "Yeah. I guess I should be glad, since it's only the worst job in the world."

Mrs. Colley watched as Margery took a number of items out of the freezer to start supper: a bag of Tater Tots, package of corn, fish fillets stuck together in the shape of a brick. Mrs. Colley said, "I saw somewhere that fish can give you mercury poisoning."

"Not if it's frozen, I don't think."

They didn't say anything else about the hours cutback, and after a while Mrs. Colley took herself home.

It didn't used to be that husband and wife both had to work to put food on the table. She and Mr. Colley had managed. But there had not been so many things to buy back then, and there hadn't been a stock market, or there had been but it wasn't full of crooks who sucked all the money out of the world overnight. Times were hard. Jeffy Johnson said it was the seven lean years like in the Bible. The President said there were always sacrifices in time of War. Mrs. Colley took a Rainbow pill and slept for nine and a half hours.

June was cherry pie month, one of Mrs. Colley's favorites, even though cherry juice stained like the dickens. Mrs. Colley still got up on a stepladder and picked cherries from her own tree. There was nothing quite as pretty as a cherry tree, the sprays of red fruit against the green leaves. The birds were never happier than in cherry season. June was always good. June was fireflies and brides. Crops were planted and there had not yet been too much or not enough rain. School got out and children planned long campaigns of play.

Mrs. Colley and Mrs. Pulliam ran cherries through the hand-cranked cherry pitter, saving the juice to can later. Mrs. Colley used a plastic form to stamp out the lattice crusts, which was cheating, sort of, but couldn't be helped. She knew her crust was not the equal of Mrs. Pulliam's, although only a longtime subscriber might notice the difference. She flattered herself that she had a better flair for the fruit pies, a more generous hand with the fillings than Mrs. Pulliam. Her best cherry pies made you wish there was such a thing as a cherry pie tree.

The last few weeks she'd kept a close eye on Mrs. Pulliam, watching for signs of discontent. But Mrs. Pulliam pitted cherries and weighed out sugar and did her share of the chores without complaint. Just as Mrs. Colley was taking the last of the last batch of cherry pies out of the oven, Mrs. Pulliam said, out of nowhere, "Bobby called."

Bobby was Mrs. Pulliam's bad son in Chicago. He did not often call. Mrs. Colley, as she was meant to, kept her eyes on the pies as she asked, "Well, how's Bobby?"

"He's part of a group now."

When Mrs. Pulliam didn't say anything more helpful, Mrs. Colley was forced to ask what kind of group.

"It's a No More War group."

You might expect as much from long-haired, pot-smoking Bobby, and Mrs. Colley was about to murmur something by way of consolation, when Mrs. Pulliam spoke again. "Bobby says we aren't winning the War, we're losing it."

This was such an unexpected idea that Mrs. Colley had no response, only stood there with her hands in oven mitts. Mrs. Pulliam went on. "He says we keep having Wars just so everyone stays all stirred up and scared."

"Now what possible reason would anyone have for wanting that?"

Mrs. Pulliam only shrugged and went back to balancing the month's accounts.

The last week in June the meatpacking plant fired all the Mexicans. The government said it was not safe to have foreigners, people of unknown, un-documented backgrounds, motives, and sympathies, at work in the sensitive area of food supply. Many of the Mexicans just disappeared. Overnight, it seemed, they were gone. They left behind cars, the children's bicycles, food in kitchens, shoes in closets. It was hard to get new workers to replace them. The worst job in the world wasn't at SuperStuff, in spite of what Margery said. Everyone knew the worst jobs were probably in the meatpacking plant, in the slaughter room, or the hide room, or the rendering room. The Texas bank that had already bought up a lot of the farms took over the plant and cut back on the shifts.

Mrs. Colley found that she missed the Mexicans, the blackeyed babies, the snatches of Spanish radio on Main Street. Some people said they must have done something criminal, clearing out like that, but Mrs. Colley wondered if they weren't just afraid. The Mexicans who remained behind were having a hard time making ends meet, and the churches in Hi Ho organized a food drive for them. The Lutheran pastor, young Reverend Higgs, gave a sermon about charity and brotherhood and overcoming differences, which made everybody feel better, since that was exactly what they'd done. Summer baseball leagues started up. There was a bank robbery in Des Moines and Mrs. Colley was terribly worried about her son, John, who worked in a bank, until she reached him on the phone and found out it was a different bank. The War was said to be winding down, although things still blew up now and then. For whole days at a time you could almost forget there was a War going on; there was too much else to crowd it out. But the War was like a pie you'd left in the oven, something nagging at you, a task left unfinished.

July was for blueberry pies. Blueberries were grown in cool places, and when you sifted through the fruit, washing and straining and picking out stems, you thought of pine trees, of gray, chill lakes and seagulls. Blueberry was the easiest of the fruit pies, nothing to pit or peel, and that was a mercy. July was always so blamed hot. The sun rode the sky all day long. There was no rain (the drought had been going on almost as long as the Wars), except for those times when a black storm swept in and sent forks of lightning and crop-shredding hail.

There was a Fourth of July parade, with the fire truck going five miles an hour and running its siren, the high school band, the Veterans of Foreign Wars (by which was meant the old-fashioned Wars that were already in the history books), marching in formation, and some convertibles donated by a car dealership. Mrs. Pulliam got her hands on a quantity of nearly flawless blackberries and donated a dozen pies to the Freedom Celebration picnic. When you cut into the pies each blackberry was still perfectly shaped, glistening with grains of undissolved sugar. No one had ever seen or tasted anything like them.

Mrs. Pulliam stood beneath the awning that covered the picnic tables, accepting compliments. Mrs. Colley was pleased to see her friend getting the recognition that she deserved, pleased also that Mrs. Pulliam seemed to be enjoying herself, after a fashion. She had even dressed up a little, for her, in a new red and white blouse that seemed more cheerful than Mrs. Pulliam herself. For there was a kind of formality, even aloofness, to Mrs. Pulliam as she acknowledged people's thank-yous, and that was to be expected. There was for every artist the awful moment when they stepped out from behind their splendid creation and revealed the meager, human-sized self that was bound to disappoint by comparison. People filled their mouths with sweet corn and potato salad and fried chicken and pie, pie, pie. The excellence of the food was some consolation for the fireworks show, which everyone agreed was not as good as last year's.

In mid-July it was announced the SuperStuff would be closing. The national chains were all cutting their losses, tightening their belts. The store hired a number of the Mexicans to stand on street corners with red, white, and blue signs that said Everything Must Go! Prices were reduced by twenty, then thirty, then forty percent and more. For a time the SuperStuff's parking lot was jam-packed and they did more business in a weekend than they might have in a month. Mrs. Colley stocked up on those items of apparel which a lady of her age and size required. People wandered the aisles. There was a pleasant sense that everything in the store was available for the taking, for free or very nearly free. Everyone in Hi Ho had new dish towels and sheet sets and garden hoses and CD players and fishing rods and generators, and then the store was shut for good.

Margery found work a few hours a week at the dry cleaners, running clothes through the machines that tumbled them and took out spots and gave them that dry cleaning smell. A while back there had been some kind of alarm about dry cleaning, about the chemicals used, but then it was determined that exposure was within acceptable limits. Mrs. Colley babysat Ronnie and Crystal to help out. Ronnie said he wanted to be a baseball player when he grew up. Crystal said she wanted to be a television lady. There was a scare about eating beef, something that had nothing to do with the Mexicans, and just like that you couldn't give beef away. Everyone knew the scare would wear off sooner or later but before it could, the Texas bank closed the meatpacking plant and hauled all the equipment down to Texas or who knows where and padlocked the gates. Most of the local farmers had long since sold off their cattle because of the drought, but still it was a blow. For a time there was talk that the state might build one of its new prisons in the county and bring back some jobs, but nothing ever came of it.

You wanted so badly to believe that life was basically good, that people were basically good. And Mrs. Colley did believe it. She might not go around announcing that she was wonderful and blessed, but she reminded herself often that there were many terrible places she could have been born into but had not. Nothing abnormally bad had ever happened to her personally or was likely to happen except for, eventually, dying, oh well. But nowadays there was so little you could trust to stay good, as if there was a pinhole at the bottom of the world and all the best things were leaking out of it.

.   .   .

In August, everyone's water bills doubled. It came out that the water utility had been bought up by a company in Belgium. Belgium! Most people in Hi Ho were unaware that you could do such a thing as sell the water, and it was unclear why anyone in Belgium should own a lot of the water in Iowa. It was some consolation that Belguim was not one of the hot countries; when people looked it up on maps, it was right up there with normal nations like France and Germany. The new Belgian water company said the increased bills reflected higher costs for security, that it was now necessary to guard against the possibility of the water supply being blown up or poisoned. That was odd, since the workers at the filtration plant still kept the side gate wide open in summer. That way they could leave their cars in the shade of the adjoining park, and take their lunch coolers out there at break time.

"Bobby says it isn't really countries that fight Wars now. It's corporations. The corporations are bigger than the countries."

"I just can't keep up with all of Bobby's ideas," said Mrs. Colley, which she hoped was a tactful way of saying she was tired of hearing about them. Bobby and Mrs. Pulliam talked a lot these days, and after every conversation Mrs. Pulliam offered up some new, outlandish opinion.

"Bobby says everything's global now. Things that happen on the other side of the world, even small things, affect everyone else. He says we are a global village."

"Well that sounds nice," said Mrs. Colley, still trying to be agreeable. "I think I would like to live there."

Mrs. Pulliam shook her head darkly. "The news we see these days isn't the real news," she began. Fortunately the oven timer went off just then.

They were in the middle of the August peach pies. Peach pies were murder. The fruit had to be perfect, firm enough to handle but ripe enough to juice up. The skins almost never came off easy, and by the time you dug the pits out, you threw away more than you saved. August was murder. Ponds turned green and stagnant, the ground dried and split into thirsty cracks. Only the air was humid, like breathing through blankets. When Mrs. Colley and Mrs. Pulliam baked peach pies they didn't even try to run the AC, just set up big fans to blow the heat away. It was a lot of effort, but a good peach pie was a triumph. Mrs. Pulliam always cut smiling sun faces into the top crusts, because the pies had the sun in them, that was what you tasted, everything yellow and ripe.

When they'd finished the last of the pies and done the washing up and put everything away, they sat on Mrs. Colley's screened-in porch to let the house cool down. It was nighttime. A haze of heat blurred the stars. The fireflies were mostly gone by August, but here and there one sent up a faint, greenish spark. Cicadas and mosquitoes bumped against the screens. Mrs. Colley had put sprigs of mint in the iced tea and they let the ice melt a little so it was good and cold. If you raised your eyes beyond the lights of town you saw, or imagined you saw, the outline of the grass-covered hills that had been there, exactly the same, for a thousand thousand years.

"What's got into you lately?" Mrs. Colley heard herself saying. It just popped out. She held her breath.

Mrs. Pulliam was silent for a moment, then she said, "I think I may have gone about as far as it's possible to go with pie."

"I don't understand. Going farther? Why do you have to go anywhere at all?"

"Maybe the world makes you restless. Maybe you just get older, and wonder if you should have lived a different life. A bigger life."

Mrs. Colley thought that all the things she loved were small. They were all close by; she could practically reach out and touch them. She muddled her words trying to explain that this was not a bad thing. She only managed, "Well mercy sakes, Joyce, you talk like life was already over and done with." Although even as she spoke she had a sense that so many things, if not over and done with, had long since been determined for her.

In the darkness Mrs. Pulliam turned toward her and gave her a look, although the look itself was invisible. "I expect you're right. Now I'd best be getting home. This heat! You could wring out the air like a dishrag."

At the end of August, the President said the War was over, and there was general public satisfaction at a job well done. But the very next week there was a new War, or rather, a return to one of the old Wars already won. It was breaking out again, like a rash, and once more there were flags and headlines and airships named after birds of prey. The following Sunday the Lutheran pastor, young Reverend Higgs, climbed up to the pulpit made of varnished blond oak and preached a sermon whose text was "Blessed are the peacemakers, for they shall be called the children of God."

The Lutheran congregation sat as if they had been given orders not to flinch. Sunlight poured through the stained glass window depicting Jesus the Shepherd of His Flock. Oblongs and lozenges of red, violet, gold, and green moved imperceptibly across the blond oak floorboards. There was a vague sense that someone might come to arrest them all on the spot. When Reverend Higgs finished his sermon and the benediction and the organist played the first chords of the recessional, there were people who went out the exit without staying to greet and visit. There were others who filed out and shook hands with the pastor without knowing what to say.

Mrs. Colley was one of these. Reverend Higgs looked pale and exhausted and noble, like Jesus. "Oh Pastor," she began. Foolish tears brimmed in her eyes. A great confusion of words was welling up in her, but she only said again, "Oh Pastor." The crowd behind her inched reluctantly forward, as if in line for vaccinations. Reverend Higgs murmured a blessing, and Mrs. Colley let her hand drop.

That night she felt unwell. She slept fitfully, and had extraordinary and disturbing dreams. There was a rainbow in the sky that drifted closer and closer until you saw that it was really poison fumes in lurid, neon colors. Margery took packages of frozen sperm out of the freezer for supper. Mr. Colley appeared, dressed in the coveralls and straw hat he always wore for gardening, asking her where she put the. The. She couldn't make out what he wanted because it was a small thing on the other side of the world. Mrs. Colley woke up with a fever and chills and a sore head and called Margery to take her to the doctor's.

The doctor said there was a lot of this going around lately and gave Mrs. Colley some new prescriptions and told her to stay in bed. Mrs. Colley dozed with her windowblinds closed against the heat and the air conditioner whispering to her. Margery fixed her meals of toast and fruit Jell-O, though she didn't have much appetite and was content to sleep. The doctor said there was a lot of War sickness going around lately. Now wasn't that silly. She knew she was dreaming. The cool sheets lulled her, the air conditioner sighed. How could you get sick from a War?

By the time Mrs. Colley felt well enough to get out of bed and open her blinds, it was already September and the yellow heat had dropped out of the sky.

"I'm still weak as a kitten," she fretted to Mrs. Pulliam over the phone. "I've never been so useless in all my days."

"Then there's no point in you even leaving the house. Make yourself sick all over again."

"But the apple pies!"

September was apple. *A* for apple in the children's schoolbooks. Red apple barns and wagons, the promise of fall. Apple pie being what it was, there were people who doubled their September orders. Apple was the queen of pies. A baker's reputation rose or fell on it.

"I'll manage fine," said Mrs. Pulliam. "The last thing I need is you getting your old germs all over the place."

"I don't have germs anymore, don't be rude."

"Or falling face down into the flour bin. I'm not going to argue with you."

"I've got the rest of the week to get my strength back," said Mrs. Colley stubbornly.

But when baking day came around she wasn't much better, still short of breath and unsteady on her feet. "I can still do the deliveries," she told Mrs. Pulliam when she called. In the background she heard water running, pans clashing like cymbals.

"Get Margery to help you. I'll leave some money for her trouble."

"Leave? Where are you going to be?"

"I'm going to visit Bobby." There was a whirring, grinding sound that Mrs. Colley knew was the device that took off apple peel in a long thin spiral, cored and cut the fruit into slices. "Don't worry, the pies will be ready."

"You're going to Chicago?" The enormity of this was enough to make Mrs. Colley wonder if she was having another fever dream, as if her sickness had loosened the top of her head like a box lid and now strange things were always falling in and out. "For how long?"

"For a spell. If a grown woman can't take herself on an occasional trip, then I don't know what. Now shoo, I have work to do."

"What is it you aren't telling me? What don't I know?"

The clatter in the background stopped. "You already know everything you need to know. You just have to let yourself believe it," said Mrs. Pulliam, and then she hung up.

Mrs. Colley woke early and drove herself to Mrs. Pulliam's house. It seemed like a long time since she had been outside, and the season had changed. There were dew-covered spiderwebs in the long grass. She noted here and there an early tree, ash or elm, getting ready to turn. The sky was still pink from sunrise. Far overhead a plane pulled a line of silver from west to east. You knew these things because you saw them. Wasn't seeing believing?

When she parked the car in Mrs. Pulliam's driveway, a cinnamon wind enveloped her, wafting from every chink and window. The back door was open. Two pieces of knowledge registered with Mrs. Colley at the same time: that the house was full of pies, and that Mrs. Pulliam was gone, like the Mexicans.

Or not really like the Mexicans, since everything was scrubbed and ordered and cleared away. There were bags of clothes with labels directing them to the Goodwill, tags on furniture, boxes of household goods stacked in the laundry room. And everywhere there were pies.

On the kitchen table, lined up on the counters. The cupboard doors were open to make space for pies. The dining room table and every chair, the bookshelves and dressers. The mattress was covered in a thin, clean sheet, and two dozen pies were set out on it. There were even pies in the bathtub, wrapped up in plastic. And on every top crust, words had been cut out, one hundred, two hundred times, pie after pie after pie:

NO

MORE WAR

Mrs. Colley both knew and believed that if she counted, there would be a pie for every household in Hi Ho. On the kitchen table was an envelope filled with money, all the proceeds from this year's subscriptions. The pies on the table were still warm. Mrs. Pulliam must have left only minutes before.

Mrs. Colley removed a pie from a chair so she could sit down. She cradled a pie in her lap as if it were a living thing, a bird or a lamb or a child. In a little while she would call Margery and they would begin their chores. Mrs. Colley would take baskets of pie to the trailer court and ask the Mexicans how you said it in Spanish, NO MORE WAR. All over town, people would be eating apple pie, swallowing the words down, NO MORE WAR, and they would put it on the license plates of their cars, and pastors would spell it out on the brick-framed billboards in front of churches, it would deck the marquee of the old Cinema, NO MORE WAR. Farmers bringing in their crops would carve the words into the earth with tractors, so that the President himself, aloft in the great sleek airship that signified the power and swiftness of eagles, could look down and read it in the green Iowa hills, NO MORE WAR.

And in this way a small thing might become a big thing, easy as pie.

Workdays and Nightshifts

20

A Day

CHARLES BUKOWSKI

Charles Bukowski earned acclaim over his lifetime as a poet and writer who focused on downtrodden and dispossessed members of society. Born in Andernach, Germany, in 1920, he was the only child of an American soldier and a German mother who moved to Los Angeles when he was still a toddler. Bukowski's upbringing was plagued with intense physical abuse at the hand of his father. As an adolescent he also suffered from bouts of acne so intense and painful that he was hospitalized. Bukowski would write about these domestic horrors in his later fiction and poetry. After graduating high school, he attended Los Angeles City College from 1939–1941 before dropping out to travel the country and become a writer. But Bukowski's publishing efforts received scant attention and he was forced to work a wide range of menial jobs to support himself. He fell into a life of drinking and debauchery, and it was not until age 35, when he developed a bleeding ulcer, that he seriously returned to writing. With his new resolve, Bukowski went on to publish more than forty books of poetry and prose as well as the screenplay for the movie *Barfly*, establishing himself as a leading counterculture figure. He died of leukemia in San Pedro, California in 1994.

Brock, the foreman, was always digging his fingers into his ass, using his left hand. He had a great case of hemorrhoids.

Tom noticed this throughout the working day.

Brock had been on his ass for months. Those round and lifeless eyes always appeared to be watching Tom. And then Tom would note the left hand, reaching around and digging.

And Brock was on his ass all right.

Tom did his work as well as the others. Maybe he didn't show quite the enthusiasm of some but he got the job done.

Yet Brock was always after him, making comments, making useless suggestions.

Brock was related to the owner of the shop and a place had been made for him: foreman.

That day, Tom finished packing the light fixture into the oblong 8-foot carton and flung it onto the pile at the back of his work table. He turned to get another fixture from the assembly line.

Brock was standing in front of him.

"I wanna talk to you, Tom . . . "

Brock was tall and thin. His body bent forward from the middle. The head was always hanging down, it hung from his long thin neck. The mouth was always open. His nose was more than prominent with extremely large nostrils. The feet were large, and awkward. Brock's pants hung loose on his skinny frame.

"Tom, you're not doing your job."

"I'm keeping up with production. What are you talking about?"

"I don't think you're using enough packing. You've got to use more of the shredding. We've had some breakage problems and we're trying to correct that."

"Why don't you have each worker initial his carton, then if there's breakage, you can trace it."

"*I'll* do the thinking here, Tom, that's my job."

"Sure."

"Come on, I want you to come over here and watch Roosevelt pack."

They walked over to Roosevelt's table.

Roosevelt was a 13-year man.

They watched Roosevelt pack the shredded paper around the light fixture.

"You see what he's doing?" Brock asked.

"Well, yes . . . "

"What I mean is, look what he's doing with the shredded paper."

"Yeah, he's putting it in there."

"Yes, of course . . . but you see how he's *picking up* that shredded paper . . . he lifts it and drops it . . . it's like playing a piano."

"That isn't really *protecting* the fixture . . . "

"Yes, it *is*. He's *fluffing* it, don't you see?"

Tom quietly inhaled, exhaled, "All right, Brock, I'll fluff it . . . "

"Do that . . . "

Brock reached his left hand around and dug in. "By the way, you're one fixture behind assembly now . . . "

"Sure I am. You've been talking to me."

"Doesn't matter, you'll have to catch up."

Brock gave it another dig, then walked away.

Roosevelt was laughing quietly. "*Fluff* it, motherfucker!"

Tom laughed. "How much shit does a man have to take just to stay alive?"

"Plenty," came the answer, "and more . . . "

Tom went back to his table and caught up with assembly. And while Brock was looking, he "fluffed" it. And Brock always seemed to be looking.

Finally, it was lunchtime, 30 minutes. But for many of the workers lunchtime didn't mean eating, it meant going down to the Villa and loading up on beer and ale, can after can, bulwarking themselves against the afternoon shift.

Some of the fellows popped uppers. Others popped downers. Many popped both uppers and downers, washing them down with the beer and the ale.

Outside the plant, in the parking lot, there were more people sitting inside old cars, each with a different party going. The Mexicans were in some and the blacks were in others, and sometimes, unlike in the jails, they were mixed. There weren't many whites, just a few silent ones from the south. But Tom liked the whole gang of them.

The only problem in the place was Brock.

That lunchtime Tom was in his own car drinking with Ramon.

Ramon opened his hand and showed Tom a large yellow pill. It looked like a jaw-breaker.

"Hey, dude, try this. You won't worry about shit. 4 or 5 hours go like 5 minutes. And you'll be STRONG, *nothing* will tire you . . . "

"Thanks, Ramon, but I'm too fucked-up now."

"But this is to *un-fuck* you, don't you get it?"

Tom didn't answer.

"O.K.," said Ramon, "I've had mine but I'll take yours too!"

He popped the pill into his mouth, raised the can of beer and took a hit. Tom watched that enormous pill, he could see it going down Ramon's throat, then it was gone.

Ramon slowly turned to Tom, then grinned, 'Look, the damn thing hasn't even hit my belly yet and *already* I feel better!"

Tom laughed.

Ramon took another hit of beer, then lit a cigarette. For a man supposedly feeling very good he looked very serious.

"No, I'm not a man . . . I'm not a man at all . . . Hey, last night I tried to fuck my wife . . . She's gained 40 pounds this year . . . I had to get drunk first . . . I banged and banged, man, and *nothing* . . . Worst of all, I was sorry for *her* . . . I told her it was the job. And it *was* the job and it wasn't. She got up and turned on the tv . . . "

Ramon went on: "Man, everything's changed. It seems like no more than a year or two ago, with me and my woman, everything was interesting and funny for us . . . We laughed like hell at everything . . . Now, all that's stopped . . . It's gone away somewhere, I don't know where . . . "

"I know what you mean, Ramon . . . "

Ramon jolted straight upright as if given a message:

"Shit, man, we've got to punch in!"

"Let's go!"

Tom was coming back from the assembly line with a fixture and Brock was waiting there. Brock said, "All right, put it down. Follow me."

They walked out to assembly.

And there was Ramon in his little brown apron, with his fleck of mustache.

"You stand to his left now," said Brock.

Brock raised his hand and the machinery began. It moved the 8-foot fixtures toward them at a steady but predictable pace.

Ramon had this huge roll of paper in front of him, a seemingly endless spool of heavy brown paper. The first light fixture off the assembly line arrived. He ripped away a sheet of paper, spread it on the table, then placed the light fixture on it. He flicked the paper together lengthwise, holding it with a small piece of Scotch tape. Then he folded the left end into a triangle, then the right end, and then the fixture moved toward Tom.

Tom sheared off a length of gummed tape and ran it carefully along the top of the fixture, where the paper was to be sealed. Then with shorter lengths he tightly secured the left end, and then the right. Then he lifted the heavy fixture, turned, walked across an aisle and placed it upright in a wall rack where it awaited one of the packers. Then he went back to the table where another fixture was moving toward him.

It was the worst job in the plant and everybody knew it.

"You'll work with Ramon now, Tom . . . "

Brock left. There was no need to watch him: if Tom didn't perform his function properly, the whole assembly line stopped.

Nobody ever lasted long as second man to Ramon.

"I knew you'd need that yellow," Ramon said with a grin.

The fixtures moved relentlessly at them. Tom tore lengths of tape from the machine in front of him. It was a glistening, thick, wetted tape. He forced himself into the quick rhythm of the work but in order to keep up with Ramon, a certain caution was sacrificed: the razor-sharp edge of the tape occasionally cut long deep slices into his hands. The cuts were nearly invisible and seldom bled but looking at his fingers and palms he could see the bright red lines in the skin. There was never a pause. The fixtures seemed to move faster and faster and get heavier and heavier.

"Fuck," said Tom, "I ought to quit. Wouldn't a park bench beat this shit?"

"Sure," said Ramon, "sure, anything beats this shit . . . "

Ramon was working with a tight crazy grin, denying the impossibility of it all. And then, the machinery stopped, as it did every now and then.

What a gift from the gods that was!

Something had jammed, something had overheated. Without those machinery breakdowns, most of the workers could not have endured. Within those 2 or 3 minute breaks they pulled their senses and their souls back together. Almost.

The mechanics scrambled wildly looking for the cause of the breakdown.

Tom looked over at the Mexican girls on the assembly line. To him, they were all very beautiful. They gave away their time, their lives to dull and routine labor, but they *kept* something back, some little thing. Many of them wore small ribbons in their hair: blue, yellow, green, red . . . And they made private jokes and laughed continually. They showed immense courage. Their eyes knew something.

But the mechanics were good, very good, and the machinery was starting. The lighting fixtures were moving at Tom and Ramon again. They all were working for the Sunray Company again.

And after a while, Tom got so tired that it went beyond tiredness, it was like being drunk, it was like being crazy, it was like being drunk and crazy.

As Tom slapped a piece of tape on a light fixture he screamed out, "SUNRAY!"

It could have been his tone or the timing. Anyhow, everybody started laughing, the Mexican girls, the packers, the mechanics, even the old man who went about oiling and checking the machinery, they all laughed, it was crazy.

Brock walked out.

"What's happening?" he asked.

He got silence.

The fixtures came and went and the workers remained.

Then, somehow, like awakening from a nightmare, the day was over. They walked to the card racks, pulled their cards and then waited in line before the time clock to check out.

Tom hit the clock, racked his card, made it to his car. It started and he pulled out into the street, thinking, I hope nobody gets in my way, I think I'm too weak to put my foot down on the brake.

Tom drove back with the gas gauge sliding into the red. He was too tired to stop and pump gas.

He managed to park, got to his door, opened it and walked in.

The first thing he saw was Helena, his wife. She was in a loose dirty housegown, she was sprawled on the couch, her head on a pillow. Her mouth was open, she was snoring. She had a rather round mouth and her snoring was a mixture of spitting and gulping, as if she couldn't make up her mind whether to spit out her life or swallow it.

She was an unhappy woman. She felt that her life was unfulfilled.

A pint of gin was on the coffee table. It was 3/4's empty.

Tom's two sons, Rob and Bob, age 5 and 7, were bouncing a tennis ball against the wall. It was the south wall, the one without any furniture. The wall had once been white but now was pocked and dirty from the endless banging of tennis balls.

The boys paid no attention to their father. They had stopped banging the ball against the wall. Now they were arguing.

"I STRUCK YOU OUT!"

"NO, IT'S BALL FOUR!"

"STRIKE THREE!"

"BALL FOUR!"

"Hey, wait a minute," Tom asked, "can I ask you fellows something?"

They stopped and stared, almost affronted.

"Yeah," Bob said finally. He was the 7-year-old.

"How can you guys play *baseball,* bouncing a ball against a wall?"

They looked at Tom, then ignored him.

"STRIKE THREE!"

"NO, BALL FOUR!"

Tom walked into the kitchen. There was a white pot on the stove. Dark smoke was rising from it. Tom looked under the lid. The bottom was blackened, with burnt potatoes, carrots, chunks of meat. Tom slid the pot over and shut the flame off.

Then he went to the refrigerator. There was a can of beer in there. He took it out, pulled the tab and had a gulp.

The sound of the tennis ball against the wall began again.

Then there was another sound: Helena. She had bumped against something. Then she was there, standing in the kitchen. In her right hand she held the pint of gin.

"I guess you're mad, huh?"

"I just wish you'd feed the kids . . . "

"You just leave me a lousy twenty each day. What am I supposed to do with a lousy twenty?"

"At least, get some toilet paper. Every time I want to wipe my ass I look around and there's just a cardboard roll hanging there."

"Hey, a woman has *her* problems too! HOW DO YOU THINK I LIVE? Every day, you go out into the *world,* you get to go out and see the world! I've got to sit around *here!* You don't know what that's like day after day!"

"Yeah, well, there's that . . . "

Helena took a hit of her gin.

"You know I love you, Tommy, and when you're unhappy, it hurts me, it hurts my heart, it does."

"All right, Helena, let's sit down here and calm down."

Tom walked to the breakfastnook table and had a seat. Helena brought her pint and sat across from him. She looked at him.

"Jesus, what happened to your hands?"

"New job. I've got to figure a way to protect my hands . . . Adhesive tape, rubber gloves . . . something . . . "

He had finished his beer can. "Listen, Helena, got any more of that gin around?"

"Yeah, I think so . . . "

He watched as she went to the cupboard, reached high, and got a bottle down. She came back with the pint, sat down again. Tom unpeeled the bottle.

"How many of these have you got around?"

"A few . . . "

"Good. How do you drink this? Straight?"

"You can . . . "

Tom took a good hit. Then he looked down at his hands, opening and closing them, watching the red wounds open and shut. They were fascinating.

He took the bottle, poured a little gin into one of his palms, then rubbed it around on his hands.

"Wow! This shit bums!"

Helena took another hit at her bottle. "Tom, why don't you get another job?"

"Another job? Where? There's a hundred guys want *mine* . . . "

Then Rob and Bob ran in. They skidded to a stop at the breakfastnook table.

"Hey," said Bob, "when we gonna *eat*?"

Tom looked at Helena.

"I think I've got some weenies," she said.

"Weenies again?" asked Rob. "*Weenies*? I *hate weenies*!"

Tom looked at his son. "Hey, fellow, go easy . . . "

"Well," said Bob, "how about a fucking drink then?"

"You little bastard!" Helena yelled.

She reached out, open-handed, and slapped Bob hard on the ear.

"Don't hit the kids, Helena," said Tom, "I got too much of that myself when I was a kid."

"Don't tell me how to handle my kids!"

"They're mine too . . . "

Bob was standing there. His ear was very red.

"So, you want a fucking drink, eh?" Tom asked him.

Bob didn't answer.

"Come here," said Tom.

Bob walked over near his father. Tom handed him the bottle.

"Go on, drink it. Drink your fucking drink."

"Tom, what are you *doing*?" Helena asked.

"Go on . . . drink it," said Tom.

Bob lifted the pint, took a gulp. Then he handed the bottle back, stood there. Suddenly he looked pale, even the red ear began to pale. He coughed. "This stuff's AWFUL! It's like drinking *perfume*! Why do you *drink* it?"

"Because we're stupid. You've got stupid parents. Now, go to the bedroom and take your brother with you . . . "

"Can we watch the tv in there?" asked Rob.

"All right, but get going . . . "

They filed out.

"Don't you go making *drunks* out of my kids!" Helena said.

"I just hope they have better luck in life than we've had."

Helena took a hit from her bottle. That finished it off.

She got up, took the burnt pot from the stove and slammed it into the sink.

"I don't *need* all that god damned noise!" Tom said.

Helena appeared to be crying. "Tom, what are we going to *do*?"

She turned the hot water into the pot.

"Do?" asked Tom. "About what?"

"About the way we have to *live*!"

"There's not a hell of a lot we *can* do."

Helena scraped out the burnt food and poured some soap into the pot, then reached into the cupboard and got another pint of gin. She came around, sat down across from Tom, and peeled the bottle. "Got to let the pot soak a while . . . I'll get the weenies on soon . . . "

Tom drank from his bottle, sat it down.

"Baby, you're just an old sot, an old sot-pot . . . "

The tears were still there. "Oh yeah, well, *who* do you think *made* me this way? ONE GUESS!"

"That's easy," answered Tom, "two people: you and me."

Helena took her first drink from the new bottle. With that, at once, the tears vanished. She gave a little smile. "Hey, I've got an idea! I can get a job as a waitress or something . . . You can rest up awhile, you know . . . What do you think?"

Tom put his hand across the table, put it on one of Helena's.

"You're a good girl, but let's leave it like it is."

Then the tears were coming back again. Helena was good with the tears, especially when she was drinking gin. "Tommy, do you still love me?"

"Sure, baby, at your best you're wonderful."

"I love you too, Tom, you know that . . . "

"Sure, baby, here's to it!"

Tom lifted his bottle. Helena lifted hers.

They clicked their pints of gin in mid-air, then each drank to the other.

In the bedroom, Rob and Bob had the tv on, they had it on *loud*. There was a laugh-track on and the people on the laugh-track were laughing and laughing and laughing

and laughing.

21

Scales

LOUISE ERDRICH

Louise Erdrich, the daughter of a German American father and a mother of French and Turtle Mountain Chippewa Indian heritage, was born in 1954, in Little Falls, Minnesota. The eldest of seven children, she was raised in Wahpeton, North Dakota, where her parents worked as teachers for the Bureau of Indian Affairs. Erdrich earned her BA from Dartmouth College in 1976 and her MA in creative writing from Johns Hopkins University in 1979. One of the most influential voices in American letters, Erdrich broke new ground with her short stories and novels that explored the tensions and ruptures that occur in both Native American and European American cultures, especially when the two worlds collide. Her first novel, *Love Medicine* (1984), won the National Book Critics Circle Award. She has written twelve novels in addition to collections of poetry, children's books, and a memoir on motherhood. Erdrich owns an independent bookstore in Minnesota called Birchbark Books. In addition to short stories, novels, and poetry, she is also a prolific essayist and literary critic.

I was sitting before my third or fourth Jellybean, which is anisette, grain alcohol, a lit match, and small wet explosion in the brain. On my left sat Gerry Nanapush of the Chippewa Tribe. On my right sat Dot Adare of the has-been, of the never-was, of the what's-in-front-of-me people. Still in her belly and tensed in its fluids coiled the child of their union, the child we were waiting for, the child whose name we were making a strenuous and lengthy search for in a cramped and littered bar at the very edge of that Dakota town.

Gerry had been on the wagon for thirteen years. He was drinking a tall glass of tonic water in which a crescent of soiled lemon bobbed, along with a Maraschino cherry or two. He was thirty-five years old and had been in prison, or out of prison and on the run, for almost half of those years. He was not in the clear yet nor would he ever be, that is why the yellow tennis player's visor was pulled down to the rim of his eyeglass frames. The bar was dimly lit and smoky; his glasses were very dark. Poor visibility must have been the reason Officer Lovchik saw him first.

Lovchik started toward us with his hand on his hip, but Gerry was over the backside of the booth and out the door before Lovchik got close enough to make a positive identification.

"Siddown with us," said Dot to Lovchik, when he neared our booth. "I'll buy you a drink. It's so dead here. No one's been through all night."

Lovchik sighed, sat, and ordered a blackberry brandy.

"Now tell me," she said, staring up at him, "honestly. What do you think of the name Ketchup Face?"

It was through Gerry that I first met Dot, and in a bar like that one, only denser with striving drinkers, construction crews in town because of the highway. I sat down by Gerry early in the evening and we struck up a conversation, during the long course of which we became friendly enough for Gerry to put his arm around me. Dot entered at exactly the wrong moment. She was quick-tempered anyway and being pregnant (Gerry had gotten her that way on a prison visit five months previous) increased her irritability. It was only natural then, I guess, that she would pull the barstool out from under me and threaten my life. Only I didn't know she was threatening my life at the time. I didn't know anyone like Dot, so I didn't know she was serious.

"I'm gonna bend you out of shape," she said, flexing her hands over me. Her hands were small, broad, capable, with pointed nails. I used to do the wrong thing sometimes when I was drinking, and that time I did the wrong thing even though I was stretched out on the floor beneath her. I started laughing at her because her hands were so small (though strong and determined looking, I should have been more conscious of that). She was about to dive on top of me, five-month belly and all, but Gerry caught her in midair and carried her, yelling, out the door. The next day I reported for work. It was my first day on the job, and the only other woman on the construction site besides me was Dot Adare.

The first day Dot just glared toward me from a distance. She worked in the weighshack and I was hired to press buttons on the conveyor belt. All I had to do was adjust the speeds on the belt for sand, rocks, or gravel, and make sure it was aimed toward the right pile. There was a pyramid for each type of material, which was used to make hot-mix and cement. Across the wide yard, I saw Dot emerge from the little white shack from time to time. I couldn't tell whether she recognized me and thought, by the end of the day, that she probably didn't. I found out differently the next morning when I went to the company truck for coffee.

She got me alongside of the truck somehow, away from the men. She didn't say a word, just held a buck knife out where I could see it, blade toward me. She jiggled the handle and the tip waved like the pointy head of a pit viper. Blind. Heat-seeking. I was completely astonished. I had just put the plastic cover on my coffee and it steamed between my hands.

"Well I'm sorry I laughed," I said. She stepped back. I peeled the lid off my coffee, took a sip, and then I said the wrong thing again.

"And I wasn't going after your boyfriend."

"Why not!" she said at once. "What's wrong with him!"

I saw that I was going to lose this argument no matter what I said, so, for once, I did the right thing. I threw my coffee in her face and ran. Later on that day Dot came out of the weighshack and yelled "Okay then!" I was close enough to see that she even smiled. I waved. From then on things were better between us, which was lucky, because I turned out to be such a good button presser that within two weeks I was promoted to the weighshack, to help Dot.

It wasn't that Dot needed help weighing trucks, it was just a formality for the State Highway Department. I never quite understood, but it seems Dot had been both the truck weigher and the truck weight inspector for a while, until someone caught wind of this. I was hired to actually weigh the trucks then, for the company, and Dot was hired by the state to make sure I recorded accurate weights. What she really did was sleep, knit, or eat all day. Between truckloads I did the same. I didn't even have to get off my stool to weigh the trucks, because the arm of the scale projected through a rectangular hole and the weights appeared right in front of me. The standard back dumps, belly dumps, and yellow company trucks eased onto a platform built over the arm next to the shack. I wrote their weight on a little pink slip, clipped the paper in a clothespin attached to a broom handle, and handed it up to the driver. I kept a copy of the pink slip on a yellow slip that I put in a metal file box—no one ever picked up the file box, so I never knew what the yellow slips were for. The company paid me very well.

It was early July when Dot and I started working together. At first I sat as far away from her as possible and never took my eyes off her knitting needles, although it made me a little dizzy to watch her work. It wasn't long before we came to an understanding though, and after this I felt perfectly comfortable with Dot. She was nothing but direct, you see, and told me right off that only three things made her angry. Number one was someone flirting with Gerry. Number two was a cigarette leech (someone who was always quitting but smoking yours). Number three was a piss-ant. I asked her what that was. "A piss-ant," she said, "is a man with fat buns who tries to sell you things, a Jaycee, an Elk, a Kiwanis." I always knew where I stood with Dot, so I trusted her. I knew that if I fell out of her favor she would threaten me and give me time to run before she tried anything physical.

By mid-July our shack was unbearable, for it drew heat in from the bare yard and held it. We sat outside most of the time, moving around the shack to catch what shade fell, letting the raw hot wind off the beet fields suck the sweat from our armpits and legs. But the seasons change fast in North Dakota. We spent the last day of August jumping from foot to numb foot before Hadji, the foreman, dragged a little column of bottled gas into the shack. He lit the spoked wheel on its head, it bloomed, and from then on we huddled close to the heater—eating, dozing, or sitting blankly in its small radius of dry warmth.

By that time Dot weighed over two hundred pounds, most of it peanut-butter cups and egg salad sandwiches. She was a short, broad-beamed woman with long yellow eyes and spaces between each of her strong teeth. When we began working together, her hair was cropped close. By the cold months it had grown out in thick quills—brown at the shank, orange at the tip. The orange dye job had not suited her coloring. By that time, too, Dot's belly was round and full, for she was due in October. The child rode high, and she often rested her forearms on it while she knitted. One of Dot's most peculiar feats was transforming that gentle task into something perverse. She knit viciously, jerking, the yarn around her thumb until the tip whitened, pulling each stitch so tightly that the little garments she finished stood up by themselves like miniature suits of mail.

But I thought that the child would need those tight stitches when it was born. Although Dot, as expecting mother, lived a fairly calm life, it was clear that she had also moved loosely among dangerous elements. The child, for example, had been conceived in a visiting room at the state prison. Dot had straddled Gerry's lap, in a corner the closed circuit TV did not quite scan. Through a hole ripped in her pantyhose and a hole ripped in Gerry's jeans they somehow managed to join and, miraculously, to conceive. When Dot was sure she was pregnant, Gerry escaped from the prison to see her. Not long after my conversation with Gerry in the bar, he was caught. That time he went back peacefully, and didn't put up a fight. He was mainly in the penitentiary for breaking out of it, anyway, since for his crime (assault and battery when he was eighteen) he had received three years and time off for good behavior. He just never managed to serve those three years or behave well. He broke out time after time, and was caught each time he did it, regular as clockwork.

Gerry was talented at getting out, that's a fact. He boasted that no steel or concrete shitbarn could hold a Chippewa, and he had eel-like properties in spite of his enormous size. Greased with lard once, he squirmed into a six-foot-thick prison wall and vanished. Some thought he had stuck there, immured forever, and that he would bring luck like the bones of slaves sealed in the wall of China. But Gerry rubbed his own belly for luck and brought luck to no one else, for he appeared, suddenly, at Dot's door and she was hard-pressed to hide him.

She managed for nearly a month. Hiding a six-foot-plus, two hundred and fifty pound Indian in the middle of a town that doesn't like Indians in the first place isn't easy. A month was quite an accomplishment, when you know what she was up against. She spent most of her time walking to and from the grocery store, padding along on her swollen feet, astonishing the neighbors with the size of what they thought was her appetite. Stacks of pork chops, whole fryers, thick steaks disappeared overnight, and since Gerry couldn't take the garbage out by day sometimes he threw the bones out the windows, where they collected, where dogs soon learned to wait for a handout and fought and squabbled over whatever there was.

The neighbors finally complained, and one day, while Dot was at work, Lovchik knocked on the door of the trailerhouse. Gerry answered, sighed, and walked over to their car. He was so good at getting out of the joint and so terrible at getting caught. It was as if he couldn't stay out of their hands. Dot knew his problem, and told him that he was crazy to think he could walk out of prison and then live like a normal person. Dot told him that didn't work. She told him to get lost for a while on the reservation, any reservation, to change his name and although he couldn't grow a beard to at least let the straggly hairs above his lip form a kind of mustache that would slightly disguise his face. But Gerry wouldn't do that. He simply knew he did not belong in prison, although he admitted it had done him some good at eighteen, when he hadn't known how to be a criminal and so had taken lessons from professionals. Now that he knew all there was to know, however, he couldn't see the point of staying in a prison and taking the same lessons over and over. "A hate factory," he called it once, and said it manufactured black poisons in his stomach that he couldn't get rid of although he poked a finger down his throat and retched and tried to be a clean and normal person in spite of everything.

Gerry's problem, you see, was he believed in justice, not laws. He felt he had paid for his crime, which was done in a drunk heat and to settle the question with a cowboy of whether a Chippewa was also a nigger. Gerry said that the two had never settled it between them, but that the cowboy at least knew that if a Chippewa was a nigger he was sure also a hell of a mean and low-down fighter. For Gerry did not believe in fighting by any rules but reservation rules, which is to say the first thing Gerry did to the cowboy, after they squared off, was kick his balls.

It hadn't been much of a fight after that, and since there were both white and Indian witnesses Gerry thought it would blow over if it ever reached court. But there is nothing more vengeful and determined in this world than a cowboy with sore balls, and Gerry soon found this out. He also found that white people are good witnesses to have on your side since they have names, addresses, social security numbers, and work phones. But they are terrible witnesses to have against you, almost as bad as having Indians witness for you.

Not only did Gerry's friends lack all forms of identification except their band cards, not only did they disappear (out of no malice but simply because Gerry was tried during powwow time), but the few he did manage to get were not interested in looking judge or jury in the eye. They mumbled into their laps. Gerry's friends, you see, had no confidence in the United States Judicial System. They did not seem comfortable in the courtroom, and this increased their unreliability in the eyes of judge and jury. If you trust the authorities, they trust you better back, it seems. It looked that way to Gerry anyhow.

A local doctor testified on behalf of the cowboy's testicles, and said his fertility might be impaired. Gerry got a little angry at that, and said right out in court that he could hardly believe he had done that much damage since the cowboy's balls were very small targets, it had been dark, and his aim was off anyway because of three, or maybe it was only two, beers. That made matters worse, of course, and Gerry was socked with a heavy sentence for an eighteen-year-old, but not for an Indian. Some said he got off lucky.

Only one good thing came from the whole experience, said Gerry, and that was maybe the cowboy would not have any little cowboys, although,

Gerry also said, he had nightmares sometimes that the cowboy did manage to have little cowboys, all born with full sets of grinning teeth, Stetson hats, and little balls hard as plum pits.

So you see, it was difficult for Gerry, as an Indian, to retain the natural good humor of his ancestors in these modern circumstances. He tried though, and since he believed in justice, not laws, Gerry knew where he belonged (out of prison, in the bosom of his new family). And in spite of the fact that he was untrained in the honest life, he wanted it. He was even interested in getting a job. It didn't matter what kind of job. "Anything for a change," Gerry said. He wanted to go right out and apply for one, in fact, the moment he was free. But of course Dot wouldn't let him. And so, because he wanted to be with Dot, he stayed hidden in her trailerhouse even though they both realized, or must have, that it wouldn't be long before the police came asking around or the neighbors wised up and Gerry Nanapush would be back at square one again. So it happened. Lovchik came for him. And Dot now believed she would have to go through the end of her pregnancy and the delivery all by herself.

Dot was angry about having to go through it alone, and besides that, she loved Gerry with a deep and true love—that was clear. She knit his absence into thick little suits for the child, suits that would have stopped a truck on a dark road with their colors—bazooka pink, bruise blue, the screaming orange flagmen wore.

The child was as restless a prisoner as his father, and grew more anxious and unruly as his time of release neared. As a place to spend a nine-month sentence in, Dot wasn't much. Her body was inhospitable. Her skin was slack, sallow, and draped like upholstery fabric over her short, boardlike bones. Like the shack we spent our days in, she seemed jerry-built, thrown into the world with loosely nailed limbs and lightly puttied joints. Some pregnant women's bellies look like they always have been there. But Dot's stomach was an odd shape, almost square, and had the tacked-on air of a new and unpainted bay window. The child was clearly ready for a break and not interested in earning his parole, for he kept her awake all night by pounding reasonlessly at her inner walls, or beating against her bladder until she swore. "He wants out, bad," poor Dot would groan. "You think he might be premature?" From the outside, anyway, the child looked big enough to stand and walk and maybe even run straight out of the maternity ward the moment he was born.

The sun, at the time, rose around seven and we got to the weighshack while the frost was still thick on the gravel. Each morning I started the gas heater, turning the nozzle and standing back, flipping the match at it the way you would feed a fanged animal. Then one morning I saw the red bud through the window, lit already. But when I opened the door the shack was empty. There was, however, evidence of an overnight visitor—cigarette stubs, a few beer cans crushed to flat disks. I swept these things out and didn't say a word about them to Dot when she arrived.

She seemed to know something was in the air, however; her face lifted from time to time all that morning. She sniffed, and even I could smell the lingering odor of sweat like sour wheat, the faint reek of slept-in clothes and gasoline. Once, that morning, Dot looked at me and narrowed her long, hooded eyes. "I got pains," she said, "every so often. Like it's going to come sometime soon. Well all I can say is he better drag ass to get here, that Gerry." She closed her eyes then, and went to sleep.

Ed Rafferty, one of the drivers, pulled in with a load. It was overweight, and when I handed him the pink slip he grinned. There were two scales, you see, on the way to the cement plant, and if a driver got past the state-run scale early, before the state officials were there, the company would pay for whatever he got away with. But it was not illicit gravel that tipped the wedge past the red mark on the balance. When I walked back inside I saw the weight had gone down to just under the red. Ed drove off, still laughing, and I assumed that he had leaned on the arm of the scale, increasing the weight.

"That Ed," I said, "got me again."

But Dot stared past me, needles poised in her fist like a picador's lances. It gave me a start, to see her frozen in such a menacing pose. It was not the sort of pose to turn your back on, but I did turn, following her gaze to the door that a man's body filled suddenly.

Gerry, of course it was Gerry. He'd tipped the weight up past the red and leapt down, cat-quick for all his mass, and silent. I hadn't heard his step. Gravel crushed, evidently, but did not roll beneath his tight, thin boots.

He was bigger than I remembered from the bar, or perhaps it was just that we'd been living in that dollhouse of a weighshack so long I saw everything else as huge. He was so big that he had to hunker one shoulder beneath the lintel and back his belly in, pushing the door frame wider with his long, soft hands. It was the hands I watched as Gerry filled the shack. His plump fingers looked so graceful and artistic against his smooth mass. He used them prettily. Revolving agile wrists, he reached across the few inches left between himself and Dot. Then his littlest fingers curled like a woman's at tea, and he disarmed his wife. He drew the needles out of Dot's fists, and examined the little garment that hung like a queer fruit beneath.

"'S very, very nice," he said, scrutinizing the tiny, even stitches. "'S for the kid?"

Dot nodded solemnly and dropped her eyes to her lap. It was an almost tender moment. The silence lasted so long that I got embarrassed and would have left, had I not been wedged firmly behind his hip in one corner.

Gerry stood there, smoothing black hair behind his ears. Again, there was a queer delicacy about the way he did this. So many things Gerry did might remind you of the way that a beautiful woman, standing naked before a mirror, would touch herself—lovingly, conscious of her attractions. He nodded encouragingly. "Let's go then," said Dot.

Suave, grand, gigantic, they moved across the parking lot and then, by mysterious means, slipped their bodies into Dot's compact car. I expected the car to belly down, thought the muffler would scrape the ground behind them. But instead they flew, raising a great spume of dust that hung in the air a long time after they were out of sight.

I went back into the weighshack when the air behind them had settled. I was bored, dead bored. And since one thing meant about as much to me as another, I picked up her needles and began knitting, as well as I could anyway, jerking the yarn back after each stitch, becoming more and more absorbed in my work until, as it happened, I came suddenly to the end of the garment, snipped the yarn, and worked the loose ends back into the collar of the thick little suit.

I missed Dot in the days that followed, days so alike they welded seamlessly to one another and took your mind away. I seemed to exist in a suspension and spent my time sitting blankly at the window, watching nothing until the sun went down, bruising the whole sky as it dropped, clotting my heart. I couldn't name anything I felt anymore, although I knew it was a kind of boredom. I had been living the same life too long. I did jumping jacks and push-ups and stood on my head in the little shack to break the tedium, but too much solitude rots the brain. I wondered how Gerry had stood it. Sometimes I grabbed drivers out of their trucks and talked loudly and quickly and inconsequentially as a madwoman. There were other times I couldn't talk at all because my tongue had rusted to the roof of my mouth.

· · ·

Sometimes I daydreamed about Dot and Gerry. I had many choice day-dreams, but theirs was my favorite. I pictured them in Dot's long tan and aqua trailerhouse, both hungry. Heads swaying, clasped hands swinging between them like hooked trunks, they moved through the kitchen feeding casually from boxes and bags on the counters, like ponderous animals alone in a forest. When they had fed, they moved on to the bedroom and settled themselves upon Dot's king-size and sateen-quilted spread. They rubbed together, locked and unlocked their parts. They set the trailer rocking on its cement-block and plywood foundation and the tremors spread, causing cups to fall, plates to shatter in the china hutches of their more-established neighbors.

But what of the child there, suspended between them? Did he know how to weather such tropical storms? It was a week past the week he was due, and I expected the good news to come any moment. I was anxious to hear the outcome, but still I was surprised when Gerry rumbled to the weigh-shack door on a huge and ancient, rust-pocked, untrustworthy-looking ma-chine that was like no motorcycle I'd ever seen before.

"She asst for you," he hissed. "Quick, get on!"

I hoisted myself up behind him, although there wasn't room on the seat. I clawed his smooth back for a handhold and finally perched, or so it seemed, on the rim of his heavy belt. Flylike, glued to him by suction, we rode as one person, whipping a great wind around us. Cars scattered, the lights blinked and flickered on the main street. Pedestrians swiveled to catch a glimpse of us—a mountain tearing by balanced on a toy, and cling-ing to the sheer northwest face, a young and scrawny girl howling some-thing that dopplered across the bridge and faded out, finally, in the parking lot of the Saint Francis Hospital.

In the waiting room we settled on chairs molded of orange plastic. The spike legs splayed beneath Gerry's mass, but managed to support him the four hours we waited. Nurses passed, settling like field gulls among reports and prescriptions, eyeing us with reserved hostility. Gerry hardly spoke. He didn't have to. I watched his ribs and the small of his back darken with sweat, for that well-lighted tunnel, the waiting room, the tin rack of maga-zines, all were the props and inevitable features of institutions. From time to time Gerry paced in the time-honored manner of the prisoner or expect-ant father. He made lengthy trips to the bathroom. All the quickness and delicacy of his movements had disappeared, and he was only a poor weary fat man in those hours, a husband worried about his wife, menaced, tired of getting caught.

The gulls emerged finally, and drew Gerry in among them. He visited Dot for perhaps half an hour, and then came out of her room. Again he settled; the plastic chair twitched beneath him. He looked bewildered and silly and a little addled with what he had seen. The shaded lenses of his glasses kept slipping down his nose. Beside him, I felt the aftermath of the shock wave, traveling from the epicenter deep in his flesh, outward from part of him that had shifted along a crevice. The tremors moved in widening rings. When they reached the very surface of him, and when he began trembling, Gerry stood suddenly. "I'm going after cigars," he said, and walked quickly away.

His steps quickened to a near-run as he moved down the corridor. Waiting for the elevator, he flexed his nimble fingers. Dot told me she had once sent him to the store for a roll of toilet paper. It was eight months before she saw him again; for he'd met the local constabulary on the way. So I knew, when he flexed his fingers, that he was thinking of pulling the biker's gloves over his knuckles, of running. It was perhaps the very first time in his life he had something to run for.

It seemed to me, at that moment, that I should at least let Gerry know it was all right for him to leave, to run as far and fast as he had to now. Although I felt heavy, my body had gone slack, and my lungs ached with smoke, I jumped up. I signaled him from the end of the corridor. Gerry turned, unwillingly turned. He looked my way just as two of our local police—officers Lovchik and Harriss—pushed open the fire door that sealed off the staircase behind me. I didn't see them, and was shocked at first that my wave caused such an extreme reaction in Gerry.

His hair stiffened. His body lifted like a hot-air balloon filling suddenly. Behind him there was a wide, tall window. Gerry opened it and sent the screen into thin air with an elegant, chorus-girl kick. Then he followed the screen, squeezing himself unbelievably through the frame like a fat rabbit disappearing down a hole. It was three stories down to the cement and asphalt parking lot.

Officers Lovchik and Harriss gained the window. The nurses followed. I slipped through the fire exit and took the back stairs down into the parking lot, believing I would find him stunned and broken there.

But Gerry had chosen his window with exceptional luck, for the officers had parked their car directly underneath. Gerry landed just over the driver's seat, caving the roof into the steering wheel. He bounced off the hood of the car and then, limping, a bit dazed perhaps, straddled his bike. Out of duty, Lovchik released several rounds into the still trees below him. The reports were still echoing when I reached the front of the building.

I was just in time to see Gerry Nanapush, emboldened by his godlike leap and recovery, pop a wheelie and disappear between the neat shrubs that marked the entrance to the hospital.

Two weeks later Dot and her boy, who was finally named Jason like most boys born that year, came back to work at the scales. Things went on as they had before, except that Jason kept us occupied during the long hours. He was large, of course, and had a sturdy pair of lungs he used often. When he cried, Jason screwed his face into fierce baby wrinkles and would not be placated with sugar tits or pacifiers. Dot unzipped her parka halfway, pulled her blouse up, and let him nurse for what seemed like hours. We could scarcely believe his appetite. Dot was a diligent producer of milk, however. Her breasts, like overfilled inner tubes, strained at her nylon blouses. Sometimes, when she thought no one was looking, Dot rose and carried them in the crooks of her arms, for her shoulders were growing bowed beneath their weight.

The trucks came in on the hour, or half hour. I heard the rush of airbrakes, gears grinding only inches from my head. It occurred to me that although I measured many tons every day, I would never know how heavy a ton was unless it fell on me. I wasn't lonely now that Dot had returned. The season would end soon, and we wondered what had happened to Gerry.

There were only a few weeks left of work when we heard that Gerry was caught again. He'd picked the wrong reservation to hide on—Pine Ridge. At the time it was overrun with Federal Agents and armored vehicles. Weapons were stashed everywhere and easy to acquire. Gerry got himself a weapon. Two men tried to arrest him. Gerry would not go along and when he started to run and the shooting started Gerry shot and killed a clean-shaven man with dark hair and light eyes, a Federal Agent, a man whose picture was printed in all the papers.

They sent Gerry to prison in Marion, Illinois. He was placed in the control unit. He receives his visitors in a room where no touching is allowed, where the voice is carried by phone, glances meet through sheets of Plexiglas, and no children will ever be engendered.

.   .   .

Dot and I continued to work the last weeks together. Once we weighed baby Jason. We unlatched his little knit suit, heavy as armor, and bundled him in a light, crocheted blanket. Dot went into the shack to adjust the weights. I stood there with Jason. He was such a solid child, he seemed heavy as lead in my arms. I placed him on the ramp between the wheel sights and held him steady for a moment, then took my hands slowly away. He stared calmly into the rough, distant sky. He did not flinch when the wind came from every direction, wrapping us tight enough to squeeze the very breath from a stone. He was so dense with life, such a powerful distillation of Dot and Gerry, it seemed he might weigh about as much as any load. But that was only a thought, of course. For as it turned out, he was too light and did not register at all.

22

Something That Needs Nothing

MIRANDA JULY

Miranda July is a versatile writer, filmmaker, performer, and visual artist. Born in Barre, Vermont, in 1974, she was raised in Berkeley, California, where in her teens she began writing and directing plays at local venues, including the 924 Gilman collective. July attended the University of California, Santa Cruz, for a stint before dropping out to move to Portland, Oregon, where she began a career in performance art. Her videos, performances, art, and Web-based projects have been featured at the Museum of Modern Art, the Guggenheim Museum, the 2002 and 2004 Whitney Biennials and the 2009 Venice Biennale. Her collection of short stories, *No One Belongs Here More Than You*, was published in 2007 and won the Frank O'Connor International Short Story Award. Her fiction has also been printed in *The Paris Review*, *Harper's*, and *The New Yorker*. In 2005, July wrote, directed, and starred in her first feature-length film, *Me and You and Everyone We Know* (2005). The film earned her a special jury prize at the Sundance Film Festival and four prizes at the Cannes Film Festival, including the Camera d'Or.

In an ideal world, we would have been orphans. We felt like orphans and we felt deserving of the pity that orphans get, but, embarrassingly enough, we had parents. I even had two. They would never have let me go, so I didn't say goodbye; I packed a little bag and left a note. On the way to Pip's house, I cashed my graduation checks. Then I sat on her porch and pretended that I was twelve or fifteen or even sixteen. At all those ages I had dreamed of this day; I had even imagined sitting on this porch, waiting for Pip for the last time. She had the opposite problem: her mom *would* let her go. Her mom had gigantic swollen legs that were a symptom of something much worse and she was heavily medicated with marijuana at all times.

We were anxious to begin our life as people who had no people. And it was easy to find an apartment when we got to Portland, because we had no standards; we stood in our tiny new studio and admired *our* door, *our* rotting carpet, *our* cockroach infestation. We decorated with paper streamers and Chinese lanterns and we shared the ancient bed that came with the apartment. This was tremendously exciting for one of us. One of us had always been in love with the other. One of us lived in a perpetual state of longing. But we'd met when we were children and we seemed destined to sleep together like children, or like an old married couple who got married before the sexual revolution and are too embarrassed to learn the new way.

Next we focussed on employment; we went hardly anywhere without joyfully filling out an application. But once we were hired—as furniture sanders—we could not believe that this was really what people did all day. Everything that we had always thought of as "The World" was actually the result of someone's job. Each line on the sidewalk, each saltine. Everyone had a rotting carpet and a door to pay for. Aghast, we quit. There had to be a more dignified way to live. We needed time to consider ourselves, to come up with a theory about who we were and set it to music.

With this goal in mind, Pip came up with a new plan. We went at it with determination—three weeks in a row we wrote and rewrote and resubmitted an ad to the local paper. Finally, the *Portland Weekly* accepted it; it no longer sounded like blatant prostitution, and yet, to the right reader, it could have meant nothing else. We were targeting wealthy women who loved women. Did such a thing exist? We would also consider a woman of average means who had saved up her money.

The ad ran for a month and our voice-mail box overflowed with interest. Every day we listened to hundreds of messages from men, waiting for that one special lady who would pay our rent. She was slow to appear. Perhaps she did not even read this section of the paper. We became agitated. We knew that this was the only way we could make money without compromising ourselves. Could we pay Mr. Hilderbrand, the landlord, in food stamps? We could not. Was he interested in the old camera that Pip's grandmother had loaned her? He was not. He wanted to be paid in the traditional way. Pip grimly began to troll through the messages for a man who sounded gentle. I watched her boyish face as she listened and I realized that she was terrified. He would have to be a withered man, a man who really just wanted to see us jump around in our underwear. Suddenly, Pip grinned and wrote down a number. The woman's name was Leslie.

The bus dropped us off at the top of the gravel driveway that Leslie had described on the phone. We'd told her that our names were Astrid and Tallulah, and we hoped that Leslie was a pseudonym, too. We wanted her to be wearing a smoking jacket or a boa. We hoped that she was familiar with the work of Anaïs Nin. We hoped that she was not the way she'd sounded on the phone. Not poor, not old, not just willing to pay for the company of anyone who would come all the way out to Nehalem, population 210.

Pip and I walked down the gravel path toward a small brown house. A woman stepped onto the porch. Her age was difficult to determine from our vantage point—a point in our lives when we could not bring older bodies into focus. She was perhaps the age of my mother's older sister, Aunt Lynn. And, like Aunt Lynn, she wore leggings, royal-blue leggings, and an oversized button-down shirt with some kind of appliqué on it. My mind ballooned with nervous fear, and I looked at Pip, and for a split second I felt as though she were nobody special in the larger scheme of my life. She was just some girl who had tied my leg to hers before jumping off the bridge. Then I blinked and I was in love with her again.

Leslie waved and we waved. We waved until we were close enough to say hi and then we said hi. She said, "Come on in," and we went in. Pip asked for the money right away, which was something we'd decided to do beforehand. It is always terrible to have to ask for anything. We wished we were something that needed nothing, like paint. But even paint needs repainting. She told us that we were younger than she'd expected. We sat on an old vinyl couch, and she left the room. It was an awful room, with magazines piled everywhere and furniture that looked as if it had come from a motel. We didn't look at each other or at anything that was reflective. I stared at my knees.

For a long time we didn't know where she was, and then slowly I could feel that she was standing right behind us. I realized this just before she pulled her fingernails through my hair. I hadn't been able to imagine her as the sexual type, but now I realized that I didn't know anything. It had begun, which meant that every second brought us closer to the end. I told myself that long nails meant wealth; the idea of wealth always calmed me down. My head relaxed and I did that exercise where you imagine that you are turning into honey. My mind slowed to a rate that would not have been considered functional for any other job. I was alive only one out of every four seconds; I registered only fifteen minutes out of the hour. I saw that she was standing before us in a slip and that it was not really clean and I died. I saw that Pip was taking off her shoes and I died. I saw that I was squeezing a nipple and I died.

· · ·

On the long ride home neither of us said anything. We were kites flying in opposite directions attached to strings held my one hand. The money we'd just made was also in that hand. Pip stopped to get a bag of chips on the way home from the bus station and then we had $1.99 less than our rent. It seemed obvious now that we should have charged more. Pip put the money in an envelope and wrote Mr. Hilderbrand's name on it. Then we stood there, apart, bruised, and smelling like Leslie.

We turned away from each other and set about tightening all the tiny ropes of our misery. I decided to take a bath. Just as I was stepping into the tub I heard the front door close and I froze mid-step; she was gone. Sometimes she did this. In the moments when other couples would fight or come together, she left me. With one foot in the bath, I stood waiting for her to return. I waited for an unreasonably long time, long enough to realize that she wouldn't be back that day. But what if I waited it out, what if I stood there naked until she returned? I had done things like this before. I had hidden under cars for hours. I had written the same word seven hundred times in an effort to alchemize time. I studied my position in the bathtub. The foot in the water was already wrinkly. How would I feel when night fell? And when Pip came home, how long would it take her to look for me in the bathroom? And would she understand that time had stopped while she was gone? And, even if she did realize that I had performed this impossible feat for her, what then? She was never thankful or sympathetic.

I left the bath and paced around our tiny room. It didn't even occur to me to go outside; I had no idea how to navigate the city without her. There was only one thing that I couldn't do when she was with me, so after a while I lay down on the couch and did this. I closed my eyes and ran through my memories from our childhood. We were under the covers on her mom's foldout sofa, or on the top bunk of my bunk bed, or in a tent in her back yard. Every location was potent in its own way. No matter where we were, it would begin when Pip whispered, "Let's mate." She'd scoot on top of me; we'd clamp our arms around each other's backs and rub ourselves against each other's small hipbones trying to achieve friction. When we did it right, the feeling came on like a head-rush of the whole body.

But just before I got there I noticed a clicking noise in the air. It was distractingly present, quietly insistent. Above my head, our five Chinese paper lanterns were rocking slightly of their own accord. As I reached toward them I suddenly realized why, but I was too late to stop myself. I shook a lantern and cockroaches came pouring out. They were crawling on each other even as they fell. They were determined and surviving as they passed each other in the air. They were planning the conquest of wherever they landed before they had even touched down. And when they hit the ground they didn't die—they didn't even think of dying. They ran.

When Pip finally came home, we agreed that the Leslie job had not been worth the money. But a few days later we saw Nastassja Kinski in the movie "Paris, Texas." She was wearing a long red sweater and working in a peepshow. I thought it looked like a pretty easy job, so long as Harry Dean Stanton didn't show up, but Pip didn't agree.

"No way. I'm not gonna do that."

"I could do it without you."

This made her so angry that she did the dishes. We never did this unless we were trying to be grand and self-destructive. I stood in the doorway and tried to maintain my end of our silence while watching her scratch at calcified noodles. In truth, I had not yet learned how to hate anyone but my parents. I was actually just standing there in love. I was not even really standing; if she had walked away suddenly, I would have fallen.

"I won't do it—never mind."

"You sound disappointed."

"I'm not."

"It's O.K. I know you want them to look at you."

"Who?"

"Men."

"No, I don't."

"If you do that, then I can't be with you anymore."

This was, in a way, the most romantic thing she had ever said to me. It implied that we were living together not because we had grown up together and were the only people we knew but because of something else. Because we both didn't want men to look at me. I told her that I would never work in a peepshow, and she stopped doing the dishes, which meant that she was O.K. again. But I wasn't O.K. In ten years we had touched only three times, not including the thing with Leslie. It seemed as though we'd stopped mating on the day we learned what fucking was.

These were the three times:

When she was eleven, her uncle tried to molest her. When she told me about it, I cried and curled up in a ball for forty minutes until she uncurled me. I kept my eyes shut as she pulled my knees away from my chest, and I knew that if I didn't open my eyes it would happen, and it did. She slid her hand under my tights and felt around until she had located the thing she knew on herself. Then she shook her finger in a violent, animal way. When it was over she told me not to tell anyone and I didn't know if she meant about this thing with me or about her uncle.

When we were fourteen, we got drunk for the first time and for a few minutes everything seemed possible and we kissed. This encounter felt promisingly normal, and in the following days I waited for more kissing, perhaps even some kind of exchange of rings or lockets. But nothing was exchanged. We each kept our own things.

In our last year of high school, I momentarily had one other friend. She was just an ordinary girl. Her name was Tammy. She liked the Smiths. There was no way I could ever have fallen in love with her, because she was just as pathetic as me. Every day she told me everything that she was thinking, and I guessed that this was what most girls did together. I wanted to talk about myself, too, but it was hard to know where to begin. So I just hung out, in a loose imitation of Pip. Pip did not think much of Tammy, but she was mildly intrigued by the normalcy of our friendship.

"What do you guys do?"

"Nothing. Listen to tapes and stuff."

"That's it?"

"Last weekend we made peanut-butter cookies."

"Oh. That sounds like fun."

"Are you being sarcastic?"

"No, it does."

So Pip came along the next time I went to Tammy's house. As predicted, we listened to tapes. Pip asked if we were going to make peanut-butter cookies, but Tammy said that she didn't have the right ingredients. Then she threw herself down on the bed and asked us if we were girlfriends or what. An appalling emptiness filled the room. I stared out the window and repeated the word "window" in my head. I was ready to *window window window* indefinitely, but suddenly Pip answered.

"Yeah."

"Cool. I have a gay cousin."

Tammy told us that her room was a safe place and we didn't have to pretend, and then she showed us a neon-pink sticker that her cousin had sent her. It said "Fuck Your Gender." We all looked at the sticker in silence, absorbing its two meanings—at *least* two, probably more. Tammy seemed to be waiting for something, as if Pip and I were going to obediently fall upon each other the moment we read the sticker's bold command. I knew that we were a disappointment, meekly sitting on the bed. Pip must have felt this, too, because she abruptly threw her arm over my shoulder. This had never happened before, so, understandably, I froze. And then very gradually I recalibrated my body into a casual attitude. Pip just blinked when I sighed and flopped my hand onto her thigh. Tammy watched all this and even gave a slight nod of approval before shifting her attention back to the music. We listened to the Smiths, the Velvet Underground, and the Sugarcubes. Pip and I did not move from our position. After an hour and twenty minutes, my back ached and my hand felt numb and unaffiliated with the rest of my body. I asked Tammy where the rest room was and then ran out of the room.

In the powdery warmth of the bathroom I felt euphoric. I locked the door and made a series of involuntary, baroque gestures in the mirror. I waved maniacally at myself and contorted my face into hideous, unlovable expressions. I washed my hands as if they were children, cradling first one and then the other. I was experiencing a paroxysm of selfhood. The scientific name for this spasm is the Last Hurrah. The feeling was quickly spent. I dried my hands on a tiny blue towel and walked back to the bedroom.

I knew it just the moment before I saw it. I knew that I would find them together on the bed; I knew that I would be stunned; I knew that they would spring apart and wipe their mouths. I knew that Pip would not look me in the eye. I knew that I'd never speak to Tammy again. I knew that we would all graduate from high school and that Pip and I would live together as planned. And I knew that she did not want me in that way. She never would. Other girls, any girl, but not me.

Now that we had paid the rent, we felt entitled to mention the cockroach situation to the landlord. He told us that he would send someone over, but that we shouldn't get our hopes up.

"Why not?"

"Well, it's not just your apartment—the whole building's infested."

"Maybe you should have them do the whole building, then."

"It wouldn't do any good. They'd just come over from other buildings."

"It's the whole block?"

"It's the whole world."

I told him never mind, then, and got off the phone before he could hear Pip hammering. We were making some renovations—specifically, we were building a basement. Our apartment was small, but the ceilings were high and there was a tantalizing amount of unused space above our heads. Pip thought that lofts were for hippies, so even though our studio was on the second floor, she had sketched out a design that would allow us to live on a low-ceilinged main floor and then, whenever we were feeling morose, descend a ladder to the basement. We would leave the really heavy things down there, like the couch and the bathtub, but everything else would come upstairs. We could both picture the basement perfectly in our heads. It had a smell—damp, mineral—but was not entirely uncivilized. Warmth and beams of light seeped through the ceiling. Up there was home. Dinner was waiting for us there.

One of the many great reasons for building a basement was our access to free wood. Pip had met a girl whose father owned Berryman's Lumber and Supply. Kate Berryman. She was just a year younger than us and went to the private high school by Pip's grandma's house. I had never met her, but I was glad that we were using her. We practiced a loose, sporadic form of class warfare that sanctioned every kind of thievery. There was no person, no business, no library, hospital, or park that had not stolen from us, be is psychically or historically, we'd concluded, and thus we were forever trying to regain what was ours. Kate probably thought that she was on our side of the restitution when she struggled to pull large pieces of plywood out of the back of her parents' station wagon. She left them in the alley behind our building, honking three times as she drove away. We hauled the wood upstairs, convinced that we had hoodwinked everyone. We were always getting away with something, which implied that someone was always watching us, which meant that we were not alone in this world.

Each morning, Pip made a list of what we needed to do that day. At the top of the list was usually "Go to bank"—where they had free coffee. The next items were often vague—"Find out about food stamps," "Library card?"—but the list still gave me a cozy feeling. I liked to watch her write it, knowing that someone was steering our day. At night we discussed how we would decorate the basement, but during the day our progress was slow. Mostly what we had was a lot of pieces of wood; they leaned against the walls and lay across the couch like untrained dogs.

We were trying to nail a post into the linoleum kitchen floor when Pip decided that we needed a certain kind of bracket.

"Are you sure?"

"Yeah. I'll call Kate and she'll bring it."

Pip made the call and then went to take a shower. I continued hammering long nails through the post and into the floor. The post became secure. It was a satisfying feeling. It wouldn't bear any kind of weight, but it stood on its own. It was almost as tall as me and I couldn't help naming it. It looked like a Gwen.

The buzzer rang and Pip ran damply to the door. It was Kate. I looked up at her from where I was sitting on the kitchen floor. She was wearing a school uniform.

"Where's the bracket?" I said.

With panic in her eyes, she looked at Pip. Pip took her hand, turned to me, and said, "We have to tell you something."

I suddenly felt chilled. My ears were so cold that I had to press my hands against them. But I realized that this made me look as if I were trying to avoid listening, like the monkey who hears no evil. So I rubbed my palms together and asked, "Are *your* ears cold?"

Pip didn't respond, but Kate shook her head no.

"O.K. Go ahead."

"Kate and I are going to live together at her parents' house."

"Why?"

"What do you mean?"

"Well, I'm sure Kate's dad doesn't want you living in his house after we stole all that wood from him."

"I'm going to work at Berryman's Lumber to pay him back. I might even make enough money to get a car."

I thought about this. I imagined Pip driving a car, a Model T, wearing goggles and a scarf that blew behind her in the wind.

"Can I work at Berryman's Lumber, too?"

Pip was suddenly angry.

"Come on!"

"What? I can't? Just say I can't if I can't."

"You are purposely not getting it!"

"What?"

She raised Kate's hand clasped in her own and shook it in the air.

Suddenly my ears were hot, they were boiling, and I had to fan my hands at either side of my head to cool them down. This was too much for Pip; she grabbed her backpack and marched out of the apartment with Kate following her.

I could not let her leave the building. I ran down the hall and threw myself on her. She shook me off; I locked my arms around her knees. I was sobbing and wailing, but not like a cartoon of someone sobbing and wailing—this was really happening. If she left, I would become mute, like those children who have witnessed horrible atrocities. Pip was prying my fingers off her shins. Kate kneeled down to help her, and I was repulsed by the touch of her puddinglike skin. I wanted to puncture it. I lunged at her chest. Pip took advantage of this moment to scuttle down the stairs and somehow Kate was behind her. I ran after them, watched them scurry into Kate's car. Before they pulled away, I shut my eyes and hurled myself onto the side-walk. I lay there. This was my last hope—that Pip would take pity on me. I heard their car idling beside me. I listened to the traffic and to the sound of pedestrians stepping carefully around me. I could almost hear Kate and Pip arguing in the car, Pip wanting to get out and help me, Kate urging her to leave. I pressed my cheek against the pavement in prayer. A pair of high heels clicked toward me and stopped. An elderly woman's voice asked if I was O.K. I whispered that I was fine and silently begged her to move on. But the woman was persistent, so finally I opened my eyes to tell her to leave. Kate's car was gone.

I slept for three days. At intervals I'd open my eyes just long enough to re-member. Then I'd drop back into unconsciousness. In dreams, I was tunnel-ling toward her—if I could only dig deep enough I would find her. The tunnels narrowed as I crawled through them, until they became impossibly knotted strands of hair that I could only tear at.

On the afternoon of the third day, the phone finally rang. It was Mr. Hil-derbrand. In some bizarre alternative reality, the rent was due again. A month had passed since we had lifted Leslie's dirty slip. I hung up the phone and looked around the room. My post was still standing in the kitchen, tactfully silent. A dangerously tall tablelike structure wobbled in the middle of the room. It was the first square foot of the upstairs. I crawled underneath it and imagined Pip and Kate eating dinner with Mr. and Mrs. Berryman. It was the kind of scenario she had often described. We could never walk past a fancy house without her presuming that its owners would want her to live with them if they only knew that she was available. She saw herself as a charming street urchin, a pet for wealthy mothers. It was a scam. There was nothing in the world that was not a con—suddenly I understood this.

I went to the bathroom and threw handfuls of water on my face. I took off the jeans and T-shirt I had been sleeping in. Naked, I crouched on the floor and sliced the legs off my pants with a box cutter. I put on what was left of the pants and they were itty-bitty. Itty-bitty teeny-tiny. I sawed through the T-shirt, leaving "If You Love Jazz" on the floor. "Honk" barely covered my small breasts, but hey. Hey, I was leaving the apartment. I was walking down the hall, and there was a small basket of old apples in front of the neighbor's door, with a sign that said, "For my neighbors—please take one." I was starving. I took an apple and the door swung open. I had never really met this neighbor, but now I could see that she was a junkie. An old junkie. She told me to take another one and then she asked for a hug. I hugged her hard with an apple in each hand. A week before, I would have been afraid to touch her, but now I knew that I could do anything.

I had no money for the bus, so I walked. It was an incredible distance. A horse would have got tired galloping there. When birds flew there, it was called migration. But it wasn't difficult; it just took time. It was a new experience to walk across the city in tiny shorts and a half shirt that said "Honk." People honked without even seeing the shirt. I had the feeling that I might be shot in the back with an arrow or a gun, but this didn't happen. The world wasn't safer than I had thought; on the contrary, it was so dangerous that my practically naked self just fit right in—like a car crash, this kind of thing happened every day.

The place I was walking to was in a strip mall, between a pet store and a check-cashing place. I asked the man at the counter if they were hiring, and he gave me a form to fill out on a clipboard. When I handed it back, he stared at it without moving his eyes, which made me think that maybe he couldn't read. He said that I could start that night if I wanted to come back at nine. I said, "Great." He said that his name was Allen. I said that my name was Gwen.

I hung out in the strip mall for three hours. The pet store was closed, but I could see the rabbits through the window. I pressed my fingers against the glass and an ancient lop-ear hopped toward me wearily. It looked at me with one eye and then the other. Its nose quivered and for a moment I felt that it recognized me. It knew me from before, like an old teacher or a friend of my parents. The rabbit's eyes darted across my clothes and sniffed my wild, sad urgency and guessed that I was up to no good. I stood up, brushed off my knees, and walked back into Mr. Peepers Adult Video Store and More.

The "and More" part was in the back. Allen left me there with a woman named Christy. She was sitting in a green plastic patio chair and wearing a pink OshKosh overall dress. Looking at the sturdy brass overall fasteners, I wondered if everything familiar was actually part of a secret sexual underworld. Christy showed me into a booth and began packing dildos and bottles and strings of beads into a sporty Adidas bag. Her tools were laid out on an old flowery towel that smelled like my grandmother. She wrapped the towel around a small empty jelly jar.

"What's that for?" I asked.

"Pee."

Even pee was in on this. She showed me the price list and the slot that money would come through. She raised the flat of her hand in the air as she described how the curtain would roll up. She cleaned a telephone receiver with Windex and a paper towel and warned me never to leave it sticky. Then, with hasty efficiency, she pulled her long, thin hair into a ponytail, swung the Adidas bag over her shoulder, and left.

The store suddenly felt very quiet, like a library. I sat on the green plastic chair and adjusted my shirt and shorts. The fluorescent lights droned with a timeless constancy. I looked up at them and imagined that they, not the stars, had hung over the long creation of civilization. They had droned over ice ages and Neanderthals, and now they droned over me. I walked into my booth. I didn't have anything to lay out on a towel; I didn't even have a towel. All I had was the key to my apartment. If I didn't make any money tonight I would be walking all the way back there. At night. In this outfit. I was in the unique situation of needing to give a live fantasy show in order to protect my personal safety.

I practiced taking the phone off the hook. I did it five times, quicker and quicker, as if this were the skill I would be paid for. I thought about the words that I would have to speak into it. I had never said any of those words, except as swear words. I tried to think of them as seductive. I tried to say them seductively into the receiver, but they came out in a swallowed whisper. What if I couldn't say them? How awkward would that be? The man would ask for his money back and I wouldn't get to take the bus. In a panic, I said all the dirty words I knew in one long curse: *Cock-sucking ball-licking bitch whore cunt pussy-licking asshole fucker.* I hung up the phone. At least I could say them.

I sat in the plastic chair for more than three hours. During this time, two different men came into the store. They both peeked at me over the racks of videos, but neither of them walked to the back. After the second man left, Allen yelled out from behind the counter.

"That's the second one you've let go by!"

"What?"

"You've gotta be more aggressive! Can't just sit on your ass back there!"

"Got it!"

Twenty minutes later, a man in a black sweatshirt came in. He peered over a rack of magazines at me and I rose to my feet and walked toward him. His sweatshirt had a picture of a galaxy on it with an arrow pointing to a tiny dot and the words "You are here." The man looked up at me and pretended to be surprised. I imagined him instinctively pulling off his hat in the presence of a lady, but he wasn't wearing a hat.

"Are you interested in a live fantasy show, sir?"

"Yeah. O.K."

He followed me to the back of the store. We parted for a moment and reunited inside the booth with the curtained glass between us. I heard a Velcro wallet ripping open, twenty dollars fell lightly into the locked plastic box, and the curtain rose. He already had his penis in one hand and the phone in the other. I lifted the receiver. But, as I had feared, I was mute. I stood paralyzed, as if on a rock over a cold lake. I was never good at jumping in, letting go of one element and embracing another. I could stand there all day, letting the other kids go in front of me forever. He was pumping it up and down, and it was a strange sight, not something you see every day; in fact, I had never seen this before. He said something into the phone, but I didn't catch it. Despite how close we were, the reception was not very good.

"Excuse me?"

"Can you take off your clothes?"

"Oh. O.K."

From the start, one is trained not to take off one's clothes in front of strangers. Keeping one's clothes on is actually the No. 1 rule for civilization. Even a duck or a bear looks civilized when clothed. I pulled down my shorts, slid off my underwear, lifted my shirt over my head. I stood there, naked, like a bear or a duck. The man looked at me with grim concentration, my pale breasts, the puff of hair between my legs, back and forth between these poles. And he checked occasionally to make sure that I was looking at him. I diligently stared at his penis and hoped that this was enough, but after a few seconds he asked me if I liked what I saw. Again I was on the rock; kids splashed below me yelling "Jump!" I knew that jumping was like dying. I would have to let go of everything. I considered what I had. She hadn't called, she wouldn't call, I was alone, and I was here—not in some abstract sense, not here on earth or here in the universe, but really here, standing naked before this man. I pushed my hand between my legs and said, "Your big hard cock is making me so horny."

At 5 A.M., I was gliding through the night on a bus. The bus was just a formality, though—actually I was flying, in the air, and I was taller than most people are, I was nine or twelve feet tall, and I could fly, I could jump over cars, I could say "cock" ravenously, gently, coyly, demandingly. I could fly. And I had three hundred and twenty-five dollars in my pocket. Standing with one foot in the bathtub until Pip returned wasn't just a way to stop time—it was also a ritual to bring her back. I would be Gwen until she came home.

I bought a lime-green negligee, a dildo, which I de-virginized myself with, and a bobbed chestnut-colored wig. I hated my job, but I liked the fact that I could do it. I had once believed in a precious inner self, but now I didn't. I had thought that I was fragile, but I wasn't. It was like suddenly being good at sports. I didn't care about football, but it was pretty amazing to be in the N.F.L. I told long involved stories that revolved around my own perpetually wet pussy. I spread open every part of my body. I told customers that I missed them, and these customers became regulars and these regulars became stalkers. I learned to stay inside until the moment before my bus came, and then dash past anyone who was waiting in the parking lot, waving and yelling, "Come see me on Thursday!"

And I missed her terribly.

One evening, the bus was late and a customer followed me out to the curb. He stood beside me at the bus stop and I ignored him, and then he started spitting. First he spat on the pavement, then more generally in the air. I felt tiny wet specks blow onto my face and I pressed my lips together and stepped back. His harassment relied on a logic so foreign that I felt disoriented. I couldn't gauge whether this was terrifying or silly, and it was this feeling that told me to go back inside. I walked, then ran, slamming the door behind me. Mr. Peepers was not exactly a safe haven, though, and I couldn't stay there forever. I asked Allen to go outside and see if the customer was still there. He was. Couldn't Allen tell him to leave? Allen felt that he could not, because (a) he wasn't breaking the law, and (b) he was a good customer. Allen thought that I should call a friend or a cab to pick me up.

I had been waiting for this moment, and I marvelled at how organically it had arisen. I usually imagined poisoning myself or getting hit by a car. Someone official—a cop or a nurse—would ask me if there was anyone I wanted to call. I would gasp her name. "She works at Berryman's Lumber and Supply," I would say. This situation was not as dire, but it did involve safety, and, more important, it hadn't been my idea to call her. I had been ordered, almost commanded, by a superior, Allen.

I called Berryman's Lumber quickly, almost distractedly, modelling myself on the kind of person who would have a question about replacement saw blades. But the moment the line began ringing my senses dilated, winnowing out everything that was not the sound of my own heart.

"Berryman's Lumber and Supply. How can I help you?"

"I'm trying to reach Pip Greeley?"

"Just a sec."

Just a sec. Just two months. Just a lifetime. Just a sec.

"Hello?"

"It's me."

"Oh, hi."

I knew this wouldn't do. This, *Oh, hi*. I couldn't be the person who elicited a response like this. I straightened my wig. I smiled into the air the way I smiled when customers unbuckled their belts, and I made my eyes laugh as if everything were some version of a good time. I began again.

"Hey, I'm in a bind here and wonder if you could help me out."

"Yeah? What?"

"I'm working at this place, Mr. Peepers? And there's this really creepy guy hanging around. Do you have a car?"

She was silent for a moment. I could almost hear the name Mr. Peepers vibrating in her head. It described a man with eyes the size of clocks. She had devoted her whole life to avoiding Mr. Peepers, and now here I was, cavorting with him. I was either repulsive and foolish or I was something else. Something surprising. I held my breath.

She said she guessed she could borrow and van and could I wait twenty minutes until she got off work? I said I probably could.

We didn't talk in the van, and I didn't look at her, but I could feel her looking at me many times with bewilderment. I usually changed my clothes and took off my wig before I went home, but I had been right not to do this today. I looked out the window for other passengers in love with their drivers, but we were well disguised—we feigned boredom and prayed for traffic. Just as her former home came into view, Pip made a sudden left turn and asked if I wanted to see where she lived now.

"You mean Kate's?"

"No, that didn't work out. I'm living in this guy I work with's basement."

"Sure."

The basement was what is called "unfinished." It was dirt, with a few boards thrown down here and there, islands that supported a bed and some milk crates. Pip waved a flashlight around and said, "It's only seventy-five dollars a month."

"Really."

"Yeah, all this room! It's more than fifteen hundred square feet. I can do anything I want with it."

She walked me between the beams, describing her plans. Then she slipped the flashlight into a hanging loop of string and a dim spotlight fell on her pillow. I stretched out on the bed and yawned. She stared at the length of me.

"You can stay here if you want—I mean, if you're tired."

"I might just nap."

"I have some cleaning up to do."

"You clean up. I'll nap."

I listened to her sweeping. She swept closer and closer, she swept all around the edges of the mattress. The she laid the broom down and climbed into bed with me. We lay there, perfectly still, for a long time. Finally, Pip adjusted her shoulders so that the outermost edge of her T-shirt grazed my arm; I recrossed my legs, carelessly letting my ankle fall against her shin. Five more seconds passed, like heavy bass-drum beats. Then we turned to each other, and our hands grabbed urgently, even painfully. It seemed necessary to be brutal at first, to mime anger and concede nothing. But once we had wrestled deep into the night and turned off the flashlight, I was surprised by her gentle attentions.

So this was what it was like not to be me. This was who Pip was. Because, make no mistake, I kept my wig on the whole time. I believed it had made all of this possible, and I think I was right. The wig and the fact that I did not cry, even though I desperately wanted to cry, to tell her how miserable I had been, to squeeze her and make her promise never to leave again. I wanted her to beg me to quit my job and then I wanted to quit my job.

But she didn't beg, and in fact Mr. Peepers was essential. Each night she picked me up in the Berryman's Lumber van, took me under the house, and made love to me. And each morning I went home and took off my wig. I scratched my sweaty scalp and let my head breathe for two hours before getting on the bus to go to work. I lived like this for eight beautiful days. On the ninth day, Pip suggested that we go out to breakfast before I went to work.

"I wish I could, but I have to go home and get ready."

"You look great."

"But I have to wash my hair."

"Your hair looks great."

Our eyes locked and an unfriendly feeling passed between us. Of course it was a wig—I knew she knew this—but she was suddenly determined to call my bluff. I imagined for a moment that we were duelling, delicate foils raised high.

"O.K., then, let's have breakfast."

"I can drop you off at Mr. Peepers."

"Fine. Thank you."

Everyone knows that if you paint a human being entirely with house paint he will live, as long as you don't paint the bottoms of his feet. It only takes a little thing like that to kill a person. I had worn the wig for almost thirty hours straight, and as I stripped and jiggled and moaned I began to feel warm, overly warm. But after each show a new customer appeared. By mid-day, sweat was running down the sides of my face, but the men just kept coming. It was a day of incredible profits. Allen even patted me on the back as I left, saying, "Good work, champ." Pip was waiting in the van, but the walk across the parking lot felt long and strange. I thought I recognized a customer crouching by his car, but, no, it was just a normal man huddled over something in a cage. He murmured, "That's right, we're going to take you home."

Pip put me right to bed and even borrowed a thermometer from her co-worker upstairs. But she did not suggest that I take off my wig, and in my fever I understood what this meant. I saw her in the clearing with a pistol and I knew without even looking that my hands were empty. But I could win by pretending to have a pistol. If I said "Bang!" and let her shoot me, I would win. If I died this way, as Gwen, would the rest of me go on living? And what was the rest of me? I fell asleep with this question and tunnelled through the night ripping at the knotted strands until finally the wig came off. I didn't put it on in the morning and Pip didn't ask me how I was feel-ing; she could see that I was fine. She didn't offer to drive me to work, ei-ther, and we both knew that she wouldn't be there to pick me up.

I sat in the green plastic chair under the fluorescent lights. It was a slow day. It seemed as if all the men in the world were too busy to masturbate. I imag-ined them out there doing various things, solving crimes and teaching their children how to do cartwheels. It was the last hour of my eight-hour shift and I had not given a single show. It was almost eerie. I watched the clock and the door and began to place bets between them. If no customers came for me in the next fifteen minutes, I would yell Allen's name. Fifteen min-utes passed.

"Allen!"

"What."

"Nothing."

There were only twenty minutes left now. If no one came in the next twelve minutes, I would yell the word "I," as in *me, myself, and.* After seven minutes, the door dinged and a man cam in. He bought a video and left.

"I!"

"What?"

"Nothing."

It was the final eight. If no customers came in, I would yell the word "quit." As in *no more, enough, I'm going home.* I stared at the door. With each breath I took, it threatened to open. With each passing minute. One. Two. Three. Four. Five. Six. Seven. Eight.

23

Equal Opportunity

WALTER MOSLEY

Walter Mosley was born in Los Angeles, California, in 1952. He earned his BA in political science from Johnson State College in 1977. During the next several years, he worked primarily as a computer programmer. Over time, he found himself increasingly drawn to literature and creative writing, and in 1985 he enrolled in the creative writing program at the City College of the City University of New York. In 1990, Mosley published his first novel, *Devil in a Blue Dress*, which was a commercial and critical success and later adapted into a major motion picture. He followed that success by publishing more than thirty books during the next nineteen years, establishing himself as one of the most prolific living American writers. His books run the gamut from detective fiction (with signature Sunshine Noir) to erotica to graphic novels and nonfiction. *Devil in a Blue Dress* was the first novel in a series of eleven books Mosley published in the Easy Rawlins mystery series, named for the protagonist, a World War II veteran living in South Central Los Angeles. Mosley has also contributed nonfiction to *The Nation* and *New York Times Magazine*. He is the winner of numerous awards, including an O. Henry Award. "Equal Opportunity," the story featured in this collection, originally appeared in Mosley's *Always Outnumbered, Always Outgunned* (1998) and is part of his Socrates Fortlow series.

{1.}

Bounty Supermarket was on Venice Boulevard, miles and miles from Socrates' home. He gaped at the glittering palace as he strode across the hot asphalt parking lot. The front wall was made from immense glass panes with steel framing to hold them in place. Through the big windows he could see long lines of customers with baskets full of food. He imagined apples and T-bone steaks, fat hams and the extra-large boxes of cereal that they only sold in supermarkets.

The checkers were all young women, some of them girls. Most were black. Black women, black girls—taking money and talking back and forth between themselves as they worked; running the packages of food over the computer eye that rang in the price and added it to the total without them having to think a thing.

In between the checkout counters black boys and brown ones loaded up bags for the customers.

Socrates walked up to the double glass doors and they slid open moaning some deep machine blues. He came into the cool air and cocked his ear to that peculiar music of supermarkets; steel carts wheeling around, crashing together, resounding with the thuds of heavy packages. Children squealing and yelling. The footsteps and occasional conversation blended together until they made a murmuring sound that lulled the ex-convict.

There was a definite religious feel to being in the great store. The lofty ceilings, the abundance, the wealth.

Dozens of tens and twenties, in between credit cards and bank cards, went back and forth over the counters. Very few customers used coupons. The cash seemed to be endless. How much money passed over those counters every day?

And what would they think if they knew that the man watching them had spent twenty-seven years doing hard time in prison? Socrates barked out a single-syllable laugh. They didn't have to worry about him. He wasn't a thief. Or, if he was, the only thing he ever took was life.

"Sir, can I help you?" Anton Crier asked.

Socrates knew the name because it was right there, on a big badge on his chest. ANTON CRIER ASST. MGR. He wore tan pants and a blue blazer with the supermarket insignia over the badge.

"I came for an application," Socrates said. It was a line that he had spent a whole day thinking about; a week practicing. *I came for an application.* For a couple days he had practiced saying *job application,* but after a while he dropped the word *job* to make his request sound more sure. But when he went to Stony Wile and told him that he planned to say "I came for a application," Stony said that you had to say *an application.*

"If you got a word that starts with *a, e, i, o,* or *u* then you got to say *an* instead of *a,*" Stony had said.

Anton Crier's brow knitted and he stalled a moment before asking, "An application for what?"

"A job." There, he'd said it. It was less than a minute and this short white man, just a boy really, had already made him beg.

"Oh," said Anton Crier, nodding like a wise elder. "Uh. How old are you, sir?"

"Ain't that against the law?" Like many other convicts Socrates was a student of the law.

"Huh?"

"Askin' me my age. That's against the law. You cain't discriminate against color or sex or religion or infirmity or against age. That's the law."

"Uh, well, yes, of course it is. I know that. I'm not discriminating against you. It's just that we don't have any openings right now. Why don't you come in the fall when the kids are back at school?"

Anton leaned to the side, intending to leave Socrates standing there.

"Hold on," Socrates said. He held up his hands, loosely as fists, in a nonchalant sort of boxing stance.

Anton looked, and waited.

"I came for an application," Socrates repeated.

"But I told you . . ."

"I know what you said. But first you looked at my clothes and at my bald head. First yo' eyes said that this is some kinda old hobo and what do he want here when it ain't bottle redemption time."

"I did not . . ."

"It don't matter," Socrates said quickly. He knew better than to let a white man in uniform finish a sentence. "You got to give me a application. That's the law too."

"Wait here," young Mr. Crier said. He turned and strode away toward an elevated office that looked down along the line of cash registers.

Socrates watched him go. So did the checkers and bag boys. He was their boss and they knew when he was unhappy. They stole worried glances at Socrates.

Socrates stared back. He wondered if any of those young black women would stand up for him. Would they understand how far he'd come to get there?

He'd traveled more than fourteen miles from his little apartment down in Watts. They didn't have any supermarkets or jobs in his neighborhood. And all the stores along Crenshaw and Washington knew him as a bum who collected bottles and cans for a living.

They wouldn't hire him.

Socrates hadn't held a real job in over thirty-seven years. He'd been unemployed for twenty-five months before the party with Shep, Fogel, and Muriel.

They'd been out carousing. Three young people, blind drunk.

Back at Shep's, Muriel gave Socrates the eye. He danced with her until Shep broke it up. But then Shep fell asleep. When he awoke to find them rolling on the floor the fight broke out in earnest.

Socrates knocked Shep back to the floor and then he finished his business with Muriel even though she was worried about her man. But when she started to scream and she hit Socrates with that chair he hit her back.

It wasn't until the next morning, when he woke up, that he realized that his friends were dead.

Then he'd spent twenty-seven years in prison. Now, eight years free, fifty-eight years old, he was starting life over again.

Not one of those girls, nor Anton Crier, was alive when he started his journey. If they were lucky they wouldn't understand him.

{2.}

There was a large electric clock above the office. The sweep hand reared back and then battered up against each second, counting every one like a drummer beating out time on a slave galley.

Socrates could see the young assistant manager through the window under the clock. He was saying something to an older white woman sitting there. The woman looked down at Socrates and then swiveled in her chair to a file cabinet. She took out a piece of paper and held it while lecturing Anton. He reached for the paper a couple of times but the woman kept it away from him and continued talking. Finally she said something and Crier nodded. He took the paper from her and left the office, coming down the external stairs at a fast clip. Walking past the checkers he managed not to look at Socrates before he was standing there in front of him.

"Here," he said, handing the single-sheet application form to Socrates. Crier never stopped moving. As soon as Socrates had the form between his fingers the younger man was walking away.

Socrates touched the passing elbow and asked, "You got a pencil?"

"What?"

"I need a pencil to fill out this form."

"You, you, you can just send it in."

"I didn't come all this way for a piece'a paper, man. I come to apply for a job."

Anton Crier stormed over to one of the checkers, demanded her pencil, then rushed back to Socrates.

"Here," he said.

Socrates answered, "Thank you," but the assistant manager was already on his way back to the elevated office.

Half an hour later Socrates was standing at the foot of the stairs leading up to Anton and his boss. He stood there waiting for one of them to come down. They could see him through the window.

They knew he was there.

So Socrates waited, holding the application in one hand and the borrowed pencil in the other.

After twenty minutes he was wondering if a brick could break the wall of windows at the front of the store.

After thirty minutes he decided that it might take a shotgun blast.

Thirty-nine minutes had gone by when the woman, who had bottled red hair, came down to meet him. Anton Crier shadowed her. Socrates saw the anger in the boy's face.

"Yes? Can I help you?" Halley Grimes asked. She had a jailhouse smile—insincere and crooked.

"I wanted to ask a couple of things about my application."

"All the information is right there at the top of the sheet."

"But I had some questions."

"We're very busy, sir." Ms. Grimes broadened her smile to show that she had a heart, even for the aged and confused. "What do you need to know?"

"It asks here if I got a car or a regular ride to work."

"Yes," beamed Ms. Grimes. "What is it exactly that you don't understand?"

"I understand what it *says* but I just don't get what it means."

The look of confusion came into Halley Grimes's face. Socrates welcomed a real emotion.

He answered her unasked question. "What I mean is that I don't have a car or a ride but I can take a bus to work."

The store manager took his application form and fingered the address.

"Where is this street?" she asked.

"Down Watts."

"That's pretty far to go by bus, isn't it? There are stores closer than this one, you know."

"But I could get here." Socrates noticed that his head wanted to move as if to the rhythm of a song. Then he heard it: "Baby Love," by Diana Ross and the Supremes. It was being played softly over the loudspeaker. "I could get here."

"Well." Ms. Grimes seemed to brighten. "We'll send this in to the main office and, if it's clear with them, we'll .put it in our files. When there's an opening we'll give you a call."

"A what?"

"A call. We'll call you if you're qualified and if a job opens up."

"Uh, well, we got to figure somethin' else than that out. You see, I don't have no phone."

"Oh, well then." Ms. Grimes held up her hands in a gesture of helplessness. "I don't see that there's anything we can do. The main office demands a phone number. That's how they check on your address. They call."

"How do they know that they got my address just 'cause'a some phone they call? Wouldn't it be better if they wrote me?"

"I'm very busy, sir. I've told you that we need a phone number to process this application." Halley Grimes held out the form toward Socrates. "Without that there really isn't anything I can do."

Socrates kept his big hands down. He didn't want to take the application back—partly because he didn't want to break the pudgy white woman's fingers.

"Do me a favor and send it in," he said.

"I told you . . ."

"Just send it in, okay? Send it in. I'll be back to find out what they said."

"You don't . . ."

"Just send it in." There was violence in this last request.

Halley Grimes pulled the application away from his face and said, "All right. But it won't make any difference."

{3.}

Socrates had to transfer on three buses to get back to his apartment.

And he was especially tired that day. Talking to Crier and Grimes had worn him out.

He boiled potatoes and eggs in a saucepan on his single hot plate and then cut them together in the pot with two knives, adding mustard and sweet pickle relish. After the meal he had two shots of whiskey and one Camel cigarette.

He was asleep by nine o'clock.

His dream blared until dawn.

It was a realistic sort of dream; no magic, no impossible wish. It was just Socrates in a nine-foot cell with a flickering fluorescent light from the walkway keeping him from sleeping and reading, giving him a headache, hurting his eyes.

"Mr. Bennett," the sleeping Socrates called out from his broad sofa. He shouted so loudly that a mouse in the kitchen jumped up and out of the potato pan pinging his tail against the thin tin as he went.

Socrates heard the sound in his sleep. He turned but then slipped back into the flickering, painful dream.

"What you want?" the guard asked. He was big and black and meaner than anyone Socrates had ever known.

"I cain't read. I cain't sleep. That light been like that for three days now."

"Put the pillow on your head," the big guard said.

"I cain't breathe like that," Socrates answered sensibly.

"Then don't," Mr. Bennett replied.

As the guard walked away, Socrates knew, for the first time really, why they kept him in that jail. He would have killed Bennett if he could have right then; put his fingers around that fat neck and squeezed until the veins swelled and cartilage popped and snapped. He was so mad that he balled his fists in his sleep twenty-five years after the fact.

He was a sleeping man wishing that he could sleep. And he was mad, killing mad. He couldn't rest because of the crackling, buzzing light, and the more it shone the angrier he became. And the angrier he got the more scared he was. Scared that he'd kill Bennett the first chance he got.

The anger built for days in that dream. The sound of grinding teeth could be heard throughout Socrates' two rooms.

Finally, when he couldn't stand it anymore, he took his rubber squeeze ball in his left hand and slipped his right hand through the bars. He passed the ball through to his right hand and gauged its weight in the basket of his fingers. He blinked back at the angry light, felt the weight of his hard rubber ball. The violent jerk started from his belly button, traveled up through his chest and shoulder, and down until his fingers tensed like steel. The ball flew in a straight line that shattered the light, broke it into blackness.

And in the jet night he heard Bennett say, "That's the last light you get from the state of Indiana."

Socrates woke up in the morning knowing that he had cried. He could feel the strain in the muscles of his throat. He got out of bed thinking about Anton Crier and Halley Grimes.

{4.}

"You what?" asked Stony Wile. He'd run into Socrates getting off a bus on Central and offered to buy his friend a beer. They went to Moody's bar on 109th Street.

"I been down there ev'ry day for five days. An ev'ry day I go in there I ask 'em if they got my okay from the head office yet."

"An' what they say about that?"

"Well, the first day that boy, that Anton Crier, just said no. So I left. Next day he told me that I had to leave. But I said that I wanted to talk to his boss. She come down an' tell me that she done already said how I cain't work there if I don't have no phone."

"Yeah," asked Stony Wile. "Then what'd you do?"

"I told 'em that they should call downtown and get some kinda answer on me because I was gonna come back ev'ryday till I get some kinda answer." There was a finality in Socrates' voice that opened Stony's eyes wide.

"You don't wanna do sumpin' dumb now, Socco," he said.

"An' what would that be?"

"They could get you into all kindsa trouble, arrest you for trespassin' if you keep it up."

"Maybe they could. Shit. Cops could come in here an' blow my head off too, but you think I should kiss they ass?"

"But that's different. You got to stand up for yo' pride, yo' manhood. But I don't see it wit' this supermarket thing."

"Well," Socrates said. "On Thursday Ms. Grimes told me that the office had faxed her to say I wasn't qualified for the position. She said that she had called the cops and said that I'd been down there harassin' them. She said that they said that if I ever come over there again that they would come arrest me. Arrest me! Just for tryin' t'get my rights."

"That was the fourth day?" Stony asked to make sure that he was count-ing right.

"Uh-huh. That was day number four. I asked her could I see that fax pa-per but she said that she didn't have it, that she threw it out. You ever hear'a anything like that? White woman workin' for a white corporation throwin' out paperwork?"

Stony was once a shipbuilder but now worked on a fishing day boat out of San Pedro. He'd been in trouble before but never in jail. He'd never thought about the thousands of papers he'd signed over his life; never won-dered where they went.

"Why wouldn't they throw them away?" Stony asked.

"Because they keep ev'ry scrap'a paper they got just as long as it make they case in court."

Stony nodded. Maybe he understood.

"So I called Bounty's head office," Socrates said. "Over in Torrence."

"You lyin'."

"An' why not? I applied for that job, Stony. I should get my hearin' wit' them."

"What'd they say?"

"That they ain't never heard'a me."

"You lyin'," Stony said again.

"Grimes an' Crier the liars. An' you know I went down there today t'tell'em so. I was up in Anton's face when he told me that Ms. Grimes was out. I told him that they lied and that I had the right to get me a job."

"An' what he say?"

"He was scared. He thought I mighta hit'im. And I mighta too except Ms. Grimes comes on down."

"She was there?"

"Said that she was on a lunch break; said that she was gonna call the cops on me. Shit. I called her a liar right to her face. I said that she was a liar and that I had a right to be submitted to the main office." Socrates jabbed his finger at Stony as if he were the one holding the job hostage. "I told'er that I'd be back on Monday and that I expected some kinda fair treatment."

"Well that sounds right," Stony said. "It ain't up to her who could apply an' who couldn't. She got to be fair."

"Yeah," Socrates answered. "She said that the cops would be waitin' for me on Monday. Maybe Monday night you could come see me in jail."

{5.}

On Saturday Socrates took his canvas cart full of cans to the Boys Market on Adams. He waited three hours behind Calico, an older black woman who prowled the same streets he did, and two younger black men who worked as team.

Calico and DJ and Bernard were having a good time waiting. DJ was from Oakland and had come down to L.A. to stay with his grandmother when he was fifteen. She died a year later so he had to live on the streets since then. But DJ didn't complain. He talked about how good life was and how much he was able to collect on the streets.

"Man," DJ said. "I wish they would let me up there in Beverly Hills just one week. Gimme one week with a pickup an' I could live for a year offa the good trash they got up there. They th'ow out stuff that still work up there."

"How the fuck you know, man?" Bernard said. "When you ever been up Beverly Hills?"

"When I was doin' day work. I helped a dude build a cinderblock fence up on Hollandale. I saw what they th'owed out. I picked me up a portable TV right out the trash an' I swear that sucker get ev'ry channel."

"I bet it don't get cable," Bernard said.

"It would if I'da had a cable to hook it up wit'."

They talked like that for three hours. Calico cooed and laughed with them, happy to be in the company of young men.

But Socrates was just mad.

Why the hell did he have to wait for hours? Who were they in that supermarket to make full-grown men and women wait like they were children?

At two o'clock he got up and walked away from his canvas wagon.

"Hey," Bernard called. "You want us t'watch yo' basket?"

"You could keep it," Socrates said. "I ain't never gonna use the goddam thing again."

Calico let out a whoop at Socrates' back.

On Sunday Socrates sharpened his pocket knife on a graphite stone. He didn't keep a gun. If the cops caught him with a gun he would spend the rest of his life in jail. But there was no law against a knife blade three inches or less; and three inches was all a man who knew how to use a knife needed.

Socrates sharpened his knife but he didn't know why exactly. Grimes and Crier weren't going to harm him, at least not with violence. And if they called the cops a knife wouldn't be any use anyway. If the cops even thought that he had a knife they could shoot him and make a good claim for self-defense.

But Socrates still practiced whipping out the knife and slashing with the blade sticking out of the back end of his fist.

"Hah!" he yelled.

{6.}

He left the knife on the orange crate by his sofa bed the next morning before leaving for Bounty Supermarket. The RTD bus came right on time and he made his connections quickly, one after the other.

In forty-five minutes he was back on that parking lot. It was a big building, he thought, but not as big as the penitentiary had been.

A smart man would have turned around and tried some other store, Socrates knew that. It didn't take a hero to make a fool out of himself.

It was before nine-thirty and the air still had the hint of a morning chill. The sky was a pearl gray and the parking lot was almost empty.

Socrates counted seven breaths and then walked toward the door with no knife in his hand. He cursed himself softly under his breath because he had no woman at home to tell him that he was a fool.

Nobody met him at the door. There was only one checker on duty while the rest of the workers went up and down the aisles restocking and straightening the shelves.

With nowhere else to go, Socrates went toward the elevated office. He was half the way there when he saw Halley Grimes coming down the stairs. Seeing him she turned and went, ran actually, back up to the office.

Socrates was sure that she meant to call the police. He wanted to run but couldn't. All he could do was take one step after the other; the way he'd done in his cell sometimes, sometimes the way he did at home.

Two men appeared at the high door when Socrates reached the stairs. Salt and pepper, white and black. The older one, a white man, wore a tan wash-and-wear suit with a cheap maroon tie. The Negro had on black jeans, a black jacket, and a white turtleneck shirt. He was very light-skinned but his nose and lips would always give him away.

The men came down to meet him. They were followed by Grimes and Crier.

"Mr. Fortlow?" the white man inquired.

Socrates nodded and looked him in the eye.

"My name is Parker," he continued. "And this is Mr. Weems."

"Uh-huh," Socrates answered.

The two men formed a wall behind which the manager and assistant manager slipped away.

"We work for Bounty," Mr. Weems said. "Would you like to come up-stairs for a moment?"

"What for?" Socrates wanted to know.

"We'd like to talk," Parker answered.

The platform office was smaller than it looked from the outside. The two cluttered desks that sat back to back took up most of the space. Three sides were windows that gave a full panorama of the store. The back wall had a big blackboard on it with the chalked-in time schedules of everyone who worked there. Beneath the blackboard was a safe door.

"Have a seat, Mr. Fortlow." Parker gestured toward one of the two chairs. He sat in the other chair while Weems perched on a desk.

"Coffee?" asked Parker.

"What's this all about, man?" Socrates asked.

Smiling, Parker said, "We want to know what your problem is with Ms. Grimes. She called the head office on Friday and told us that she was calling the police because she was afraid of you."

"I don't have no problem with Ms. Grimes or Anton Crier or Bounty Supermarket. I need a job and I wanted to make a application. That's all."

"But she told you that you had to have a phone number in order to complete your file," said Weems.

"So? Just 'cause I don't have no phone then I cain't work? That don't make no sense at all. If I don't work I cain't afford no phone. If I don't have no phone then I cain't work. You might as well just put me in the ground."

"It's not Bounty's problem that you don't have a phone." Parker's face was placid but the threat was in his tone.

"All I want is to make a job application. All I want is to work," Socrates said. Really he wanted to fight. He wanted his knife at close quarters with those private cops. But instead he went on, "I ain't threatened nobody. I ain't said I was gonna do a thing. All I did was to come back ev'ry day an' ask if they had my okay from you guys yet. That's all. On the job application they asked if I had a car or a ride to work—to see if I could get here. Well, I come in ev'ry day for a week at nine-thirty or before. I come in an' asked if I been cleared yet. I didn't do nuthin' wrong. An' if that woman is scared it must be 'cause she knows she ain't been right by me. But I didn't do nuthin.'"

There was no immediate answer to Socrates' complaint. The men looked at him but kept silent. There was the hum of machinery coming from somewhere but Socrates couldn't figure out where. He concentrated on keeping his hands on his knees, on keeping them open.

"But how do you expect to get a job when you come in every day and treat the people who will be your bosses like they're doing something wrong?" Weems seemed really to want to know.

"If I didn't come in they woulda th'owed out my application, prob'ly did anyway. I ain't no kid. I'm fifty-eight years old. I'm unemployed an' nowhere near benefits. If I don't find me some way t'get some money I'll starve. So, you see, I had to come. I couldn't let these people say that I cain't even apply. If I did that then I might as well die."

Parker sighed. Weems scratched the top of his head and then rubbed his nose.

"You can't work here," Parker said at last. "If we tried to push you off on Ms. Grimes she'd go crazy. She really thought that you were going to come in here guns blazing."

"So 'cause she thought that I was a killer then I cain't have no job?" Socrates knew the irony of his words but he also knew their truth. He didn't care about a job just then. He was happy to talk, happy to say what he felt. Because he knew that he was telling the truth and that those men believed him.

"What about Rodriguez?" Weems asked of no one in particular.

"Who's that?" Socrates asked.

"He's the manager of one of our stores up on Santa Monica," Weems replied.

"I don't know," Parker said.

"Yeah, sure, Connie Rodriguez." Weems was getting to like the idea. "He's always talking about giving guys a chance. We could give him a chance to back it up with Mr. Fortlow here."

Parker chewed on his lower lip until it reddened. Weems grinned. It seemed to Socrates that some kind of joke was being played on this Connie Rodriguez. Parker hesitated but he liked the idea.

Parker reached down under the desk and came out with a briefcase. From this he brought out a sheet of paper; Socrates' application form.

"There's just one question," Parker said.

{7.}

"What he wanna know?" Stony Wile asked at Iula's grill. They were there with Right Burke, Markham Peal, and Howard Shakur. Iula gave Socrates a party when she heard that he got a job as a general food packager and food delivery person at Bounty Supermarkets on Santa Monica Boulervard. She made the food and his friends brought the liquor.

"He wanted to know why I had left one of the boxes blank."

"What box?"

"The one that asks if I'd ever been arrested for or convicted of a felony."

"Damn. What you say?"

"That I musta overlooked it."

"An' then you lied?"

"Damn straight. But he knew I was lyin'. He was a cop before he went to work for Bounty. Both of 'em was. He asked me that if they put through a check on me would it come up bad? An' I told him that he didn't need to put through no checks."

"Mmm!" Stony hummed, shaking his head. "That's always gonna be over your head, man. Always."

Socrates laughed and grabbed his friend by the back of his neck.

He hugged Stony and then held him by the shoulders. "I done had a lot worse hangin' over me, brother. At least I get a paycheck till they find out what I am."

24

The Passenger

MARISA SILVER

Marisa Silver has received considerable acclaim as both filmmaker and writer. She was born in 1960 in Cleveland, Ohio, and raised in New York City. While studying at Harvard University, she wrote and directed a feature film, *Old Enough*, which earned her the grand prize for a dramatic work at the 1984 Sundance Film Festival. With that early breakthrough, Silver launched a successful career as a screenwriter and director. Her films include *Permanent Record*; *He Said, She Said*; and *Indecency*. She also directed an episode for the television series *L.A. Law*. Silver made her fictional debut in *The New Yorker* in 2000 with "The Passenger." The following year she published *Babe in Paradise* (2001), a collection of short stories that was named a New York Times Notable Book of the Year and a Los Angeles Times Best Book of the Year. She has since published two novels, *No Direction Home* (2005) and *The God of War* (2008), the latter named a finalist for the Los Angeles Times Book Prize for fiction. Her fiction has been anthologized in *The Best American Short Stories* and in *The O. Henry Prize Stories*.

I have a ring in my nose and a ring in my navel, and people make assumptions about me. None of them are true. I'm not a punk or a slave, a biker chick or a fashion hag.

I drive a limo. I take people where they want to go—to parties and airports, to score drugs at a ranch house or a piece of ass at a hotel bar. On any given night, I'll be taking the curves on Mulholland, hitting a prom in Northridge, or, if I'm lucky, flying the straight shot out the highway to Malibu. People think Los Angeles is the same everywhere—all palm trees and swimming pools. But some nights you need a passport and a two-way dictionary just to get from Hancock Park to Koreatown.

Ruthanne's my dispatcher. I've never met her, but she's probably the person I talk to the most. Once I saw her red jacket hanging off a chair at the office. It had a dog appliquéd across the back. Normally, someone who wore that kind of jacket would have nothing to say to me, and so, in a sense, not meeting has brought us closer. Right now, her voice crackles over my car radio.

"Ex-Lax," she says, using her helium-balloon voice. "Who wants to shit or get off the pot?"

"Ex-Lax" is her shorthand for a pickup at Lax, the airport. She says "Re-lax" when you have to make a second airport trip. Ha, ha, ha, right? But I'm smiling.

I pick up my handset. "Twenty-two. I'm all over it." We're required to use our call number, but Ruthie never does. She calls me by my name, Babe.

"O.K., Babe," she says. "You're picking up two Chins outside International baggage."

"No way."

"Yes way," she says. "You'll have to circle the drain."

I click off. The usual airport routine is that I park the limo and wait at the arrivals gate, holding a piece of cardboard with a stranger's name on it. Finally, a passenger comes off the plane. He'll smile when he sees his name, delighted that he's the same guy he was before he took off. Sometimes he'll be so relieved that he'll shake my hand, like I care one way or another. It's moments like these that kill me.

But meeting someone outside baggage is an ordeal. Security is tight, and you can't wait by the curb for more than twenty seconds before some uniform appears, telling you to scram. So you have to drive around and around until you actually see the pickup.

I click on my radio again. "It could take an hour," I complain.

"You vant I should give it to someone else, *daah-link*?" Ruthie answers, doing her Gabor sisters impersonation.

"No," I say quickly. International is promising in other ways—people are often confused by the exchange rate. I once got a hundred-dollar tip from an Indian family that had fastened their suitcases together with electrical tape. I felt bad about taking it, but not so bad about having it.

I'm twenty-three. I live alone in a second-story box on Lincoln Boulevard. I had a boyfriend for a while. I liked him, then I didn't. It was like a sugar rush and just after. I have a few friends left over from high school, and we go drinking sometimes, but lately I'm not sure why. We get together and moan about rent, or we get worked up telling stories we've told before. Then we end up staring into our drinks because facing each other is like looking into a mirror in bad lighting.

A few years ago, my mother left L.A. to join a spiritual community in the desert. This makes it sound like she's living in a collection of gassy, glowing matter; in fact, it's a bunch of trailers on a scrubby piece of land near a Marine base.

After she left, I worked as a waitress, a copy-shop clerk, a messenger—all those jobs that you get when you have nothing but a couple of community-college credits in highly useless things like World Literature. The difference between me and the other employees was that I didn't want to be something else. With all the other people it was, "I work in a copy shop, but I really want to act." Or, "I sell subscriptions over the phone, but I have this great idea for an Internet company." Not that I want to drive a car for the rest of my life, but I'm willing to say that driving is what I do for now.

The fifth time I circle International baggage, people begin to pour out the doors. Most of the passengers wear wrinkled nylon track suits and baseball caps with American logos—walking advertisements for a place they're seeing for the first time. They look dazed. All but a few are Asian, and I have no idea how I'm going to find my fare. Then I see a man and a woman standing at the curb with a very large black suitcase between them, and for some reason I know that they are my Chins. She's wearing a neatly cut jacket and a matching skirt. Her black heels are so polished they reflect the lights overhead. He wears a double-breasted suit that hangs loosely over his thin body. His hair is swooped back into a gentle pompadour, and it's shiny with whatever goop he put into it. You'd never guess that these two had just spent the day on an airplane.

"Mr. and Mrs. Chin?" I call out the passenger-side window.

They don't respond for a moment, but then they nod enthusiastically. I pop the trunk and hop out of the car. I reach for their suitcase, but Mr. Chin waves me away and points toward the back seat.

"It's safer to put it in the trunk," I explain. "If the car stops suddenly, the case could fly into your face."

The Chins smile, as if I've said something amusing but not exactly funny, and I realize that they don't understand a word I'm saying. I go for the suitcase again, but Mr. Chin steps in front of me, shaking his head. Mrs. Chin slides into the back seat like a swan, her legs pressed together, and holds out her hands to take the suitcase, which Mr. Chin pushes inside. Finally, he tucks himself neatly into the space left over and waits for me to shut the door. I think for a minute about pressing the point: it's company policy to put luggage in the trunk. If the Chins got hit with that hard plastic bag, they could sue and I'd be out of a job in the blink of an eye. But I let it go. People do things a million different ways. It's when you interfere that guns are drawn.

I get into the driver's seat, and Mr. Chin hands me a piece of paper through the privacy window. They want to go to Tarzana. I'm surprised. I would have thought they were visiting relatives in Monterey Park or staying in one of the downtown hotels. I call my destination in to Ruthanne.

"Tarzana," she repeats after me, and gives her trademark jungle yodel.

I start the car and head toward the 405. It's still early and I have eight hours of road ahead.

The first time my mother tried to off herself, I was nineteen, already living on my own, working shifts at an industrial-laundry center on Highland. So she called to tell me.

"Babe," she said. "I'm leaving now."

"You're calling to tell me you're leaving the house?"

"I'm leaving," she said. "In the final sense of the word."

"Delia," I said, the way I did when I wanted to get her attention, "what the hell are you talking about?"

She said she'd taking an entire bottle of Xanax. She was getting yawny and slurry as we were talking, and I couldn't get her to tell me how many pills had been in the bottle. But, since she usually avoided taking her pills when she needed them, I figured that "entire" might be the truth.

"Don't move," I said. "Don't do anything."

When I got to her shabby rental in Laurel Canyon, she was sitting on the couch with her legs crossed underneath her. Her orange dress, missing half its sequinned flowers, covered her knees like a tent. Bubbles of spit shone on her chin, and there was vomit on the dress.

"Babe!" she said, as if I were dropping in for a surprise visit.

"How many did you take?" I asked. The bottle of pills was on the coffee table.

"Just a couple," she said. "I started to gag and then everything just came up and out." She giggled and covered her mouth like a girl on a date. "Want some tea? Or I could make us some lunch?"

"I have to get back to work," I said. "They'll dock my pay."

"O.K.," she said, pouting. She played with the sequins on her dress. "I'm fine, I guess."

"I'll come back later," I said. "I'll bring you dinner."

"That would be nice." Her voice was drifting away, like some balloon a kid had let go of. She closed her eyes. "How's the laundry, Babe?"

"How?"

"Yeah. What's it like?"

"It's like dirty sheets getting clean."

"Um," she said. She smiled and nodded as though she were remembering some favorite childhood dessert. Her long hair had begun to make her look older, and I could see age spots on her chest.

I went to work, where I unloaded soggy restaurant tablecloths and hospital sheets from the washing machines and crammed them into the carriers strung from the ceiling. After eight hours, my apron was soaked and my hands were waterlogged, and I was a little high off the dryer fumes. When I walked out onto Highland, I had the feeling I was swimming. The noise of the traffic was like the rubbery sounds you hear underwater.

Later that night, I brought bad Mexican take-out up to my mother. She was asleep in her bed. Her forehead was sweaty and cool. I watched her breathe a few times, then turned on the TV so she would have some company when she woke up. I put the food in the refrigerator with a note reminding her to take the burrito out of the Styrofoam container before she reheated it.

Mr. Chin has something stuck in his teeth. He's working at it, first with his forefinger, then with the nail of his upside-down pinkie. Finally, he gives up, runs his tongue across his teeth, stares out the window. The traffic is starting to get a little thick for my taste, and the radio crackles on: Ruthanne, announcing a pickup in Sherman Oaks at eight-thirty.

I reach for my handset. "Twenty-two. I'll take it."

"Goody," she says. "Recording studio. Could be a *gen-u-ine* rock star."

"Goody," I shoot back. "I'll make sure he doesn't pee in the ashtray."

I cut across two lanes and exit the freeway at Sunset. I hop onto Sepulveda to save ten minutes, so I can get to the fare in time. The Chins don't register the route change, so I don't explain it. Sepulveda dips and bends beneath the freeway's underpasses, and as we swing around the curves the Chins sway back and forth in perfect unison. *Weebles wobble but they don't fall down!* I remember this from TV somewhere as a kid. St. Louis? Cleveland? Driving sometimes puts me in this dreamy place where I remember strange details from my life: in one city, a bedspread covered with pictures of Cinderella; in another, the way you had to move the kitchen table to open the refrigerator. Miles go by like this without my noticing them; sometimes I'll reach a destination and have no idea how I got there.

Orange lights are flashing somewhere in my consciousness, like an alarm clock sneaking up on your sleep. My attention snaps back to the road. Up ahead, I see emergency vehicles and warning lights. We slow down and soon we aren't moving at all.

Mr. Chin bends forward to look out the windshield.

"Traffic," I explain. "Probably an accident."

He leans back and says something in Chinese to his wife. From her handbag she takes out a mirror and lipstick, which she applies with two perfect swipes. She purses her lips together, judges the result disinterestedly.

Ten minutes later, we are sitting in the same place, boxed in on one side by a line of cars; on the other, the road gives way to a gully. News choppers hover overhead. I pick up my radio.

"This is Twenty-two. Come in, Dispatch."

"I'm coming, I'm coming, I'm—unh!" Ruthie groans.

"You're a freak, you know that?" I say.

"This is what you're hogging the frequency to tell me?"

"It's molasses out here. Better take me off the Sherman Oaks."

"Not to worry. I think it was Captain and Tennille."

"Who?"

"You're making me feel old, Babe."

"I'm gonna need a lot of quickies later to make up on my tips," I say.

"I'll take care of you," she says. "Just sit tight."

"That's all I can do."

I sign off and watch the traffic flowing easily on the southbound side of Sepulveda. You can be stuck or you can be going places. Usually it's just a matter of luck.

When I was eleven, my mother and I lived in Cleveland. All winter, the city was the color of dirty dishwater. People wore heavy coats and boots over their shoes and worried their way across icy streets, as though the road were covered with nails. We'd come up from Pensacola and had nothing warmer to wear than sweatshirts, so my mother took us over to the Salvation Army, where I picked out a hot-pink snow jacket and some blue boots that were a size too big. When I walked, my heels rubbed up and down inside, and after a few weeks all my socks had matching holes.

We lived in a part of town where every house was cut up into four equal apartments, like a kid's baloney sandwich. We had the bottom left-hand quarter. At school, a girl told me I lived in the "bad" part of town. What she really meant was that it was the black part of town, and it was true: we were the only white people on our block. But we had just come up from shitty neighborhoods in the South, and we knew how to get along.

The only nice thing for blocks around was a temple. It had a big gold dome and walls of polished stone, and had been built when this was still the good part of town. Now it was stuck here with no place to go, like the fat girl at a dance. After school, I often took the bus to the temple, where my mother worked as a cleaning lady. She'd make me sit quietly in the pews as she dusted the altar. The pews were covered with a rough maroon material and scratched the backs of my legs when I wore a skirt. I'd pass the time staring up at the dome, wondering whether all that gold was real or fake and whether I could climb up and scrape it off with my fingernails.

My mother hated Cleveland. She said that it was an ugly city, that the lake was so polluted it had caught on fire once, the months without sun made the people depressed and crazy. I wondered why she'd picked Cleveland if she felt this way, but I never asked. I already knew that certain questions made her nervous.

One day, after my mother was finished up at the temple, we took a bus to a part of town I'd never seen. All the buildings were one-story brick, with matching green roofs. There were no stores, there were "shoppes." Everything was very clean. We stopped in at a coffee shop and sat at a booth. Usually when we ate out, I understood that I was to order the cheapest thing on the menu or share whatever my mother had. But this time she said, "You want the steak plate? Have the steak plate. That's what I'm having."

I ordered the steak plate. We didn't talk much, and about twenty minutes later a man came in with a girl a few years older than me. The coffee shop wasn't crowded, but when he got to our booth he stopped and asked if they could sit with us. My mother said yes, if they wanted. The man sat down. The girl looked upset, but he told her to sit, and she did.

The waitress came with our plates, and the man ordered a B.L.T. for himself and a grilled cheese for the girl. I felt embarrassed about my steak and I stopped eating.

"Eat your food," my mother said, so I did.

The man had a wide face with two strong lines that cut down each cheek like the biggest dimples I'd ever seen. He didn't take off his coat and hat, and he drank his glass of ice water with his gloves on. He caught me looking at him, and before I looked away I saw him smile. My mother didn't talk to him, and he didn't talk to her. We just ate, and when the waitress brought their food the man and the girl ate, too. The girl had long hair, and it kept getting in her way. At one point, she found a hair in the melted cheese of her sandwich and started to pull. She pulled and pulled for what seemed a long time, concentrating as though she were playing a game with herself.

"It's mine," she determined when it finally came out, and continued to eat.

"You have long hair," my mother said. "You have to take care of that hair."

This seemed to stop everything. The man stopped chewing and put his sandwich down. The girl looked at him as if she wasn't sure what she was supposed to do.

"Answer the lady," he said.

"I brush it a hundred strokes in the morning and at night."

"Somebody must have taught you that," my mother said. I wasn't sure whether she was asking or telling. The girl didn't say anything.

We finished our steaks, and my mother washed hers down with coffee, then reached behind her and inched herself back into her coat. She slid out of the booth and turned to me.

"All right, Babe," she said. "We're done."

I was confused. We hadn't asked for a check and we hadn't left any money. But I put on my pink parka and followed my mother out the door and onto the street.

"I think we forgot to pay," I said once we were headed into the freezing wind toward the bus stop.

"We paid, all right," she said.

Another twenty minutes, and the traffic on Sepulveda hasn't moved a foot. I turn to talk to the Chins.

"Don't worry about the time. It's a flat rate."

They both smile, having no idea what I just said.

Ten minutes later, the Chins start to argue. He thinks one thing, she thinks another. That's all I can make out. She gestures once or twice toward the suitcase. Their voices yo-yo up and down like a twelve-year-old boy's.

I see a cop about fifty feet in front of us. He's moving down the line of cars.

"Look!" I say. "Policeman here! He tell us!" I'm talking like a racist pig, but it seems like they might understand me if I skip some words.

Mr. Chin makes a low, deep rumble in this throat. I open my window and call out to the cop. He comes up to the car.

"What's up?" I ask.

"Accident," he says. He has a narrow face and his nose bends to the right.

"Just when I decide to take the fast route, right?"

"Happened over two hours ago."

"Oh," I say, realizing it doesn't take two hours to clean up a fender bender. "Somebody die?"

The cop nods. "Kids." There's a sad disgust in his voice. "My daughter wants one of those," he says, looking at my nose ring. "I told her it looks like you have a piece of dirt on your nose, or worse. No offense or anything."

"She's not doing it for you," I say. "No offense or anything."

For a second, he looks like he's going to get mad, but then he smiles.

"Ain't that the truth," he says.

He looks back at the Chins, who have gotten very quiet. I don't blame them. They've probably heard about the L.A.P.D. Someone told me that Rodney King video was shown something like five hundred times a day all over the world.

The cop nods toward the Chins. "Airport?"

"Don't speak a word of English, either."

"Welcome to L.A.," he says. I can't tell if he's talking about the Chins or to them. Then I hear a sound, like a muffled moan, coming from the back seat. I look in the rearview. Is Mrs. Chin getting sick in my car?

"Are you all right back there?" I say.

Mr. Chin looks up. His face has come alive, as though someone flipped a switch.

"O.K.," he says. "Everything O.K. here."

"You speak English?" I say, amazed and a little pissed.

The cops leans into the car to get a closer look at the Chins.

"There's been a bad accident," he says. "Car crash." He mimes driving, then slaps his hands together, looking pleased with his little bit of community service.

"Yes, yes," Mr. Chin says. "Absolutely car crash." He nods his head, trying to look like he understands what's going on. Suddenly I feel sorry for him.

"Well, that's all she wrote," the cop says, slapping his palms down on my door. "You'll see it all on the ten-o'clock news." He motions with his chin toward the sky where the choppers circle, their tails hovering above their bodies like wasps.

Just as he leaves, I hear the sound again. It's coming from the suitcase. The Chins start arguing loudly.

"Jesus," I say to nobody in particular. "What the hell is going on back there?"

Mrs. Chin cries out as if she'd been stabbed, and Mr. Chin screams at her. The car in front of me inches forward, the first movement in about an hour. In the rearview, I see the cop turn around and begin to jog back toward the scene of the accident.

"Here we go," I say, as I put my foot on the gas. But just then Mr. Chin opens his door.

"Shut the door!" I yell. "We're moving!"

But Mr. Chin is already out on the side of the road, gesturing back at Mrs. Chin to hand him the suitcase. Before she has a chance to, he reaches in and yanks it from the car. Mrs. Chin follows, her skirt sliding up her thighs. The car in front of me has moved at least twenty feet, and the ones behind me are honking.

"Are you crazy?" I scream at the Chins. "Get back in the fucking car!"

By now, every car on Sepulveda is honking at me. A police cruiser moving in the opposite direction flashes its lights.

"Move the limo now!" a voice commands over the loudspeaker. Suddenly, the Chins throw the suitcase back into the car, slam the door, and take off, scrambling awkwardly down the embankment and disappearing under the freeway underpass.

I pull forward and grab my radio.

"God damn it, Ruthie, they bolted on me."

"Who? The little green men in your head?"

"My fare. My fucking Chins. They just dumped out of the car."

"Did they pay?"

"No, they did not pay!" I scream. Company policy: if a driver fails to collect a fare, the driver is responsible for said fare.

Another sound comes from the suitcase. It's louder now, like the wail of a feral cat.

"Something's in their goddam suitcase, Ruthie."

But Ruthie's moved on the other things. She's calling out a pickup in Malibu. It's a big fare, and two drivers start in on who's the closest.

At the next red light, I turn around and look at the suitcase lying on the back seat. I reach back and rap on it lightly. No sound. O.K. Batteries dead. Fine. But then I hear another muffled cry.

I pull a hard right off Sepulveda, cross the freeway, and start to threat my way into the dark hills on Mulholland. I find a small outcropping on the side of the road, some unofficial scenic spot. I head toward the edge of the cliff, stopping when I see the grid of lights down in the valley below me. With the car lights on and the motor running, I pull the suitcase from the back seat and lay it carefully on the ground. It's an old-style case and I have to push the metal tabs apart so the clasps flip up. My heart feels as heavy as a basketball, and, after I finally get up the nerve to pull the tabs I jump back in the car and slam the door. The suitcase doesn't open. Whatever is in there hasn't moved. I turn off the ignition and get out of the car. I find a stick in the bushes, hook it under the suitcase's lid, and lift it open. I hear somebody scream "Oh my God, Oh my God," but then I realize that the sound is coming from me. I look down and my mind finally understands what some part of me has already figured out: inside the suitcase is a baby.

The baby is almost new, maybe one or two months old. It's lying on a soiled yellowish cloth, making weird stuttery noises that don't exactly sound like breathing. A small tank likes next to it, and an oxygen mask that must once have covered its nose and mouth hangs down around its chin. A rank, rotten smell reaches me, and I see that the baby's wormy legs are caked with mustardy shit. I run over to the trees and puke.

After I pull myself together, I grab the jacket I keep in the trunk for cold nights and go back to the suitcase. The baby stares up at me with eyes as dark as black beans. I must be a monster to this kid. I pull the mask off over its sweaty head, lift the baby up, and cover it with my jacket. It weighs no more than a chicken and goes all limp and floppy in my hands. I have to keep it close to my chest so that it doesn't slip.

When I finally get the jacket tucked around the baby, I hold it out and take another look. It's awake, but its eyes wonder off to the right as if they're tracking some lazy fly. Then its face seizes up in a look of pain, and, just as quickly, relaxes. Its eyes close.

I get this hot tingling sensation all over my body, the way you do when your gut realizes something before your head does: The baby's dead, I think. I hear myself moan out loud. I hold its body up to me again, its stink clouding my nostrils, my tears wetting its face. Then I feel air against my cheek. The baby is not dead, but it's as close to it as I am to its reeking stench. In a second, I have the baby in the car, strap it as best I can into the front seat, and I'm flying down the hill.

At the emergency room, the doctors treat me as if I were a criminal. They grab the baby and disappear behind a wall of green curtains. A nurse looks at me the way some of the teachers I remember from high school did. She probably thinks I'm the one who did this to the kid. I look around. The room is full of people slumped in yellow plastic chairs, their heads in their hands, staring off into the corners. One man is pressing a bloody rag to his arm. I find a seat, but another nurse comes to tell me that I have to wait in a different room. I can come on my own, she says, or security can escort me. Two guards in uniforms stand behind her, their hands casually crossed in front of their stomachs.

The second time my mother tried to kill herself, she used a razor blade to cut her wrists fifteen minutes before I was scheduled to go over for dinner—which gave me some idea of how serious she was. When I got to the house, she was standing at the bathroom sink, running water over her wounds.

"You'd think there would be a lot of blood," she said. Pink fluid ran over her forearms and into the cracked porcelain basin.

"You missed the vein," I said, lifing her arms out of the water and wrapping a towel tightly around the one she'd managed to cut into.

"I'm just a chickenshit, I guess," she said, allowing me to handle her like a rag doll.

I led her over to the bed, and she sat there silently for a long time as I held her arms, putting pressure on the cuts.

"You know," she said, "when it comes down to it, it's very difficult to kill yourself. The whole time you're doing it, your body is saying 'No! No!' and you're going 'Yes! Yes!'"

"If you really mean it, you use a gun."

"Oh," she said, shivering, as if the idea made her think of snakes or spiders. "I could never fire a gun."

"Then we're in luck."

I took off the towel. We watched a pearl of blood bubble up from the wound.

"I'm going to have a scar. I'll have to wear long sleeves from now on."

"You should have thought of that first."

"I'm not very good at thinking ahead."

I felt a fissure open up inside me, like one of those cracks in the sink. "You get by," I said. "You do O.K."

"I lose things," she said. "Then I regret it, but there's nothing I can do."

I had no idea what she was talking about. "You worry too much," I said. "And about all the wrong things."

"What are the rights things to worry about?"

I stood up and got a box of Band-Aids from the bathroom cabinet.

"This is all you have?" I say, waving a "Star Wars" Band-Aid in the air.

"They were on sale. I guess the craze has died down."

"Well, there's one thing you don't have to worry about," I said. "No more Boba Fett fanatics on Hollywood Boulevard."

She smiled and cocked her head to the side, as if to admire me from another angle.

"Stay for a while," she said.

"Eventually I'll have to go."

"That's always the way."

The detention room is actually a closet. Inside is a metal table and a couple of chairs just like the ones in the waiting room. I try the knob; the door's locked from the outside. The only fresh air comes from a ventilation grate high up above the door. Somebody has left a copy of a fitness magazine on the table, as if you might want to tone up on your way to prison. I flip through it and read about busting flab.

About half an hour later, a cop comes in. She's young. She's taken a lot of time on her looks: her hair is done up in a neat twist, and she's outlined her maroon lipstick with a lip pencil. She has two gold posts in each ear. She takes out a notepad and asks me a lot of questions. Who am I? Where do I live? When did I have this baby?

"It's not my baby."

"We can have you examined."

"Fine. Examine me. I've never had a baby. I'm tight as a drum."

"Don't be nasty," she says.

"Let me tell you where I got this baby."

"Tell me."

I tell her the whole story. She doesn't believe a word I say. I tell her to call Ruthanne. I tell her about the cop at the traffic accident. She asks for his name. I don't know it. I tell her where I left the suitcase on Mulholland.

"Did you get a good look at the baby?" I ask her, when it becomes clear that nothing I'm saying is convincing her. "It's fully Asian."

She looks at me blankly, as if the logic escapes her.

"You think I'd stick my baby in a suitcase and then bring it to the emergency room?

She shoots me a look that says I'd better shut up before I sink myself. I realize how serious this is, how close I am to getting arrested, and how there is nothing in my life—no person, no job, no past—that will make me seem legit.

She takes some notes, says something unintelligible into her radio, then leaves the room.

After what feels like a long time, the cop comes back in with a man in a suit. A badge hangs off his lapel. He introduces himself to me; he's from Immigration. He's holding the suitcase. He lays it on the table and takes out his own notepad.

"Is this the case you found in your car, Ma'am?" the man says, writing on the pad.

"Yes."

"You're sure?"

I have the feeling that if I say the wrong thing I'll be shoved up against the wall with my hands behind my back.

"It ought to have a tank inside," I say. "An oxygen tank. I took it off the baby when I found him. Or her. I don't even know what sex it is."

Neither of them answers me. The man nods at the cop, and she puts on plastic gloves and opens the case. A rancid odor rises up out of it, and the cop and the man reel. The soiled blankets are balled up in the corner. The tank is there with its tiny mask, looking sinister, the way all hospital equipment does. I hear a small moan, and for a minute I think my mind is playing tricks on me and I'm hearing the baby again. But when I look up I see that the cop has her hand over her mouth and she's crying.

I visited my mother once at her dessert community. Everyone smiled and hugged me all the time. She's happy there; she now believes that all her breakdowns happened for a reason. If she hadn't lost it in Texas, for instance, we'd never have made it West, where she'd have the opportunity to lose it in L.A. It's disaster justification.

When she decided to move, I went to her house in Laurel Canyon to help her pack. She didn't have much—mostly clothes, a few decorative pots and pictures she'd picked up at flea markets. The rest of the furniture had come with the rental.

"You move around as much as we do," she said, "you learn to live light."

"I'm not going anywhere."

She looked at me. "You like it here, don't you?"

I shrugged. "It's no different from anyplace else. So what's the point of leaving?"

"I wish I felt that way. But somehow, after a while, a place just starts to seem like a splinter, you know? Like something you have to get rid of before it gets infected."

"I remember Florida," I said. "The electric eel at the aquarium. That was Florida, right?"

"Um," she said, distracted by packing. Or maybe she was packing to be distracted.

"And Washington, right? And Texas? That man who tried to get you to ride a horse?"

"He was a fool, that's for sure," she said.

"Cleveland was cold. Remember that man and the girl at the coffee shop?"

The look that shot across her face startled me. It made me think about all the people she must have dropped along the way. And then I thought: I really had no idea about the things that went on in my life.

"You have some memory," she said, finally.

"Who were they, those people?"

"Strangers."

She didn't say anything else for the rest of the time we packed. I felt the way I always had—that I couldn't ask any more. I'd reached the limit of what she could give me, or wanted to.

When we were finally done and her bags had been stuffed into the small car, she took my face in her hands.

"I'm going to forget everything that's ever happened to me," she said, smiling. "My life begins now."

I'm standing in the parking lot outside the emergency room. People move in and out between the cars, coming and going. It's after midnight, and all this activity stands out against the hour. Bad luck happens day or night, but things that happen in the dark can trouble you to the core. On television, you see pictures of fires against the night sky, and it looks like there's nowhere to run. Or the bewilderment of a nighttime blackout leaves you wary and alone. The baby was a girl. They told me that much once they let me off the hook. It was a baby girl, and it's likely she was for sale. Maybe the Chins—that's probably a fake name—were going to make the money, or maybe they were just the ride, taking her from one place to another.

In either case, some mother gave that baby away. Maybe she needed the cash, or maybe she thought her baby would do better without her. Maybe she'd once seen a postcard of a palm tree or a movie star and thought that in Los Angeles, U.S.A., her little girl would find Paradise. Who knows, maybe she will.

About the Editors

WENDY MARTIN is Vice-Provost and George and Ronya Kozmetsky Professor of Transdisciplinary Studies. She is also Chair of the Department of English and Professor of American Literature and American Studies at Claremont Graduate University. She is the author and editor of numerous books, including *The Cambridge Introduction to Emily Dickinson* (2007), *The Cambridge Companion to Emily Dickinson* (2002), *We Are The Stories We Tell* (1990), *More Stories We Tell* (2004), *The Art of the Short Story* (2006), *The Beacon Book of Essays by Contemporary American Women* (1996), and *An American Triptych: Anne Bradstreet, Emily Dickinson, Adrienne Rich* (1984).

CECELIA TICHI is William R. Kenan, Jr., Professor of English and Professor of American Studies at Vanderbilt University. She is the author of several novels and scholarly books, including *Exposés and Excess: Muckraking in America, 1900–2000* (2004), *Embodiment of a Nation: Human Form in American Spaces* (2001), *High Lonesome: The American Culture of Country Music* (1994), *Electronic Hearth: Creating an American Television Culture* (1991), *Shifting Gears: Technology, Literature, Culture in Modernist America* (1987, 2009), and *Civic Passions: Seven Who Launched Progressive America (And What They Teach Us)* (2009).